CW00833470

The Connecticut Corpse Caper

The Connecticut Corpse Caper

A Triple Threat Mystery Book 1

Tyler Colins

Contents

This novel is dedicated to those who enjoy old-school whodunits.

The Arrival

"Hell" was the best word to describe the Moone Connecticut estate. The mansion resembled a demon's lair and could serve as a horror film director's dream setting. Dark and untamed, it promoted an underworld quality. Yet everything on the sweeping grounds also held a sense of harmony, as if the neglect, almost perfect in its precision, had been carefully executed.

A thick arc of dead rosebushes encircling a lopsided fountain of capering cherubs boasted stark, disconcerting symmetry while a large overrun garden, lifeless herb patch, and circular clump of dogwood possessed an oddly unsettling order. Situated on the far eastern corner of the estate was an elaborate stone gazebo enfolded by lifeless ivy twisted like sinewy, arthritic arms. Beyond it stood a perfectly aligned grove of cedars. With its unique aesthetic quality, the land was reminiscent of Futurist artist Giacomo Balla's later figurative works.

Wind speed was zero and precipitation nil, and there was a subtle but pleasant hay-like scent in the air. It was quite warm for the middle of November in the Nutmeg State, but a chill capered up my spine nonetheless. I chuckled. Leave it to Mathilda Reine Moone (born Fonne), my ever enchanting and dotty aunt, to live in a pleasingly gruesome place like this. And leave it to her to devise this crazy one-week extravaganza, which involved several people having to remain on the deceased grande dame's estate for seven days to each inherit two-hundred thousand dollars. Catch: the hundred-and-fifty-year-old house was haunted. A ghost named Fred roamed the upper hallways. Apparently he didn't swing chains, moan or groan, or bang on walls, but he was known to belt out a mean round of "Little Brown Jug".

Thomas Saturne, a Manhattan lawyer who'd overseen the reading of the will, had different theories as to who the six-foot-tall spook was: a) a nineteenth-century gun-and-whip wielding outlaw who'd fled north in an attempt to escape legal retribution; b) a lascivious servant who'd pissed off the stableman by playing house with said stableman's wife; c) a hobo who'd snuck into the house and gotten trapped in a passageway or cubbyhole, or; d) a combination thereof.

The drive from Wilmington, North Carolina had been tiring, but then I'd only had about six hours of sleep in the last three days thanks to Tom and Ger, who'd suddenly become stricken with the flu (yeah, and there were Chinook winds in Cuba). Tom and Ger were fellow anchors at a local Wilmington television station where I worked as a meteorologist. The young, loud, self-absorbed sportscasters – jocks – got away with a lot because they were young, loud, and GQ good-looking.

Yes, I could have, should have, taken a flight, but a scenic drive promised more of an adventure. And truth be known, I wasn't a keen flyer, not after having been on a Miami-bound plane that had been struck by lightning. Referring to that as one of the scariest moments of my life would have been an understatement.

To maintain energy on the trip here, I'd devoured a dozen Belgian chocolate truffles and four Cokes. When I'd stopped to stretch legs in Greenwich, two industrial-size creamy caffeine-infused drinks had put pep in my pace and oomph in my air. Four walkers, one French bulldog, and twin beagles at Greenwich Point Park were probably still determining if the entity they'd seen whiz past was a bird, plane, or person who'd sucked back a Red Bull four-pack.

Had I mentioned if all seven guests managed to stay the course, each one would receive the same amount? If one departed early, his or her share would be divided among the remaining lot. If six people departed, the last person standing would receive the whole shebang. And if *everyone* left? Select charities would share it all. How fabulously movie-time was that?

Speaking of movie-time, squatted on opposite ends of a long mold-flecked balcony were two chubby gargoyles. Even fifty yards back from the set-like façade you could see a ragged crack running the length of the leering face on the right. The one on the left appeared bored, like he was weary of sitting there for too many decades, and yet a hint of devilry showed in the cat-like eyes, as if he was waiting for the right moment to embark on mischief.

"Hey Floyd," Cat's Eyes said with an impish grin, "after all these years, my delivery's finally cracked you up."

"It's not your delivery, Marv, it's your stony, butt-ugly face." Guffaw, guffaw.

Prime fodder for *Two on a Guillotine* meets *Comedy Central* or what? "Whadya think boys? Jill Fonne weather announcer cum comedy writer?"

The twins responded with baleful gazes.

Okay, no quitting the day job.

Civil dusk was about an hour away and the bright setting sun was an odd Mirabelle-plum yellow. I had to squint as the Chrysler Sebring glided down the remainder of a wide, winding driveway lined with desiccated shrubs, straggly weeping willows and crisp vivid autumn leaves. At the end rested that huge house in all its astonishing glory: a multi-winged neo-Gothic number that would send shivers of gleeful anticipation up and down the spines of paranormal seekers. All that was missing was pea-soup-thick fog.

A Bruno Mars song announced a call was coming through on my Smartphone as I drew up alongside a two-tone 1958 Bentley SI. Thomas Saturne's, no doubt. Who else would drive a car like that? Not Mathilda Reine, deceased owner of the magnificent manse. She'd always been into sporty cars and had owned a few in her day, including a 308 GTsi Ferrari and a Jaguar XKR. Said she liked her cars like her men: long and fast. Mathilda Reine had never been one to mince words.

"You're late, as always. We had lunch eons ago – to which you were expected – and we also finished tea. Where the frig are you?"

"It's great to be loved and missed. Be there in two my little Bundt cake. Kiss, kiss."

My beau Adwin sounded pissed. He made it a habit to perpetually watch his language because he worked with people who cursed and swore too much; he claimed it made his naturally straight hair curl up like that of a Bichon Frise. The guy was everything you'd presume a pastry chef to be (introspective and creative and committed) and much like you'd expect a hair stylist to be (leaning toward the fey). But having been raised by four older sisters and two aunts could promote the "feminine" in anyone.

Not overly tall, but Ichabod-Crane skinny, it was hard to believe the guy could inhale a concrete-block sized chunk of wild-blueberry cheesecake and three caramel-cashew brownies in one sitting. Adwin was so not my type, but the two of us had been together two years. Everyone had said it wouldn't last more than three weeks, which went to prove that people often did not know what they were talking about.

I shoved the paisley-skinned Smartphone into a glove compartment jammed with crumpled M&M wrappers, tissue packs, and a large can of liquid carbonated energy. The wireless contraption had spent enough time glued to my ears and thumbs over the last few days and I was tired of incessant talking and texting, catering to producers' and sponsors' egos, and working what felt like 24/7. And maybe I was also a little weary of being a meteorologist – or weather-girl as the jock-guys would snicker. Don't get me wrong. Despite the apathy that had kicked in recently, I still very much liked the work, although the hours could occasionally prove tough. Even if I was a morning person, three a.m. was a bit *too* morning sometimes. And guys like Tom and Ger had taken the wind out of my sails more than once. Now that I had arrived in Connecticut, however, I felt rejuvenated and strangely tempted to check out the history of the house and its former inhabitants.

In addition to telling viewers about weather conditions, I also covered interesting and fun events like fairs, pet shows, store and mall openings, and anything that fell under the local-interest umbrella. Being a meteorologist had its perks, like being privy to the latest news (some the public never heard), receiving freebies, and having people greet you at the market like you were a favorite cousin. On occasion, mind you, they could get vocal about having been told to wear a fleece sweater and not advised to sport galoshes.

I grabbed the energy drink and chugged warm fake berry-flavored bubbles, and grimaced. Taste: 0. Vigor: 1. Dear Aunt Mathilda. Most of the Fonne family considered her a kook. I'd always found her enjoyably eccentric. Matty, or Aunt Mat as I called her, was my mother's sister, one of six. From oldest to youngest we had Mathilda Reine, Rowena Jaye, Ruth June, Jane Sue, Sue Lou, and Janis Joy. Think the names were funny? You should have met the duo who picked them: Jocasta Genvieve and Elmer Finkston Fonne. My grandmother (Gram JoGen to the family) had worked at her father's small-town soda fountain on weekends and one sticky-sweet July afternoon the perpetual pranksters' eyes met over a root-beer float and the rest, as the saying went, was history. My grandfather had spent the next thirty years as manager, general manager, and then vice-president of a company specializing in joke novelties and fun gizmos, many of which had graced Fonne mantels for decades.

At eighteen, Aunt Mat had met a quirky old-world gent with the stuffy name of Reginald Charles Moone IV. None of the Fonnes were overly keen about the relationship, particularly the fact Reginald Moone was twenty years her senior, but she married him regardless. Off to France they flew for a few months. She'd kept in touch with a couple of siblings, like my mother Janis Joy and her sister Rowena Jaye, and stuck her tongue (and finger) out at the rest of them. Maybe the family had been jealous that she'd found true love and/or married into wealth; it sure seemed like sour grapes to me.

Mom had only visited Matty once after she'd broken a leg and arm in a water-skiing accident twenty-seven years ago when I'd been five. We were living in Dallas at that time but eventually returned to Wilmington, the Fonnes' original home base, where Mom opened a fairly successful "wellness" B&B. When the two-and-a-half-week visit to Connecticut was over, she'd come back ten pounds lighter and three shades paler, and had never spoken of the trip. Even talk of "Kooky Matty" became limited and the family figured the two sisters had had a falling out, but those in the picture (Aunt Rowena Jaye and me) knew they kept in touch regularly.

Aunt Mat had written me often, first via post and then later email, and called every few months over the years. She'd claimed I was her favorite, although she'd never explained if that was favorite niece, person, pen pal, or cracker-upper.

Were the others spending the seven days at the Moone manor – a Thursday through Thursday affair to be precise – "favorites" too? They had to be or why would they have been invited? There was Cousin Reynalda, Aunt Rowena Jaye's only child who, as I'd stated, had also kept in touch with Aunt Mat, but to a lesser degree. Rey was a temperamental snot and an aspiring actress, California based these days of course. She got her start as a dancing drupe in a fruit-juice commercial and gigs as a hulaing ham, tangoing tomato, and waltzing widget followed. She moved on to small B-movie parts and was currently playing a conniving bitch on a second-rate dramatic show about a rich northern California town overrun by werewolves and zombies. In our younger years, when we got along, we did so famously; when we didn't, claws lengthened and fur flew. This last decade we'd gotten along fairly well, probably because we'd matured enough to turn a blind eye to each other's irritating mannerisms. That we only saw each other a few days a year probably didn't hurt, either.

Aunt Mat's will had stipulated Reynalda have Linda Royale, her best (inseparable) friend of six years, attend. It had also specified I bring my boyfriend, Adwin Byron Timmins. He'd caught a red-eye flight the previous night as I'd had to deliver six and seven a.m. sports highlights for Tom, who was probably on a beach somewhere with his brunette of the month. Aunt Mat had talked to Adwin on a few occasions and they'd always seemed to get along, maybe a little too well; more than twice I had had to pry the phone from Adwin's bony fingers. And why had he never laughed that heartily at *my* jokes?

Other members of the Seven-Day Extravaganza Crew were Aunt Mat's brother-in-law, London barrister Jensen Q. Moone, long-time neighbors and friends, sister and brother Prunella and Percival Sayers, and Thomas Saturne, the likely owner of the Bentley. Also along for the ride and possibly to ensure all ran smoothly because of her solid and sane business sense was Aunt Mat's long-time friend, May-Lee Sonit. A successful business analyst turned successful antique shop owner, she was a handsome woman with smooth skin the color of a Starbucks Frappucino. *The Pied Piper* had flourished from the day she'd opened the shop's bright cranberry-red doors in 1999. Her classic navy-and-gold ensemble whispered, didn't scream, I'm-doing-extremely-well-thank-you.

There'd be a maid and butler who had been with my aunt practically since she came to Connecticut, which had to make them pretty damn old in my estimation, and a cook, who'd been in her employ over ten years.

Would Aunt Mat have made sure skeletons – *real* ones – were tucked into closets? Would she have placed severed rubber hands and heads in drawers and cupboards? Would there be luminescent ghouls and ghosts peering through mirrors and windows? Or would Fred be the sole spirit? The sweet old gal had always had a thing for murder-mystery weekends and whodunits and grand finales, so much so she'd made sure she'd gone out with a bang. The sexagenarian died with a splendid swoon at an opera – Carl Nielson's *Masquerade.* You might have thought of a fainting Scarlet O'Hara as she tumbled with great finesse over a balcony and landed ever so gracefully on the lap of a dumbstruck neurosurgeon. She'd made sure her funeral – extravagant flower arrangements, well-regarded

well-wishers and curious viewers, and music performed by a twenty-piece orchestra – equaled a
Kennedy or Rockefeller memorial service. A notable Shakespearian actor, one who'd preferred
to keep his name out of the headlines (because
of the stiletto and champagne episode perhaps),
delivered the details of her will with the heart
and soul of King Lear while Thomas Saturne had
melted into a far wall with a groan and a grimace. This upcoming week, however, had to be
the masterpiece.

I was starting to suspect that this mini trip
wasn't going to be so bad after all. In fact, it could
end up being a lot of fun. If nothing else, downtime – having been at a premium lately – would
be more than welcome.

I scanned the gray-stone structure that didn't
look like it belonged on this side of the Atlantic
and took two deep breaths, turned off OneRe-
public and the car, and tucked gloves and scarf
into a tote. Grabbing a laptop and two Burberry
carry-all bags, I marched up narrow steps leading to ebony-black doors. A dragon's head door-
knocker rested at chin level. What? No bloodshot
eye peering through a peephole? No repugnantly

repelling servant hovering beyond the lace curtains lining the oval window to the left of the doors? How disappointing. If you knew Aunt Mat like I knew Aunt Mat, you'd have expected something dramatic and over-the-top.

2

Walk this Way

The heavy brass knocker resounded like a tom tom and thump-thump-thump-thump echoed throughout the huge dwelling as if the sounds had been amplified by a boom-box loudspeaker.

A manservant wearing an Edwardian butler's outfit opened the door. His face was as weathered as the shrubs and trees, and his hands, although obscured by white cotton gloves, seemed slender and half the size they should be. Maybe they'd shrunk in the wash (the hands, not the gloves).

He began to bow. If the old geezer bowed too low, he'd topple like a windblown sapling. "Madam."

Was this part of the act? Okay, I'd bite. "Sir, I'm Jill Jocasta Fonne, Mathilda Reine Moone's niece."

"You're late." Eyes, wafer-flat and vulture-dark, stared long and hard but his face, like his tone, revealed no expression. He may as well have said, "My but the weather is frightfully pleasant for this time of year."

I smiled and offered an easy shrug. "I took a left instead of a right back at –"

"Enter." He gestured the foyer and a grand one it was – full of black-veined marble and gilt, and one gawd-awful statue of a nondescript Greek god situated between two large rectangular mirrors trimmed with aureate roses. Or maybe he was Roman. Either way, he was ugly. He didn't even have a nice –

"Leave your bags by the mirrors and your keys on the balustrade. I'll see that your car is taken care of. Walk this way."

I was tempted to re-enact a classic comedy scene and walk as he did: with stooped shoulders and a pronounced limp.

We entered a large drawing room or salon that could have entertained the characters of Sir Arthur Conan Doyle. The predominant colors were crimson, chestnut and old gold, the heavy fabrics velvet and damask. Victorian- and

Edwardian-influenced furniture was situated on and around an immense Persian rug that covered three-quarters of a dark-stained hardwood floor. It smelled faintly of sandalwood, fresh and warm, not as heavy as incense, but subtle like good-quality men's cologne. Over an exquisitely carved fireplace of *Citizen Kane* proportions hung the largest portrait I'd ever seen: the likenesses of Mathilda and Reginald Moone, painted decades ago, were flawless.

She appeared happy. Ecstatic actually. And young. No more than thirty. A choker comprised of sizeable diamonds and sapphires decorated a long delicate neck. Dressed in an azure-blue silk crepe off-the-shoulder gown and long white gloves, she had the face and features of a Bolshoi ballerina: thin and exaggerated, and exotic. Her hair was much like I'd seen it in a photo she'd posted on Facebook three years back – wheat-blonde and thick – but instead of curling around her shoulders as it had in recent years, it was worn à la Jane Mansfield in *Too Hot to Handle*.

Reginald looked tense. Either he disliked posing or he wasn't comfortable in the elegant tux and top hat. Possibly both. The man was handsome in a Clark Gable sort of way (he had the same ears), but had unusually dark eyes. Mine had been described as loon black, but his were as dark and cavernous as chasms. It seemed as if you could be sucked so far into them, you'd never escape. At the base of a Grecian nose was a Dick Dastardly mustache (long and pencil-thin), black like the full head of wavy hair that crowned a spherical face. The only word that came to mind: eerie. I'd never met or talked to the man who'd died when I was twenty-three. Mom and her sisters rarely mentioned him and Mom never had had any photos of him or I'd have remembered *that* face. The only thing I knew about him was that he'd dealt in antiquities.

"Per your aunt's wishes, make yourself at home. Beatrice, our maid, will be in shortly."

I turned to find the butler limping hurriedly from sight.

Adwin rose from a long sofa that looked as if it had been newly lined with chestnut-colored velvet. He'd dressed up for the occasion, which in this case meant black cotton pants instead of jeans and a pecan-brown, cable-stitch sweater instead of a hoodie. Removing square-shaped

Nike glasses, he strode forward, grabbed me around the waist and brushed thin lips against my forehead. He wasn't the most romantic fellow – except on Valentine's Day when he baked the most awesome gifts – but he was mine. "How's my little butter tart –"

"It's Jilly. Always was a weath-ther girl, she always knows what's goin' on. Always was a weath-ther girl." Cousin Reynalda sang the introduction or greeting, or whatever the hell it was, to Tori Amos' "Cornflake Girl". I was pretty sure I'd never listen to that song the same way again.

Grinning, drink in hand, the lanky woman stood alongside an early nineteenth-century mahogany sideboard that also served as bar. At five-foot-eleven she was tall to begin with, but with those frightfully thin four-inch heels she towered above everyone in the room. The rocks glass held rye and ginger, no doubt; she'd had a thing for that combination since the day she'd first discovered nightclubs and lounges. Over the last half decade, Rey had lost twenty pounds and a hooked nose, and instead of limp sand-colored hair lining her back, she wore short spiky platinum hair. Gone were thick glasses she'd sported since the age of eight and grass-green eyes sparkled in place of ash-gray ones. Funny, I'd never noticed how globe-round they were. The woman looked great, a prime example that people could indeed change, at least physically. I wasn't so sure the prickly personality had improved.

Best friend Linda Royale wore designer jeans identical to Rey's and a tight gooseberry-hued wool sweater that showed off well-toned arms, but didn't do much for cream-toned skin or intriguing latte-colored, almond-shaped eyes. Standing beside a tall old-fashioned lamp, her wavy chin-length mocha hair was partially covered by a beaded lampshade of gold velveteen. She didn't appear drunk enough to want to do a lampshade dance, so maybe she was attempting to fade into the background. She looked somewhat ill at ease, as if she wasn't sure she should be here. Or perhaps she wasn't looking forward to facing singing ghosts and surly servants over the next few days. Or maybe she didn't care for the drink she'd been sipping. It looked like thick red goo, Nosferatu's liquid pleasure. Nothing like setting a mood. Dinner would probably consist of ghost-shaped pasta and eyeball pralines.

"What can I get you?" Adwin asked, moving to the sideboard.

I gestured Linda's port. "Is that O-positive or AB-negative?"

"B+." Linda's button lips formed a droll smile. "Kind of like the port itself. A nice little number, not quite A+ perfect, yet still too sweet for this lover of lager."

I laughed, glad to see Linda had developed a sense of humor; you had to have one serving as sidekick to Reynalda Fonne-Werde.

A short-haired black cat took me by surprise when it rubbed its long corpulent body along my leg and then flopped on my foot. Wow – ow. This fuzzy fellow was no featherweight. "Who are you?"

"Fred," my cousin responded on the feline's behalf. "He's the official owner of the house now."

"Not Fred as in 'Fred the Ghost'?"

"Fred as in Fred Frou-Frou Fat Cat." She arched heavily penciled eyebrows a couple of times.

"How Aunt Mat." I gazed from the cat to her and back again. "Hey Fat Cat, you're crushing my toes."

Adwin, white knight and lover of all things fuzzy and non-human, came to the rescue; Fred found a new resting spot on a black-and-gold velveteen ottoman.

Percival and Prunella Sayers stood and everyone started talking excitedly. I exchanged an amused glance with Adwin as I accepted a glass of Shiraz, my preferred drink, and sat on the edge of a Victorian mahogany-framed chaise longue that might have graced a Windsor Castle hallway back when.

My beau settled alongside me and draped a slim arm around my shoulders. I settled back, content to watch the oddball collection before us. Observing people and imagining what was running through minds was something I enjoyed doing, and this bunch was certainly tweaking my imagination. No question, this was going to be an interesting if not enlightening event.

3

What Were They Thinking!?

While I'd never actually written film or TV scripts, I had penned a few five- and ten-minute specials, primarily on national travel, and health and beauty tips. But being a film writer had always lingered in the back of my mind, kind of like a scar from a childhood fall off a family apple tree. Creating a "mental" script happened at the oddest moments ... like now.

REY

(eyeing her cousin over her drink, running a long finger along the rim)

What's with the bags under Jilly's eyes? Hasn't she heard of concealer?

She hasn't lost that artsy look she's had for too many years. Look at all that black: pants, turtleneck, and those weird shoe-boots. Does she think she's in the Outback? At least she got rid of "Goth girl". She was too even-tempered to play the part twenty years ago, and she doesn't seem much different now.

Smart move growing her hair shoulder length and putting burgundy highlights in that raven-black hair. Now, if she only added color to those high cheekbones and Angelina Jolie lips.

(sips thoughtfully)

What about that Adwin? She obviously turned his head. He's kinda cute: Justin Bieber meets Criss Angel. So not a perfect couple, but at least they're together. Other than a handful of two-week stands, I haven't had a relationship in three years. Linda says I'm too demanding, high-strung and high maintenance. Screw that. I'm an actress for effing's sake! My three exes – doorknobs – didn't learn that quick enough.

LINDA

(eyeing the port)

Shoulda opted for rye and ginger like Rey. Who needs a fortified liquid sugar overload? Dang-crap. When Rey had said "fun in picturesque Connecticut", I was expecting galleries and shops and restaurants, not a sleepy countryside and stuffy mansion. Jeez, the place smells like someone died here. Hey, wait a sec. They did!

MAY-LEE

(looking guardedly from Percival to Prunella)

This promises to be an intriguing affair, especially with the Sayers:Miss Nutbar and Mister Weird.

ADWIN

(putting his glasses back on)

I'd rather be perfecting my latest mousse cake: acai-goji berry surprise.
Maybe I should go with less cognac the next time.

(glances at Jill)

She looks sleep-deprived, which means she'll give another new meaning to the word "bitch".

PAN OUT. BEATRICE THE MAID lumbers across the room as if she weighs three-hundred pounds instead of one hundred and starts to replace an empty bottle of Australian Shiraz with a new one. THOMAS SATURNE grabs it before it touches the sideboard.

Thomas, whose eyes are as dark and shiny as Bela Lugosi's cape, refills his glass while PERCIVAL SAYERS exchanges a glance with his sister, PRUNELLA SAYERS, and then watches her stroll to the sideboard to refresh whiskies and sodas.

THOMAS

(gazes circumspectly around)

What a long and dreary stay this is going to be. Damn, why is Matty making me partake of these shenanigans? I'm too old for this, and much too professional.

The woman had always been a wing-ding and I rather liked that about her. She was Fruit Harvest cereal to bland porridge when it came to the perpetually boring clients I've had to deal with.

Thomas loosens his tie, scratches a red-flecked neck and sits in one of two fabric-arm accent chairs. He regards a man strolling into the room.

THOMAS

At least there's one person I can relate to: Jensen Moone. He reminds me of Dr. Abraham Van Helsing. Maybe it's that melancholic or haunted look about him, like a man of great knowledge and experience who has suffered more than his fair share over the last half century or so. Or maybe it's that huge gold crucifix protruding from that stiff shirt. Strange. What is it about that face – that's it. He looks like he sucks prunes all day – a result of the stodgy London legal arena, no doubt – but at least we can chat law.

JENSEN

(nods at Thomas and reclaims his drink from a long marble mantelpiece)

That man is too moody, much like an old brooding bachelor-uncle stuck in a somber postwar household, and eating too much Bubble'n'Squeak from the looks of those tubes around his belly. And why hasn't he applied ointment to those bizarre blemishes on his neck and face? He's sitting there scratching himself like a flea-infested mongrel. No, make that walrus.

If the chap isn't going to wear tailor-made suits, he could make an effort to press and co-ordinate his ready-to-wear attire. What was the man thinking when he tucked that two-sizes-too-small sky-blue shirt into those clay-brown trousers? And where did he purchase that hideous brown-and-cream tie? Marks & Spencer ... 1974?

(nods at Prunella, who slips past with a demure smile)

Now there's a striking woman. Nicely shaped. Energetic. Rather Laura Ashley, though, for someone of her years. The long braid and Birkenstocks really must go. But striking, to be sure.

PERCIVAL

(noticing Jensen's appraising glance)

I'll have to keep an eye on that one. Prunella is too pretty and much too ingenuous for her own good. Better she keeps her sights on her feathered friends and sticks with her associates at the Plume & Bill Guild. Matty's brother-in-law is too moneyed and sophisticated, and way too serious for his own good. Why, Mr. London Barrister looks like he sucks on lemons – no, make that prunes – all day and is suffering from the repercussions of doing so. Shit. I can't wait for these seven days to be over and done with.

PRUNELLA

(hands her brother a glass with a huge grin)

This is going to be so much fun, I just know it. Matty always threw parties to die for!

PERCIVAL

(smiles gaily and downs the drink)

Shi-it.

4

The Dinner Bell Tolleth

Even if the eccentric hostess was in absentia, dinner embraced the wacky. Hematite-black name cards with silver scroll-like print had been placed around a long rectangular mahogany dining table, but everyone played illiterate and sat beside those he or she felt most comfortable with.

Diffused lighting was provided by two ornate silver candelabras on the table, two Victorian floor candleholders in the westernmost corner, one four-arm wrought-iron candleholder chandelier suspended in the center of an unusually narrow room, and four two-tone brass wall sconces. Save for the sconces, plasma-red candles burned brightly in all.

Cutlery was early American chunky-clunky while the china had to have been made especially for the occasion. Or Halloween. The color combination again was hematite-black and silver and the motif was ectoplasm. What else could the protoplasmic substance design in the middle of the plates be? Okay, maybe a San Francisco fogbank. But if you considered the black linen napkins were secured by tiny nooses instead of napkin rings, well, ectoplasm it had to be.

If I didn't know better, I'd have bet dollars to donuts that Aunt Mat was lurking behind one of the dark-grained panels lining three walls. I'd also bet if I looked away, sparkling ginger-brown eyes darting with cyclonic speed would appear in one of six landscape paintings; either that or eyes belonging to one of several animal heads on the far wall would twinkle with merriment. Actually, nix that. If she were around, she'd probably be hiding behind one of several large colorful square and rectangular plates lining a handsome Italian-styled credenza (fashioned of alder possibly, but what would the queen of Swedish assemble-yourself furniture know). Spindly Beatrice would lift one and there she'd be, grinning and yelling, "Surprise! Yolk's on you!"

Save for the retro platters, the furnishings and colors were old-world, nice in their day, but tired and stuffy now. Aunt Mat had never been into modern, but she did have eclectic and sometimes bawdy tastes. Missing were nineteenth-century bordello layers of reds, blacks and purples, and velvets and satins.

Beatrice did her lumbering thing and heavy brown orthopedic shoes clop-clop-clopped across a gleaming hardwood floor. Graceful was not a word in this woman's vocabulary. She poured more Chardonnay into heavy multi-colored goblets reminiscent of a Kandinsky abstract painting ... gone wrong.

Everyone had dressed up in eveningwear, the sort appropriate for a dance club more than a fine family dinner at a local castle. It seemed we females had sent telepathic messages down the long second-floor hallway: do slinky and/or glitzy and pink. How scary was that?

We'd finished the soup and salad courses – mushroom and mushroom respectively. There must have been a sale on the button ones at the supermarket. Or maybe they'd been picked at a local farm. It wasn't hard to envision Porter the household cook traipsing around with a large wicker basket, giving edible fungi a critical eye. The man, who was as round as a teepee and about as tall, loved his food as much as it loved him. Porter, by the way, wasn't his real name; Aunt Mat thought it made a better cook's name than Ralph.

"So May-Lee, what are your thoughts? Do you find us a behaved, civilized group this lovely November evening?" Prunella chuckled, fingering a long gold bird-claw pendant she'd been wearing earlier. The talons were decorated with tiny diamonds and the pendant, like the thick ropey chain, looked old and expensive. Aunt Jane Sue, a bird enthusiast much like Prunella, would have loved the expensive, antique piece. She'd introduced me to the world of birds when I was ten, and while I'd learned a few things about the feathered creatures, I'd never developed the same passion.

The antique shop owner smiled prettily, showing tiny pearly teeth. "For the moment, Prunella darling. For the moment."

"Why wouldn't we be behaved or civilized?" Linda asked curiously over her wine glass.

May-Lee's smile evolved into a diva's smirk. "Dear Matty's been known to entertain guests from … *curious* walks of life."

I felt as confused as Linda appeared, but decided to stay out of whatever odd little face-to-face the two ladies were engaging in.

Adwin glanced at me and I offered the barest of shrugs. He leaned close and whispered, "Is it just me or is there tension?"

"There's tension," I whispered in return. "But does it stem from jealously, rivalry, or simple, mutual dislike?"

He crossed his eyes in response and reached for his wine.

"What's everyone gonna do with their share?" Rey asked, fiddling with a thin fuchsia strap that insisted on falling off a lean shoulder, her eyes glassy from two triple-ounce drinks tossed back in the last twenty minutes. But who was counting?

That question was bound to come up at some point. I flourished my hand like an over-enthusiastic student. "I'd set up my own business –"

"You mean your own weather station," Adwin said with a wave of a sesame seed encrusted breadstick. (Was it my imagination or did it resemble a severed limb?)

"No, not at all. I'd produce one of the screenplays I've always considered writing. There are four floating around in my head. A sci-fi, comedy, and two dramas. The money would help make a creative future reality."

Weather forecasting hadn't been my initial career choice. I'd studied film for two years, hence the interest in scriptwriting, but decided the egos that tended to congregate in that industry would be too much too endure for long. Thinking it might be better to save the world, protect endangered species, and contribute to the termination of global warming, I moved into environmental studies. It was a noble thought that had never materialized. Instead I got an admin job at a local cable station so student loans could be paid off. Two years later I stepped from behind a desk in front of a camera.

I watched Beatrice plunk a basket of crusty mushroom-shaped buns in front of Adwin. The perpetually sour expression (which did nothing to enhance a face that could *not* launch a thousand ships but could well *sink* them), suggested she had a lot to say if someone would listen. "I'd also go to the Galapagos Islands for a couple of months."

"With two-hundred thou?" my cousin snorted. Evidently Beatrice wasn't the only graceless one.

Adwin grinned and grabbed a bun. "Jill loves those turtles –"

"Tortoises."

"Whatever. She loves those green guys with the shells that move like they're on Diasepam."

"That's so cool." Linda.

"Actually, that's so *hot* – as in tropical hot and not Miley Cyrus hot." He offered a seductive pose more feminine and credible than any model's pose I'd ever seen.

It was tempting to grab the butter knobs shaped like sleeping porcupines or sea urchins – round and spiky – and throw them at my beau, but he'd probably catch them between those thin yet sensual lips and offer a victory cheer. Maybe the silver butter dish shaped like an antique apothecary mortar would have a better effect. I grabbed it and mimicked a toss.

Adwin feigned a duck.

"What about you, Jilly's boyfriend?" Rey asked, her eyes twinkling and not necessarily from merriment. She spooned two tiny ice spheres from a teeny silver bucket into her glass.

"I'd go solo and start up my own restaurant, and ask Jill to move in with me," he stated.

"With two-hundred thou?" my cousin snorted, sounding like a firing propane burner in a hot-air balloon.

I saw myself stuffing one of those ice spheres up a slim nostril any moment – whoa. *Move in with me?* Six blocks separated our homes, and with our crazy schedules, peculiar leanings and inclinations, living together had simply never been a topic of conversation before. Of course it was also highly likely we both boasted aversions to commitments and concessions.

"I'd buy a cottage for me, my brother and sister so that we could spend time together during summer and fall, and holidays," Linda offered. "And I'd go back to school."

"For what?" my cousin snorted.

Adwin grabbed my hand as it reached for the ice bucket and shot a dour look.

I sighed and chugged Chardonnay as if it were Gatorade and I was a boxer who had just done ten rounds. You hadda love that Beatrice. She had my glass refilled at the last gulp.

"Journalism. And some sort of forensic course." She wasn't the least put off by her best friend's mocking. The poor thing was probably accustomed to it.

My cousin made a yeah-right-whatever face. "I'd have a total makeover and get a trainer. And buy a huge new wardrobe."

I snorted. "What a –"

Playing peacekeeper, Adwin squeezed my thigh and gave a quick let's-play-nice look. Hey, what was wrong with a harmless little scrap between cousins?

"That might be fun," Prunella said, looking thoughtful. "But I get enough exercise hiking and fencing. No, I couldn't waste money on extravagances like that. I'd have to support my bird sanctuaries and the like."

"How charitable," Rey cooed, crossing her eyes when Prunella turned away.

"And you, boyo, I wager you'd finally move to Ireland and buy a wee spot of land to raise sheep and grow some Campanula rotundifolia and Globeflower," Prunella said with a bad Irish-English accent, giving her brother's lean shoulder a playful poke.

"Yes, and you'd be coming with me," he grinned, grabbing her thin sun-burnished hand and squeezing it. He, too, sported an accent, but he'd had it since my arrival. Unlike the accent his sibling just used, Percival's was consistent – and fake – but it fit his affected air perfectly.

May-Lee let out some sort of grunt, or maybe the wine had traveled down the wrong passage. She offered a quick smile and pressed a napkin to Joan Crawford lips: full, well-defined, and primrose red.

Aunt Mat did favor odd people, as May-Lee had pointed out, and this brother and sister were about as odd as they got. The hair on the back of my neck stood on end as if it had been veiled by an artic sea spray.

Thomas almost cracked a smile. That must have hurt.

"What about you, May-Lee darling-dear?" Prunella asked with a sugary smile. "You've been unusually quiet all evening."

May-Lee imitated the smile. "I believe I'd partake of a grouse and/or partridge shooting ex-
pedition. I've always wanted to experience the
thrill of a hunt under various cover types, with a
flusher or a pointer at my side. What fun!"

The Sayers sister paled and took hasty sips of
water.

"What about you, Jensen?" Rey asked, leaning
forward to look at the barrister seated at the end
of the table, hacking a huge chunk of ice-cold
butter. Give her points for attempting to engage
everyone in the group.

He lay the butter knife aside and smiled
tightly. "I'd buy the helpmate a diamond bracelet
and a three-month trip to Brazil, a country she's
always wanted to visit."

To get her out of my hair, I could imagine him
adding if he were sitting at a table with intimate
friends. Something in the way his kelp-green,
jellybean-shaped eyes darkened, just for a blink,
suggested it wasn't love he felt for the woman.
His Queen's English accent was flawless, but
then three-plus decades in England would lend
itself to that; so would elocution lessons and a
sincere desire to present a perfect image.

Thomas, seated on the opposite side from Jensen, nodded to Beatrice and Hubert, who had entered with silver salvers. Saved by dinner. You could almost hear the fleshy man's "phew" as he methodically chewed a sizeable piece of butter-slathered bun and fingered a cluster of tiny red splotches at the base of one ear. He'd acquired more marks since the late afternoon and served as the perfect ad for Poe's "Red Death". Looking at him made *me* want to scratch and I asked Hubert if there was Calamine lotion to be had. There wasn't.

Flank steak, scalloped potatoes and sautéed mushrooms kept the mushroom theme constant. Dessert was a mushroom-shaped mousse that tasted vaguely of, well, yes, more 'shrooms. "Curious" was what Adwin's furrowed brow suggested as the thick chilled dessert slid along his discerning tongue.

Hopefully Porter had other motifs and ideas in mind for the week. Or was this part of the test – how long someone could eat fungi prepared five dozen ways before he or she screamed "enough!" and ran into a raven-black night?

5

Done ... Like Dinner

"The man hasn't moved since we sat down in here." Salmon-pink lips pursed, Prunella stared over her sherry at Thomas Saturne. "I thought he was being aloof or meditative. You're sure he's dead? How can you tell?"

The lawyer was slumped along an armrest on the drawing room sofa, flaccid lips slightly parted, unseeing eyes *very* open. Drool trickled down a pointy chin.

Once again Poe came to mind and the rumbling words "besprinkled with the scarlet horror" pushed through a developing headache. The red marks had grown darker, more intense and defined since dinner. It seemed like an unskilled or inebriated hand had used a permanent red marker to convert him into a connect-the-dot picture. Or maybe it was that he'd grown paler and the marks merely seemed more pro-nounced. Either way, he appeared pained, and more bloated than ever with that blubber around his middle section. He resembled Tinky Winky, Adwin's favorite Teletubby (there was something about the frolicsome "tubbies" that had never ceased to entertain my little vanilla-oat scone).

"*Very* dead, I'd say," Percival murmured, war-ily pressing the man's wrist and neck.

"Dang." Sitting before a huge hissing and spit-ting fire, Linda continued sucking on a bottle of Harpoon Belgian Pale Ale.

"Dang," Cousin Reynalda agreed, pouring a rye and ginger and moving alongside a side table that sported two large egg-white ceramic vases with two-dozen dahlias each – black ones. (Aunt Mat *had* to be beyond the walls.) Drink in hand, she stood there watching with narrowed eyes; a fledgling forensic scientist ready and willing to take on the required responsibilities of the job, or an actress ready to throw herself into the role of a lifetime.

Rain thrummed the roof as if it were a stringed instrument. Monotonous and endless, the per-formance was as flat as a freshly cleaned nopal leaf. We'd been in the room about an hour, listening to distant thunder, getting drunker than we'd been by end of dinner, nibbling on homemade pralines shaped like zaftig buttocks or breasts, depending on your perspective. Made of bittersweet chocolate and containing a crunchy center of nougat and nuts, it was hard not to want to devour them by the handful. Even Thomas had sucked on a sweet when we'd first sat, making an odd mmm-yumm-numm sound so very out of character. Then he'd withdrawn, and grown quiet and solemn.

Rey, Percival and I had chatted amiably over nothing in particular while Adwin had listened with a sunny smile and perpetually topped glass of Pinot Noir. May-Lee had made notes in a leather-bound journal and the rest had retreated into ebooks and magazines. The next thing we knew, there was a shocked gasp, like someone who knew he was about to collide with a locomotive and he wasn't going to be the one choo-chooing into the vibrant horizon. Then ... he was done like dinner.

"We'd better call a doctor." Prunella's lips disappeared altogether as she continued to stare at the dead lawyer.

"It's kind of late for that," Adwin declared, leaning into the chaise longue as he sat on the floor. He looked paler than usual, and that was pretty damn pale.

Fred the Cat, as opposed to Fred the Ghost, meandered in. He looked around, focused on Thomas and evidently decided the deceased lawyer would make the best resting place. Up he leaped, curled and purred.

"I'll ring the police," Jensen volunteered, looking around the room and frowning. "By jove, where's the blasted phone?"

I swallowed a chuckle. Apparently Cousin Rey wasn't the only one for melodrama and mediocre acting. "I saw one in the *blasted* kitchen."

"I'll go!" Percival spun from sight like a dust devil swirling across ploughland.

"Man, can you believe this?" Rey laughed, spilling her drink on her slip-dress and not caring.

Adwin glanced over the top of his glasses, an eyebrow arched impossibly high.

"Isn't it great? I mean, this is like so-o Aunt Matty!"

Linda eyed her friend as if she wasn't sure whether she was screaming drunk or having a nervous breakdown. "Maybe we should have coffee."

My cousin eyed her with similar concern. Are you demented, her inner voice clearly demanded.

"What do you suppose killed him?" Prunella picked at a pink lace handkerchief she'd tucked into the sleeve of a cashmere sweater she'd been carrying with her like Charlie Brown's Linus did his security blanket.

Adwin suggested a heart attack; Jensen an aneurism. Linda said it may have been an allergic reaction to something, which Rey pooh-poohed – with a snort.

"What do you think it was?" Linda asked her best friend flatly.

Posing like Caesar about to launch into a long-winded speech, she announced dramatically, "I think the man was *poisoned*. Most likely by a slow-acting, undetectable substance."

Which resulted in another snort – from me. Adwin bit his lip and Linda spewed forth the beer she was about to swallow.

Prunella's wren-brown eyes widened and she looked from Rey to the deceased lawyer in wonderment.

"Let's wait for the authorities to determine the cause," May-Lee suggested matter-of-factly, her handsome Montblanc pen poised. A calm and gauging woman, her former business analyst persona shone through.

"The police will be here as soon as they can," Percival announced as he tramped back in, looking like a sergeant about to descend on a platoon. "There's a nasty multi-vehicle accident two miles from here, thanks to the rain, and everyone and their mothers have been called to the scene. Porter's preparing a huge urn of coffee. Hubert fainted. Beatrice is helping him revive. I think we're on our own for the interim."

Weren't we before? I took a deep breath and grabbed a praline, was about to bite into it when I recalled my cousin's suggestion about poison. I eyed the sweet treat for several seconds before placing it on a napkin on the mantelpiece. What if she was right about the toxic substance? The now full-blown headache gave way to queasiness and I asked Adwin for a glass of water. Which he ended up getting for everyone in the room, save for poor, very dead Thomas Saturne.

Then another telepathic thing happened: we all toasted him at the same second. You'd have thought you were looking at a family reunion portrait, with Uncle Thomas presenting a man-that-punch-I-spiked-was-a-hit grin.

6

Deadly Desserts

It was one a.m. when the body was finally removed and everyone's statements had been taken by Sheriff Lewis and Deputy Gwynne. Porter had ended up making two urns of strong French roast coffee. Needless to say, with all the caffeine and commotion, it was unlikely anyone under Aunt Mat's roof would be sleeping any time soon. Hubert had returned to his former stiff self while Beatrice had clumped around, serving coffee and cherry strudel that the guys with the body bag grabbed to go and the police ate with great relish, and whipped cream.

A couple of local eager-beaver reporters had arrived and hung around by the tall wrought-iron gate in the warmish misty early morning, hoping to get details. None of us felt like making their lives easier, although Rey volunteered to personally inform them about our no-comment position. Linda's firm grip on my cousin's slim wrist and my threatening glare quickly nipped that bigheaded intention in the bud.

"What a night," Adwin muttered, dropping his glasses onto a nightstand and flopping belly-first onto an oak-paneled half-tester bed.

"What a *day*," I exclaimed as I began changing into a pair of baby-blue flannel pajamas with a kitty-cat pattern, a birthday gift from the pastry chef whose face was now buried in a cotton quilt with an elk-and-deer motif; a hunter's dream. "You know, I overheard the M.E. telling the sheriff that he'd never seen anything like it – what with the ugly rash and all that – and that at this juncture *anything* could have contributed to Thomas' death."

"Anything as in *murder* maybe?" Eyes brown like crimini mushrooms squinted my way. "I was wondering what you'd overhear hanging on the old guy's shirttails. I'm surprised you didn't crush his feet. You were practically stepping on them."

"You can't work at a news station and *not* want to gather facts," I sniffed, sitting before an intricately carved mirror that graced a lovely empire-style marble-top chest.

In truth, I'd never much wanted to follow in the footsteps of Diane Sawyer, Gigi Stone or Soledad O'Brien. News and current events, power struggles and politics were either too depressing or too overwhelming. I did, though, have a passion for research and investigating fads, food, and fashion – anything fun. Nice, tame, interesting stuff that didn't want to make you question the egocentricity or stupidity of leaders and the fate of mankind. Thomas Saturne's death, however, did pique my curiosity, maybe because he died here, right in front of us, an old-school *Murder She Wrote* mystery screaming to be solved.

Adwin struggled upright. "You tell people the weather, and sometimes you discuss community or local events, but you never go beyond the happy-go-lucky stuff, even if I've told you I think you have it in you to be a brilliant investigative reporter."

Someone was reading my mind. Scary.

He grabbed a pair of folded forest-green pajamas from the topmost corner of the bed. "Branch out, Jill. Move beyond demonstrating the virtues of taffy-making and modeling rainslickers."

I grabbed a brush resembling a misshapen turtle, tempted to use it on him rather than my hair. Sleep-deprived bitch mode was setting in, something he had to be aware of and, for some strange reason, wasn't avoiding. "Screw you," I said, eyeing a tired reflection in the looking-glass mirror, feeling like Alice must have after being in the company of the Mad Hatter, March Hare and Dormouse.

"Now that you mention –"

"Forget it."

I started to put fifty strokes through waves heavy with spray and gel needed to obtain a "natural" look, and walked to the window.

He shrugged and slipped into the sleepwear. "If it was poison, who do you suppose administered it? And why?"

"Good questions and ones we're going to find answers to, my little crostata." I peered to into the darkness. The rain had passed and the moon was attempting to break through pitchy clouds. Slivers of light emanated from the cottage or shed or whatever it was that was situated four-hundred feet to the west of the mansion, and then it was gone. It was probably moonlight bouncing off a window or puddle. I turned and leaned into a wall.

Adwin's tired expression suggested he was merely making conversation; he cared less.

I shrugged. "It may have been something as simple as an insect bite that killed him."

"Huh?"

I shrugged again. "I noticed a bite under his left ear. Maybe you saw it? It was beside a very noticeable bird-shaped blotch. It could be he had a reaction to a spider bite or some winged creature that thirsted his way."

My beau smirked. "Have you been reading those old Agatha Christie books of your mom's again?"

That was neither here nor there. "Listen, butter boy, we're stuck here until next Thursday. We may as well have fun."

"When did detecting and murder – or *potential* murder – become fun?"

I stared across the dimly lit guestroom and swallowed my irritability. "You enjoy challenges. Here's a mother of one."

He was about to speak when "*Ha, ha, ha, you and me, Little brown jug, don't I love thee!*" resounded outside the thick oak door. The voice had an Earl Jones quality: deep, rich and sensuous.

"By jove, that must be dear Aunty Mat's ghost-host, Fred." I gave my best English accent (a Liverpudlian, Manchesterian and Yorkshirish mishmash) and stood column straight, as wide awake as if I'd ingested a half-pound bag of chocolate-covered espresso beans. "Let's greet the old boy." I scampered across the room.

"I guess we were destined to meet him sooner or later." Adwin looked none too pleased as I reached for a brass rosette doorknob. "What's the difference between a ghost and a spirit; do you know?"

"I've heard it explained that one passes into the After Life and can come and go at will, while the other is trapped here for one reason or purpose or another." I took a deep breath and opened the door. "But in both cases, they're pretty dead."

The long corridor was lighted softly by four incandescent ceramic wall sconces. There was nothing to be seen except a worn runner, two

cherry-finish hallway tables, a half dozen coun-
tryscapes, and a large suit of armor at the far end
by a tall domed window. (The defensive covering might have belonged to a medieval knight
as easily as to the host of a costume party for
all anyone in the group could tell earlier that
evening, but it had made for a few good zingers
and chuckles.)

"Fred, you there?" I called.

Adwin perched his chin on top of my head.
"Are you nuts?"

"You're not afraid of a singing ghost, are you?"

"Don't be silly. I meant: are you nuts waking
up everyone?"

"Do you think we're the only ones who can
hear him?"

"I – shoot. Did you see that?" It sounded as if
Adwin had dropped his jaw – to the root cellar.

"If you did, I did."

"Hey, what's going on?" Linda stepped into
the hallway from the opposite room. And I
thought my kitty cats were cute. Coupled
with clown-sized fuzzy neon-yellow slippers,
the dancing perky-eared raccoons on her knee-

length nightgown beat my kitties by a mile. She held a tiny flashlight.

"Is that a light for Minnie Mouse or a weapon for Mickey?" I smirked.

"Prunella says the electricity in this place can go out like that." She filliped.

"Of course it can. Why wouldn't it? I bet lightning and thunder streak through the night on cue, too." Adwin peered down the corridor with a frown. "Did you see anything?"

"Like a ghost?" she grinned.

"Like Fred."

"I thought I heard someone singing."

"What about Rey?" I asked. "Did she hear someone, too?"

"She's out. She won't wake before ten tomorrow. That last rye and ginger knocked her off her feet."

"I'm surprised she wasn't knocked off earlier."

Linda and Adwin's expressions rested somewhere between amused and aghast.

"You know what I mean – who's that?"

We squinted at a shadow near the dormant knight and Linda called out, "Is that you Percival?"

"Ssh, you'll wake the dead," I warned.

Again the expressions.

Wearing a cinnamon-brown cashmere robe over cream flannel pajamas, Percival strolled toward us as if engaging in a Sunday constitutional. "It seems that only a handful of us are actually fortunate enough to sleep tonight."

"Did you hear anything?" Linda asked.

He shook his head. "Nothing except a dog and an owl, and a train. I'm feeling a bit chilled and am going to make myself a pot of hot cocoa. Is anyone interested in joining me?"

Adwin shook his head while Linda and I nodded.

Talk over a pot of hot cocoa had to bring a few things to light... Didn't it?

* * *

Tired and cocoa-saturated, the three of us plodded back to our rooms. No Fred the Ghost on the shadowy stairwells or hallways at 2:30 a.m. There was Fred the Feline, however. Even in the dimness, I could see his big furry head peeking from beneath the blankets as he rested alongside my beau's chest. What a cute couple. I turned on an overhanging cast-iron lighting fixture that could have graced a nineteenth-century inventor's workroom and grabbed a Nikon camera I'd tucked into a drawer. Click, click. Click, click.

Adwin shifted and opened one eye, groaned, and opened the other. Fred looked annoyed and crawled deep under the blankets, prompting a giggle from his bedside partner. Adwin shrugged. "Can I help it if I'm ticklish?" He rubbed his disheveled hair, looking like the lucky kid at the science center who got to rub a balloon in the pursuit of *hair-raising* knowledge. "How'd the hot-chocolate party go? Did you learn anything of interest?"

I dropped beside the lump at the foot of the bed. It shifted, but stayed put. I could love cats, really I could, if it wasn't for the allergy. In their presence too long and I looked like I'd been on a three-day bender. Red-rimmed eyes and blotchy skin didn't do much on the pretty scale. Nor did raucous sneezing and a runny nose.

"I learned that Linda loves white chocolate and whipped cream, strawberries and cherries, reading and writing, anything Bollywood, and fringe theater. Lager is her choice of drink and she leans toward jazz. Percival is into obscure poetry and landscaping, writes gardening articles as well as said obscure poetry, and is fifty-one but doesn't feel a day over forty-one. He likes Turkish Delight, cookies, and savory scones." I patted the lump. "According to the radio that was on in the background, the temperature is dropping rapidly and we could see some major snowfall come early aft."

Adwin pulled himself into a seated position and stretched willowy arms. "I was referring to Thomas Saturne."

"Linda and I are inclined more than not to believe he was murdered. Percival prefers to believe he died of a natural or accidental cause."

"Everyone seems so calm about this death." He smiled wryly. "You're approaching it like you're sitting down to watch and chat about the tasty tidbits *Entertainment Tonight* has to offer."

I smiled wryly in return. "Percival thought Thomas was weird. So did Linda."

"Being weird doesn't mean you're murder material."

I rubbed my itchy nose. Oh-oh. "Both of them noticed the mark."

"The bug bite?" He frowned. "How could anyone notice it among that mess of red?"

"The blotches were scarlet and this teensy weensy mark was a deep ruby color. Also, there was a miniscule hint of blood. Linda noticed it when Gwynne stepped over to reprimand that cute young cop who'd scarfed the last piece of strudel."

One eyebrow arched.

"Linda's a screenwriter's assistant and wannabe mystery writer. She's never viewed a real murdered body up close. She wanted details."

Adwin shook his head. "Great, I'm stuck with a bunch of Nancy Drews for the week."

"Percival may take umbrage with that."

"Okay, Nancy Drews and *one* Hardy Boy." He watched Fred jump from the bed and pad across the room. "Did either one of them mention seeing … you know?"

I stood and disrobed. Sleep was but seconds away. "The stories didn't change during the liquid sugar rush. Linda hadn't seen what we saw and Percival hadn't heard or seen anything out of the ordinary." I slipped under the covers.

"Maybe we imagined seeing ... you know."

"We saw a *ghost*, honey bun. A tall translucent man with a hint of a silvery mist twirling around his, uh, spirit-ness. He was dressed in clothes of yesteryear and happily ambling down the corridor." My heavy head sank into a wonderfully soft pillow.

"It could have been a trick. You know, a hologram or something."

"It could have been, but it wasn't." Like the old War song, I began "slippin into darkness".

7

Breakfast Beckons

A few minutes before 8:00 a.m., I entered a kumquat-colored mini gym with the intention of spending an hour losing calories and gaining energy. The exercise room was on the second floor on the west side, away from guest rooms and main foot traffic. A tall unadorned narrow door leading into it could easily have served as an entrance to a storeroom for anyone knew.

"Oh." I'd not expected company.

"Miss Fonne," Jensen Q. Moone greeted me with a bow of the head. Dressed in navy-blue Nike nylon pants and a well-pressed ash-gray sweatshirt promoting the Hawaiian Islands, he was seated on a sleek g-Force RT Lemond stationary bike, cycling at a slow but steady pace. A thin layer of sweat lined a high smooth brow. *Forbes* was on his lap.

I stepped onto a Smooth elliptical trainer. "Have you been here long?"

He glanced at a Swiss Army watch. "About forty minutes. I did weight training," he motioned the Boflex home gym machine, "and now I'm doing cardio. Another fifteen minutes and I'll have a pot of Earl Gray. And prior to lunch, I'll partake of the hot tub and sauna."

"Aunt Mat has a hot tub and sauna?"

He pointed down, to the north. "They're off the deck, accessible through that huge oak door to the left of the den."

"She has a deck?" Why was that so surprising?

He laughed. "Not in the traditional sense. It's more of an elaborate patio, with a built-in barbecue and 'picnic' area which, in summer, is graced with clemitis, English ivy, and bougainvillea. The in-ground hot tub is set up like a pergola – the sunlight can stream through the top during good weather, but when it's frightfully wretched out, the 'roof' can also be closed. It's rather an elaborate structure."

And a costly one from the sounds of it. But it did sound welcoming. "Maybe I'll partake of the hot tub, too."

He offered a quick smile, flipped a page in the magazine, then glanced up. "I'm sorry about your aunt."

I sensed he genuinely meant that and gratitude was reflected in my expression. "She'd lived a very good life."

"She had indeed." He seemed to weigh the worth of offering the next comment. "I hear people truly believe Thomas Saturne may have been murdered."

I smiled wryly and upped the resistance level on the elliptical. The current one wouldn't have been challenging to a seventy-year-old with bursitis. "I believe Cousin Reynalda actually set that rumor in motion last night, but I thought people had opted to forget it."

He smiled as well. "She reminded us when she went around knocking up people to inquire about migraine-strength pain killers. It's more than a 'rumor' now."

"What do you think?"

"You're very inquisitive, aren't you?" He eyed me curiously. "Are you hoping to help your cousin prove the 'rumor' is actually fact?"

I chuckled. "Let's say it's the investigative reporter in me."

He smirked. "I thought you were a weather-girl?"

"Meteorologist," I corrected automatically, then smiled. "With an investigative reporter buried deep within."

"I must confess, I am curious about the man's unusual passing." His fleshy lips thinned. "The man wasn't overly likeable, and he did ruffle feathers."

"Prunella's?" I grinned. "Or her flying friends'?"

He laughed heartily. "I couldn't speak for our Audubon enthusiast, but I understand he'd angered and irritated several clients and associates. I'd hardly imagine one of them, however, would steal onto Mathilda's estate and do away with the man."

"Never say never," I murmured.

"Beg pardon?"

I met his puzzled gaze. "It's unlikely, but not impossible."

His expression darkened. "We'll leave it to the police to determine."

"When was the last time you saw Aunt Mat?"

He hesitated, then smiled. "That would have been about four months ago, just three days before she passed, at an after-theater event. We'd both attended the opening of a local production: *Arsenic and Old Lace.*"

"Did you see Aunt Mat often?"

"Yes, fairly regularly. I fly here four or five times a year for business and pleasure."

"I'd enjoy hearing about some of your visits."

"I'd enjoy recounting a few," he responded amiably.

I listened with great interest as he detailed entertaining accounts of silly, fun-filled Mathilda Moone affairs.

* * *

I acknowledged Percival Sayers' entrance into the exercise room with a nod. "Who'd have imagined this place would prove so popular?"

Jensen had finished his exercise regime five minutes ago. Prunella had popped in, intending to use the Bodyguard T200 treadmill, but said she'd return. "Nothing against you, Jill," she'd stated with a fleeting smile, "but I like working out in complete solitude. I'll come back later in the evening."

"It appears we're all fitness freaks." He removed a thick white bath towel with gold brocade from his shoulders and laid it on a Bowflex bench.

Why didn't it surprise me to see him sporting a pressed, blinding white T-shirt tucked into long, baggy cotton shorts and tall, thick knee socks? It wasn't a flattering look on any man of any age, but when knobby, scarred knees entered the equation – yow.

"But your sister prefers exercising in 'complete solitude'."

"She's funny that way." He smirked. "I believe she has a phobia about people seeing her sweat." He climbed onto the bike Jensen had recently occupied and keyed a program. "You're not lounging about downstairs, discussing homicide theories with your cousin and friend?"

"We've exhausted all possibilities. For now."

He laughed. "Prunella likes the murder-by-blowgun theory."

"Blowgun?"

"Didn't you suggest last night – at least a couple of times – he was poisoned? And that there was something on his neck – a tiny hole or something?"

"Linda did the suggesting, based on my cousin's creative speculation. But yes, there was an odd dot, a puncture mark. It could have been made by a dart or tiny shaft, or something similar … like a blowgun."

"Which is a weapon that would lend itself to poison – a substance like curare. It's like something in a plot from an old black-and-white movie: very classic and very 40s. I love it. Prunella thinks it's hilarious. We could use the entertainment." He laughed vigorously. "You ladies do make for great arguments and the dramatic."

I stepped off the elliptical and moved to the Bowflex where I started doing lateral shoulder raises. "What if it's *not* entertainment? What if he truly *was* murdered?"

"As we discussed last night," he responded casually, "*I* don't believe it was murder. I haven't changed my mind. That mark, if it was a puncture, could have been the result of something completely innocuous."

"But what if it's true," I persisted, "that he *was* killed?"

Percival frowned and stared at the bike monitor. "Then we have a killer amongst us, and we'd better pray that he doesn't kill again." He straightened and smiled. "Let's retreat from such forbidding fantasies, shall we?"

I nodded and did several biceps curls before speaking again. "What did you know about the man, besides his leaning toward the dispassionate?"

"I only met him perhaps four times during the last decade at one Matty Moone affair or another, and only briefly at that. We exchanged a few words about work, weather, that sort of inoffensive, mild type of thing. He wasn't very likeable or warm. He didn't inspire you to delve into lengthy discussions."

I wondered what had made the Manhattan lawyer tick. Where had the somberness, the moodiness, stemmed from? Had he hated life, people, himself? "Was your sister of the same mind?"

"Possibly. I can't recall that Thomas Saturne had ever been a topic of conversation between us, but we do tend to view people in the same light." One lean shoulder presented a lame shrug. "She had known him better than I. They sat on the same board for several years. How much actual interaction they had, I've no idea."

"He must have made for fascinating meetings."

Percival laughed and altered his cycling program.

* * *

The telepathy that had started at dinner the night before continued in the morning and weary faces showed up for a late breakfast at 9:55 a.m. in another dining room used for casual meals. The cozy room was smaller, more plain and simple, than the one of the night previous. Butter-yellow walls were accentuated by egg-white crown molding along the ceiling, and lace valances and tiers with a rose design graced three square windows. There were no decorations save for a house cuckoo clock on the south wall that looked very Black Forest with its moving waitress and coachman and Bavarian Biergarten. I noted it was 10:00 but no cuckoo informed us so.

We were seated at a long rectangular table with a white linen tablecloth and butter-yellow napkins. The china was white: Wedgwood (I had to look). Care to guess what Porter served? Yup, mushroom omelets. Mind you, there was an alternative option: mushroom frittatas. I requested jasmine tea and rye toast with buckwheat honey and got orange pekoe and wheat toast with strawberry jam – the kind with pectin, that substance sometimes described as any group of water-soluble colloidal carbohydrates (I learned that during a shoot at a jam manufacturing plant). How tasty sounding was that? As tasty as over-flavored, brightly-colored jam.

Speaking of tasty – as in tasty bit of information – ten quick minutes of Internet research after the exercise session had garnered a condensed history of the Moone family. They'd resided in Connecticut for several generations after having emigrated from Brighton England. Money had never been an issue. It seemed Travers "Simian Eared" Moone had been highly successful either as a celebrated privateer or fearsome pirate, depending on which story was to be believed. (No, he wasn't referred to as "Simian Eared" in anything I'd read and seen, but with those ears the nickname sprung quickly to mind.)

On a whim I'd texted Ger, who'd responded quickly with a phone call. Maybe he'd truly been ill. Or maybe he wanted to ensure I didn't think he was playing hooky. Either way, I suspected I was going to owe big time.

"You want me to find out about your resident spook Fred, huh?"

"Do you think you can do it, Gerben?" He'd been named after a long-time dead-ago Dutch uncle. "Kher-bunn" was the actual pronunciation he'd told me after three margaritas at a permanent bon-voyage party for the last station GM, who thought she was simply headed for two weeks of play and pleasure in Antigua, and wasn't it nice of everyone to see her off?

"Of course I can, but it'll cost you."

I could see the guy flashing a dazzling white buffoonish grin at everyone in the vicinity before swinging sneakered feet onto a desk and slurping a can of club soda. Three of the station's notorious gossipmongers claimed he'd been kicked in the head with size twelve cleats. Two sometimes gossipmongers claimed he'd gotten whacked with a Titleist wedge. My take? Margarita Boy had drunk one too many of those tart tequila cocktails and sucked on one too many cheap cigars.

"Doesn't it always?"

"Hey, babe, that hurts."

I bit my tongue, offered a chuckle that probably sounded as fake as it felt, and ran down what I was looking for. It probably wasn't the wisest thing to do – asking Ger to conduct actual research – but maybe it wouldn't hurt. He'd have a chance to use some brain cells (if there were any left).

"You're looking wide awake and ready to tackle the day," Percival commented across the table before forking fluffy eggs between his lips.

"The workout equaled five espressos," I said cheerfully, stirring milk into a mug with a character resembling Count Chocula on it and taking a surreptitious glance around to see if any eyes were peering merrily around a corner or through a window.

"Gawd, you're actually eating," Rey groused, semi-staggering into the room. She was dressed in black jeans, black Roslynn UGGs (same as mine), and a cashmere fern-green turtleneck that would have offset her eyes quite nicely if they hadn't been bloodshot.

"The frittatas are delicious." Prunella beckoned my cousin to the chair beside her.

"Ugh. I'll just have some java." She plunked herself down and gazed from one face to another, as if attempting to recollect who each one belonged to and why they were here at the table. She gulped back Linda's coffee, sighed deeply, and nearly smiled. "Any more news on our weird lawyer?"

"Our weird *dead* lawyer," Linda said, eyeing her empty cup with a frown.

"There hasn't been any word," Jensen responded, spreading something resembling mushroom paté on a thick slice of white bread. I'd half expected him to request Marmite.

Rey's brow puckered and she watched Beatrice carry in a bone china coffeepot. "Are we still expected to stay, considering?"

"Yes Miss Fonne-Werde. 'Regardless of what may occur', so our mistress stipulated." The maid offered a near smile. What an interesting if not unnerving voice she had: a hint of an Ingrid Bergman accent coupled with a Humphrey Bogart timber. The maid refilled more cups and did her lumbering thing across the room, leaving a whisper of rosewater behind.

"Let's hope no one else suffers a fatal accident," Jensen said with a dry smile.

"What 'accident'? The man was murdered!" Rey was being melodramatic again.

"Come now, young lady –"

"He was murdered!"

Jensen's haunted look was replaced by one of amusement.

"Did anyone hear any singing last night?" Adwin asked, attempting to navigate the conversation into less choppy waters.

"I did, I think." Rey frowned and peered into her cup as if its steaming contents would confirm her uncertainty. "A happy-go-lucky kind of song. Remember, Linda? You were coming out of the washroom when I mentioned it?"

Hadn't Linda said Rey was passed out? "Was that before or after you complained about the spins and hung your head out the window?" she smirked.

"Fun-nny gir-rl."

"Now that you mention it, I remember thinking someone had the radio on too loud, but it wasn't on for long, so I turned my attention elsewhere." Prunella looked at her brother. "Perc, do you recall? You'd been staring out the window and talked about hot cocoa."

Brother and sister shared a bedroom? How gruesome.

"I didn't hear anything," the brother responded, the barest crinkling of his forehead suggesting he was perturbed.

What was he staring at out the window? Did it matter?

"What's on the agenda for today?" Prunella asked, pushing her empty plate forward, and starting to finger the bird pendant. "Surely we aren't expected to sit and eat all day?"

"We're not allowed to leave the estate, but that doesn't mean we can't stroll through it. It wouldn't hurt to get fresh air while the weather's still decent." I replied lightheartedly. I motioned the necklace. "That's most interesting. Is it … a vulture?"

"Why yes. How perceptive," she twittered.

"It looks old."

"It's eighteenth-century and belonged to Detlef Huhnfuss, a very wealthy and rather loopy baron who'd been known for elaborate week-long soirees," Percival explained. "We were quite fortunate to have found it – at a decent price – while in Bavaria twenty years ago. Prunella loves it so much, she's rarely without it."

"It's my lucky charm," she grinned, slapping his hand gently. "Just like you."

"Didn't the baron have at least six huge estates with large, intricate mazes?" Linda asked.

"He had eight and they did indeed have large mazes – outdoors and *in*," Prunella nodded. "He loved puzzles and riddles, and parties and galas where hide-n-seek was one of the major 'events'."

"Didn't he jump off a bell tower?"

"I believe he *flew*." She twittered again. "He thought he could fly like an eagle."

"Or a vulture," Linda said flatly. "Loopy was right."

Rey agreed. "Now, how about we check out the property? I'm in."

"That'll kill three hours if we're lucky," Linda murmured. "Okay, I'm in, too."

"Great. We can hunt for clues while we're at it."

"Clues?" Percival.

"To who and what killed Thomas Saturne."

"We're back to that, are we?" Jensen.

Rey sniffed. "Someone offed him. Who agrees? Hands up!"

Linda and I exchanged glances and raised ours. Jensen's remained on his cup, Percival's on his fork, May-Lee's on the table, and Adwin's under his chin. Prunella's partially raised limp hand resembled a spent tulip drooping in a breezeless, arid afternoon.

"My dear, you do realize that by suggesting *murder* you're also suggesting that one of *us* is the killer." Jensen's smile was a cross between sour and smug.

Prunella's hand flopped. "I don't think I like that."

"It could be one of the servants," Rey pointed out, "or someone hidden away in the house. I never meant to imply it was one of us."

Cousin Reynalda had never been one to think things through.

"I think I like that even less." Prunella gazed worriedly at her brother and picked nervously at the pendant. "Good Lord, what if she's right? What if it's one of the servants? Who's to say we won't be poisoned next? Or even worse maybe, what if there's a lunatic lurking in the cellar or leering through a wall?"

"Listen, if Thomas Saturne was murdered, and that's a big 'if', he was killed by someone who had specifically targeted him." Adwin's voice was as silky as one of his double cream puddings and he took her hand as gently as if it were a Grand Marnier souffle. "If his killer is sitting here, he or she had personal grounds for doing the man in. If the killer is someone *outside* this little group, he or she has got to be long gone. Look, no one else has been killed. No one's been threatened, have they?"

We all shook our heads.

"Then let's not get panicky. We don't even know for sure that it was murder, do we?

We're getting overly theatrical," he gazed sternly at Rey, "and assuming the most sensational scenario possible. The man had a rash. He more than likely had an allergic reaction to something he ate or something he came in contact with. Maybe it took a while to get into his system before it killed him. Or he had a simple heart attack. Unless the police tell us differently, let's not assume things. Now, we've got a few more days here. Let's simply go with the flow." My beau's smile was as serene as his tone. The apprehension that had started to cloak the breakfast party like a heavy cerement began to lift.

"Let's confirm you're right," Rey challenged, suddenly bright-eyed and awake. "Let's check out his room and belongings –"

"The police already did that," Prunella pointed out.

"They checked out what they believed belonged to a man who'd died of natural causes, not someone they believed had met foul play." Good old melodramatic Rey.

82

But she had a point. Maybe they'd not been a thorough as they might have been had Thomas Saturne received a bullet or dagger between those eerily darksome eyes.

"What can it hurt?" I asked, draining my tea and standing. "It might be fun – like one of those Aunt Mat's dinner-mystery weekends I've heard so much about."

"She did have spectacular ones," Percival nodded, smiling in recollection. "The one with the captain and the mermaid – ah, well, yes." He cleared his throat and stood. "I'm in!"

And one by one we filed upstairs.

8

Surprise, Surprise

Rey took the lead and assigned everyone something specific to search. I got the carved maple armoire in the far corner, Adwin the Queen Anne maple highboy, Prunella the small adjoining bathroom, Linda the closet, Percival the three-drawer night tables and four-poster bed, Jensen the compartment chest and small kidney-shaped writing desk. May-Lee got the nooks and crannies while, for herself, Rey chose the worn leather luggage and attaché case. Gauging from the animated expressions on everyone's faces, the little game would prove an enjoyable time-waster.

The armoire doors were heavy and stuck, and when I finally managed to force them open, I jumped upon seeing a distorted reflection in a long narrow mirror behind the left door. Inside hung three ugly suits, three beige shirts, a taupe polo shirt, a navy wool sweater, and a mocha cablestitch turtleneck. Nothing save a clean hanky, some coins, and a number of folded and bent business cards were to be found in the pockets of the various articles of clothing that smelled faintly of peppermint and perspiration.

"In addition to the usual toiletries, there are large bottles of Tylenol, Pepto, and Immodium, and a bottle of prescription medication," Prunella announced when she stuck her head into the room. "Quinapril." She popped back into the bathroom.

"There's a man who likes to be prepared for any contingency," I said to Adwin, whose head was buried in a bottom drawer. "Did you find something of interest, sugar loaf?"

"Cream puff, would you have expected him to be the sort of man who," he pulled out a pair of yellow-and-green polka-dot boxer shorts, "wears these?"

"We all have our secret sides," Linda giggled, peering over from the closet. She held up racing forms and two Kinky Friedman books.

"More of same," Jensen murmured, looking bemused as he held up a copy of *Horse Illustrated*. "Also found: numerous cheap pens and several small notepads. None used." He returned to the chest.

"This guy was more than a man of many moods," I said.

"Many *moony* moods," Linda said, stepping back into the closet.

Adwin looked at her, then me, and crossed his eyes.

"There's nothing here," Percival sighed, looking disappointed. Plopping onto a rumpled bed, he casually patted and poked folded wool blankets.

"Did you check underneath the bed? Bugbears have been known to hide there," I said with a grin and turned back to a pile of socks in a bottom drawer. The man of "moony moods" had an overabundance of argyles. The word weird didn't do him justice.

Percival's shriek startled me and I slammed my head against an armoire door.

Prunella raced into the center of the room, her face as white as an Easter Lily, bumping into

Linda and Rey, who'd done the same – raced and bumped, that is.

"Keee-rist," Percival exhaled, standing shakily and pointing at the bed.

We all looked, but weren't too eager to get an extreme close-up of what he'd discovered. From where we stood, it was clear enough what had been curled within the covers: a rattler. A Sidewinder to be precise.

"What do we do?" Percival asked under his breath.

"Kill it," Prunella hissed, "before it kills us."

"And which one of us is going to do that?" demanded Rey.

"Well, don't look at me," Prunella puffed.

Noticing it hadn't moved or made any odd sounds, I slipped forward slowly.

Adwin's eyes widened, as did Rey's, but no one spoke.

I passed Percival. Eyes the color of Wildwood beach sand held a glazed look and a grimace pulled at lips shaped like those old-time bright red waxy jobs nowadays found at specialty candy stores.

I peered closely at our legless comatose friend. "It's stuffed!" Apparently it had encountered the same talented taxidermist the creatures in the large formal dining room had. The Sidewinder looked very lifelike and very frightening, enough to cause a heart attack under the right circumstances. Why was it here? To make sure that if poison didn't work, its scaly scary presence did?

"I could do with fresh air." Prunella looked distraught.

"We all could," her brother agreed. "I say we take a long walk and clear our heads and collect our thoughts." His smile almost came across as cheery. "Put on your hiking shoes, scarves, and gloves everyone. Last person in the foyer has to instruct Porter to stuff the mushrooms – and not with crab!"

I glanced at Adwin, who glanced at Linda, who shrugged. We dashed from the room.

* * *

Adwin took my hand as we rounded a toppled fountain. "It's a pretty decent-sized property."

"Four acres, give or take," Percival said. "It used to be much bigger, but parcels were sold off over the decades."

He and his sister were alongside us, Rey and Linda ahead, Jensen and May-Lee behind. We had dressed appropriately for the day: jeans, thick sweaters under heavy jackets, decent walking shoes or boots, and hats, gloves and/or scarves. It had gotten much colder since yesterday and even colder since early this morning. The mist that had veiled the area last night had disappeared before dawn. Considering all that had transpired, everyone appeared in relatively good spirits, but then a lemon sun, the crisp smells of fall, and the tranquility of a countryside afternoon could do the soul good. A distant train rumbled and sounded, a couple of horns honked like cross Canada geese, and a trio of playful dogs raced along a neighbor's property line.

"Too bad it's gone to seed," Rey said over her shoulder.

"Gone to seed?" Percival laughed. "My dear girl, it bloody well always looks like this." With each passing hour, the man was sounding more and more artificially British.

My cousin stopped in her tracks and turned. "You're joking?"

"Not in the least. The Moones have always had eclectic tastes." He laughed again and motioned her onward, down a winding fine-pebbled path that lead to the rear of the property. Wizened shrubs and weeds – or maybe the desiccated things had been flowers at one time – lined the length.

With a creased brow, she looked from him to Prunella, who had Swarovski Pocket Tyrol binoculars focused on some trees, to the fountain and back. "Uh yeah, whatever. Okay, I say we walk to the fish pond at the far rear. Or is it a swamp?"

"A fish pond," May-Lee confirmed, adjusting a silk twill scarf with an Inuit motif over auburn waves.

She smirked. "With piranha, no doubt."

"We-ell, there –"

Her hand flew up. "Man, I do so not want to know, thanks."

"Oh my!" Prunella grabbed her brother's arm and pointed. "Look Perc, a Western Kingbird!" She nearly jammed the optical instrument into his eyeballs.

"A *Tyrannus verticalis*? You're sure?" He didn't sound half as excited, but trained the binoculars where she'd pointed.

"What?" Adwin asked under his breath. "No yellow-bellied Sapsucker?"

I jostled him gently.

"It's gone now." Percival passed back the binoculars.

"But I saw it!" she shrilled.

He chuckled and hooked an arm around her shoulders. "I don't doubt you. How exciting. Almost as thrilling as the time you sighted the *Sphyrapicus varius.*"

Linda asked what that was.

"A yellow-bellied Sapsucker."

Adwin did a Rey thing and snorted, and sent an elbow not so lightly into my ribs. I reciprocated. Linda bah-hah-hahed (I thought only cartoon characters and drunken barrel-bellied frat boys laughed like that) while Prunella returned to her binoculars.

"Did you know pigeons pop?" Linda asked, her expression one of young Lindsay Lohan I-did-no-such-thing innocence.

Okay, I'd bite. "They 'pop'?"

"Yes," she twinkled. "Once, right beside me, a cab ran over one. Pop the pigeon went – pop! You know, like that fun bubble-wrap packaging you squeeze for fun." She demonstrated with her fingers. "Pop, pop!"

Rey laughed like a kid embarking on her first rollercoaster ride. I grinned like I'd received the compliment of my life while May-Lee turned to the horizon, biting her lip. Prunella lowered the binoculars and appeared appalled, her face as pale as ostrich down.

Linda winked and Jensen gave a you-little-vixen look.

"Okay, let's move forward fellow detectives! We'll double back around from the swamp-pond." Rey indicated a path and moved on like an excited Scouter, Linda in firm tow.

The rest of us were about to follow when something extraordinary occurred. A bird circled nigh.

"Look Perc, look! A Harris sparrow!" Prunella shouted, pointing excitedly.

"Are you sure? They're very rare around here."

She gave him a withering look and he held up his hands in a gesture that suggested: you're-right-I'm-wrong, it-was-a-Harris-sparrow. Maybe her raspberry beret (one that would have inspired Prince to sing about a trilby instead) annoyed the winged finch, or maybe her gawking did. Damn if it didn't fly close with amazing speed … before landing on her head. It let out a loud chirp, pecked twice, and flew off again.

May-Lee covered her mouth with a gloved hand to contain laughter while Adwin and I, keeping our expressions as neutral as possible, scurried after the two young women.

"That was priceless," I said under my breath.

Adwin glanced back and chuckled. "Brother and sister still look shocked. May-Lee's all but rolling on the ground."

"Those two ladies seem to be at constant odds."

"There does seem to be a perpetual degree of tension." He nodded. "Speaking of 'them', what about your cousin and her friend? Do you think they have a thing going?"

They were walking arm in arm.

"Does it matter, my little Linzer Torte?"

"No, my dear saffron bun." He offered a thin smile. "I just can't imagine getting into a serious relationship with that cousin of yours and not wanting, at some point, to shove her head into a pecan pie – heavy on the nuts."

"She and Linda get along really well – like a couple married too long." I glanced upwards and noticed the sky was evolving into a formless layer of charcoal gray. Nimbostratus clouds would soon obscure the sunlight. "It looks like rain's on its way."

"Accompanied by thunder and lightening, no doubt." He laughed. "How perfect would that be?"

"When Aunt Mat goes all out, she goes all out."

"She has Mother Nature in her back pocket, huh?"

"Aunt Mat could charm the socks off Red Skull."

"Another villain?" He smirked. "You've got to stop stealing your nephew's comic books."

My nephew Quincy's penchant for comics and graphic books had rubbed off on me not long after he'd moved in with my mother five years ago. My sister, Reena Jean, had been a thrill-seeker, or wing-nut as her nonconformist ex called her (he who parasailed and freefall-skydived regularly). During her last adventure, she'd been washed out to sea when she'd stood on a pier during a Category Four hurricane. So much for trying things at least once, which had been her motto since youth.

We stopped alongside Rey and Linda, and waited for the others.

Linda turned to Prunella and pointed at a cross-hipped roof visible beyond a line of tall spindly pine trees. "Is that your home over there?"

"That would be it," she replied with a proud smile.

"Have you been neighbors long?"

"Twenty years," Percival said with a sad smile. "Twenty wonderful fun-filled years."

Everyone ambled to the pond in silence. The opposite side of the Moone property was fairly barren while this stretch was much busier – with the pond and a gazebo, a rose garden, and spo-radically placed wrought-iron benches. Halfway between a six-car garage and the gazebo stood the small outbuilding I'd seen last night. It might have served as a studio or cottage, or even fancy storage shed. Whatever it was, the structure seemed out of place; it didn't match the grand house in any respect, except for gray-green slate roofing. A small-town carny ride stuck in Disneyland.

As the others continued forward, Adwin and I strolled up to the dwelling and wiped at a side window with dried-up leaves to peer inside.

"What do you suppose she kept in here?"

"Too bad the sun's pretty much gone. I can't see much through this tiny opening between the shades, except some sheet-covered furniture... Maybe visitors stayed here, ones who preferred privacy to a house filled with people. Or maybe the servants use this place."

"For what purpose? To pluck chickens and clean pond piranhas?"

"Do piranhas have scales?"

"You'd still have to skin them."

We chuckled feebly – to match the humor – and moved along a narrow semi-worn path to the entrance.

"Maybe Fred resides in there."

"Fred the Ghost or Fred the Feline?" I asked, scanning two tall windows bearing specially-designed blinds lining both sides of the door. A third, small arched window with a stained-glass leaf motif was positioned overhead.

"Why not both?" Adwin stood on my heels. "Ghosts need pets like anyone else, especially if they're stuck on earth for perpetuity."

A hand-forged pull handle was loose. Too bad the door it was attached to wasn't. "Pooh."

"You're as fixated on finding clues and bodies as Rey."

"Hardly. I'm merely curious."

Adwin clicked his tongue and grabbed my elbow, and led us toward the rest of the group gathered on the topmost step of the statued white marble gazebo, which was pretty much the size of my studio condo back in Wilmington.

"Did you find anything of note, Detective Reynalda?" I asked, stepping up behind her.

"Not yet," she sniffed, "but I will." She stood five feet from a sizeable pond that four dozen Koi would have been happy to call their home had the water been cleaner. Noticing my gaze, she nodded. "Looks kinda murky."

"It certainly does," Prunella agreed softly, looking uncertain about moving any closer than Linda, as if the pool of water might suck her into its unknown depths.

"Are you expecting to find a body in there?" Adwin joked, swinging around a pillar and nearly bumping into Jensen, who appeared to be humoring us by appearing keenly interested in all that lay before him.

"I'm not," Linda replied with a droll smile, "but Rey is."

"Fun-nny gir-rl." My cousin ambled past the two women and stopped inches from the edge, ignoring Prunella's caution about getting too close. She crouched. "Man, this baby could use a serious cleaning. If there were ever fish in here, they'd have to be dead."

"Or slime suckers," Adwin offered.

"Well, great detective, are you going to squat there? Or *detect*?" Percival asked, again appearing to keep mirth in check.

"Patience my not-so-favorite lackey," my cousin responded, removing a knitted glove, rolling up a fleecy sleeve, and sticking her hand beneath the surface.

"Oh, for the love of –"

"Hold on. I can feel – yes, there's something here. Gawd!"

Who'd have guessed trim, gangly Prunella could emit such a bloodcurdling scream?

* * *

Percival released a low and lengthy whistle, lurching backward and grabbing the zaftig thigh of a pillar-goddess he'd lurched into. "Keeee-rist, doesn't that want to make you spill your frit-tatas?"

Adwin and I clasped hands and gaped, while May-Lee's response was to glance at Percival and arch her right eyebrow.

"Damn." Jensen suddenly seemed very serious as he regarded the item my cousin clutched.

Shocked-looking Rey held a head by mud-thick curls. Rubbery kelp-tinged skin was daubed with slime and bulbous eyes gazed back defiantly while chubby, deformed lips were pulled back in a badger snarl. It was a prime *CSI/Bones* moment.

"Who's that?" Adwin asked, releasing me and crouching alongside Rey, who hadn't moved or spoken since she pulled the hideous find from the dank wetness. She seemed staggered, incapable of moving or speaking. This was a truly rare occasion. Mom would want to hear about it.

"The Incredible Hulk?" I suggested.

"A superhero or comic book champion this guy – uh, head – ain't," Linda said. "Any ideas Rey?"

"Cousin?" I urged when she remained still.

Rey looked up, focused, and frowned. "What am I – psychic? I don't know who this dude is." She scanned the head, cursed softly and let it fall, then studied her hand as if to ensure it wasn't contaminated with a flesh-eating virus or cooties.

"Has anyone gone missing in the area lately?" I asked as I crouched alongside Adwin.

"Someone inevitably always goes missing." Percival's voice was as dark as his expression.

Jensen sighed. "We'd best ring the police."

"Hold on." I peered closer and then poked the head.

"Are you crazy?" Linda asked, stepping up alongside me.

"No. *Curious*," Adwin answered for me with a smirk.

"Too funny, humorless pastry boy," I said, smirking in return. I poked again. "This is a fake head."

"What?" Prunella moved beside Rey. "A fake? As in a *joke*?"

"It's an odd place to put a joke," I replied, "but that's what it appears to be. See?" I yanked a misshapen rubber ear, and then rubbed oily sludge from my fingers on a patch of spiky grass. Strange. It felt like grease or petroleum jelly.

"I don't get it," Linda murmured.

Rey laughed and we all stared. "Come on! It's Aunt Matty's idea of fun. I bet she's stashed a dozen of these around the place, and some legs and arms, too!"

I found myself laughing as well, remembering what I'd been thinking yesterday. "She probably figured we'd go exploring at some point, so she made sure to have all bases covered." I held up glistening fingers. "Even the pond scum is for show."

"I don't find this funny," Prunella said, annoyed.

"Oh come on, you were one of her best friends. You must be accustomed to this stuff."

The bird benefactor tilted her head one way and then the other, and the pout evolved into a grin.

"Do you think she placed the snake in the bed, too?" Percival asked.

I glanced at Rey and she at Percival. "No," my cousin and I replied simultaneously.

"Why not?" He kicked the head as if it were a soccer ball. Back into the pond it went.

"She's dead," we responded at the same time.

His brow furrowed like a kiwi past its prime (the fruit, not the bird).

"Our aunt passed a while ago," I explained. "That snake was put there recently – to scare Thomas, or warn us, or maybe both. It's unlikely Snakey's been lying there since her funeral."

"Why not?" Percival challenged.

"You have me there." It was time for my brow to furrow. "Maybe when she'd planned this inheritance affair, one of the pranks was to scare Thomas. She'd probably requested one of the servants put the reptile in his bed when an opportunity presented itself."

"Do you think all the staff may be in on this?"

"Anything is possible," I said with a shrug.

"Keeee-rist, I need a tea. With a shot of brandy." Percival removed his Ascot cap and ran a hand through loam-colored hair as dense as wool.

"*Need*? I *want* one. A double." Jensen turned on the heels of his Bally loafers and started toward the house.

"Hey! We've got more exploring to do," Rey called.

"I've endured enough foolish pranks for today, thank you." He waved a long thin hand limply behind him.

"Spoilsport." She thrust out her lower lip, looking like a birthday brat-uh-child who'd not received enough ice-cream with cake.

"Let him go. He thinks he's too grand for the likes of us anyway," Percival said quietly, watching the London barrister take a shortcut beyond the bungalow-cottage-shed.

There was a touch of hostility in the tone and gaze, and I got the impression the London barrister affronted the poetry and gardening lover in some way. In fact, there appeared to be a lot of ill-feeling among the group.

We shared another telepathic moment and simultaneously headed for a narrow path that led to the other side of the Moone estate.

The dark sky hovered ominously overhead, but the rain it promised didn't arrive, at least not during the next ninety minutes. We enjoyed the solitude of the estate, Mathilda Reine Moone's crazy landscaping notions, and the two heads, three hands, and one leg placed in more strategic locations than the pond.

Dear Aunt Mat. You had to love the old gutsy gal.

9

A Tour of the Manse

Tea-time saw a spicy blend served with mushroom tartlets and shortbread cookies shaped like multi-legged creatures, maybe octopi or spiders. It was a silent affair. We were hungry – or peckish as Jensen may have said – and it appeared we felt like entering Zen zones again. Forty minutes later our sated re-energized group, save Jensen, marched along a west-wing corridor lined with ornaments and weaponry. Longswords, battle axes and quarterstaffs, and unusual pieces of chainmail added an interesting if not disquieting dimension to the interior decoration. King Arthur and his knights would have felt perfectly at home.

The plan was to move throughout the first floor, from back to front, starting with the larder and kitchen. If nothing else, it was something to do to kill time. Oops, maybe "kill" wasn't the best word under the circumstances.

"Where's that London barrister?" Rey peered circumspectly around one of two tall long metal shelving units in the large dim larder, as if anticipating finding a body tucked between cases of granola and pickling barrels. "He become too good for us?"

Linda dropped the lid to a mammoth freezer. She looked disappointed, as if expecting to find a corpse inserted between forty containers of soup and stew and twenty tubs of ice cream, but finding nothing more than freezer burn. "Become? The man was *born* too good for us."

Percival snickered like a sibling watching his parents' favorite child being dissed and chomped into a chocolate chip cookie. When he saw the stares, he passed his sweet find on.

Adwin glanced at the bag, frowned, and handed it to Rey. Pre-fab desserts did not play a part in the life of my little dough boy.

Cookies in hand, we moved through an old-fashioned but immaculate kitchen into a large somber room that was a mix of library, study, and museum. It smelled "old". One tall partition supported russet-stained shelves and books. Another wall was lined with oil paintings of old-world landscapes and hunting scenes; yet another wall supported two huge portraits.

Like the King Arthur corridor, the room possessed an unusual if not disturbing effect. Or maybe it only seemed disturbing because there was something perturbing about the man in the first portrait, which resembled an early twentieth-century photograph with predominant shades of browns and creams. A solemn man in his late forties, he was dressed in a dark tail coat and trousers. What was it that was so bothersome? The fixed stare? The graveness? The big Dumbo ears? The huge solitary eyebrow perched over dark beady eyes? The handlebar mustache that looked as if it had been pasted in the middle of a pail-shaped head for some unidentified effect? And what about those lips? They were so fat and flabby you might have thought the guy had encountered a collagen-happy cosmetic surgeon. This had to be Reginald Charles Moone II.

Prunella stood so close behind, my eyes began to water. Obsession was an intense and intoxicating scent when dabbed delicately behind ears or on wrists, but not so pleasant when the body had been completely doused with it. "I can't say why, but that man always came across as eerie."

I was glad to know I wasn't alone in my feelings. "Did you ever meet him?"

She chuckled. "He was way before my time. Moone Number Two died in the early 1930s."

"And the other?" I gestured the second portrait. Like Moone Number Two, this fellow had one huge eyebrow; it was perched over onyx-black eyes just as beady as the sire's. He had the same ears and the same sober – almost grim – air. That was where the similarities stopped. Unlike his father, Moone Number Three was clean-shaven, his skin slightly scarred, possibly from a childhood ailment. His lips were well-defined, almost sensual, as if they belonged on a silent movie star. The face was remarkably thin, a dramatic contrast to the father's. His smart and fashionable if not expensive suit consisted of a double-breasted vest worn with a single-breasted jacket and matching trousers.

"I never knew him, either." She leaned close. "Matty once told me that Reginald rarely talked of his family. There'd been a falling out between brothers and uncles. Hence, the limited number of portraits. I understand many were removed, if not destroyed, over the years."

That wasn't hard to doubt. The male Moone kinfolk were much too serious for anyone's good. "What about Aunt Matty's hubby, Moone Number Four? Even though he was my uncle, I never met him. What was he like?"

Searching for the right words, she studied a cabinet filled with curios – everything from teapots to vases to statues. "Aloof. Frosty. Weird – no, maybe I should say *different*. He, too, had a few falling-outs, including one with Jensen, his youngest brother, but they made up when Reginald celebrated his sixtieth. He was extremely knowledgeable about antiquities and history." She offered a lean smile. "Reginald didn't talk much, except after a couple of glasses of Madeira. Good gracious, then he would get caught up in the Renaissance and Reformation, or the Napoleonic Wars, and that mouth seldom closed." She smiled thinly.

I'd forgotten Reginald and Jensen were brothers. Other than sharing a somber demeanor, they bore little resemblance. Maybe Jensen took after the mother. I motioned the cabinet. "Is that his only collection of curiosities?"

"Oh my no. Oddments and showpieces fill a large room on the third floor, as well as the entire tower." Her voice became a conspiratorial whisper. "I wouldn't go there alone, sweetie. It might turn that lovely dark hair of yours a stark shade of white." She turned to her brother, who had sidled up alongside us.

"Lookee here!"

We whirled and found Linda holding a 10 ½" X 13" hardcover comprised of black cloth, gilt lettering, and gilt page edges. It was very old and in pristine condition.

"It's a book," she announced.

We offered surely-you-jest looks.

"It's all about old-world treatments and remedies!" She flourished an arm like a heralding trumpeter might a majestic banner. "In fact, half this shelf is about medicines and herbs, poisons and toxins. There are some awesome first editions."

Rey sped across the room with the velocity of a tempest. "How perfect is that?"

"Perfect for what?" Percival asked flatly.

"For Thomas Saturne's killer. Everything he or she needed to know about committing the perfect murder was – is – right here in this room."

"Sure. His 'killer' came in here the day of his death and researched all these books to find the perfect poisonous substance."

"It's merely a coincidence, dear," May-Lee added quietly. "If Thomas was murdered, and we must assume it's an 'if', then it's unlikely his murderer would have had time to research poisons, never mind find one that satisfied his or her needs, much less acquire it."

"Unless it was the help. They'd have had access to this information at any time and could have researched poisons days, weeks, maybe months in advance." My cousin's chin rose with defiance. "That could hold true for a lot of folks."

Adwin offered a placating smile. "If I were going to kill someone – as in *predetermined* murder – I'd have made sure that my research, method of murder, and timing had been methodically devised. There'd be no leaving things to chance or examining last-minute details. I'd have had all my ducks in a row."

My cousin pouted. "I say we move onwards and upwards, and hit the second floor."

"I say we hit *her*," Percival said under his breath.

His sister's response sounded like the haunting laughter of a hyena.

But upwards and onwards we did troop – along a narrow rear staircase to an unchartered wing of the house.

Rey sneezed, Linda coughed, and I held my breath as long as possible, and when I had no option but to suck in air, my sneeze and cough were of booming Jolly Green Giant properties. We were in the first room at the top of the stairs, a large L-shaped room that hadn't been aired for some time and where Swiffer hadn't yet given new meaning to cleaning. Egg-white sheets, layered thinly with dust, covered most of the furniture.

"Another guestroom?" Linda asked, throwing a Werther's Caramel Apple candy between those unusual button-like lips.

"I think this may have been Reginald's parents' room."

We turned to Percival, who was peering beneath a covering draped over what appeared to be a huge dresser. He pulled out a small oval gold-framed photograph of a young couple and held it up for all to see.

"That would be Moone the Third and Theadora," Prunella agreed, taking the photograph.

"Theadora?" Rey smirked.

"I don't remember any Theadora," I searched my mental family files.

"She came from Bohemian parents."

"Unlike most Bohemians, however, her parents had lots of money," Percival explained with a knowing look.

"Which made her very suitable wife material," I responded.

He tapped the tip of his nose with an index finger and pointed.

Rey yanked a sheet from a carved cherry armoire and sneezed. She sounded like a backfiring Mack truck. Delicate did not appear to be these two cousins' middle names.

"Should you be doing that?" Prunella asked, her high forehead crinkled like a linen pantsuit that had been worn on a transatlantic flight.

"Why not? We're exploring."

"We don't have to explore *every* little thing."

"Come on, Rey," Linda coaxed, "if we look behind and beneath every stick of furniture, we'll be here at the end of next month."

"Let's stick to *cursory* exploration, shall we?" Percival suggested. "Which means quick strolls into rooms, peeks under beds and into cubbyholes."

"And closets," Rey added, pulling open a wide, heavy door beyond the armoire.

"And closets," he sighed, rolling his eyes and then nearly having them leap from their sockets when she offered a strident scream or curse, or combination thereof.

We hastened forward.

… And found Jensen perched on a shelf, sporting an unlikely and most mischievous grin, looking like an office mail-boy who'd pulled one over on the ever-critical boss. In his vein-lined hand was beige floral-etched stationary and written on it in large ornate script was: having fun yet?

"It took you bloody explorers long enough. My word, I thought I'd be here well into the midnight hour."

* * *

Jensen Q. Moone, dressed in designer jeans and an alpaca mock turtleneck, hopped to his size fourteen loafers. How come we'd never noticed those clodhoppers before? They stood out like yams amid fingerling potatoes. And that crucifix – it could anchor a small boat. He no longer seemed so stiff though. In fact, considering the flexibility he'd displayed, he was very much the opposite. Even his accent seemed less severe or forced.

"What's going on?" Percival demanded, stepping before him. "This isn't at all funny."

"No?" he smiled. "You should have seen your face from where I was."

Prunella pulled her brother back gently. "You did have a rather interesting expression." She smiled, then giggled.

Rey chuckled. "It *was* priceless. I thought you were going to pis –"

"Let's not go there," Adwin suggested hurriedly. "What's your story, Jensen?"

"Mathilda had requested my services some time ago and I acquiesced."

"Services?" Rey asked curiously.

The serious demeanor returned. "I was asked that when this collect-your-inheritance week came to pass, I assist matters along." He smiled darkly and then chuckled. "I must say, that *was* rather fun."

"And Thomas?" Adwin asked acerbically. "Was he part of assisting matters along?"

Jensen shook his head. "His death was an unfortunate, unexpected event."

"I have to say, considering Aunt Mat's sense of humor, that you playing closet peek-a-boo isn't up to her usual wit," I said.

"Who's to say I'm all there is?" His expression waffled between mirth and flippancy, suggesting more pranks and tricks were afoot.

I smiled drolly. "*That's* more like Aunt Mat."

"Can we move on now?" Rey asked impatiently. "Anywhere we should look or go that *you* haven't been?"

The barrister shook his head. "I haven't seen that much of the house."

"But you lived here once upon a time ago," I stated.

"I stand corrected." He bowed his head. "I haven't seen that much of the house since I left to attend university."

"Good." Tossing her head, Rey led the way.

10

The Never-Ending Manse

Twelve rooms later, we were dusty, weary and leaning toward cranky. The lighting, for the most part, was dim at best and in some rooms we'd had to use flashlights when there were no lamps or bulbs. We'd found a huge hairy spider the size of a Smart car hanging from invisible wires in a sewing room and a shrieking skeleton in a vintage brass-bound trunk in a room that served as a hobby and/or art area, a plastic job with fake black roses in one hand and another note from kooky Aunt Mat in the other. Miss me? (That's all she wrote.)

Percival swung around a wooden antique room divider and groaned, wiping a thick sticky cobweb from his face and lips. "I vote we stop. I'm ready to sit back and enjoy a nice cool martini." He glanced at his Rolex, a Yacht-Master I was pretty sure, having done a piece the previous Christmas about outrageous gifts for the abundantly wealthy. "Dinner's a good two hours away."

"Ooh, a classic martini would be lovely. With three Hondroelia olives," Prunella purred, grabbing her brother's forearm as if it were a life preserver.

"Hell, I'd settle for Manzanillas."

"That does sound frightfully good – with a twist of lemon *and* lime," Mr. Jensen Peek-a-Boo Moone piped in, stepping from a small storage room he'd been investigating. He tossed a large rubbery lizard at our feet.

I wasn't a martini gal, but it sounded tempting. "Count me in. Adwin, you make a mean Cosmo. You're in charge."

"Okay, but we continue checking out the place after dinner," Rey insisted, looking petulant.

Percival eyed her. You could see a disparaging comment poised on his taut lips. He caught his sister's glance and read something in it, smiled wryly, and slapped my beau on the back, nearly sending the slim baker of sweets into the brass-bound trunk. "Make two pitchers each: classic *and* cozz-moh."

"Bloody hell, make several," Jensen ordered brusquely, stepping over Mr. Lizard. "I'll meet you in the drawing room in half an hour."

We watched him stroll into the hallway.

"My my, but someone's testy," Rey said, standing akimbo.

"It's been a long day," May-Lee reminded her, dabbing her pert Hollywood-sculpted nose with a small tissue.

"A grimy one at that," Prunella agreed, wiping dust from arms reminiscent of heron legs. "I could do with a quick shower."

"Not a bad idea," Linda concurred, rubbing her face. "Even my eyes feel like they're layered with dust."

Clunk, thump. Groan. Clunk, thump. Clunk, thump. Eerie old-movie laugher echoed down the hallway.

Everyone glanced at one another and smiled feebly.

"Your aunt's moved beyond plastic and rubber toys," Linda said with a tired chuckle. "Now she's making sure that spooky sounds entertain us.

We'll probably be listening to ghosts and ghouls all night."

"I wonder what else she got Jensen to do," Rey said, peeking behind a painting of a stone-faced woman sitting in a rocking chair on a verandah. Norman Rockwell it wasn't. But Marcel Duchamp might have felt a kinship for the unconventional piece. "Who'd have thought Jensen could be the jokey sort?"

"She probably paid him well enough," Percival said, hooking his sister's arm. "I say we get back at him."

My cousin scanned his face. Her lips curled upward slowly, reminding me of The Grinch before his heart expanded. "I like the way your mind works. Yes, let's."

We spent three quick minutes planning revenge before racing to our rooms to wash faces and/or take hurried showers, brush teeth, and grab sweaters or jackets. Within thirty minutes we'd regrouped downstairs, eager to sample the fruits of Adwin's bartending skills.

Back in the room where Thomas Saturne had spent his last moments, no one sat on the sofa or spoke of him. Observers might have thought we were being respectful of the dead. In reality, we had other things to focus on – like icy-cold curl-your-toes martinis.

"Delicious." Percival toasted Adwin.

"Even with common supermarket olives," Prunella agreed, perched on an armrest by her brother's side.

He slapped her thigh playfully. "Aren't we the snob?"

She giggled.

"For a woman who has to be fifty, she sure acts half her age," Adwin whispered in my ear as we sat on a long, hard divan near the double-door entrance.

"What's wrong with that?" I asked.

"Nothing I guess. It just kind of rubs me the wrong way." He shrugged, sipped thoughtfully, and shrugged again, looking like someone struggling with contrary thoughts. "Or maybe it's her… She's icky."

"Icky?" I laughed.

"Icky," he repeated with a grin, then gestured. "At least she's not wearing that creepy Morticia Adamms bird necklace."

"Oh come on. What's wrong having a buzzard decorate cleavage?" I joked.

"So where's the mood music?" Linda asked as she placed logs on a fire she'd managed to start with great effort. Obviously she'd never aspired to be a Girl Scout during her early years.

"Yeah, we only got two minutes worth." Rey.

"If I know Matty," Percival said with a wry smile, "we'll be hearing two *hours* worth around one in the morning."

"Where's Jensen? His martini's getting warm." Linda brushed sooty hands on her jeans and reached for her glass. "Do you suppose he's gearing up for another 'fright'?"

"Let's hope this one is more scary than the last." Rey held out her martini glass for Adwin to top up. "It was kinda lame."

"It worked," Prunella commented, nodding at her brother.

"To a degree," he said with a salty smile. "A very small one."

May-Lee smirked and sipped. The attractive middle-aged woman seemed far from the shy sort; she was discerning and cautious, obviously selecting comments carefully lest she aggravate or insult someone. That was a smart thing – less chance of making enemies.

Beatrice's familiar footfalls caught our attention. She stood in the doorway, looking as sour as always. This time, instead of sporting an old-world maid's uniform in charcoal gray, she wore one of navy blue, and the starched apron was more lacy and formal, with a subtle trim of cornflowers. Shriveled liver-colored lips looked as if they'd kissed a pot of peach-colored lip gloss.

"Dinner is precisely one hour and forty minutes away." With what was either an attempt at a smile or an expression suggesting tummy troubles, she left.

"Shall we place bets as to how the mushrooms will be served tonight?" Prunella asked.

"I'm in. I bet five dollars there's some sort of mushroom stew." Linda.

"Five we get soup." Percival.

"Ten we see a casserole." May-Lee.

"Ten for quiche," Adwin piped in.

Prunella and May-Lee and I exchanged smiles, and I got the classic martini pitcher from the sideboard and started refilling glasses. A re-topping of the "cozz-moh" version followed.

124

Twenty minutes later, feeling galvanized if not smashed, we headed up softly lit stairs to change for dinner and see who'd win the mushroom bet.

Prunella stumbled to a stop. "I think I'll go see where our London barrister is. I'd hate for him to have decided to stay in his room all night and miss our joke."

Percival clasped her wrist. "We can play the joke anytime on the old stuck-up sour puss."

"Don't be rude, brother dear. Like us, he's a guest," she interrupted, pulling free. "We should all try to get along."

"Now, where have I heard that line before?" Rey asked, bemused.

"Why don't we all stop by his room?" Linda suggested.

Percival's eyes gleamed. "Good idea. Let's visit the 'old boy'."

We stopped in front of Jensen's door and Rey gave an urgent knock-knock-knock. Any louder and they'd have heard it on the next estate; any harder and the door would have given way.

"He must be power-napping," Rey said, grabbing the doorknob when there was no answer.

Prunella clutched her hand. "If he is, it wouldn't be right to wake him."

Rey looked at her sharply, stunned or startled, and yanked back her hand. "Why not? He'd do the same." She marched in like a bandleader leading a high-school ensemble down a football field during half-time.

Prunella sighed loudly, but followed Linda, who had followed Rey. Percival was right behind his sister of course, and Adwin trailed him – after rolling his eyes and giving a you-can't-win look. I took up the rear with May-Lee.

"Ouch!"

"I can't see a thing –"

"Turn on the frigging light –"

"I can't find the damn light switch."

"Stop standing in the fucking way –"

"Oh for the love of –"

"Ou-ouch!"

A mandarin sheen veiled the room and showed an astounded-looking Adwin by an art-deco night-table lamp, Linda standing on Percival's foot, Prunella on her butt on the hardwood floor, and Rey holding a hand to her reddened forehead. May-Lee and I were inches from the bed and each other: a near collision.

Rey snorted. "The joke's on us ... again."

"He's not here." Prunella sounded and looked awed as she slowly got to her feet.

"He'll probably show up in a closet or trunk or something," Linda said, leaping back from the writer of obscure poetry and gardening articles as if he were an aphid-infested rosebush she'd crashed into.

Percival frowned and regarded his foot as if making sure it was still its original shape and size.

"He's probably downstairs, waiting with one of those snide, smug smiles," Rey suggested. "Or he's getting decked out in a florescent ghost or padded monster suit, and is going to surprise us during dinner."

I smiled at an image of Jensen decked out like Frankenstein's monster. "For the record, ladies, I won't be wearing pink this evening."

* * *

Porter stood by a neon-blue four-oven cooker, stirring contents in a big Le Creuset pot. Two other ones simmered on back burners. He was dressed in chefwear: baggy striped pants and white short-sleeve shirt, a chefband, and black kitchen clogs. His hair was wild, cotton-candy dense, the color of butterscotch. Clairol? He had to be fifty-five if he was a day, so that was not his own color.

"More mushrooms for dinner?" I asked cheerily as I strolled across the cork flooring.

The portly cook turned and scanned my face with curiosity. "Marcel McIntyre – a respected local produce vendor – had a sale. I like them. Don't you, miss?" His New England accent sounded a bit stiff, slightly off. Artificial maybe.

"I do. I'm Jill Jocasta Fonne, by the way."

"Madam's niece." His voice was somewhat high-pitched, almost feminine. It didn't suit the frame or face. It also held little emotion and was thin, like non-sodium vegetable broth; a hint of flavor, but not much depth.

My gaze fell to a silver pinky ring with etched geometric patterns on his left hand, which was holding a long wooden spoon and stirring a fragrant mixture. Tiffany maybe. I'd seen a similar ring a few months back when an assistant producer and I were picking out a gift for her boyfriend's birthday.

I moved closer and peered in. Stew, it appeared. With lots of mushrooms, of course. "This smells great," I said cheerily.

"It's lamb stew. I'll be freezing it." The smile was as spare as his lips and he reached for a long thin plastic cutting board on which approximately three tablespoons of chopped herbs rested. "What brings you to my domain, Miss Fonne?"

"Jill, please. I've heard wonderful things about your cooking over the years from my aunt. I've liked what I've tried so far and thought it was time to officially meet you." I leaned into a counter that supported two sets of rustic-red ceramic canisters and a mobile phone. "My boyfriend's a pastry chef. He says you're very good at what you do." It was a bit of an exaggeration, but not a lie.

Another spare smile. He moved to a large French-door fridge and removed a fat ivory pitcher. "I don't normally spend time with guests."

"So I've heard, but I'm a niece, not a guest."

This time he chuckled and the teddy-bear rumbles sounded cute. "I don't spend time with them, either."

I stepped up to a deep stainless-steel sink in front of a small steamed-up window, and grabbed a crisp Granny Smith apple. I tossed the green globe and caught it. "You've been here quite a while."

He looked at me as if that went without saying, turned off the stove, and moved the pot with the stew to another burner.

"Did you know Thomas Saturne?"

"Only by name and sight." He shuffled back to the fridge and removed butter and eggs.

"So you wouldn't know if anyone hated him enough to kill him?"

Porter's ruddy chipmunk cheeks performed a hamster shuffle (invisible nuts shifted from one facial pocket to the other and back again). A sizeable trident-shaped scar graced the lower left cheek. That injury must have hurt like crazy. "Are the police saying he was murdered?"

"No." I smiled trimly. "Not yet."

More hamster shuffles. Close-set ash-gray eyes stared into mine. "Do *you* think he was murdered?"

"I'm a budding reporter," I shrugged. "It's my nature to be nosy and presume or assume the worst – until proven otherwise."

He marched to the pantry like a soldier on a mission. "Anything else, Miss Fonne?" he asked when he returned with a fresh bag of sorghum flour and bottle of agave nectar. His visage conveyed nothing: no curiosity, annoyance, or joy. The man was hard to read.

I shook my head.

"The final touches to dinner require undivided attention. You don't mind if I continue my work – in solitude?"

I shook my head again.

"Miss." He bowed a cantaloupe-shaped head and ambled back to the counter with the cutting board while I moved on to the library-study, hoping to find an entertaining book to read later in bed.

I was scanning the inside jacket of Lee's *To Kill a Mockingbird*, a book I'd not read since high school, when May-Lee Sonit entered.

She jumped upon seeing me. "You startled me!"

"Apparently," I smiled, tucking the book under my arm.

She laughed anxiously and strolled to the shelves that housed fiction books. "I seem to be in a reading frame of mind and thought I'd grab two or three more novels."

"Good books beat TV any day."

"I agree. There are too many reality shows and not enough quality programming anymore." She scanned two shelves and removed Hemingway's *For Whom the Bell Tolls* and Twain's *Life on the Mississippi*. "I never tire of either."

"The books? Or the authors?"

She regarded me for several seconds. "You look like Mathilda. You have her cheeks and mouth."

Instinctively I touched my face. "No one's mentioned that before."

"They've probably never seen the two of you together before."

"Either have you."

"But I have. Here you are and there she is." She gestured three large photos in ornate silver frames on one of two antique oak carved pedestal tables. One was of Aunt Mat and Reginald by a willow tree in a vast hilly park during their early years. Gauging from the nearby flowering trees and colorful tulips, it was early spring. Another was of Reginald receiving an award or certificate from a man who bore a striking resemblance to Christopher Lloyd in *Back to the Future.* The third was a medium shot of my aunt in a forest-green sequined number at a black-tie gala, probably taken five or six years ago. "There's definitely a resemblance."

"You two were close."

"Very." She glanced wistfully at the third photo. "We shared many enjoyable moments together."

"You also shared a lot of interests."

"We did, yes – antiques, art, theater, opera, viticulture and the resulting fine wines." Another wistful glance.

"Did you know Thomas at all?"

She hugged the books to her chest. "We'd met a few times over the years, primarily here at the estate." She smiled sadly. "Mat did have a flair for in-house parties and celebrations."

"What did you think of the man?"

"He was stuffy, self-absorbed, anxious, preoccupied. He wasn't overly friendly and he wasn't one to open up to others and make them feel welcome or liked." She shrugged. "I suppose I shouldn't be so judgmental, considering the man's deceased."

"But that's certainly the impression he gave," I agreed. "Do you think someone could have disliked him enough to have killed him?"

Eyes the color of Red Rose tea widened. "The man's death was an accident, wasn't it? I know what your cousin has been claiming, and what's been said, but I can't believe his death was anything but an accident."

I smiled fleetingly and sauntered to the door. "Of course it was an accident. It's very easy to get caught up in Rey's penchant for the melodramatic."

She scanned my face, chuckled lightly, and moved into the hallway.

Forget Cousin Reynalda's nonsense. I'd allowed myself to become absorbed in the dramatics. Of course Thomas' death was an accident. So I'd keep convincing myself.

11

Come Out, Come Out, Wherever You Are

Dressed in black linen pants and a white silk shirt with a polka-dotted white and teal scarf, a gift from Aunt Mat several months back, I swung into the main dining room, Adwin not far behind. I wasn't surprised to find the other gals wearing shirts and pants as well, in different shades of gray and brown, but I did raise a curious brow at the array of polka-dotted scarves. I'd not even have worn mine had it not been draped on the same hanger as my shirt, kind of like a prompt or Post-It note. This was becoming way too co-incidental.

"Nice scarf. A gift from Aunt Mat?" I asked Rey flatly.

"Yeah. I forgot I had it. In fact, I'm pretty sure I forgot to bring it along." She glanced down, bemused. "Because I forgot I even had it."

The Sayers presented puckered brows while Linda, May-Lee, and I eyeballed each other's neckwear.

"Soup's on," Adwin announced as Hubert limped in with a large white ceramic tureen and set it in the middle of the table. This time there were no bizarre dinner service motifs. A thick beige linen tablecloth and eggplant-colored napkins, and tall cream-colored candles adorned the table. It was all quite staid, which made me wonder what Mathilda Moone had in store for the evening (the others might lower their guards, but mine was on red alert).

"What the hell is this?" Rey asked, looking into the tureen.

"I believe it's a pepper pot," Percival replied cheerfully.

She peered closer. "What's in it? I see mushrooms and veggies, but there's lumpy meat-like stuff in here."

"That would be tripe, dearie," Prunella said with a smile as wry as her brother's. "Dumplings and tripe."

"Lovely," Rey murmured, wrinkling her nose. She leaned toward Linda and quietly asked, "What the frig is tripe?"

"The lining of a bovine stomach."

My cousin's face took on a corpse-like hue.

Prunella inhaled deeply and said, "It smells absolutely divine."

Hubert nodded and, as if on cue, began to serve.

Talk was limited as we dove into the pepper pot. Alright, maybe we didn't exactly dive; we sniffed, tested gingerly, sniffed again, and *then* dove in. It was tasty … for bovine stomach lining.

"I won the bet," Percival said after emptying his bowl. "I said soup."

"You did," Prunella nodded, "but this wasn't mushroom soup per se. It merely had edible agaric in it."

No one won the bet that evening. The pepper pot was followed by chicken schnitzels, spaetzle (Austrian noodle thingies) and creamed mushrooms. Dessert was a dense, spice-laden pumpkin pie – and a very good one judging from the way Adwin's lips curled upward between mouth-fuls.

Later, after dinner and a few treks upstairs, we adjourned to the Drink & Death Room, as Linda called the drawing room. We were sipping mint tea and avoiding eye contact, ensconced in those little Zen zones we'd become quite familiar with in the last twenty-four hours, when ghost-like booing started to flow softly around us like milk-weed filaments propelled by a westerly wind.

"How Abbott and Costello," Linda commented.

"That explains why Jensen didn't show up for dinner," Percival said with a roll of his eyes, jerking a thumb upward. "He's hovering near a vent, doing a Casper impression."

"It's kinda lame," Rey sniffed, pouring more tea into her cup.

"Why don't we sneak up on him and give him a scare?" Linda suggested, standing. "I don't want him thinking he can get away with this all night."

"If the lot of us 'sneak up on him', we'd hardly catch him unawares," Prunella pointed out dully.

Rey threw back her tea. "Let's give it a try. If it doesn't work, it doesn't work. We'll get back at him with our original plan."

"Never mind the fact there have to be hidden rooms and walkways in an old place like this," Linda added with a nod.

"Let's split up," I proposed. "Rey and Linda can take the west wing. Adwin, you and I will take the east. Prunella and Percival could –"

High-pitched staccato laughter echoed throughout the dwelling.

Linda snorted. "Geez, now we've got freaking Fred Flintstone's Uncle Giggles running amok."

Percival looked blank, but Adwin and I laughed.

"Okay guys, let's do as my cousin suggested and take different parts of the house," Rey said, stepping past.

I grabbed her forearm. "Let's *not* make too much noise. We want to surprise him."

"How're we going to see anything? We can't exactly go turning on lights if we're aiming for the element of surprise," Adwin pointed out.

"Let me get those flashlights we put back in the pantry earlier." Percival strolled from the room; a man with a target.

* * *

The lighting in a rectangular music room was as dim as it was everywhere else in that wing of the house. A lone bulb in a shade-less lamp was 40W at best. Different sized cloths in various shades of beige and taupe, ranging from silky-soft to scratchy-coarse, had covered two classic pianos, an Erard harp, a long wooden trunk, and one tall cabinet in which clarinets rested. They now lay on a smooth maple hardwood floor that would have gleamed had it been waxed. Textured wallpaper, a dusty rose and pale peach-puff combination, did little to brighten the place. Dusting appeared to be regular, but it didn't look as if music lovers hadn't frequented the room in years.

Adwin gazed at a John Brinsmead Art Case Upright while running fingers lovingly over a 1880s French Pfeiffer Cottage Upright, its wrinkled cover lying at its pedals like a shorn shroud. His expression was similar to the one he sported when putting finishing touches on a five-layer hazelnut butter torte. Music had been the pastry chef's first love, but an incident with a flaky if not skittish piano maestro and the lid of a grand piano terminated a successful music career before it started. Fortunately, those long graceful fingers hadn't been too damaged and they went on to create other magnum opuses: delectable ones.

I could imagine May-Lee regarding both pianos with appraising eyes, calculating their worth if they were to find their ways into her shop. Or perhaps she'd simply admire the workmanship and marvel at the history.

I could see the Moones going for the pianos and the harp, but clarinets? Pleased to demonstrate how far his know-how extended, my beau-slash-music-expert pointed out one was an A-flat clarinet and the other a bass clarinet (his Australian cousin Henry played the former in a military band). Given Aunt Mat's taste for the odd and different, I could imagine her tooting on the former, but not the latter, a heavy version with a floor stand.

"What's up?"

I brushed dust from the jersey cardigan I'd slipped on before the exploration began. It was getting progressively colder out and it seemed as if the chilly external air were seeping in through windows and cracks. Earlier, the Weather Channel had posted a winter storm watch, which had already gripped Georgia, where highways were experiencing icy white-out conditions, freezing fog, and multiple pile-ups. It would impact at least six states over the next few hours. Airports had already started to delay and cancel flights. From the feel of it, the ice storm was approaching rapidly. Closing a case, I asked, "Do people toot?"

Adwin laughed. "Only if they're taxis."

"Ha, ha." I walked over to see what he'd found in a strongbox. "Anything of note?"

He held up a small pile of printed songs. "It's hard to hide body parts among compositions."

"What a funny boy you are ... not."

"Are you ready to move to the next room?"

"I'm ready to call it a night."

He draped an arm around my shoulders and we strolled to the door. "Where's that investigative reporter instinct?"

"I'm a weather gal," I replied with a droll smile. "I only need to look out a window to get my story."

Adwin laughed as we stepped into the shadowed hallway – only to freeze as a sound that fell between a shriek and a screech pierced the air.

"You've got to wonder if there are amplifiers hidden beyond these walls." He peered into the darkness. "What do you think – was that part of the show?"

The hairs on the back of my neck stood on end. "I doubt it." I grabbed Adwin's hand and we raced forward, making it across the house in seconds, only to stop at a flight of shadowy stairs, unsure which direction to take.

Adwin gestured upward. "That way."

I pointed down the hallway. "That way."

"Is anyone down there?" Percival's voice boomed from above.

We hastened up the stairs, stopping before the writer, who stood at the base of a narrow winding staircase that led to the tower where Prunella claimed Reginald kept additional "oddments". He held a pewter candelabrum in which five fat white candles burned. The golden light made his angular face glow eerily, giving him the appearance of a specter visiting from an other-world.

Adwin glanced around. "Where is everyone?"

"I have no idea, but I heard a scream. I thought it came from up there," he motioned, "but the door is locked and there doesn't appear to be anyone beyond it. I was heading down to find someone to help me open it. Now that you're here, the three of us should easily be able to break it down."

Adwin smiled wearily. "It's another joke … probably."

"The scream sounded like one of Pruney's," Percival claimed, his expression bordering on pained.

Pruney? Oh boy. The more time spent in their company, the weirder the brother-sister duo was becoming. "Maybe she and the girls decided to turn tables and scare Jensen, and/ or us," I said with a wink.

Percival looked from me to Adwin and back again. The knots in his brow softened. "I wouldn't put it past your cousin to think up something silly like that."

Adwin had to agree. "Let them have their fun —"

Another shriek-screech erupted. We scurried up the steps, bumping into walls and jostling one another like the Ghostbusters pursuing the Stay Puff Marshmallow Man.

Percival rammed the candelabrum into Adwin's chest, nearly knocking him over.

He clutched it, barely avoiding a singed neck, a curse seen but not heard.

Prunella's anxious brother rattled a heavy, clunky lock that would have nicely graced a medieval castle. It wouldn't give so he banged on the heavy wooden door and shouted his sister's name several times before Adwin kneed him in the butt. The action was very unlike my beau, but then so was the, "Will you get a frigging grip, dude? She's not answering the frigging door!"

The lock was sturdy and secure. I was about to request suggestions as to how to open it with no hairpins or sharp implements in reach when something movie-time popped into my head. I reached upward and felt along the doorsill. Nothing. So much for ingenious flashes. Not completely discouraged, I moved onward.

Percival gestured. "Help me break it down."

Adwin scanned the door that had to be as solid as a fortress gate. The look he gave the middle-aged gent suggested he thought the man two screws short of demented.

"Do you have a better idea?" His question held enough chill to form ice crystals on Adwin's thin upper lip.

"I do." I held up a brass key I'd found secured to the underside of a staircase banister.

Ignoring Percival's outstretched hand, I unlocked the door. Despite its thickness and size, the door swung inward as easily and lightly as if it were a feather fan.

Adwin slipped in first, lighting the way for several feet. "Wow."

The round room was filled with artifacts and curiosities and Prunella's "oddments". "Wow" didn't begin to describe it. Numerous showcase pieces, made primarily of bone and horn, were so simple and crude they could only have been homemade. But made in whose home? The mad scientist, Dr. Moreau's?

A tiny control, cleverly camouflaged to blend into roughhewn bricks alongside the door, proved to be a light switch. A soft glow, pale as moonlight, swathed the room.

"Maybe we should have stuck with candle-light," Adwin said with a tight smile, position-ing the candelabrum in the gauntlet of a 16th-century knight. "Hang onto that, willya Lancie?"

"What a hodgepodge," Percival muttered.

"You've never been in here?" I asked. I'd come to believe brother and sister did everything to-gether. So how had Prunella known what was in here? An educated guess? Or a personal invita-tion?

"Never had the, mmm, privilege."

"How ugly is this guy?" Adwin's face was an inch from a wrought-iron griffin. The winged monster stood as tall as he.

"Not half as hideous as this one," Percival said, eyeing a terra cotta cherub corbel near a high and narrow arched window. "Keeee-rist. The thing looks possessed!"

I'd have argued that a bronze fountain top I'd nearly crashed into beat theirs by a mile or two; a crazed-looking eagle with pointed wings that nearly touched the ceiling clasped a misshapen world in sharp, oversize talons.

Thunk. Swish. Cheep-chirp-chitter. Strange subdued sounds emanated from the area of a carved Gothic gargoyle gracing the wall across from the window.

We exchanged glances that wavered between baffled and frightened.

"Is this where we poke our guardian against evil in the eye and he steers us to a secret room?" Adwin stepped forward and pressed one eye and then the other. Nothing happened.

"Try the ears," Percival suggested.

Nothing happened.

"Go for the Donald Trump backcombed coif," I offered.

Adwin looked at me with a furrowed brow, then ran fingers across the gargoyle's head. Something caught his interest. A jiggle here, a joggle there, and ta-da, a three-by-five-foot portion of the wall slid sideways, sounding like a dull spade scraping pebbled earth.

"Keee-rist."

"Cool." Adwin peered inside. An impossibly narrow flight of stairs lead downward into blackness. "Grab a candle, plum dumpling, and place it in that holder-type thing on the windowsill."

"… Got it, my little banana flan."

Percival groaned and waited for me to lead the way.

* * *

"Anyone here?" Percival shouted.

Bumping into Adwin, who'd stopped in the middle of the narrow corridor, I rubbed my ear, hoping the damage from the strident question was temporary, and elbowed Percival not so lightly in the ribcage.

"Hey!"

"Hey yourself," I muttered, turning back to the tight ash-colored passageway. Forty feet ahead, it forked. "We could split up," I suggested.

"It would be better to stay together until we find the others," Percival advised. "If this is all a stupid game, fine; if not, why play into some fruitcake's hand?"

Adwin and I glanced at each other and nodded, and the three of us marched solemnly to the left.

The bricked walls and rough flooring weren't dirty or overly dusty, which suggested the hidden passage had been in use throughout the years. Or maybe dust and dirt didn't collect in walled-off places. What did I know? It did smell moldy, though, and I fought an urge to sneeze.

"Did you hear that?"

"Hear what?" I asked.

Percival's voice grew urgent. "I heard something. It was soft, hushed, and seemed to come from there." He pointed to the left.

Adwin and I turned to each other and shrugged simultaneously. "Left it is." He grasped the candle holder and took the lead. For an introspective laid-back kind of guy, he was being as valiant as one of the men sporting Reginald's armor centuries ago might have been.

"Ach-choo!"

"*Gesundheit*," my valiant beau murmured as we halted. There was nowhere to proceed; solid wall lay immediately ahead.

Percival pressed a monogrammed linen hankie into my hand. After another violent sneeze and the blowing of my itchy nose, I pressed it back into the pocket of his sweater.

"Thanks." You could hear the wince rather than see it.

I pointed a thumb to the rear. "As Rey would say: about face!" Making a crisp turn, I started to head back when Percival grabbed my forearm.

"Listen."

We faced the wall. Subtle sounds suggested there was something or someone beyond the barrier. I ran fingers along uneven bricks on the left. Adwin, seeing what I was doing, did the same on the right. Percival inspected the barren floor and low irregular ceiling.

It was nimble-fingered Adwin who discovered a loose brick that – with a push and a pull – resulted in a wall shifting inward. "Just like in the movies," he said with a triumphant smile.

"Too much so," Percival said with a sigh. "If Mr. Hyde or the Wolfman pops out of nowhere, I won't be held responsible for what I may do."

He wasn't intending to be funny, but I laughed.

An apricot light glimmered in the nearby distance and we moved toward it. The search for missing persons and goblins was on again as we picked our way down a short slope.

Adwin stopped dead in his tracks, prompting me to bump into him and Percival to stumble into me. "Speaking of horror-movie nasties, what's this? A lair?"

"Someone's been here," Percival said, nodding to one of two antique parlor lamps that provided the gentle lighting. "Hey!"

The opening had slid back in place with a whoosh-thunk. We were in a square room of meadow green with a low beamed ceiling and walls finished with plaster. It resembled a cross between an old-world library and study, and would have made a great Victorian England stage setting. Had this been Reginald's little get-away? It was certainly reminiscent of the library-study in the main part of the house. Or could this be Aunt Matty's hideaway?

Adwin blew out the candle and we spent a couple minutes attempting to find a lever or switch that would reopen the wall, gave up, and decided to investigate the intriguing surroundings that suggested we'd walked into another era. We strolled around, entranced by quality furnishings and fine details, tempted to touch things, but knowing better.

"Oh-oh."

Adwin and I turned to Percival, then to what he was viewing. Oh-oh was an understatement.

Jensen Q. Moone was reclining on an elaborately carved mahogany recamier in a far corner niche, a slender pine stake wedged into his heart through a fine designer shirt and the gold chain and cross he'd sported since arrival draped around the stake. If you looked beyond the blood-covered chest, you might have claimed the barrister was sleeping, so serene was his expression. Hadn't the man protested or fought? Or had he known his killer? And if he had, why would he have allowed that person to drive a wedge of wood into his body? Maybe the killer had been swift, surprising? Or had Jensen Q. Moone been drugged, his senses dulled so he couldn't react?

"So much for the crucifix. It didn't do him much good," Percival murmured, peering over my shoulder.

"Vampires are the ones to get stakes through the heart, and they don't wear crosses – at least not in the movies I've seen," Adwin said.

"He was a bloodsucking lawyer, Addy boy. They're a different, hardier breed."

I swallowed a chuckle and attempted to appear grave. Okay, maybe "grave" wasn't the right word, considering.

"My word, what a spot of bad luck," Adwin said with a West-Country English dialect.

I roared. Adwin tittered. Percival looked at us as if we'd lost it, but seconds later, he was laughing like someone who'd sucked in too much nitrous oxide.

Several tears and gasps for breath later, Adwin was checking out a large handcrafted oak fireplace that hadn't seen a fire in years, if ever. Percival was investigating a beautiful mahogany bookcase with a lovely brass swan neck he swore was from the Chippendale period, while I was searching a handsome handcrafted nineteenth-century oak armoire with satyrs and other mythological creatures lining triple-paneled doors. Besides the wall that had swung back into place, there had to be an alternative exit somewhere.

I was about to test the rear panels of the armoire when a grinding sound from beyond the unit drew my attention. I glanced across the room to see if my cohorts had heard it. They had and their expressions mirrored mine: wary.

Like a loaded car carrier, slowly and noisily, the heavy armoire slid aside.

12

Hyde-n-Seek

"You found it!" Linda, smiling jubilantly and waving a waterproof lantern, rushed forward. Her left cheek sported dirt shaped like a top hat while the tip of her ski-slope nose missed a couple of layers of skin.

Rey raced in from behind, followed by Prunella and then May-Lee.

"What? The room?" I grabbed the intense light and switched it off. I was already suffering from partial hearing loss, no thanks to good ol' Perc, so partial blindness wasn't on the rest of the agenda.

"The entrance to the hidden passageway." She motioned the corridor from which they'd emerged.

"It was *you* who found it." Peering past her shoulder, I viewed only exaggerated shadows and darkness. I motioned the opposite wall. "We came across the other one during our travels."

"They actually loop around. It's kind of weird and wacky the way things connect, but this place is really cool," Rey exclaimed, pulling cobwebs and dust balls the size of marsh plants from disheveled hair.

"It has a certain fun factor," Prunella agreed, stepping alongside her brother. Her costly cashmere sweater was layered with grime and a three-inch tear graced one sleeve. A jagged scrape bloodied one cheek and an abrasion divided an eyebrow the size of a Tootsie Roll.

"Did you ladies meet a mad ghoul along the way?" Adwin joked.

She fingered the wound and smiled dryly. "It was more like erratically positioned pipes and cobweb-mad spiders."

Percival regarded her worriedly.

She waved his unvoiced concern aside. "A huge repugnant arachnid caught me by surprise. I panicked and smacked iron ... face first." She grinned. "Then, just for effect, I did it again."

"Pruney, that's *one* fabulous scream you have," Rey declared with a wide smile, sticking an index finger in one ear and jiggling it back and forth.

Pruney appeared to be the name of choice and endearment this evening. Well, there were worse names to answer to.

May-Lee swung around from the rear. She suppressed a sneeze. "I believe I have had more adventure in the last few hours than I have in the last five years." Sighting something crawling along her stretch linen-blend jeans, which had to cost more than the six pairs of denim I owned, she cast it aside with a soft wail.

Percival stepped on it when it landed by his foot. "What did you find, besides multi-legged companions?"

"Besides bugs – and looping corridors – we discovered a couple of alcoves and another secret room, a smaller version of this one, with a concealed bar and fridge, just off the tower," Linda offered. "We didn't find Jensen, though."

"We did." I pointed at the recamier.

The women raced across the room like runners in a track-and-field sprint.

Prunella's tiny lips disappeared while Rey and Linda peered so closely they could have administered mouth-to-mouth. May-Lee simply appeared resigned, but took one long stride rearward.

"You didn't tell us he was dead," Rey said flatly.

"You didn't ask."

"He wasn't here when we passed through earlier." Linda.

"When was that?" I asked.

She glanced at a pumpkin-orange Swatch watch and shrugged. "Twenty minutes ago, give or take."

"More like fifteen." Rey.

"More like thirty." May-Lee.

"Thirty, at the very least." Prunella.

"You're certain he wasn't here when – whatever time – you moved through here?" Adwin asked, baffled.

They looked at one another, then at Jensen, and shrugged simultaneously.

Percival's eyebrow arced like a gooseneck. "We'd better call the police."

"What do we do with Jensen the Jokester?" Linda asked, jerking a thumb.

"He's not going anywhere," he replied.

"Dead bodies always disappear in the movies," she said.

"Then why don't you sit beside the unfortunate bugger and make sure he doesn't – wait a minute. Has anyone checked that he *is* dead? He's already played one prank."

We regarded Percival as if he'd offered a dramatic and enlightening disclosure.

"Well?" he asked.

I pressed Linda's lantern into his hands, marched forward and scanned Jensen's tranquil expression, his torso, legs and arms. The digits of his right hand were crusted with blood. Was this all fake? Was it theatrical make-up? I wasn't inspired to check that closely. Besides, there was no way someone could remain that inactive for that long and not be dead – hold on. CPR 101, courtesy of a ten-minute segment I'd hosted on first aid, kicked in. I pressed two fingers alongside the outer edge of his trachea to feel the pulse of the common carotid artery.

"What's the verdict, Dr. Fonne?" Rey asked.

"He's as dead as Fred the Ghost."

"Let's hope he doesn't start singing anytime soon," Adwin said.

"He's not going anywhere," Percival repeated, moving into the opening the trio had emerged from. "But you're all welcome to keep him company."

We were on his heels faster than kids on cotton candy at an annual state fair.

* * *

The witching hour found a steady stream of ice-heavy rain saturating the state and spreading towards Pennsylvania, New York, and eastern Canada. It also found the return of our two favorite law enforcers.

Thanks to temperamental locks and those "looping" corridors, it took a quarter of an hour with skeptical Sheriff Lewis and surly Detective Gwynne in tow, to find the way back to the secret room. And wouldn't you know it? As sure as the sun rose in the east, Jensen Q. Moone wasn't where we'd left him. There was no blood, no weapon ... nada.

Back to the drawing room we traipsed, where coffee and sugary treats and an immense roaring fire awaited. Lewis, fifty if he was a day, had an easy-going air about him. When he smiled, sea-green eyes sparkled with sincerity. He'd probably seen a lot of mischief in his youth. Gwynne, on the other hand, leaned toward the somber. He couldn't have been more than forty, but appeared to have seen it all. Or maybe fourteen years on the Bronx police force had taken its toll; made him familiar with violence and, consequently, indifferent.

The sheriff had a soft Massachusetts accent that recalled fond memories of cherry clams, colorful falls, and saltbox houses. "It's nawt that I don't believe you, but there's no body and no blood."

"Bring out the Luminol. You'd find trace amounts of it," Linda suggested with a hint of smugness.

Lewis laughed and took a chocolate-walnut cupcake from a large oval plate. "This isn't one of those police procedural shows, Miss."

"What about the fact that Thomas Saturne died?"

Gwynne sighed. "It was an accidental death –"

"For *sure*?" Linda challenged. The screenwriting assistant was becoming feisty.

"For *now*." Lewis drained his coffee and stood. "Matty Moone was a good lady and she made a tasty pear crumble pie –"

"Pear crumble pie?" Rey and I asked simultaneously. Our aunt *baked*?

"Your ahnt enjoyed baking in the fall. Never did it any othah time of the year, except for the week around Christmas, of course. She dropped off a couple of pies, like clockwork, every second Friday throughout the autumn months." He smiled wistfully and gazed into the distance, as if a slice were within reach.

"Shouldn't you check out the entire property?" Linda asked.

"I was going to say, before I was interrupted, she made tasty pear crumble pies but she made even greatah jokes." Lewis glanced at me, then at Rey. "As her nieces, you'd know that bettah than anyone. She probably got this Jensen Moone fellow to play anothah prank."

"But –"

Gwynne's concentrated stare silenced Linda.

She frowned and turned to the mammoth fireplace.

"If you won't find him, we will," Rey stated haughtily, standing.

"When you find him, I'm sure he'll be roaring with laughtah," Lewis said with a grin, smoothing his shirt over a belly that had enjoyed many of Mathilda Moone's pear pies and more. "We'll see ourselves ount. Please thank the team in the kitchen for the hospitality."

"Do you believe that?" Linda asked angrily, watching the two men leave.

"You can't blame them," Percival said, attempting to stifle a yawn. "I wouldn't believe us, given the situation: *no* corpse."

Adwin sipped green tea. May-Lee nibbled a pecan tart and stared into the distance. Linda rubbed her raw nose and Pruney continued to pick at a large bandage on her cheek. I was too tired to care. If Jensen were indeed playing a joke, we'd get him back threefold. If he wasn't, then the million-dollar question was where was he? Which prompted the two-million dollar question: if he were truly dead, who the hell had moved his body?

"I'm annoyed," Linda announced, crossing her arms and adopting one of Rey's peevish moods.

"I'm curious," Rey offered.

"I'm itchy." Pruney pulled at the bandage and winced as it came off, with a couple of layers of skin. A tissue quickly found its way to bleeding flesh.

"I'm ready for bed," May-Lee announced, standing.

"I'm gone." Percival marched from the room.

"I am, too." Adwin followed.

"I say we go searching." Rey.

"I say we get some sleep and start our search with fresh eyes and a decent breakfast in our stomachs." Keeping the tissue pressed to her wound, Prunella rose slowly.

"I agree. We need to recharge," I said.

"Hear, hear." May-Lee strolled into the hall-way.

Rey did her pouty thing and Linda sighed, and we ambled upstairs.

13

Come Out, Come Out, Wherever You Are

"Oh!" With thoughts back in North Carolina and eyes on the cork flooring, I hadn't immediately sighted Beatrice ten feet in front.

"Ma'am."

On a small acacia-wood serving tray sat a steaming floral mug and slice of poppyseed strudel. She was wearing an Empire night-gown under a long matching cotton robe, belt loose, and a padded, quilted bonnet, something I thought could only be found in PBS sagas and epics. A thin sheen of oil glistened on her shriv-eled face. It seemed a little late in life for moistur-izing and/or attempting to soften those "fine fa-cial lines", which she had more of than an Asian bitter melon.

"I've heard a few footfalls traipsing hallways this late evening," I smiled. "I guess I'm as restless as you and the others. Maybe hot cocoa will help me relax."

"Warm milk and honey works as well as any sleeping pill, and is much healthier." She nodded to the mug and her lips twitched. A smile? "Ma'am." With the tray held firmly in both hands, off she ambled like a devoted lady departing church with the Good Book.

The milk was easy to find: there were three large cartons in the fridge. The honey took longer to locate, but finally showed up in a cupboard – the sixth of fourteen. There was a selection, too: blueberry, clover, apple blossom and fireweed. The fireweed sounded novel.

Two minutes later, as I was whisking a liquid "sleeping pill", Percival Sayers walked in, wearing the same bedtime attire as the evening previous.

"You couldn't sleep, either?"

Percival shook his head and leaned into the counter alongside me. "I like the slippers."

He was referring to a pair of fabulously fuzzy Pandas that warmed my feet and ankles, a birthday gift from my nephew. "They're perfect for chilly nights."

"I'll have to find me a pair," he laughed, sounding like Santa Claus approving of a child's gift list. The hearty sound was oddly comforting.

I motioned the fridge. "Grab the carton of low-fat. Beatrice swears this works better than hot cocoa."

He peered into the pot, appeared dubious, then stepped across the kitchen. "Would you care for cookies? We can sit here and chat until fatigue kicks in."

"There's a package of oatmeal-raisin in the second cupboard to your left. They'd go nicely with hot honeyed milk."

"Wouldn't Oreos make a better pairing?"

"Oreos?" I stopped whisking. "I don't recall seeing any."

His smile was sly. "That's because there were only a couple of packages and I hid them behind the kidney beans in the pantry."

"You devil." I whirled and pointed. "Oreos, Mr. Sayers! And fast!"

He complied and I quickly whisked in more honey to compensate for the extra milk. After filling two large clunky mugs to the brim, I ambled to the breakfast nook and sat across from the middle-aged writer. I grabbed several Oreos from a plastic plate in the middle of the table and placed them on a paper napkin sporting a picture of pasta.

"Do you think we'll find that sour-faced barrister?" He sniffed the milk-honey mixture and took a small taste. His expression suggested he wasn't sure whether he liked it, but he took another sip and bit into a cookie.

"More likely he'll find us – when he's ready."

"You don't believe he's dead then?"

"I don't know what to think. He looked pretty dead and felt pretty dead, but anything is possible. He may have taken something to simulate death. And the mess in his chest could have been special effects. I didn't touch the stake. Until his body shows up, I am going to refrain from voicing thoughts or suppositions." I scanned his face and tried not to stare at the left jaw, which sported a jagged Z-shaped scar.

"I acquired the wretched thing while on a safari in Kenya."

"*Really*?" I'd never have expected him to be a man of adventure.

He laughed. "Nothing exciting or perilous transpired. I fell from a Jeep ... in the hotel driveway ... after one brandy too many."

I also laughed and happily munched a couple of cookies.

He drank thoughtfully. "Your boyfriend seems an interesting sort."

"And so not me?"

"You two are very different, but you do mesh well. I understand he's a celebrated pastry chef."

"He has a following," I replied with a proud smile. "The Food Network will be airing a show next month featuring pastry chefs from around the country. Adwin's in the first three episodes."

"He never mentioned it."

"No, he wouldn't. He leans toward the private and understated. I only found out two weeks ago when I saw a trailer for the show – and there he was."

Percival chuckled. "I'm not sure 'understated' and Adwin are synonymous. He looks like the front man to an eclectic ... offbeat band." He grabbed another cookie and this time unscrewed the chocolate wheels. "Adwin's an un-usual name."

"His first name is actually Adwin-Byron."

"He had imaginative, creative parents, I take it?" He licked the sweet white cream like a sugar-starved five-year-old. It wasn't like him – a stuffy, academic gent channeling his inner child – and I found the action and expression endearing in an odd sort of way.

"His mother was a ceramics artist, his father an architect. Both were killed in one of Almafa's medieval alleys when he was three."

"The poor fellow."

"Fate's not always kind," I said quietly.

"Fate happens for a reason … if you believe in Fate."

"Do you?"

His smile was quick. "How did you two meet?"

"I was showcasing popular Wilmington restaurants two springs ago and as my cameraperson was following Adwin around the kitchen and getting in his way, Adwin tripped and literally fell into my arms … with an unbaked chocolate-raspberry cake. That was the first and last time I wore a lovely caramel-colored linen suit."

We chuckled and drained our mugs.

"Care for another round?"

"Why not?" Percival wiped tiny brown flecks from his chin. "I could get to like it if I drank it enough."

I was strolling across the kitchen when May-Lee entered, wearing much what I'd expect from a woman of her caliber: a floral Coromandel robe and lace-trim pajamas. She flinched upon seeing Percival and a fleeting look passed between them. It wasn't one of love or admiration, nor did it seem to be one of hatred or anger. What was it? Annoyance? Avoidance?

"This seems to be a night for not sleeping. We're having hot milk with honey."

"And Oreos." Percival held one up as if he were displaying an Olympic medallion. "You always liked them."

"I've outgrown them," she said with a hint of dryness. Just like I've outgrown you, her expression added. She turned to me and smiled. "If you don't mind making me one – to go – I'll take you up on your offer. Thanks."

I offered a regal bow. Casually I said, "I imagine you two have known each other for several years, courtesy of my aunt."

Percival snapped a cookie in half. "We go back."

She tossed her head. "Way back."

"Way *way* back." Both halves found themselves in his mouth.

An undercurrent of enmity passed. I looked from one to the other as I whisked. What was between these two? Mutual dislike? An unpleasant bygone incident? A bad business deal? I decided it best to steer the conversation – and mood – elsewhere and asked May-Lee if she knew Jensen well.

"I'd met him through Matty a few times over the years here ... and once in London when the two of us had traveled there for a week of theater and shopping. He'd taken us to the Tamarind Restaurant in Mayfair for dinner and then a cruise on the Thames. He'd also brought his wife along. They seemed very civil and very proud to show us the city and sites."

"Did anything out of the norm stand out?"

The antique-store owner eyed me curiously. "Such as?"

I poured steaming milk into mugs. "I don't know, to be honest. Was he anxious? Was he getting along with his wife?"

She walked over and took the mug I held forth. "That wasn't quite two years ago. I can't imagine anything having happened then that would bear any significance now." She pursed her lips and stared into her mug. "For what it's worth, I do recall two things. First: he made several phone calls, which I suppose isn't that unusual, given his profession. But during a couple of calls he was visibly tense, even stressed. And during one of the more 'stressful' moments, he muttered good-bye in German." She shrugged and stared flintily at Percival for five full seconds before returning to me. "Second: he and his wife behaved more like casual acquaintances. If was as if they tolerated each other, but barely."

Somewhat like you and Percival I was tempted to say.

"Sleep well Jill." She smiled and offered Percival the barest of nods.

I glanced at him. He smiled, took a handful of Oreos, and came to get his mug.

"Another one of these and I will sleep like a baby."

I hoped I would as well, but I suspected I'd be lying around, wondering what was between May-Lee Sonit and Percival Sayers – and come to that, what was between May-Lee Sonit and Prunella Sayers.

* * *

Adwin was under the blanket with Fred the Cat. The feline was snoring up a storm while the feline lover murmured in his sleep. It was nearly 3:00 a.m. and, yes I was tired, but I was also interested in seeing if jock-meister Ger had a response re Fred the Ghost. I grabbed the laptop and slipped into the dim hall. Prunella had done the same.

"I thought you were sleeping," were our simultaneous, suspicion-tinged comments.

"I have messages that need checking." I scanned her silky crimson robe with – what else? – a bird motif running along the collar and sleeves. Puffins. Fat, tripping-the-light-fantastic puffins. The robe hung loosely, drawing attention to a 36C chest with ripples of cord-like scarring starting at the cleavage and stretching to sights thankfully unseen. High-heeled red satin slippers with huge furry pompoms matched nicely. With her hair uncharacteristically loose and wavy the way it was, the freshly scabbed cheek and abraded eyebrow, the bird lady held an unexpected sexy if not raw edge.

"I'm in need of peppermint tea," she said with a trim smile. "My stomach's acting up."

"Too much excitement?"

"Too much rich food. Porter's a good cook, but he uses much too much butter."

I watched her sashay down a recently vacuumed Kashmar rug. Not that I made a habit of watching women's behinds, but hers had a seductive sway going on. Interesting. I moved onward with the intention of finding an empty guestroom, but ended up in Aunt Mat's bedroom. It was one place the gang had agreed it wouldn't encroach upon (showing consideration for our hostess and respecting the dead and all that).

Adjusting the lighting, I sat at a Queen Anne vanity set, a cherry ensemble much like Aunt Mat: pretty and feminine, delicate yet sturdy. Logging on, I found a lengthy email response with two scanned documents from Ger.

Fred Maxwell – our resident spook – was a relative of Pete Maxwell, the guy who tipped off Sheriff Garrett about Billy the Kid's whereabouts after that spectacular escape from the Lincoln courthouse in 1881. That's where the association between Fred and the Kid ended, although the former wasn't considered that upstanding a citizen either, having hung around with cattle rustlers, small-time bank robbers, and working women.

Fred liked ladies. A lot. He enjoyed spending earnings on them. A lot. Because he wasn't that careful about staying in the shadows or keeping a low profile after a bout of thievery or rustling, his wayward ways had made mention in local papers. Were the ladies to blame? Or the libido?

One such lady, Mahogany Belle, didn't take kindly to Fred's overzealous if not controlling affections and Fred didn't take kindly to having his overzealous if not controlling affections snubbed.

Mahogany Belle skedaddled to Big Chester, a local merchant and town cleaner-upper, who ran Fred out of town with a bag of feathers in one hand and a bucket of tar in the other. Gambling, questionable women, and debatable judgment resulted in Fred being jailed thrice for petty crimes and nearly being lynched once. Maybe the man found God, or at the very least peace, because he ended up settling in Norfolk Virginia for three years.

This was more information than I'd have expected, given the limitation of documents and chronicles in the 1880s, but our Fred showed up in a few records and the like, including a diary from young Anna Mae Bellamy, who'd first met him one afternoon when he'd delivered her father's newly shod Arabian Stallion. Apparently chaperons and parental units weren't as abundant as you might have thought, given the times. The eighteen-year-old spent a couple of hours with Fred, chatting over life, his mainly. In addition to youthful female feelings, she chronicled all she'd learned, such as his fall from grace and his respect for the "gentler sex", his traveling from state to state until he rode into Virginia, and his subsequent discovery of honest work: blacksmithing. It was a trade he'd originally learned from his father, but he'd only worked at it for a few short years. Evidently running with rustlers had had more appeal.

Lucky for me, Anna Mae's small leather-bound diary was part of an on-line archival collection at Duke University and that Ger had taken the time to assist with my request.

Fred had been a cowboy kind of guy, for a while anyway, one who'd seen and done wrong, then found purpose and tranquility along the way. Though how he'd ended up in Connecticut and, more specifically, in Aunt Mat's house was anyone's guess. Maybe we'd never learn, unless *he'd* left a diary in the walls he surreptitiously strolled along.

I requested Ger to uncover what happened to Fred between Virginia and Connecticut. The timeframe would have been 1885-1890.

Was it important to discover more about Fred? No. But I was curious. I stared past the window and saw that the rain had stopped. It was probably gathering momentum. I scanned an indigo sky filled with brilliant specks of silver, scrutinized the constellation Perseus, picked out Algo, the second brightest star in Perseus, and gave myself a mental pat on the back for remembering parts of the magnificent celestial sphere, thanks to a brief foray into astronomy. It looked frightfully cold out there. When the storm returned in all its pre-winter fury, and I had no doubt that it would, it was going to be a nightmare. Traveling would be challenging if not treacherous. The wisest thing would be to hunker down, preferably by a roaring fire with lots of blankets and a big pot of cocoa or milk and honey.

My thoughts returned to the two men who'd just died. Why not ask Ger to help with that, too? "I need all the facts you can find on the Moone mansion. If you're too busy, please ask Angela. In fact, have her learn all she can about Thomas Saturne and Jensen Moone. Please have her summarize the important/interesting facts in point-form. Need ASAP. Love ya." Like root canal. If anyone could unearth unusual or hard-to-find data, Angela could. The woman was a whiz at ferreting out remote facts, but what would you expect from a former corporate research analyst?

Did I feel like sleeping or sleuthing? Jensen's murder, real or not, had me wondering. Where was that man? Hiding in another secret room, laughing and gleefully rubbing his hands like a movie baddie? Or was he stuffed in a cubby-hole somewhere? He'd certainly looked dead, but special-effects make-up could achieve amazing results and death could be feigned, as I'd intimated to Percival. Severe hypothermia, for example, could make someone appear dead. But that could be ruled out in Jensen Moore's case; it was pretty unlikely someone had dunked him into Greenwich Harbor. There were "zombie drugs" of course, but that was a stretch. I doubted anyone here was into voodoo, but never discount the improbable. What other drugs were there – say, didn't tetrodotoxin cause paralysis?

I was reaching for the keyboard when a strange sensation overcame me. It felt as if someone were watching. I turned slowly and froze. I could have sworn ... I saw Aunt Mat beyond the armoire mirror.

Hopping to my feet, I hastened to the ornate wardrobe, and yanked open the heavy satinwood door. It was empty inside. *Completely* empty. No clothes hung from a rod on the right; nothing was folded and sitting on four shelves on the left. How sad. Once you were gone you were consigned to memory and the Sally Ann.

The inside of the door held nothing save a panel of soft, clean puckered paisley fabric. Decorative to be sure, but decorative to whom? Dust fairies? Absently I fingered it and then pulled it gently. The panel of fabric swung outward, revealing the rear of the mirror. Pressing my face to the back painting proved nothing. It wasn't a two-way mirror or a magic one. No illusion. Merely a delusion – mine. My imagination was having a figment of some sort.

Stifling a yawn, I stepped into the hallway and stopped, my eyes as wide as my mouth. "*Ha, ha, ha, you and me, Little brown jug, don't I love thee!*"

Stunned, awed, and frightened, I watched Fred the Ghost saunter past. He glanced sideward, smiled, and I felt myself being twirled around in a dosy-do. Then he entered a wall. I wasn't sure if I was more startled by the fact he'd greeted me, danced with me, or that he wasn't more than thirty-five years of age. Anna Mae, the young diary keeper, had described Fred as possessing a "funny crooked smile" and being as strong and striking as a vaquero. She was right. Those sky-blue eyes, surrounded by tiny crinkles – laugh lines made more noticeable by regular exposure to frontier sunshine – twinkled with mischief. The coffee-brown beard was full and the hair shaggy and short. He was of average build and average height, with broad shoulders, and his clothing typical of the period: plaid pants and double-breasted jacket, and cravat. Had he borrowed the outfit from the householder, or had Fred always held a sense of fashion? Or was it possible he'd been a guest of the Moones back when? It was difficult to imagine Fred, coming from a very different social force, hobnobbing with a Moone, but never discount the improbable, right?

This time I'd had the privilege of seeing him for several seconds as opposed to viewing him for a blink. Tonight he hadn't appeared like a will-o'-the-wisp or a flickering light or image, or a movie ghost, all translucent. Nor had he appeared hazy or filmy like the spirits in the footage our station had presented in a two-part documentary on local supernatural phenomena. I'd done a portion of the voice over and had absorbed a lot of information. The subject had never been a fascination of mine prior to that, but for several weeks after the project wrapped up I'd found myself scanning shadows and watching darkened windows and empty fields.

Fred looked pretty damn life-like. Human. Real. I hurried to the wall, tapped and slapped. My fingers tracked wrought iron candleholders and swirled paint, but couldn't locate levers or buttons or springs. What blood-and-bones person walked through a wall as solid as the Hoover Dam? *None.*

I hastened into the bedroom and dove under the covers, caring little if Fred the Cat was there or if the fuzzy beast minded that I'd hugged him to my chest like a teddy bear.

Adwin rolled forward, asking sleepily, "That you, my little Twinkie?"

"Go back to sleep, my beloved Ho Ho." The whiskered teddy bear began purring and the low rumbling sound was soothing and pleasant. With a stifled sneeze, I settled in for what was left of the night.

"Where've you been?"

"Dancing with a ghost."

14

1-2-3, You're It

Dressed in faded Diesel jeans and a Nautica full-zip sweatshirt, Adwin strolled into the bedroom and dropped bundled items into a small wooden hamper in a corner. With towel-dried hair and a Dennis-the-Menace cowlick hanging between the eyes, he looked impishly cute. "What are you doing?"

"Reading up on the history of the property, courtesy of our station's research associate, Angela. Ger texted her before going on air and she was on it pronto. She sent me what she found on the property so far. She'll get back to it when she's put out a few fires at the station."

He moved to a grooming kit on a nightstand and placed a drop of Joop at the base of the neck; never more, never less. "And?"

"The property dates back to 1860."

"Antebellum?" He searched through a drawer for socks. "I'd have thought it was built later."

"The property was initially five times as big. Besides this house – which has been renovated, extended and expanded at least three times since then – there were stables, a barn, a circular drive, parterre garden, kitchen garden, and a carriage house, which burned down in 1904.

"The main house had been designed and built for the Smith family by an architect named Montague Black. The Smith family, sadly, met with continual tragedy. Caine Granton Smith became very ill three years after they'd settled here and nearly died. His health never fully returned. He was a scientist of some sort and had hired an assistant by the name of Horatio who helped with experiments and the logging of findings. Smith came from money, so there was more than enough for him to carry on with scientific studies." I scanned Angela's notes. "In 1867, Scientist Smith died. Three years later Moone Number One bought the place for a legal tender note or two."

"He got it cheap, did he?" Adwin asked over his shoulder as he padded back into the bathroom. It was mousse and dryer time.

"Absurdly cheap." I followed to observe the morning ritual.

"How did Smith finally die?"

"He was crushed under the wheels of a fast-moving stagecoach."

"Those accidents happened all the time back then – like car crashes today."

I glanced in the mirror and decided I could partake of my own morning ritual. I gestured my beau to pass the mousse and applied some to unruly waves. "They never found the stagecoach, never mind a driver – only Smith's broken body along a common stagecoach route."

"A phantom coach." He pulled and twisted spikes as if they were fondant being molded into cake turrets. "I see a movie in the making."

"Then his wife, Elisabeth Mary, who continued to live here with the servants and three kids, died."

"Courtesy of another phantom?" On went the blow-dryer.

I waited for him to finish. "Poison forever silenced her speech. There's no mention whether it was self-administered or dispensed by another hand."

Adwin scanned my reflection. "What about the kids?"

"A rich aunt took them to Boston to live with her. One became a doctor, another had something to do with the Zeppelin airship, and the whereabouts of the third remain unknown as he went off to China on a mission of humanity and was never heard from again."

"Kudos to Angela." He gave a thumbs up. "She discovered a lot in a short period of time."

"Thanks in part to an autobiography written by one of the great-grandkids, Sue Smith. There's a blog dedicated to the Smiths and their history, and another related to Sue's writing. Both are maintained by a proud family member with the initials L.L. It seems the misfortunate Mr. and Mrs. Smith spawned intelligent and inventive offspring; they, in turn, spawned a whack of extraordinary and prominent offspring. Some proved more prominent than others, while a few suffered the early Smith misfortune."

"You mean stagecoach hit-and-runs and/or poison?"

"Destitution, dementia, devilry, and other hardships." I keyed and motioned him to the screen. "Here's an old layout of the property – a bad one – but it does give an idea of what it originally looked like." I moved to another image. "Here's a newer layout."

He stared for several seconds. "Go back to the old one." He waited and pointed. "The original property was much larger – as you said – but the cottage was L-shaped and longer, and not as close to the Sayers property."

"It was obviously rebuilt and relocated." I flipped between the old and new views. "Maybe the original one burned down or was torn down. You're right though; it's pretty close to the Sayers property. I hadn't noticed."

"Either had I, until we looked at these plans."

"I should ask Percival about the history of his place. Maybe it belonged to a relative or friend of the Smiths ... hence the proximity."

Adwin smiled dryly. "Be prepared for an afternoon of excitement."

A loud knock demanded our attention.

"Hey-ho, anybody here?" Rey's sing-song voice asked.

Adwin rolled his eyes and passed the dryer. He put on a ten-thousand-dollar smile and slipped from the bathroom. "Hey-ho, we're doing our hair."

I scanned my reflection, gave up the notion of doing anything else, and grabbed a cosmetics bag. Some color on the cheeks and lips wouldn't hurt, and the bags under the eyes needed concealing.

When I entered the room, Rey was on the edge of bed, dressed in Hilfiger jeans and a fitted baby-pink turtleneck, and sporting full make-up. She looked pretty and unusually cheerful and perky.

"You look like the cat that swallowed the canary, her mate, the babies, *and* the nest," I commented, grabbing a lightweight chocolate-brown suede bomber jacket from the closet and slipping it on.

Rey's grin widened. "Linda did some laptop detecting."

"Jill's associate checked out the history of the place and discovered a few interesting things. Maybe Linda found something equally cool," Adwin suggested, slipping into a pair of black Converse All Stars.

My cousin glanced at me, her gaze wavering between bemused and surprised. "I guess we have some info exchanging to do."

"First please, Number Two Cousin, provide facts found." I bowed my head and perched myself on the edge of a narrow windowsill.

"Thank you, most honorable cousin who does not-so-bad Charlie Chan impression." She bowed her head in return. "Linda ran a search on Thomas Saturne."

Pooh. Beaten to the punch. "And she learned … ?"

"Not a helluva lot. He'd been in the legal biz for about a quarter of a century. Did some pro bono work for a few charities and non-profit orgs. Was linked to some strange non-profit scandal, but was cleared when it turned out that someone at the non-profit was proven to be the actual guilty party. He also sat on a half-dozen boards and committees over the years – one of a company owned by Reginald Moone."

Adwin leaned into the back of the door, expressing exaggerated interest. Although he leaned toward the mild Clark Kent type, he could be quite a jokester and mocker when inclined. "And?"

"And, Jilly's boyfriend, he attended a few black-tie functions."

"And?" Adwin and I challenged in unison.

"And there are a few photos of those functions." She leaned back on her palms, the look shy of gloating. "At a dozen different functions in the last eight years he had the same escort."

We continued the game. "And?"

"The date was a woman with long hamster-colored hair and sexy clothes, and a decent body, too, for someone who has to have been in her mid to late forties at the time."

"So he had a date, a girlfriend with rodent hair?" Adwin exhaled loudly and crossed his arms. "Do we get three guesses as to who she is – was?"

My cousin laughed and rubbed her hands gleefully, playing smugness to the hilt. "I'd give you five, but you'd never guess, so I'm going to tell." She glanced from him to me, her smile widening to the point I thought her lips would touch her ears. "Prunella Bird-Lover Sayers."

My eyes bulged to the point you might have thought I was suffering from hyperthyroidism, while Adwin's mouth pretty much dropped to his bony knees. But then I recalled Percival's mention of the two being on the same board and it made sense that they would attend the same functions and be photographed together.

Another knock. This one sounded as if someone were using a brick instead of a fist. Percival stuck in his head. "Everyone's waiting at the breakfast table. They have delicious looking frittatas."

Rey said, "I don't like frittatas."

He smiled gaily. "The other option is quinoa-and-flaxseed waffles."

"That sounds healthy," Adwin said.

"With Vegemite."

"Nummy." Rey clasped my forearm. "Come on. We can't let the waffles get cold and hard." She leaned close. "Like Jensen Moone must be this morning."

* * *

195

The rain – more sleet really – returned after noon. Visibility was minimal. The storm was making an official entrance. Fortunately, the in-ground hot tub and its "pergola" (I'd have been more tempted to call it a sun lounge) was completely covered. With its ergonomically-designed seats and invigorating jets, the ceramic tub was proving to be a great stress-reliever. It bubbled and steamed, and created a fine mist that veiled our faces. Sporting conservative bathing suits that Beatrice had provided from a guest stash, Adwin, Percival, May-Lee, Rey and I reclined and relaxed, and sipped a light fruity wine. Perhaps it wasn't appropriate, considering Jensen's death and/or disappearance, but really, for all we knew, he could be playing a fantastic joke. The "body" hadn't yet been found, so quite possibly "it" was alive and well, and scooting surreptitiously between rooms.

Sitting in the hot tub was preferable to sitting in the drawing room, which lent itself to the somber. And remaining in our rooms waiting for a late lunch to be served didn't seem that pleasing, either. Linda had opted for chips and dip and soda with Prunella in the den, along with Sea-son One of *The Big Bang Theory*. Prunella didn't seem the sort to watch frivolous television, but when Linda stated that was what she was doing, the older woman quickly asked if she could keep her company.

"Think we'll find him?" Rey asked, stretching long lean legs onto an empty seat.

"That depends on if he's really dead," Adwin replied.

"He looked pretty dead to me," she said flatly.

I took a long sip and exhaled through my mouth, watching my breath float across the sizeable tub before restating what I'd thought and said previously. "It could have been make-up and special effects. I only checked the pulse, not the stake... I wasn't exactly inclined to touch it to see if it was real."

Percival gestured with his glass. "If one of us had checked more carefully, we might have discovered the stake *was* fake."

May-Lee grimaced. "Or we might have discovered a *real* corpse with mutilated flesh and pulp for a heart."

Adwin looked aghast and threw back his drink.

"Whatever the case, until he shows up – hopefully alive and simpering like a self-satisfied prankster – the police think we're, as you might say Reynalda, 'loony tunes'." Percival reached for a second bottle of wine perched in an ice-filled bucket and refilled glasses.

Rey gazed from one moist face to the next. "I don't suppose we want to go searching –"

"No" was the firm, unanimous response before she could complete the question.

"Then where do we go from here?" she sniffed.

"We let the police do their job and wait," I replied, rubbing a warm hand across my cold nose.

"*If* he was killed, *why* was he killed?" May-Lee.

"Let's say, for the moment, Thomas Saturne *was* murdered," I offered. "Perhaps Jensen saw something he shouldn't have in relation to the killing and was silenced as a result."

"Then why not die within minutes or hours of Thomas? Why give a witness an opportunity to spill the beans, so to speak?" May-Lee asked, slipping lower into the hot frothy water. It was getting progressively colder around us as outside elements began to pummel the enclosure like an over-zealous masseuse.

"Maybe Jensen didn't witness anything in terms of the actual murder, but bumped into the killer as he or she was getting rid of evidence," Adwin proposed. "Jensen may not have been aware of what he was actually seeing, but in the killer's eyes that would have made him a serious liability."

"That would explain the stake," Rey declared. "It's the type of weapon you'd use in the heat of the moment."

"A spontaneous action, or reaction," Adwin agreed.

"Speculation is a decent time-waster, but does little for unraveling a mystery or providing a resolution." Percival drained his glass and draped a fleecy towel over his head. "I'm feeling more wrinkled than usual. See you later, my sodden-faced friends."

* * *

Rey proved to be a chatterbox during lunch. She possessed enough decorum, however, not to say anything about Prunella and Thomas as possible lovers, but it was obvious – with those long knowing glances and salty smiles – that she was dying to reveal what she had discovered. Unfortunately, I'd not had a chance to tell her what Percival had disclosed about the two: that Thomas and Prunella were business acquaintances who had attended a few functions together and had bona fide reasons for being there. This would have flipped those patronizing smiles upside down. And I'd have bet a weeklong sports-casting stint that was precisely what Prunella would maintain should she have been put on the spot.

Who in their wildest dreams could imagine Thomas and Prunella an item? Thomas Tinky Winky Saturne wasn't exactly hunky, charming, likeable, or wealthy. A hanky-panky infused relationship between lawyer and birder seemed as plausible as a union between Mother Goose and the Brothers Grimm.

Waving away the coffeepot that Beatrice held over me like an aspersorium, I rose. "What's first on the agenda after some serious teeth-brushing?"

"We search for Jensen Moone ... and we try to locate your Fred," Rey replied.

"Fred the Cat?" Prunella appeared perplexed. "He was lapping up cream in the kitchen a few minutes ago when I got a glass of Perrier."

"Fred the *Ghost*." Rey smirked. "Remember him? The singing spirit that *nobody* has seen except Jilly and her cake-maker boyfriend." The smirk evolved into an askew smile as she stared at us for confirmation.

We presented malevolent looks in response.

"I say we opt for Fred the Ghost and forget the barrister." Percival patted a napkin to his lips and stood. "Jensen Moone is – pardon the pun – a dead end. At least for the moment."

Prunella groaned and slapped her brother's butt.

"Shouldn't we wait until midnight?" May-Lee asked, pushing aside her plate. "Ghosts don't come out during the day, do they?"

"Sure they do."

"How would you know?" Percival appeared genuinely intrigued by the fact Rey would know.

"I did research for a film where I played a priest's daughter. You may remember the film – I was the town librarian who shot one of the lesser evil spirits, Tedworth, with a silver arrow."

Priest's daughter? Town *librarian*? I looked at her blankly.

"Oh, come on – you know the movie! The one where blond hunk Myles Milestone annihilates the freaks and lackeys who serve Cienne, the master evil spirit."

"Sure," I smiled, not having a clue. "You remember the film, don't you, truffles?"

Adwin nodded. "Demented Demons go Delinquent."

Reynalda beamed.

I stared at my beau. I'd forgotten he liked cheesy B films.

"Are evil spirits the same as ghosts?" Prunella looked skeptical.

"Some of them in the movie were."

"That was a movie, not reality," I pointed out. "You've never met a ghost, have you?"

"No," she sneered. "I haven't been as lucky as you."

"Let's hold off ghost trekking," Adwin suggested. "Fred seems to be more of a night spirit."

"We could play bridge," Prunella offered. "Or Scrabble or Monopoly. I saw board games in a closet."

"Or tag. One-two-three, you're it," Rey said sarcastically.

Linda elbowed her.

"Count me in," Adwin said, draining his cranberry juice. "Corpse and ghost hunting are getting boring."

"Only because they're not cooperating," Rey said with a pout.

"Tell you what, Rey," he said with a wry smile. "You get Jensen or Fred to cooperate, and I'll be happy to –"

A shriek, bloodcurdling enough to send shivers skipping up spines, erupted.

"Right on cue," I grinned.

"That sounded real to me." Linda peered pensively around the dining room. "Where'd it come from?"

"The kitchen."

"Outside."

"No, the garage."

15

What a Jam

We raced to the kitchen and bumped into Beatrice who, astonishingly, was careening around a corner like an Impreza WRX STI rally car. Then we knocked over Hubert, who was lurching toward us, wild-eyed and wild-haired (apparently hair, no matter how sparse, did stand up on end when its owner was frightened out of his or her wits). Percival and Adwin both hooked an arm through the butler's and, like an assortment of Mexican jumping beans, we stumbled and bumbled our way through the walkway to the attached six-car garage.

On the far side of the large, tidy structure stood my rented Sebring, Thomas' two-tone '58 Bentley, and Reginald's prized pearl-black Bentley S3 Continental. Oil stains on the far side of the Bentley, before Linda's Accord, indicated where two additional cars once stood, probably Aunt Mat's sportscars.

Leaning to the side of the partially open trunk of Reginald's car was Porter, his face flour-white, and his frozen expression a combination of dread and fear. Who'd have expected someone of that mass to emit such a high-pitched shriek?

"What's wrong with him?" Concern lined Adwin's low forehead.

"He seems to be dazed," Prunella responded, stepping beside the cook and draping an arm around his broad back. "Are you all right my friend?"

Percival instructed Beatrice to get water and a first-aid kit, and flounced across the garage to his sister's side.

"Should he be moved?" Linda asked worriedly.

"Perhaps he needs to catch his breath," Hubert suggested softly, peering around Linda's shoulder.

"He doesn't appear hurt," May-Lee said. "Merely bewildered."

A worried-looking Percival whispered something to Prunella and she scanned his face before turning back to Porter and murmuring into his ear. He gave the barest of nods ... before straightening and toppling like a lightning-struck sapling.

"I'll find smelling salts." The butler limped hastily from view as Rey and I hurried forward.

"He's looking awfully pale," I murmured.

"How can you tell? He's always pasty," Rey stated.

"As white as button mushrooms," Linda agreed.

I scanned the prone body dressed in a black traditional-fit chef's coat with knotted cloth buttons and baggy white houndstooth pants. Small, maybe size nine, Wolverine shoes graced his wide feet. The cook's pudgy hand, now sporting a sizeable sapphire on the middle finger in addition to the silver pinky ring, had a tiny blood drop near the thumb. It appeared to be the only wound suffered.

Beatrice arrived with a large plastic tray supporting a first-aid kit, two small bottles of water, and a fleece covering, which Percival grabbed and passed to his sister.

She folded the soft cover under Porter's head.

"I've called for an ambulance," the maid announced, "just in case."

Frowning, Prunella peered at her patient. "Hopefully he's not in need of paramedic assistance."

"Has anyone looked into the trunk or car to see what might have caused Porter to faint like that?" May-Lee asked inquisitively.

"Ten bucks we find a body inside," Linda declared.

"I'll bet fifty it's Jensen," Percival stated.

"Well it ain't gonna be Fred the Ghost's," Rey responded with a smirk.

My cousin and I moved forward, swung open the trunk as far as possible, and peered inside.

"One, two, three, you're so-o it," Rey said softly.

Though pale as custard and looking as flaccid as taffy, Jensen Moone's face was as serene as it was last night. You might have thought the man had snuck into the trunk to get away from it all and take a nap. There was no sign of blood or trauma, and the stake was gone, as was the designer shirt. In its place was a thick navy-blue flannel number, something cheap, a workman's choice. Why the change of shirts? He was dead. What difference would it have made if the shirt were nice and clean or ripped and bloody? Or was it that the killer couldn't bear to view the mutilation? Maybe he or she felt a pang of remorse? And why play hide-n-seek with the body? I voiced my thoughts to my cousin.

She scanned Jensen up and down. "The killer probably removed the stake to better transfer and store the guy. Maybe, like you said, he or she couldn't stand looking at the cavity in his chest. Here – hold on." Jaw clenched, she undid two buttons and peered beneath the fabric. "He's thickly bandaged. I'm guessing our killer didn't want to leave a trail of body fluid and fleshy bits," she said with a tight smile. "… Do we call the cops again?"

"Someone should." I gestured the grim-faced cook who'd not yet found his tongue. His head fell back. With that glazed, dazed expression and static pose, Porter could have passed for a top-pled giant wind-up toy. I picked up keys that lay not far from his feet and tucked them in Rey's two-pocket tunic. "Maybe you could call them," I suggested.

She looked down at Porter, who was staring up at her. "Are you up to joining me, Chef?" Grabbing his right arm, she motioned Percival to grab the left.

Porter's lips moved. Then he fell into a stupor.

I crossed my arms and leaned into the side of the car. "Apparently the excitement's been too much for him."

"It's proving too much for me," Adwin said dryly. "*I'll* go and call the police."

"Rey and I will stay here." I nodded toward Jensen. "This time our pseudo British barrister remains in full sight."

"Unless he pulls a Fred the Ghost," Rey said wryly.

Hubert hobbled quickly into the garage. "I've found them," he announced triumphantly, brandishing smelling salts like a track marshal waving a red flag.

* * *

Swallowing the last of a large pecan cookie, Percival appeared happy and smug. "They believed us this time." He was leaning against the

209

four-oven cooker in the massive kitchen. An ugly pinto-bean brown corduroy jacket worn earlier had been exchanged for an ugly pea-green cardigan, but a brick-brown Hugo Boss tie remained.

We'd all put on new clothes. Heavy sweaters, jeans and runners were the order for most. Something about finding dead bodies tended to make you want to re-shower and re-dress. And we'd had the time. Lewis and Gwynne, although scheduled for duty later in the day, had been immediately contacted by the officer who'd taken Adwin's call. The two men elected to make the return trip themselves, but due to multiple traffic accidents and a lost dog incident (the Sheriff's), hadn't managed it as quickly as intended. The ambulance had arrived in a more timely manner, but Porter had pulled himself together, at least enough to utter that he would not <bleep, bleep> be going to the <bleep, bleep> hospital. No amount of persuasion or argument could convince the jittery cook otherwise.

Once the two officers had viewed Jensen's supine body, and determined the barrister was indeed deceased, things moved as quickly as they could given the extreme weather. Law enforcement folks, media types, and curious neighbors willing to brave the angry weather collected and collided. A couple of tempers flared and fisticuffs weren't far behind. Two reporters rolling and grappling around the glacial ground would have been comical under less serious circumstances.

We'd all taken a bit of private and personal time between questions, face-offs and flare-ups. Mine was spent checking messages. Angela had sent an email stating there was little of interest to be found on the two dead gents. Her findings were basically the same ones Rey had revealed earlier, but Angela had listed actual boards and committees Thomas had sat on over the years: two non-profits, one telecom firm, two pharmaceutical companies, and Igloonomics Inc., a company that made plastic igloos for pets and ice-fisherpeople.

In terms of Jensen Q. Moone, he'd been a successful barrister in South Kensington for several years and had been involved with prestigious organizations and charities not only in England but in the United States. He had a socialite wife named Winda who looked like a bow-collared

Pomeranian but possessed a pit bull personality. There were no kids. My belief the first evening hadn't been far off the mark re little love being lost between the two. Two photos, five years apart, showed a couple that obviously barely tolerated each other. Frosty glares were scarcely concealed and tension was evident in squared shoulders, while smiles were faker than those of politicians making promissory oaths. They reminded me of two welterweights at a televised press conference trying to be civil prior to the big match.

There was also a photo of Jensen with Reginald at Reginald's sixtieth birthday party. Held at an exclusive country club outside Greenwich, it was *the* do to attend that fall. It seemed the brothers had ceased being at odds and had come to an understanding at the grand shindig. Who'd arranged for the brothers to finally bury the hatchet? Aunt Mat?

"Wasn't that Gwynne fellow as sour as tamarind when he laid eyes on the body?" Prunella asked with a sneer. "It serves the bugger right."

Adwin glanced at her, bemused, while May-Lee quelled a smirk.

"The next time we call, they won't be so quick to pooh-pooh us," Prunella said crisply.

"There won't be a next time," Percival responded lightly, then frowned deeply, perhaps concerned he could have spoken too soon.

Rey, seated at a small rectangular table that served as part of a breakfast nook, poured more coffee. It was her fourth, but instead of being revved, she looked calm, concentrated, deep in thought. That wasn't good. What was even worse was that I could read her mind. What was even *more* worse was that I wanted to do precisely what she was contemplating doing, so before she suggested it, I did. "It's a few minutes after four. Porter's out for the count for the afternoon and probably the evening, despite what he mumbled about an 8:00 p.m. dinner, so we're on our own. And since we've all indulged our sweet tooths, I don't see us eating anytime soon. What's say we kill – uh – pass time by retracing steps? Maybe we'll figure out Jensen's along the way."

Adwin jerked a thumb toward the window. "And get in the way of the last of the legal sorts?"

"They can't be everywhere at once, and their main focus is the garage," I pointed out with a patient smile.

"I believe they're heading out as quickly as they can, given what they're required to do, before the storm hits full-force," May-Lee said.

"It's pretty forceful right now," Percival declared. "According to the news, it won't be long before this encroaching nor'easter topples power lines and tree limbs. Flights have been cancelled in a few states and several interstates are evolving into colossal skating rinks and parking lots."

"That's probably why they haven't asked us to leave the estate," Prunella murmured, absently fingering a fresh bandage on her cheek.

"They should post an officer here to keep a watchful eye," Adwin said.

Percival snorted. "Why? Are you expecting more murders?"

Before Adwin could answer in the affirmative, I jumped in. "Let's do as I suggested and retrace steps. It's better than twiddling thumbs, sitting idle, or scarfing endless supplies of baked goods."

Percival shook his head. "I'm up for nothing more than a nice little nap."

"Okay Grandpa, suit yourself," Rey said with an exaggerated toss of her head.

May-Lee chuckled.

Linda finally tuned into the conversation, which had taken a rear seat to a bowl of strawberry-cheesecake ice-cream she'd been devouring with noisy gusto. "Count me in for detecting." She looked at May-Lee.

Who motioned her chin where a bit of berry clung, nodded, and then turned to Prunella with a defiant gaze.

"Fine. Count me in, too," the bird lover said haughtily and turned to her brother.

He shook his head again.

Prunella shrugged. "I need to do a couple of things. Give me a few minutes."

Percival turned to Adwin, his expression dry. "And you, Addy?"

He glanced from one set face to another and turned up his palms in a what-choice-do-I-have gesture. "I'm with the girls – er, women."

With a sow-like snort, Percival took his sister's elbow. "I'll escort you up."

"Let's all meet in twenty minutes by Reginald's room of gloom," Rey said cheerily, waving them off.

"What strange siblings," Linda murmured, watching them saunter from sight.

"They're more like an odd couple," May-Lee responded with an expression of irritation. "With very heavy emphasis on 'odd'."

"They're fucking freaks," Rey declared.

Adwin grimaced and strolled from the room, muttering something about meeting us in ten or doing Zen. Or maybe he'd called Rey a disagreeable hen.

* * *

"Whose hand's on my ass?" Rey cried out in the darkness.

"Not mine." Adwin. "I wouldn't touch that butt if you paid me," followed under his breath.

"I heard that."

"You were meant to."

"We'll talk later, Jilly's boyfriend. We're hanging a left everybody, right dear cousin?"

"Right."

"No, *left*," Percival affirmed. He'd decided to accompany us at the last moment. Maybe Prunella had convinced him to or maybe lying in bed like a bull's eye – considering two men had recently died unpleasant deaths – had prompted him to change his mind.

"I meant –"

"Let's not go there," I advised, scenes of old tired comedy and cartoon routines flooding my head.

"Not go left?"

"Rey!" I all but shrieked.

"Left!" Percival and Adwin shouted.

Like daycare kids hanging on to a group tether device, we proceeded down a corridor leading from the "room of gloom" to Jensen's "burial chamber" (Prunella's contribution). We were without benefit of light because Rey's large flashlight had died two-hundred feet into the bricked passageway and no one else had thought to bring an extra one. Determined we were. Smart? That was questionable.

"Ouch. Watch it! I don't need a scab on top of an already scabbed nose," Linda crabbed.

"I can't bloody well see, so pardon me-e," Percival groused.

"Fuck!" Rey.

"Watch that mouth, sister." Adwin.

"I hit my frigging head against a wall." A couple of curses followed, these ones soft. "We must be at the end. Who opened this panel last night?"

"I did." Adwin brushed past. "Let me at it. Okay. I think ... yes ... got it!"

No one wanted to move forward in the blackness and stub a toe or break a limb by crashing into furniture, so we stood there for a few seconds like deer caught in convoy headlights.

"I think I remember where the lamps are." Arms outstretched and feet moving at a snail's pace, I stepped forward cautiously. A bang into wood, a table from the shape and weight of it, made my eyes water, but I managed to locate one of the parlor lamps and turned it on. An apricot glow warmed the room. May-Lee hastened to turn on the second one.

"See if you can find a flashlight or candle that we can use to illuminate the passageways," I instructed Adwin and Linda, and turned to Rey, who now stood beside Prunella. "Should we take that loop you four did last night? Or see if there's another corridor that Jensen may have doubled around?"

Percival gazed around dubiously. "We pretty much cased the entire joint last night."

I kept a straight face. Barely. "You sure we checked *everything*, Bugsy?"

He shrugged.

"I'll try a wall or two," Prunella said merrily.

"Me, too," Rey offered excitedly.

"I'll sit." He dropped into the recamier, realized Jensen's corpse had rested there, and leaped up as if someone had set his Gucci jeans alight.

"I found one." Linda held up a sturdy cream-colored candle two inches in diameter and eight inches high. "Smells like," she sniffed and made a face, "liniment."

No one had a match or lighter, so the oversize candle ended up on an end table.

"Come here guys!"

Rey had discovered a hollow sound behind the wall she was examining, suggesting the presence of open space.

"Kee-rist, how many hidden corridors lead to this little room?" Percival asked, stunned.

"The two leading from opposite directions and this one, if it is one," I answered, eyeing Rey, who was madly attempting to find a way of shifting the wall.

"Maybe this is a panic room of some sort," she suggested. "Strange area for a secret place, doncha think?"

"There were different periods in history where families wanted and needed somewhere safe to escape." Linda stepped alongside her best friend to assist.

"For which period had this one been built?" Percival scanned the room. "Panic rooms, or safe rooms as they're sometimes called, were really more a result of terrorist threats and attacks, and kidnappings. They didn't exist, per se, at the time this house was built."

"No, but rooms or vaults to conceal valuable possessions, women and children, did. The house has gone through various renovations. This could have been built during the Spanish-American War, the First World War, or maybe even the Second. There were always threats and dangers of one kind or another." Linda returned to the wall.

"It's certainly a suitable place to hide," he commented, "but one you could easily perish in if your enemy set fire to the dwelling or cornered you." His tone sobered and he gazed around nervously. "This room could have become your tomb."

"Maybe one of the Moones simply wanted a place to get away from the family for a while," Adwin suggested. "We all like having our own space now and again."

"Hey people, take a look," Linda requested. A narrow opening led into more darkness.

"Do we dare?" Prunella asked softly, peering in. "Good heavens. It smells dusty and old, and wretched – like death."

Adwin leaned forward into the opening. "Jensen may have found it and decided to hide in it to pull another prank."

"Or explore," May-Lee offered.

"He didn't seem the overly curious sort," Percival said, stepping alongside Adwin.

"Do you suppose someone killed him down there in the foul darkness?" his sister asked skeptically.

"We need light," Linda said. "What's the point of heading down it if we can't see a thing? For all we know, there's a fifty-foot drop a few yards down. Does absolutely *no one* have a light for the candle?"

There was no reply.

"Someone is going to have to backtrack and get –"

"Oh, screw it." Percival pulled a silver lighter from his cardigan pocket and lighted the candle.

"You're smoking again, aren't you?" Prunella asked with obvious disgust. "Probably those vile, reeking French cigarettes. No wonder you've been smelling so minty!"

His expression wavered between apologetic and defensive. "We all need a vice or two."

She looked furious and gestured the candle, which he quietly passed forward. She eyed him up and down with something akin to loathing. "I'll lead. You, Mr. Tobacco Head, *you* take up the rear."

When that gal got mad, she got downright plucky. Rey and I exchanged amused glances while Linda, May-Lee and Adwin fell in silent, cautious step behind Pissed-Off Prunella. Another measured progression began, but at least we could see in the shadowiness – unpleasant things like thick cobwebs and layers of mold, patches of dust and dirt, and scratches and nicks in irregular walls. The sloping floor was rough and strange little things crunched beneath our soles. With the odd pipe-rattling and house-settling sounds that resounded every so often, it made for a perfect slasher setting.

"Stop, Prunella." I squeezed past the two before me. "Curiosity being what it is, let's check the floor."

She lowered the candle and we scrutinized old, uneven planking.

Percival asked, "What's that slimy black patch? Blood?"

"It could be oil or jam, or any one of a dozen things. Let's see. We have rodent droppings, a cigarette butt – yours Perc? – and, hmm, this could be old gum." I stifled a sneeze and rose. The smell and dampness seeped through my skin like a west-coast fog.

Prunella frowned and continued onward, only to stop thirty feet ahead. "Get closer everyone. We have tight, uneven stairs to descend – and it's a lengthy flight from what I *can't* see. Be careful everyone. They may not be safe."

The stairs creaked and groaned, and the air grew thicker, heavier, and damper (and maybe I was growing a little claustrophobic). The descent was painstaking, even if it wasn't that great of one, but all went fairly well considering that everyone was stressed and testy to some degree.

Rey pulled Prunella's arm gently. "Let's take a quick look below again."

This time we all stooped to see if there was anything to be found, scanning the area as if we were forensic pros.

"We should have brought tweezers and plastic bags," Percival jested, running a finger cautiously along what appeared to be an old rusty protruding pipe at the base of a cracked wall.

"And a camera and swabs," Linda chimed in.

"Look at these marks here," Rey pointed. "These could have been someone being dragged. Whadya think?"

I squatted alongside her and motioned Prunella to pass the candle. "Could be. That looks like a heel mark. And that could be blood."

"Whose?" Rey asked grumpily. "Jensen's? Or a rat's? Could be anyone's or any thing's."

"Or it could be our imaginations running wild," May-Lee suggested.

Rey stood. "Let's show our police pals."

"They might take umbrage with our having disturbed evidence… If it *is* evidence," the antique dealer stated, looking below dubiously.

"We didn't disturb it too much," Linda said. "And we shouldn't keep this to ourselves."

"Keep *what* to ourselves? Mouse crap? Dead bugs and *possible* scuff marks and blood? Or *jam*?" Percival snorted. "This hardly qualifies as police-grade 'evidence'."

"Listen here –"

"Can it kids!" I put a stop to the discord before it got started. "Let's get out of here first. We can decide what to do second."

"That's a wise idea, dear." Prunella took charge and started guiding us as if we were a slow-moving human caravan on its way from Kumbum to Lhasa.

16

Fall of the Fungi

We shuffled into a room so dark it was barely possible to see the outline of a chain and light bulb hanging from a low beamed ceiling. In fact, Percival managed to smack his forehead against one of several heavy beams, resulting in a soft but colorful curse. Rey snickered and Linda yanked the thick brassy chain like a frantic passenger might an emergency hand brake in a vintage train. A hundred-watt luster flooded an H-shaped room. Peeling paint clung to chipped bricks while ailing pipes groaned and listed as if age were taking its toll. Asbestos and other un-seen toxic substances probably abounded, and you didn't have to see mold and dust to know they were there; you merely had to hear the sneezes and coughs.

Cluttering two corners were canvas-covered chairs and chests, wooden crates, stacked sheets of cardboard and wood panels of different shapes and sizes. In another corner, protected by lightweight see-through plastic, were four French portable trunks with iron handles, eight small trunks with leather edging and corners, and six large storage cases with leather handles, brass clasps and chrome fittings. Also stacked to one side were a dozen vintage Samsonite suitcases in pristine condition, spanning different decades. May-Lee eyed them appraisingly.

"This must be the basement," Percival murmured.

"Ya think?" Rey asked sarcastically.

"It ain't the attic, sister," he replied, matching her tone.

Rey raised an eyebrow and smirked, and cast aside a checkered sheet suspended from an old thick cord, which was attached to a pine step-back cupboard and strung to one of six tarnished cast-brass hooks. "Wow, bad art."

Three, maybe four dozen canvases were stacked against the side of the cupboard. Rey pulled out five. Themes ranged from misshapen fruit to surreal landscapes. If they'd been painted on velvet they might have fetched a couple of bucks at a flea market. Who'd painted them? Reginald or Aunt Mat? I couldn't imagine either as the artist, nor could I see the servants serving as wannabe Picassos. Behind them, tucked into a recess, were long tubes, some skinny and some fat. They sported labels: theater, art shows, and concerts. Posters most likely. Others had big black block letters identifying what was inside: estate, landscaping, township, and state. Maps and blueprints no doubt. I pressed the one marked ESTATE into Adwin's hand.

Next, I pulled open the uppermost cupboard drawers. Old cooking and homemaker magazines, store receipts and recipes were stacked in two of them; unused tea towels, kitchen gadgets and ugly cutlery cluttered another. A bottom drawer revealed boxes of nails and pins and thumbtacks, packages of batteries, and two flashlights. I grabbed the larger of the two and found it worked.

Percival jerked a thumb to the side. "There are stairs over there. Let's get out of this cramped, unpleasant place."

"Shouldn't we look around?" Rey asked, sounding like a mope.

He sighed. "By all means. Go ahead – alone – Miss Fonne-Weird."

"That's Fonne-*Werde*."

"Well, go ahead and sort through these Goodwill donations. It looks like no one's been down here in a dog's age, so the chance of finding anything of interest or use is highly unlikely."

Rey's mouth opened, but Linda managed to speak first. "You don't believe Jensen's been down here?"

"There's nothing to indicate he was here, much less met up with his killer," May-Lee answered, sounding bored.

I picked my way across timeworn floorboards that had seen decades of shoes and boots, lots of dirt and dust and stains, and circled around again. I eyed walls painted wheat once upon a time. "Here are a couple of fingerprints, courtesy of dried blood … or chocolate."

"If that were Jensen's blood," Linda commented, stepping alongside me, "there would be lots of it. The man had a hole in his chest the size of a catch basin."

"Those marks are my doing," Percival announced. "And yes, it is chocolate."

We all turned.

He smiled guiltily and wiggled his fingers. "I nibbled a partially melted Godiva bar – dark chocolate with raspberry – in the corridor."

Rey slapped me on the back. "Good detecting, either way."

I aimed the flashlight at a small, barely discernible workroom on the far left. "Seeing as we're here, we may as well finish checking out the place. Then we can officially take it off our checked-for-clues list."

Chain/brake-puller Linda turned on another light. Carpentry and gardening tools were suspended from one wall, discarded kitchen equipment lined shelves on another. Everything was perfectly aligned, not one item one inch farther than the next. "Come here," she beckoned.

A worktable against the far wall housed old cassette tapes, CDs and DVDs, and books. Most of the tapes were country and classical music, while the other items dealt with the topics of woodworking, art and folklore … and sound effects. One was titled "Haunting Horror Noises & Scares". That explained the silly spooky sounds.

"Is this for real?" Rey asked dryly.

"It's for show," I replied, regarding sixteen slender pine stakes that lined steel-wire shelving above the worktable and then running a finger along several. "There's no dust. These have been placed here recently and most likely for our benefit."

May-Lee appeared baffled. "Someone actually believed one or all of us would be inspired to come down here?"

"He or she wanted to cover all bases. Look at all the fake limbs we found on the property."

She nodded, then murmured, "Bizarre."

"It's for show, like my cousin said." Rey whirled slowly, scanning walls from top to bottom as if consigning every feature to memory.

"What's with the books and vampire slayers? Why down here?" Linda pulled out a thin book on voodoo dolls, peered inside, and frowned. "This little 'show' isn't up to your aunt's usual standards. I'd expect more from an eccentric lady having fun from the Great Beyond. Why didn't we find a coffin, a giant mummy, or a headless body?" Putting back the book, she picked up a wooden stake and eyed it critically. "We have two dead guys, one *possibly* murdered and one *definitely* murdered." She returned the stake and scrutinized the others. "These look similar to the one Jensen had sticking in his chest."

"Maybe Jensen was in the process of getting this place set up for another prank and got in someone's way," Adwin conjectured. "That would explain the partial stab at creating Scary Basement 101."

As everyone considered his assumption, I noticed an old vent on the wall above his head and pointed. "Maybe you're right. He may have been planning on sending more spooky sounds up that way."

"But where's the equipment to play the spooky sound effects?" Rey motioned the room impatiently. "I don't buy it."

"Buy what?" Adwin asked wryly. "Another pair of Manolo Blahnik knock-offs?"

Heat emanated from her blazing glare.

"Maybe he had a portable player," I suggested. "Or maybe he had help."

Linda looked perplexed. "From one of us?"

Prunella asked, "Or one of the servants?"

"I don't see Beatrice as much of a jokester," I replied.

"Porter's too introverted and unsociable," Rey offered.

May-Lee advised, "Hubert's too old, overly serious, and very by the books."

"We're back to square one," I said dully, "which is *nowhere*."

"Not necessarily," Percival said, "I believe we all concur that Jensen Moone came down here. This has helped fit together some puzzle pieces and while far from complete, a petite part of the picture is visible."

We murmured something akin to agreement, although Rey appeared somewhat blank.

"The plot thickens," Adwin jested. "Where's Inspector Clouseau when you need him?"

I gave his arm a playful punch.

"Let's summarize before we move on, so that we share the same 'petite piece of the picture'," May-Lee proposed. "Jensen came down here, started setting up for another Mathilda Moone let's-frighten-the-guests trick, was distracted – or was called away by a potential partner – and ended up in the hidden corridors where he was murdered."

"Sounds reasonable. I like it," Rey nodded.

Linda agreed.

I pointed to a half-dozen stairs leading up. "Folks, let's move onward and upward."

The procession ascended. A narrow door at the top opened easily and quietly as we stepped into the pantry. Strange. How come we'd not noticed the door when we'd been in here before? I glanced back. It was painted the same color as the walls and the small doorknob was the same color as the door. Add to that the fact we'd been preoccupied with freezers and casks and crates, never mind a mutual fondness for cookies, and small wonder it had gone unnoticed.

"Look at you," Rey jibed, poking her friend's dirt-streaked cheek.

"You're no belle of the ball with that gunk on your chin and that weal on your forehead," Linda snapped.

"Man, someone's sure touchy –"

"*Someone's* tired and in need of a piping-hot espresso and another shower," Linda interrupted, brushing past her with a scowl.

Percival laughed and Prunella chuckled. Rey tossed her head and followed her friend into the hallway, the rest of us trooping behind. Above the oven, a sardine (or maybe it was a herring) clock informed us it was fifteen minutes past six; it felt as if it should have been fifteen after midnight.

"I smell," Adwin sniffed, "soup." He ambled to the oven on which sat three pieces of cast-iron cookware, one of which was simmering on very low. "I guess Porter's going to be serving dinner after all." He removed the lid to the first pot. Having all but stuck his face into the cocotte, he announced, "We have vegetable soup – heavy with sliced mushrooms."

"I thought the poor man had taken enough sedatives to fell an elephant," Linda said, bemused, scratching her scabbed nose.

"Maybe Beatrice is filling in," I suggested. "Someone must sub for the cook when he's off."

"The soup sounds boring. What else we got?" Rey asked.

My beau checked the second cocotte and frowned. "It's a mixture of uncooked potato, celery and carrot. Could be fixings for Shepherd's Pie or stew."

"Neither sounds appealing," Linda said with a sigh. She stepped alongside him and removed the lid to the third and largest pot. Steam rose. The lid clattered to the cork floor. "Ouch, dang, hot – whoa Nelly! The mushroom king has been dethroned."

Adwin looked in. "Holy crap."

The rest of us dashed forward. In the immense pot rested a head reminiscent of a giant peanut shell. Incredulity traversed each face in the kitchen like a Sierra Nevada mudslide. Porter stared back with equal amazement.

"How unoriginal. The head-in-the-pot scene has been done *so* many times," Rey said sardonically. Then she fainted. Right into Percival's arms.

He looked from her to the pot and back again.

"That's so unlike her." Linda grabbed a tea towel and started flapping it before Rey's pale face.

"She probably passed out more from lack of food than fright," Prunella commented dryly. "This girl has more balls than any man I've met."

"Or it all caught up to her," Adwin suggested, helping Percival settle her on the floor.

"I vote for lack of food and too much booze and excitement over the last couple of days." I grabbed the tea towel from Linda, ran it under cold water, and placed it to my cousin's forehead. After several seconds, she moaned and opened her eyes, looked around, and quickly shut them again.

"Something we said?" Percival's smile bordered on snide.

"There you are. Are you folks doing more body searching?" Lewis asked cheerfully as he ambled into the kitchen, swinging an empty mug. He might have been taking a walk in the park. He glanced at Rey, who was struggling into a seated position and gazing dazedly from one face to another. "Miss, are you ahright?"

She nodded and pulled on Adwin's reedy thigh to push herself up.

"Everyone's left save Gwynne and myself. Weathah's getting worse by the minute. Powah lines are down in parts south of here and there's a fifteen-car pile-up close to the station. You'd think people didn't listen to weathah warnings.

237

I'm going to check on the cahs on the driveway and see if we can move ount." He looked doubtful.

"You can't." I pointed to the pot.

The sparkle in the sea-green eyes dimmed. "Please don't tell me that's nawt chowdah in there."

"Okay."

Lewis drew a deep breath and peered in. "Gwynne!"

* * *

"So, Miss Fonne, that's all for now," Lewis said with an unreadable smile as he closed a new small, thick notepad he'd found in a kitchen drawer. I suspected he was more comfortable with the old-school approach. He motioned a tall muscular female cop who'd arrived twenty minutes ago after an hour-long drive through increasingly perilous conditions. She was standing by – guarding – the first-floor rear guestroom door. "I hate to ask, Jeana, but would you mind getting coffee? Put in double the usual sugah for me, please. I got that Sayahs couple coming in next –"

"They're brother and sister," I clarified, staring pointedly at the brunette.

She was scanning my face as if she were a human lie detector device, determining whether she was in the company of a crazed killer. Jeana, too, offered an unreadable smile and turned to Lewis. "Two coffees coming up." She marched from the large L-shaped room like someone who could as easily have been embarking on a major drug bust as fetching liquid caffeine.

"Do you have any theories as to who the killer may be?" he asked casually, standing before an oak drop-front desk, and stretching arms upward and behind.

I shook my head. "Do you?"

He smirked and stretched again.

I looked him square in the eye. "Like the other two, Thomas Saturne was murdered, wasn't he?"

Gripping the back of a press-back rocker, he stared for a long while. "He ovahdosed on a prescription drug called quinapril –"

"Which is used for treating high blood pressure and heart failure, and for preventing kidney failure due to hypertension and diabetes. Cousin Otto takes it." I stood before one of two tall domed windows veiled by beaded light-gray lace curtains, hearing the glass being assailed by a mixture of sleet and freezing rain. When the snow finally arrived, it would be heavy and dangerous. Suspended transit services, parking bans, and city-wide precautions were already in place in abundance in nearby counties and states, but hopefully, resulting storm outages would be at a minimum.

"Thomas Saturne only stahted taking it recently. That's why the man was all rashed ount. It seems to be a side effect for first-time takers. But whoever decided to kill him wanted to be *really* sure they succeeded ... so he was also shot with curare."

The puncture wound. I whirled. "Shot? Like with a dart gun?"

"Like with a blowgun – a.40 calibah. He had a tiny hole here." He pointed to a spot below his neck. "It makes you think of old-time James Bond and the KGB."

The weapon did seem rather Cold War and spy-like. And totally unbelievable. But Percival had joked about a blowgun, so maybe it wasn't that farfetched a concept. I moved aside a lace panel and stared past misty, crusted glass. Nothing on the property was visible, save for shrubs immediately outside, and they looked like they'd not last the night; their spindly, ice-encrusted limbs were dragging the ground.

"Poor Thomas. He must have realized what was going on, but couldn't tell anyone because of the paralysis factor. No wonder he was so still and quiet." I sighed. "But why kill him?"

"That's what we're going to find ount... There was one more thing."

I turned. "What?"

"He'd also ingested Poison Hemlock. It was in his tea or drink."

"You're joking, right? He was murdered *three* times?"

His gaze grew more solemn. "If the curare didn't relax him to the point of asphyxia, the Poison Hemlock would have caused any numbah of problems, like respiratory paralysis. And if neither of those got him, the ovahdose of quinapril might've done the trick... Do you know anyone that hated the fellah enough to want to kill him three times ovah?"

"He wasn't overly friendly, but no one in our group expressed or demonstrated animosity toward him, not openly anyway."

"What about people ountside the group?"

I arched my shoulders. "I don't know anything about the personal lives of the deceased men. Like Thomas, Jensen probably annoyed a few people and clients in his day – he could be bombastic. The cook? We were all getting very tired of the many mushroom dishes, so in his case, it could have been any one of us." I smiled dryly.

A loud forceful knock preceded Jeana's entrance. If the six-foot-tall officer was surprised to see me still there, she didn't show it, merely strode forward with purpose, plastic tray in hand, and placed it on an oak side table. He grabbed a large ceramic mug and half a tuna sandwich; she grabbed the other mug and took up her previous post.

"Time for me to make a few phone calls," I said with forced cheer. "Maybe catch a show or two after."

"Good luck. The winds and ice may hamper that." Although he offered a benign smile, his gaze was stern. "Like I'm telling everyone in the group, don't plan on going anywhere for the time being."

I smirked. "I take it that's an order Sheriff Lewis?"

He grinned. "Professional advice."

"Fortunately for you, thanks to Mother Nature, we have no choice but to accept that advice." I jerked a thumb at the window as strong winds and frozen precipitation thwacked glass. "I guess you'll be staying put, too ... for the time being."

The grin dimmed.

17

Olly Olly Oxen Free

Adwin blew into thinly gloved hands to warm them up in the frosty evening. "Why are we out here? This weather's insane."

We were huddled beside a wide-slated redwood garden bench at the rear of the Moone cottage-studio-guesthouse (we hadn't yet figured what purpose it served). It was after nine and the mid-November night was more like late January in Buffalo: bitter and bracing. Our matching American Apparel hooded fleece jackets, worn under heavy oversize men's raincoats courtesy of a walk-in closet stocked with a sundry of outerwear, did little to halt the northeasterly 40MPH winds from freezing flesh.

"One, to get downtime from the group. Two, to put our heads together."

"I'd prefer to put something else together – and in the main house, where it's warm and dry. Forget this oversize toolshed, or whatever it is."

Funny, I don't believe I'd ever heard teeth actually chattering before, but his were. And how. I gave his sodden chin a playful squeeze. "Privacy is a misnomer in the Moone manse, so personal moments are few and far between."

"That is so sadly true." He squinted through the slapping wetness at an obscured sky. "People are going to wonder where we are."

"People as in Rey?"

"Or the police. But knowing your cousin, carrot cake, she's probably forming a search party at this very moment."

I chuckled and eyed the small building. "The first night, I thought I saw a light in here. Then I decided it was merely a reflection – moonlight or stars bouncing off the glass or the pond. Now I'm wondering if maybe, just maybe, our killer was in here."

"Doing what? Hiding?"

"That. Or looking for something. Maybe making plans and/or organizing murder weapons and tools. Or possibly concealing something."

"The best laid plans of –"

"Yeah, yeah, whatever." I chuckled and turned to an ice-coated wall and did a quick assessment. "There are no secret panels here, that's for sure."

"Forget about secret panels, tea loaf. What you need is a magic hairpin that will unlock the door so we can get in."

With a sly smile I reached beneath the rain-coat into a small tote I'd slung over one shoulder. "How about a hammer, courtesy of Aunt Mat's unnerving but orderly cellar?"

My bumbleberry tart grimaced and groaned when he heard the crackle-crunch. "You're going to have to replace that window."

I stepped over shards of glass, yanked Adwin inside, closed the door, and smoothed the pleated polyester blinds across the shattered pane. A raincoat sleeve had ripped when I'd slipped an arm through the shattered pain; jagged glass had missed flesh by a hair. "Feel for a light switch, but don't turn it on until I tell you."

"I doubt anyone would see any light from the house given the weather, but hold on – okay, I've got one."

Fumbling around, I made sure all four blinds were fully drawn. "Now."

Light the color of lemon gelato illuminated a cozy room.

He pulled down his hood and rubbed a Rudolph-red nose as he studied the interior. "It's nice, but nothing spectacular."

Adwin was right: it was a pleasant little cottage, and that was all. A faux Rayo lamp rested on a narrow counter running the length of what could qualify as a kitchenette. The walls were warm beige, like a skim-milk latte, the ceiling and crown molding whipping-cream white, the rug – perhaps Persian – spotless and a perfect complement to the interior. Two items of furniture were covered with freshly-washed sheets, but it was obvious one piece was a rocking chair and the other a small sofa or loveseat.

Wiping excess water from my face, I stepped toward a studio in the north-east corner, where sheets draped an artist's easel and model's stool. To their side was an old, large oval mirror with a thick braided gilt frame.

It hadn't been cool inside when we'd entered, but the newly created airway was letting in the outside chill. I glanced around and noticed a small thermostat to the left of the kitchen. Up a few degrees it went.

"Maybe we'd better clean up the mess. I see a broom by the garbage bin." Adwin strolled forward determinedly. "Check if there's cardboard or plastic around to cover up the broken window."

"Aye, aye." I saluted and opened the door of a large pine shelving unit. Inside were tubes and jars of paint, brushes, watercolor pads of various sizes, pencils and pens, and miscellaneous art paraphernalia. Now we knew where the cellar paintings had been rendered.

"It seems pretty darn clean in here."

"Huh?" I was engrossed in removing thick cardboard backings from three large pads. They would make for a decent makeshift window covering until morning, when I could locate more permanent covering back in the house.

"It looks and smells sanitary in here, like cleaning products have been used."

"The servants probably clean on a regular basis," I said, grabbing a roll of masking tape.

He sniffed. "It also smells like a lady with good taste in perfume has been here."

I sniffed. J'adore by Dior. A favorite of Aunts Mat and Sue Lou.

"Why is this place spick and span, and why are parts of the main house *not*?"

"Budget constraints? Tight schedules?" I ripped six long pieces of tape and affixed the cardboard to the broken window. Speaking of clean, the windows inside were exceptionally so, while those on the exterior were as dirty as Lower Manhattan alleyways. "Why go to the bother of cleaning the inside and not the outside?"

"What?" Adwin was concentrated on sweeping glass into a paper bag.

"The windows are spotless on the inside and filthy on the outside."

"Maybe an agoraphobic lives here." He smiled weakly and started picking carefully at the broom for tiny bits of glass. "To be honest my sweet potato pie, this place unnerves me a little."

"Really? I find it comfy and homey compared to the house." I leaned into a wall. "Care to have a quick verbal toss-around with what we know?"

"We don't know that much, but sure." Returning the broom, he perched himself on the edge of the rocking chair. "Our first two dead guys were fairly successful, sat on boards and committees, and attended functions." Adwin snapped his fingers. "We can't forget that Thomas Saturne had an affair with Prunella."

"At this stage, we can only assume he had one and that's really Rey's assumption. Percival told me his sister and Thomas were on the same board. Those photos we saw simply showed two smiling –"

"Fixated and *totally tanked* people –"

"With no *confirmed* intimate relationship."

"Moving on," he said with a roll of the eyes. "You were going to tell me about two phone calls you had before I got dragged to the sheriff's inquisition."

I sat on the stool. "You want the so-so news first or the super exciting news first?"

"You've got news more super exciting than the fact that Thomas was murdered three different ways?" He smiled wryly. "Let's start with the so-so."

"Gloria Laplante has been – *had* beenThomas' secretary for fifteen years. She was shocked to hear of his death on a noonday news show and as his assistant, she was more than outraged having learned of it via media and not an official visit or call. As she said," I switched to a Brooklyn accent, " 'I shoulda been properly informed, ya know, coz I'm his right-hand girl, the second in command, ya know'."

Adwin simulated a loud yawn.

I stuck out my tongue. "*You* didn't have to listen to ten minutes of snooze stuff before hearing something of note."

"Such as?"

"Such as Thomas had been a very discreet man in every sense of the word before he got involved with a woman who could have been – and I quote again – 'a walking advertisement for hippie and nudie health-nuts'."

"There you go." Adwin pointed. "Prunella Sayers."

"We'd *still* be assuming. The description of the woman was vague and a lot of people – like the Sayers – are into organics and cotton, and planet preservation."

251

A loud sigh drifted across the cottage. "What's the 'super exciting' news?"

"A man by the name of Harold Watermaker sat on two boards with Thomas and had known him for twenty years. They'd never been true buddies, but had hung out together now and again." I leaned forward. "Guess where they hung out."

"I couldn't and wouldn't even begin to guess," he said with enough dryness to leave you thirsting for a gallon of water.

"The race tracks. They both loved placing big bets."

Adwin's eyes widened. "They were hardcore gamblers?"

"Harold admitted he'd lost his house, bombshell wife, and cruiser racer to gents that made the bad guys in vintage Cagney and Bogart films seem like choir boys. Fortunately, his sister got him into Gamblers Anonymous and he pulled his life around."

"Not so for Thomas?"

"Harold told me that Thomas continued to go for 'bigger and better odds', but Thomas also had Lady Luck on his side – most of the time. After Harold started attending GA meetings, they rarely spoke or saw each other, but he heard that Thomas' exceptional luck started swinging between pretty good and really *really* bad. He suggested I try contacting someone who used to go by the name of Lay-a-Wager Waynie, who has since seen the light, and prefers the name he was born with: Wayne Antici. These days he lives in Boston from April to September and Tallahassee the other months."

"And?"

I smiled smugly. "I got telephone numbers and left messages for Wayne to call either my cell or the main Moone number."

"… As your crazy cousin would say: I don't buy it."

"You don't think Thomas' gambling buddies might have come after him here?"

"I can't see those kinds of thugs using three means of murder. They just break multiple limbs or shoot a .22 into the cranium, don't they?"

"Maybe they felt it safer and easier to have paid one of us to take care of Thomas. And if we're novices to murder, we might want to make sure we're successful by using three alternative methods."

"I don't buy that, either. I suppose curare and Poison Hemlock and quinti-whatever are easy enough to procure and crush up, and mix into a drink or something. But you'd have to know how his medication would react, or what would transpire when taken in large amounts –"

"Most meds are dangerous, if not lethal, when taken in large amounts –"

"But they produce different symptoms and effects." Adwin shook his head. "It's like creating a dessert. You have to have the precise amount – the right combination – to obtain the perfect result."

I eyed the talented pastry chef thoughtfully. "So Thomas' murderer would have had to have known about plants and poisons, *and* prescriptions... . Not to mention knowing as much as possible about Thomas Saturne himself."

"Or he'd have to have *planned* the murder well in advance and learned everything and anything about plants, poisons, and prescriptions ... and Thomas Saturne himself."

Hadn't I said that? "But no one knew that far in advance that Aunt Mat was going to hold this crazy win-your-inheritance affair. We were only informed three weeks ago."

"That's plenty of time to gather information. And people could have had access to her will, thereby having learned of this *weeks ago*," he said pointedly. "Regardless, if someone were consumed with killing Thomas, they'd have planned the details and waited for the perfect opportunity to perform the dastardly deed." Winds sounding like lamenting spirits circled the building. Adwin glanced around anxiously and crossed his arms. "When you intend to off someone – if you're any kind of thinking, reasoning person – you'd plan it to the letter."

I nodded. "What about Jensen? Who'd want to off him? The same person who offed Thomas? A stake in the heart seems a spur-of-the-moment act."

"It may have been the same person, but not necessarily. Maybe Jensen rubbed Thomas' murderer the wrong way. Or he stumbled onto something he shouldn't have. I'm inclined to believe that, because Thomas was annoying with a capital A. The killer simply couldn't take him anymore and put him out of everyone's misery."

"Where does Porter fit in?"

"Someone got tired of his mushrooms?" Adwin joked.

"I suggested that to Lewis," I grinned. "Another day of fungi and I might have done the 'dastardly deed'."

"He must have witnessed something," Adwin said, standing. "Why else kill an innocent chef?"

"What could he have witnessed?"

"The guy seemed so wordless when we found him in the garage."

"The guy was in shock."

"He looked more – I don't know – zoned-out than shocked."

Porter had appeared rather trance-like. *Zombie*-like. The blood drop near his fat thumb flashed before me. "Maybe …"

"Yes?"

"He was drugged – courtesy of a blowgun."

"Like Thomas Saturne was?"

"Exactly. Maybe it wasn't curare in Porter's case, or maybe it was a smaller dosage, or maybe he'd removed the tiny dart – hey!" I jumped up. "If Thomas was hit by a tiny dart and it wasn't physically stuck in his neck –"

"Then maybe it's still in the sofa or on the rug, or somewhere," he finished doubtfully. "Lewis or one of his people would have found it."

"The sheriff didn't mention finding anything." I frowned. Was the Massachusetts native holding back facts? That was his right, of course, but if he was, I'd have given up Godiva chocolate for six months to know them. "As for Porter, it's too soon to know what caused his death –"

"Besides the obvious beheading?" Adwin asked darkly.

I made a face. "I was referring more to how he became head-less. I can't see Porter allow-ing himself to be decapitated willingly." Again, I thought of the blood on his thumb. "The man had to have been drugged."

"He would have had to been drugged before the garage episode, which could have been at any time and in any place. As for Thomas, he would have had to have been shot with the blow-gun *after* we gathered in the drawing room, be-cause he didn't have that mark you noticed at dinner … or did he?"

I thought about it and shook my head. "It was after dinner, I'm certain, and the person responsible would have wanted to make sure no evidence was found –"

"So he or she would have removed it."

"Wow," I breathed, realizing the ramifications of Adwin's comment.

He whistled softly. "It *is* one of us."

"I agree." I wagged a finger. "Yet I can't entirely dismiss the possibility that it could be someone yet unknown. He or she may have been hiding beyond a wall or painting. As we've discovered, the house has a few secret places."

"That also means that he or she would have had to have an accomplice, which still points to one of us."

"Maybe we should talk to Lewis," I suggested.

"And tell him what? The obvious? Something he's probably already considered?"

I arched a shoulder. "It seems worth sharing."

"It'll have to wait. He was meeting with a creepy-looking guy with no forehead and Black Molly eyes who's been floating around the house for the last couple of hours. The guy drove in on a Ski-Doo and brought bags and stuff. I hope he leaves soon. If you think Gwynne is surly, this guy's outright disagreeable." He gazed around warily. "I've got a weird feeling … like someone is watching."

I scanned walls, furniture, floors, the cherry- and olive-colored kitchenette, and a tall polished mahogany arch-top mirror in a far corner. "Olly olly oxen free. Come out, come out, wherever you are."

"That's not funny, dumpling buns."

I moved across the floor and hooked his arm. "I could use a big mug of hot cocoa."

"Really? You mean, no more detecting or hanging around bone-chilling places?" He looked as hopeful as a kid waiting to hear if his I-feel-sick complaint had worked and he'd be staying home from school.

"No more detecting for us tonight," I confirmed, guiding him to the door.

18

What a Surprise

When I returned to the cottage a couple of hours later, it was exactly as Adwin and I had left it, albeit a little crisper. Accelerating winds, which been fairly escalated before, hadn't yet thrust the new makeshift window aside; they were too busy assaulting shrubbery, trees, and any living entities foolish enough to be outside. They'd also chilled my face several painful degrees as I'd made a lengthy slippy-slide dash from the house to the cottage. I ran a gloved hand across my forehead. Surprising. There was no mask of rime.

Ensuring the heavy front door was locked and the blinds still secure, I removed the raincoat and hooked it on one of two fat pegs on the back of the door. Turning on the faux Rayo lamp, I peeked under a sheet before sitting on the edge of a snug plum-colored corduroy loveseat. Why

I'd felt a need to return I couldn't say, but the itch had been too great to subdue.

"Hold on." I glanced back at the broken window I'd overlaid with cardboard. There was thick, see-through plastic tacked over it. "What the ..."

I experienced Adwin's earlier feeling about being watched. That investigative reporter he was certain was buried deep within me emerged. I felt a case of Poirotitis coming on and like the diminutive French detective, I surveyed walls, nooks and crannies with a critical eye. Fact: someone had been here since my beau and I had departed. Fact: sheets and coverings aside, the place was extremely clean. Fact: the dwelling had been relatively warm when we'd first arrived, as if providing lodging or shelter for a guest. Fact: there'd been a light in here on at least one occasion, and I may not have been the only person to have seen it. But I was the only one who'd admit it. Why?

Who was looking after this place? The person who'd secured the window? A scraping sound, like sandpaper rubbing rough wood and similar to the one made by the moving panels the gang had been stealing through recently, interrupted my musing. I turned, ready to pounce and/or run. My jaw dropped – as did I, right back into the backrest. "You!"

Aunt Mat stepped from a shadowy opening beyond the gilt-framed mirror, stopped in the kitchenette and leaned both elbows on the counter. She looked at me expectantly, perhaps thinking I'd either lose it and start screaming hysterically, or berate her for a joke gone horribly wrong.

Shock, anger, and happiness rolled over one another like Gloucestershire cheese rollers moving down Cooper Hill. My voice was as dry as Uncle Charly's barbecued chicken, which gave new meaning to the culinary term "blackened". "You *are* going to explain everything, I hope."

A quick smile followed a meek reply: "It's a wee bit of a long story."

"I bet it is."

Good old kooky Aunt Mat. Dressed in soft sable slacks, a maple-colored wool sweater and heavy matching shawl, wheat-blonde hair tucked behind dainty ears sporting sizeable pearl earrings, she looked like a noblewoman on a weekend getaway; casual yet stylish. And very alive. She looked me up and down. "You've lost weight, haven't you, dear? ... I like the hair."

"I'm wearing Cousin Norbett's XXL Panthers sweatshirt and track pants two sizes too big. These rainboots, owner unknown, are scuffed and worn to crap, and Adwin's thermal socks, fortunately unseen, need serious darning. Thanks to the weather, I look like a soggy rooster about to engage in the cockfight of its life." Absently I pulled at my hair. "Stop buttering me up."

She arched a knobby shoulder and turned to a bottom cupboard, rummaged past boxes of kitchen supplies, and pulled out a bottle of Hennessy Privilege. A fine woodsy-spicy cognac was how she'd once described the grape brandy in an email, her fourth that evening – drink, not email. Two Baccarat glasses followed. She poured two fingers in each and held out a glass. Alcohol was something I didn't need at this hour of the night, not that I was sure about the time. It had come to a halt; lost, forgotten. With a shrug, I took the drink and managed a slow sip. The liquid warmed nicely as it traveled downward and started softening the tension that had slipped into my neck and shoulders. We eyed each other warily. Neither one of us looked like we were sure what to say first or who would say it.

We finished our drinks and Aunt Mat poured two more. Glass in hand, she motioned the open panel and slipped inside. I followed. Anyone above a size twelve would find entry into the opening a challenge. Grabbing a large flashlight from a hidey-hole, she flicked it on, closed the panel, and started down a narrow but gentle landing. It was cool but not cold, stale but not fusty. We reached a short flight of stairs, narrow and steep, and very dark. I kept anxious eyes on the bright orange bobbing ball ahead as we took countless steps, waited for a slim narrow door to slide aside, then followed a long, winding corridor that looked vaguely familiar. But all secret passageways in huge old mansions probably looked the same.

We entered a dimly-lighted room and it took two seconds to realize it was the one where we'd first found Jensen.

"Are there a lot of these hidden corridors and concealed rooms in the Moone mansion? Seems like overkill."

"There are three that I know of: the two that circle around and the one from the cottage that leads to the house. Oh, I suppose there's a fourth, if you count the one that leads from the tower and connects to the two down here but, to me, that's merely an extension. The original owner was quite eccentric, perhaps even crazy." She shrugged. "We have a blueprint and plan or two somewhere. They may expose others."

Ah yes, the tube marked ESTATE not yet opened. Adwin had put it in the closet. Out of sight, out of mind.

I sat on an end table corner.

"Thanks for the air conditioning in the cottage, by the way."

I offered a smile and a salaam. "Was this Reginald's secret place to chill, or yours?"

"He had the tower; I had this." She flourished an arm in a semi-arc. "When I wanted absolute privacy, I came here."

"You couldn't escape in one of fourteen bedrooms?" I asked drolly.

"Someone always managed to find me," she replied equally drolly.

I put down the glass I'd emptied on the journey here. "Rey is going to be ticked off that she's not getting that personal trainer with her share of the inheritance."

"She won't right now, but in time." Aunt Mat sat on the recamier the hide-n-seek corpse had claimed as his first resting place.

"We discovered Jensen Moone on that: dead."

She scanned the scroll-patterned fabric, her brow knitted. "I thought they'd found him in the back somewhere – the garage, wasn't it?"

"We found him here, then lost him, then found him again. Or rather Porter did. He's also dead, by the way, in case no one's been filling you in."

"I figured as much from the fragments of conversations I caught here and there. What a burlesque."

"Out of curiosity, is this where you've been hiding and sleeping most of the time?"

"I've been using the cottage for the most part, and one of the unused guestrooms on the far north side of the house. You went there once; I figured you wouldn't be returning as there's not much there." She sighed softly. "Since Reggie's death, I've closed off most of the place. Entertaining isn't quite the same without him."

I eyed her guardedly. "What gives? You're alive, but Thomas, Jensen, and Porter are dead."

She took a slow sip. "It's long and complicated, and may tie in with what I've learned over the past year."

When she didn't elaborate, I urged her on.

"A number of antiques and art pieces Reggie had purchased over the decades have been replaced with counterfeits."

"How did you discover the counterfeits?"

"Ben, a former gallery director in Berlin – and Reggie's advisor – had dropped by for a few days during an East Coast visit the year previous. We were touring Reggie's tower room when Ben's observant eye caught a few obscure incongruities. He was astounded by the quality of the replicas. He said upon first glance – and second – few people would be the wiser."

"But your husband was an expert, wasn't he?"

Her smile was dry. "Reggie's eyes had deteriorated over the years. He was a bit vain when it came to glasses." She shrugged. "It's also possible he'd 'seen' them so often, he didn't give them much thought."

"Wouldn't he have spotted inconsistencies prior to, or upon, delivery?"

My aunt shrugged. "He may have found the originals sound, but the items that were shipped were fakes. Once uncrated, I doubt Reggie spent much time with them. He was all about collecting, not admiring." Another sip. "The more digging Ben and I did, the more we unearthed. We discovered someone had been pilfering, courtesy of the counterfeits. There are numerous investments, funds and foundations, and accounts, so it wasn't noticeable to the average eye. Invoices, receipts, and records, all appeared valid ... until viewed under the proverbial microscope."

"So unless there was a professional actively seeking financial inconsistencies, no one would have known differently."

"Precisely. Fortunately, Ben's sharp eye helped bring things into the open." She sighed softly. "I ended up hiring a private dick –"

I burst into laughter.

She smiled self-consciously. "I guess I've been influenced by all the old black and whites movies

I'd been watching of late. Before I start spouting more forties lingo, I'd better give them up."

"Why? They're wonderful, but maybe you could refrain from using certain words … like 'gams' and 'kisser' and 'paluka', and 'dick'." I laughed again. "You were saying you hired a detective?"

"Johnny Gorcey. He has a face like Edward G around the time of *Big Leaguer* and the heart of Bing as Father Chuck O'Malley. In terms of missing money, he said the thief was highly skilled at covering his tracks and had probably done so for some time."

"He's positive it's a guy?"

She placed her empty glass by her size five feet. "Johnny was pretty certain it could only be a handful of people who were very close to Reggie and me. He was prime for Jensen, but I was prime for Thomas. I didn't want to believe Reggie's own brother could steal from the family."

Calling that somber-faced gent hanging in the library-study Reggie seemed strange, and it sounded even stranger when Aunt Matty said it – with obvious affection, as if she were whispering the name to him over cocktails and a platter of raw oysters. "Hadn't they been at odds for years, until they finally made nice?"

"They had business connections and family ties, which kept them bonded to a degree, but they had never much seen eye to eye and had been very vocal about it to everyone. For years, they spoke through intermediaries, but finally, thankfully, made up. Reggie's relationship with Carlton, the youngest Moone brother, had also been at odds. In fact, *theirs* had disintegrated in one rage-filled moment when Carlton defied Reggie's heartfelt and logical advice." She sighed with resignation and it was obvious she wished things had been different.

"So the belief is that Jensen or Thomas may have been the pilferer?"

"There's one more possibility." She regarded me for several seconds, as if deciding whether to reveal more. Apparently she did. "Percival – through charities and businesses – had considerable dealings with Reggie during the last few years of his life. There were numerous dinners and outings, and working weekends as a result."

"What sort of dealings?"

"The two were co-owners of an antiques shop, as well as a beer company. They'd become associates in five businesses in total." As she gave a quick rundown, the sparkle in her ginger-brown eyes dimmed. I thought of the women who believed emphatically they knew their husbands well, only to realize they'd never known them at all.

"I thought Reginald was solely into antiquities?"

"He'd been into art, as well. Perc's Spanish firm handled both, which Reggie often used for buying and selling. Reggie had also funded an Asian exporting firm and had considerable stock in an Irish whiskey distillery."

"Reginald had his hands in several pots, and some with Percival," I mused aloud, unable to see Percival as a cheat or fraudster. "… Do you really believe Prunella's brother could be capable of duping you both?"

"Anything seems possible right now." She tipped her head to one side. "Why do you call him Reginald? Whatever happened to 'Uncle'?"

"I never called him 'Uncle'," I reminded her. "He never seemed like one. He never visited and never called." I chewed my bottom lip, deciding whether to ask the question that had always been at the back of my mind. What the hell. "Why'd you marry him? Money?"

Aunt Mat chuckled. "His money hadn't hurt, but no, I married him for love. He was different. Intelligent. World-wise. No one but the two of us knew he was such a compassionate and passionate man."

"He seemed the sort to leave starving kittens in a storm."

She smiled wistfully. "Quite the opposite. Reggie would have risked double pneumonia to save those starving kittens." She glanced down at the floor and frowned. "You must remember that generations of Moones have been a dour, suspicious and stern lot. Reggie played the part whenever he believed it was necessary – which was 95% of the time – but he truly despised the Moone institution and what being a Moone entailed."

"You weren't too fond of the Moones, were you?"

"They leaned toward the pretentious and judgmental. They considered themselves of an elevated social standing, which from my perspective was a pathetic illusion." A fleeting glower darkened her countenance.

I sensed Reginald's side of the family had not been overly kind to her over the years, and changed the topic. "What about all the macabre oddities around the house? Were they for show?"

"No." She grinned. "Reggie truly loved macabre oddities."

I'd have to spend some time putting the enigmatic Reginald Saver-of-Kittens Moone into perspective. Later. For the interim, I wanted to get back to Percival Sayers. To live in this area meant you had to have some money. Why had I assumed he was merely a man of middle-class means? His looks? Maybe. He didn't seem a Beluga caviar and Cristal champagne kind of person, but he did have costly designer clothes. So, in addition to writing obscure poetry and landscaping articles, the man was an entrepreneur and potential pilferer. Or was that embezzler? My due diligence was in need of less "due" and more "diligence".

"So the plan was to gather the suspects, along with some extras, under the pretext of a come-and-get-your-inheritance extravaganza?"

"It seemed an ingenious way to uncover the truth."

I rose and rubbed my backside, which was feeling a burn from sitting on a hard base. "Were you hoping one, both, or all would be so over-whelmed by your death, they'd break down and confess all sins?"

"Something like that." Aunt Mat chuckled, but not with humor, and gestured the spot along-side her. I sat with a grimace. There was some-thing disturbing about parking yourself on a place where a dead body had rested.

"Johnny was waiting to engage a hacker friend's services. Macky's the best there is, says he."

"Waiting?"

"Macky had been away for a wee while."

Being "the best" was undoubtedly why he'd been "away for a wee while" – as in "prison away". I motioned my aunt to continue.

"I was aiming for a big jaw-dropping mo-ment, when I'd walk into dinner and confront the group." She smiled ruefully. "But it appears others have had the pleasure of grabbing such moments since this get-together first began."

"So you were hoping to play Columbo and solve the crimes of fraud and thievery?" I asked.

"I was hoping more for a Magnum moment; I always liked the Aloha spirit and paradisiacal tranquility."

"I myself always liked the rumpled lieutenant's persistent one-more-question approach."

She leaned back. "I got to thinking, Jilly –"

"Oh-oh."

She offered an uncharacteristic raspberry, reminiscent of her niece Rey. "Over the last wee while, I got to thinking that Prunella could also be involved. Or *solely* involved. Her brother's not the sharpest knife in the cutlery drawer, but that may be an act."

An earlier thought returned and I held up a hand. "Does anyone in the Moone family smoke?"

She shook her head. "Reggie indulged in the very odd Cohiba, but no one smoked cigarettes. I believe we were all of the same – and rare – mind in that regard. They're coffin nails. Why?"

"Just curious. I thought I'd seen a package on an end table, and got to wondering who the smoker was, but it may have been something else," I said lightly. I'd joked about Percival being the owner of that butt in the corridor, but later as I was mentally rummaging through recent events like bric-a-brac at a garage sale, that brief scene replayed itself. Why hadn't I thought to pick it up? If it had proven to be the remainder of a French cigarette, it would have proven that Percival Sayers was a liar: he knew of, and had been in, the hidden passageways previously. That, in turn, pointed an accusatory (legitimate) finger at him.

"There's certainly more to Pruney than meets the eye," I commented, recalling her attire in the hallway.

"She's not quite the librarian or hippie she appears." Aunt Mat leaned forward, her eyes sparkling merrily again.

I leaned forward as well. We were nearly forehead to forehead. "You're going to drop a bomb, aren't you?"

"I found out that our friend of feathered vertebrates was having an affair with Thomas. Johnny provided the proof."

Rey would be overjoyed with the news, but it was hardly a bomb at this stage. "They'd been photographed together a number of times."

"Yes, yes, I know. They often attended functions and galas together." She waved a hand dismissively. "So did I. You could find thirty photos of Prunella and Thomas grinning and hugging, but you could find thirty photos of Thomas and I doing the same. *Those* photos don't prove a thing."

When she didn't continue, I urged, "But *Johnny's* photos do ... ?"

"Yes. They proved the two were intimate. It wasn't only his photos, but ones taken by the lovers themselves. Johnny found them by accident."

By accident? I wasn't going there. The less known about Johnny's private detective antics, the better. "When did this relationship end?"

"A good fifteen months ago, when his gambling got completely out of hand and he was being threatened by associates. Prunella wasn't making his life any easier by suggesting he propose to her. When she gave him an ultimatum – 'gambling or me' – he refused to meet her demand."

I took a moment to collect thoughts. "It's possible then that Thomas is – was – your culprit. And Prunella was also involved, either through him and/or Percival."

She gazed at me solemnly. "Or solely."

"Let's say she was involved with Thomas, and it ended on a sour note –"

"Then he'd want to be as free of her as she would him. It depends on who initiated the let's-dupe-Reginald-and-Mathilda-Moone   scheme. Being ex-lovers is one thing, ex-partners-in-crime another. Affairs of the heart and libido become so much more complicated when criminality's involved, don't you think?"

I sighed, feeling deflated. Where did one take it from here? How come answers didn't come as readily in real life as they did in two-hour mystery shows? "Why bring the rest of us here?"

"The gathering had to look legitimate. I'd planned to enlist your personal aid sooner than later. Things got …"

"Out of hand?"

"Who'd have expected Thomas to kick the damn bucket?"

"He was murdered – as Jensen was and as Porter was."

She scanned my face. "Obviously no one has yet been arrested for any crimes, but do we have an idea who the murderer may be?"

"… I'm tempted to place Prunella at the top of the list. Scorned women make for good suspects. Scorned and *betrayed* women make for even better suspects. But who knows? Maybe one of those associates who'd been threatening Thomas had done the deed."

"And gotten around the property and house without having been seen by anyone?" She shook her head. "No, I don't believe that's possible."

"What about the secret passageways and concealed nooks and crannies and niches? They could have sneaked through them."

She shook her head again. "No. That's not possible."

That theory wasn't meeting approval by anyone who heard it. But as Adwin and I had discussed earlier, considering timing and every-thing, if had to be someone in the group. Still, I couldn't completely discount the notion of an outside source. Not yet anyway. "What about Jensen? He said you'd asked him to play pranks."

"He was helping me have fun." Her smile was that of a little girl's, one who was certain she'd played the best April Fool's joke ever. "A few months ago, when more and more was coming to light and the concept for this seven-day affair was beginning to bud, I told him that when my time came, I wanted to have a big laugh from the Afterlife. Spooking my dearest friends and family seemed 'frightfully fun' and – for the customary legal fee – he agreed to help. He never wanted to know more than necessary and didn't ask ques-tions."

"What about Percival? He has a pretty odd re-lationship with his sister."

"She has fifty-percent control in all his ven-tures, so they have a tight professional bond. And, technically, they're half brother and sister. They shared the same wing-ding father."

"It's still odd," I said flatly.

Aunt Mat smiled darkly. "They became an item about twenty-five, maybe thirty years ago, so scuttlebutt had it."

"And scuttlebutt claimed they lasted as an 'item' for ... ?"

"Well over a decade. Actually, closer to two."

"That's ..."

"Weird?"

"Disturbingly creepy."

Aunt Mat offered a flat smile. "Almost as much as May-Lee having been married for two months to Percival when they were in their late teens."

Thump.

She gazed down, extended her hand, and helped me back into the seat.

19

A Tale with Two Tails

It was six in the morning, hours since I'd left Aunt Mat and the corridor. I'd crashed in her bedroom, not having wanted to awaken the sleepy pastry chef and his newfound pet, which would surely accompany us back to Wilmington if Aunt Mat didn't put a stop to it. Sleep had been deep but brief. I could have used lots more shut-eye, but three murders, a madcap aunt, an array of weird guests, and a happy-go-lucky ghost required attention.

As for the cigarette butt, someone had beaten me to it. Gone it was. Of course, I could have taken a wrong turn, but that was doubtful. A shiver capered up my spine as an image of that dark, dank place burst before my eyes like a Flashcube on an Instamatic camera.

I dropped to the side of the bed and jostled Adwin's shoulder, prompting him to groan and Fred to crawl under the covers.

"Huh? What?" Adwin gazed up blearily.

"She's alive!"

"Are you talking about *The Head with Two Brains*? Or is that *The Brain with Two Heads*?" He shifted onto bony scarred elbows and appeared genuinely concerned that he'd gotten B-movie titles confused.

"Aunt Matty – she's alive!" I grabbed a fur-shrouded pillow that Fred had obviously slept on and hit Adwin lightly in the head.

"Did you have a wild dream? Or has lack of sleep contributed to figments of the imagination?" He struggled out of bed and grabbed a flannel robe to cover a white T-shirt and cupcake-themed boxer shorts. He lurched into the bathroom, then peered around the doorframe. "I know! You opted for an early liquid breakfast. Maybe I'll opt for the same. A Mint Julep might be the best way to get through what will – without doubt – be another wacky day." The bathroom door closed and water started running.

I sighed and grabbed the laptop and Smartphone. Why waste time sitting around? I'd already showered, slapped on makeup, and changed into jeans and a thick jet-black wool sweater with huge fuchsia snowflakes. At this hour, I couldn't see Beatrice or Hubert preparing breakfast, or anyone else dragging his or her tail downstairs, so the kitchen would almost certainly be empty. I could whip up toast and tea. And if I was really inclined, I could assemble breakfast for the troupe: toasted English muffins, boiled eggs, oatmeal and coffee. Yeah, and an Indian monsoon would blow into Connecticut any moment.

Two chai teas and three slices of toasted rye with blackberry jam later, I was pounding at the keyboard, running more searches on the first two dead gents. Nothing earth-shattering surfaced so I moved on to the third corpse. Porter the cook, also known as Ralph Bloom-Walters and "Crackers" to his jailhouse buddies, was an interesting individual. As co-owner of a popular NYC hotspot in the early 80s, Porter/Ralph/Crackers was arrested for embezzlement. There was also mention of poison in a porcini sauce that took out mobster Jimmy Jojo James in said hotspot, but it was never proven who the killer was. There was lots of speculation, though, with Crackers' name placed amid twenty known Jimmy Jojo James haters. Murder never proven, Crackers did nine months for misappropriation.

I Googled again and discovered that Ralph Bloom-Walters had ended up cooking at *Le Cochon Volant,* an upscale French restaurant in San Fran in the mid nineties. It received six excellent reviews, five good ones, and one negative one. One day, the restaurant exploded like an over-poached perogy. Debris flew, glass shattered, and flames cavorted amid the chaos. Shock waves were felt blocks away. Bad wiring was cited as the source, but two journalists weren't sold on faulty circuitry as the cause. One suggested family crime connections of co-owner Benton Wiffleton and/or overdue funding payments acquired through questionable sources, could have played a part. The other insinuated that purposeful manipulation of gas connections may have generated the explosion.

Of the several persons knocked off their chairs, five suffered minor injuries while two people were seriously hurt: a food critic and his companion. Apparently the one who'd written the negative review had been enticed to return – financially, no doubt. Why else would he have come back to a place that served filet mignon "as succulent and savory as beef jerky left in a lost camper's knapsack" and sautéed vegetables "resembling desiccated krill"? Accident or other-wise, talk about bad timing.

You had to wonder: did Crackers get his nick-name because he liked Saltines or because he was a few bolts shy?

Linda strolled into the kitchen dressed in a black A-line skirt and bubble-gum-pink silk blouse with a black cardigan slung from one shoulder. She looked particularly bright-eyed and perky. "I slept like a log."

I smiled. "You look great." And she did. Even with a thick coating of make-up blobbed on the ugly scrape on her nose.

"Wish I could say the same for you. Those dark bags look like they could fit five suits and ten sweaters."

I ran fingertips under my eyes. They did feel dry and puffy. It was probably time to apply Nivea Eye Cream – with a spatula.

"Is there any breakfast to be had?"

I jerked a thumb at the mammoth fridge. "You're on your own. I highly recommend rye bread, toasted, with jam or honey."

Linda laughed and started preparing a pot of coffee. "What're you looking at?"

"Porter. It seems the cook was a man with a checkered past."

"You're talking about the prison term, right?"

I all but goggled. "You know?"

She poured cream into a mug with multi-colored air balloons on it. "I learned that last night. I did a search on him, the two dead guys, and the Sayers – you know, to see if anything weird stood out."

Great minds think alike. "Do you have anything of note to share?"

Out of the fridge came a loaf of sliced rye bread, jar of blueberry jam, and stick of butter. "Did you know Prunella got arrested once? She never served time. The charges got dropped: the witnesses recanted."

"Arrested? For what?" I grinned. "Leading a demonstration to save the Green-bellied Seer-sucker Warbler?"

Linda laughed hysterically as she watched the coffeemaker start to work its magic. Whatever she'd popped I wanted a dozen of. "She had a partnership in a highbrow restaurant in San Francisco that blew up in the 90s. A well-known restaurant critic got hurt. So did Prunella. She was with him when it happened. The co-owner, who owned a fair share of the place – unlike Porter's token percentage – was a stuffed shirt with too much money and time. His name was Benton Merkston Wiffleton. He ate bad sushi in 1997 and died."

Obviously I'd not read the right article. I should have been more thorough with search parameters, but in fairness, I'd not been at it that long; I'd have stumbled onto the additional details eventually. But wasn't this getting interesting if not complicated? Had Prunella known that the Moone mansion cook was the same one that had worked at *Le Cochon Volant* and that he'd owned a "token percentage"? How could she not? But during a phone chat with Aunt Mat a couple of years back, she'd mentioned Porter was an introverted cook who preferred to remain out of the limelight, regardless of how a guest gushed or cooed over a meal. I remembered her commenting on how shy and humble he was, how he'd never show his face. It was entirely possible he'd remained hidden in the Moone kitchen and out of Prunella's sight. Yeah, and penguins could fly. He'd been in my aunt's employ since about 2003, when Sergey, the first cook, decided to move his aging body to Arizona. How was it possible for a guest to never see the cook? *It wasn't.*

"Was she arrested because they thought she could have had something to do with the 'accident'?"

Linda popped four slices of bread into a mint-green retro toaster. "No, she got arrested because once she was out of the hospital she went after Wiffleton and Bloom-Walters, aka Porter, with a frozen swordfish." She smiled grimly. "She claimed they were to blame for her emotional state and financial problems. Apparently she really loved that place and had invested her heart and soul – and several thousand dollars – into it.

I think she may have had a thing for the critic, too. Maybe they broke up after the accident, or maybe he blamed her for it. I read that some individuals weren't even sure it was an accident, but there wasn't enough evidence to prove otherwise."

She pulled out a plate and knife, and prepared a simple breakfast. "Culinary critics are like actors, Jill. They have mega egos. Who knows what really happened? Did guy #1 tick off guy #2 and, as a result, guy #2 decided to exact revenge? Or was it truly nothing more than a misfortunate accident? As for Pruney Sayers, she's not about to confide in us. But we can all attest to the fact she's more than a bit out there."

She was a bit out there, all right, but enough to commit murder? Well, she'd gone after two men with a frozen *xiphias gladius*, hadn't she? That meant she had a violent streak, or at least a heated one. Being injured and scarred during an explosion, intentionally set or otherwise, could ignite a mental or emotional fuse. How intensive was the scarring on Prunella's chest? Did it matter? A little or a lot, I'd have been pissed, too.

"Apparently she lived in San Fran for a few weeks during spring months throughout the 90s. Various charities and foundations took her to different states over the years, but she's solely New England bound these days." She chuckled. "Can you see Prunella Sayers, hippie crusader and bird lover, taking a swing at someone with a swordfish?"

I chuckled. It did seem absurd, but then stranger things had been known to happen. And, very recently, they had.

* * *

At 9:00 a.m. everyone was in the small dining room – two of us musing, one obsessed with Angry Birds while sucking a green-apple lollipop, one reading *Farmer's Almanac*, one perusing Julia Childs' *The French Chef Cookbook*, and one playing with cold butter-soaked toast. Another stood at the window watching a couple of foolish media folks beyond the gate, shivering beside company vans under sodden, polar conditions. No doubt they were hoping for another body.

"Don't they have better things to do, like filming stranded people or mangled vehicles?" Prunella adjusted a lace valance and sighed loudly.

The group hadn't exchanged more than twenty words prior to her comment. We all looked worn, maybe a little worried. I'm not sure if the prevalent question on everyone's mind was, "Who the heck is next to greet the Grim Reaper?" or "When the [*insert preferred expletive*] do we get to leave?"

"I heard a cute reporter on a cheesy community news program say something about the 'medieval and morose Moone mansion' – uh, hmm." Adwin's expression changed from animated to perplexed as he brought a coffee cup to his lips.

"I was right behind you and heard the same report. She wasn't cute, not with that overbite – she looked like Mr. Ed. She said 'triple murders make for a frightening fiasco at the former' – uh, dang. I forgot." Linda frowned, placed the tablet on the table, and stood.

Percival snorted. "The young *lad* with *effete* features and voice said, and I quote: 'freakish shenanigans result in three deaths at the –' "

" 'Freakish shenanigans' my ass," Linda snapped, waving the lollipop like a conductor might a baton during the climax of Tchaikovsky's *1812 Overture*. The meds must have worn off.

"My goodness. Don't we look as cross as avid concert goers who've just been told the headline act is delayed on another continent?"

Beatrice ceased rearranging napkins. Hubert barely managed to place a shaky cup on an even shakier saucer. Prunella blanched and Percival's breath caught in his throat. Adwin merely hugged Julia to his chest and May-Lee ceased shifting toast.

"Aunt Mat! Jeez! Holy crap!" Rey appeared more insulted than shocked. Standing akimbo, glittery bangles jangled as they hit a silver knock-off Prada belt.

Linda tittered and slapped her thigh, humor apparently restored.

I swung around the sexagenarian and pecked a lightly rouged cheek. "You look as lovely as always."

Happy, pretty, stylish: that was Aunt Mat. Estrada did her justice, but the woman would look good in bargain-basement specials.

"What's the idea?" Rey demanded.

"It's a wee bit of a long story."

"That would be an understatement," I murmured.

Somewhere upstairs, a voice bellowed.

With a simper, Adwin nodded upward. "That sounds like Gwynne."

Out of the corner of my mouth, I asked, "When did Detective Surly arrive?"

Out of the corner of his, he replied, "Maybe an hour and a half ago, fit to be tied, looking like something the cat dragged in."

Aunt Mat bowed her head at the group and strolled purposefully from the room, a twinkle warming those lovely ginger-brown eyes.

"The long story just got lots longer," Adwin declared with a droll smile.

"Does someone want to provide a condensed version?" Prunella asked caustically, her furious gaze coming to rest on me.

* * *

Nancy Drew's spirit must have seized my soul, because an overwhelming desire to snoop surged through me like a menopausal hot-flash (such as the ones my mother had complained about the preceding year). I wasn't exactly sure what it was I was searching for, but nosing around became priority number one.

Thomas Saturne's bedroom was first on the agenda. Yes, we'd combed through it as a team and not found much, save for racing forms, a horse mag and Kinky Friedman books, which had provided an interesting skew to the Manhattan lawyer. The room was fairly dim so I turned on one of two antique brass candlestick table lamps.

Our stuffed reptile friend was no longer around; the police had taken possession of him when we'd mentioned our find on Friday. They'd not found the Sidewinder on the initial look-around, but they'd not been investigating a murder at that time. Agreeing it was suspicious, they'd said they'd check Snakey for clues. Clues to what, though? Stuffing and scale remnants?

If memory served correctly, Nancy the amateur detective was a pretty methodical gal, so it seemed best to start in the northwest corner where the armoire stood and work my way around. Thirty minutes later I'd not discovered anything new. I sat on the corner of the bed with Kinky's *Frequent Flyer* and *A Case of Lone Star* on my lap, and wondered if Thomas was also a closet cigar smoker. It wasn't hard to envision a Kinkycristo perched on those blubbery lips. Idly, I began flipping pages. A business card for a pizza place in Greenwich Village fell from *Flyer*. Nothing surprising there. Thomas seemed a pizza sort of man, heavy on the sausage and ground beef. I shook the other novel and a wallet-sized photo dropped to a floral wool rug.

A Linda Royale "dang" tiptoed past my lips when I saw the face. A fancy cigarette hung from the lips of the man staring back with a joyful, toothy smile; he appeared genuinely cheery as he held a crystal snifter with hairy digits. Two platinum rings with sizeable diamonds caught light from somewhere beyond the camera. That's where similarities between young Porter Dance-Club King in the photo and old Porter On Ice ceased. This silk-draped fellow, Ralph Bloom-Walters, was at least two decades younger and forty pounds thinner. Evidently food had loved

Porter as much as he had it; they'd developed a steadfast, *embracing* bond over the years.

Why would Thomas be in the possession of a photo of the dead cook? Had Prunella given it to him? That made no sense, but what made a tad more sense was that Thomas had known about her involvement with Porter back in San Francisco – whatever that relationship had entailed – and had held onto the photo for some obscure reason.

Was there something in the photo I wasn't seeing? I studied it for several seconds. There was no one in the background. The man looked cheerful; he wasn't committing any visible crime. It didn't appear to be anything more than what it was: an old, innocuous photo.

Obviously I didn't have the logic and rationale of a fiction or television detective – I was scrabbling my awkward way through. I tucked the photo into my jean pocket, put everything back in place, and turned off the light. Hopefully Jensen's room would reveal something more apparent and useful.

As I stepped in, my phone rang. "Fonne," I said instinctively, the way I usually answered at work.

"It's Ger. How is it up in the winter hinterland?" he chuckled.

"Awesomely wintery," I replied dryly. "What's up?"

"I just wanted to let you know I'm sending a bit of info your way in the next few minutes re that dead ghost guy. I'll stay on it for a bit, but I don't know how much luck I'll have finding more info."

"Great stuff. You're the best, Ger."

"Don't I know it?" He laughed and hung up.

I turned on a lovely tortoiseshell urn lamp, one of two on opposite sides of a plush bronze-colored armchair. The barrister's room was decorated and arranged much like Thomas', except that the predominant wood was cherry instead of maple and the color scheme more feminine: rose and turquoise instead of avocado and russet. In the corner nearest the door, not far from a cherry armoire with geometric etching on the doors, stood a cherry-framed cheval mirror of no aesthetic value. The contents of the armoire and cabinet drawers revealed expensive taste in designer footwear and clothes, a penchant for heavy gold jewelry, and an interest in business magazines.

This is Gonna Hurt: Music, Photography and Life Through the Distorted Lens of Nikki Sixx lay on one of two-drawer nightstands. Okay, now *that* went beyond bizarre. Jensen and Nicki? I couldn't see it, but maybe it had been a gift from a client. Or perhaps he wasn't as stuffy and conservative as he appeared. After all, he had displayed that little streak of humor in the closet, which went to prove you couldn't always judge a book by its cover. Uh, yeah.

The small bathroom, bearing a seashell theme, held nothing out of the norm. A travel-size tube of Tylenol had rolled into a corner. A royal-blue toothbrush, dental floss, and fresh tube of Marvis Aquatic Mint toothpaste rested neatly on the corner of a large oval sink. On a narrow glass shelf, a bottle of Blue de Chanel kept company with a fancy shaving brush, double-edged safety razor, Zirh Shave Foam, and Bull Dog moisturizer for sensitive skin. A handsome silver-plated hairbrush and comb, and a bottle of Korres Coriander Spray were neatly arranged one level above. Most of the British products were unfamiliar and likely not cheap.

Back in the bedroom, I spun slowly, eyeing corners, nooks and crannies. Nothing shouted, "hey, over here, clue for ya!", so I spun again, stopping at the four-poster bed. I got down on my knees, pulled aside a crepe-like ruffled skirt, and peered down the width and length. In a far corner rested a lovely leather briefcase that had to cost £1500 if it cost a pence. With awkward maneuvering and arm-stretching, I managed to retrieve it. Turning on the second lamp, I emptied contents from multiple pockets and one by one reviewed the documents.

There was a copy of Aunt Mat's will, leases and contracts related to overseas properties and businesses, ledger photocopies, emails, and a few legal articles with yellow highlighting. Seeing little of interest, I was about to stop when several pages fluttered to the floor. A familiar company name caught my eye: Ages & Artisans. This was Reginald Moone's Asian antiquity business. I flipped through pages and found another name Aunt Mat had mentioned recently, Lace & Velvet, which was a porcelain antiques shop in Kent, and a joint Reginald-Percival venture. Art pieces and antiquities were listed on a few pages, while others itemized financial transactions.

One page, tucked between the lot, had amounts and names: Thomas Saturne, Prunella Sayers, Percival Sayers, Gruber Pathos and Santana Anna Dinero. I suspected the recorded dollar amounts were relocated ones – as in relocated to accounts in Turks and Caicos and Switzerland.

Did this mean Jensen had suspected something was amiss? Or had Aunt Mat requested he check into things? She hadn't mentioned that, but maybe she'd forgotten to, or hadn't deemd it worth sharing. If either were the case, how long had he been investigating? Had Prunella stumbled upon these documents? Or had Jensen let something inadvertently slip? If the answer was yes to one or both of these last two questions, then we had a motive for Jensen's murder. But it was all still conjecture; nothing tangible.

For a second, I contemplated taking the ledger pages, but decided against it. It would be best to leave the briefcase where it was. There was no point in alerting – or alarming – anyone.

20

Big but [Not So] Bad-Ass

Upon entering the guestroom I checked for Ger's promised info and was pleased to find it in the Inbox. As he'd said, there wasn't much.

A grainy photograph near rural railroad tracks showed a dozen men with shovels and picks. It had been part of an article on expanding railways, but Ger had provided only the photo that held a couple of unremarkable sentences beneath. One name stood out, though: Fred Maxwell. It was hard to see his face, not only because of the poor quality of the photo, but the shaggy hair and beard. In the "Clinton News" section of a Connecticut paper dated May 1896, a blurb advised that Contractor Marcus F.P. Jerrold of Middleton and his men, Fred Maxwell and Peter Kelsomm, had begun working on a barn for

Joseph Crumholz in the rear of his Clinton Beach cottage.

Ger restated a promise to keep looking and signed off with "xoxoxox". Yuck. Well, what the two items did reveal was that Fred had indeed moved around doing odd jobs and subsequently – good for him – stayed out of trouble.

The cell phone started ringing. So much for a quick lay-down and freshen-up. The display said it was private investigator Johnny Gorcey. He was quick to respond; I liked that. Hopefully there was something of note to impart.

"Gorcey here. This Ms. Fonne?" He didn't wait for a response. "How's your aunt?"

"Fine, good, healthy," I stumbled, surprised. I wasn't sure what I'd been expecting, but it wasn't a deep, booming, gravelly voice that sounded as if it belonged to a big bad-ass TV tough guy. I could envision Gorcey standing six feet tall, as huge as a restaurant refrigerator, no neck, the body half muscle and half flab. He'd smoke cigarillos, drink black coffee by the potful, and eat rare steaks with sides of greasy, gravy-soaked fries. Clothes would be frumpy and baggy, not unlike the deceased Manhattan lawyer's.

"Tell her Johnny sends regards."

Who was going to argue with the brusque command? Not I. "Ummm, how can I help?"

He laughed, sounding like a staple gun operating out of control. "You were the one who called for help, Ms. Fonne."

"Right. Where shall we start?" I dropped into a chair in front of the vanity and eyed the weary face staring back. A quick sudsy shower might help. So might a triple espresso.

"Linda Royale. You probably already know this. There are no living parents. Sister Loretta Linn has lived in six states in the last eight years. She works for a few months, usually in an admin capacity, and moves on. Obviously she's not one to lay roots. Brother Lido Lawrence is a travel-documentary cameraman – or was. He's been out of work since he broke a foot and arm filming chipmunks in Canada two years ago. He got into some sort of depression. He has a son Theo he sees every three weeks. He also has a San Diego apartment and recently gave up one in L.A. due to financial woes. There are no red flags for either sibling, except for small-time theft when Lido was seventeen.

"Ms. Royale got married in her teens to a jazz musician named Chiffre Royale, who played sax on a few albums of notable artists. He died in a fleabag motel outside Chicago of a heroin overdose." Paper rustled and his cough sounded like a bear growl. He offered a few quick facts related to her current employment and life. The not-so-interesting highlights: Linda had never been arrested, had received two parking tickets in 2012, and won a large-screen television that same year.

I turned back to the mirror and found Ms. Weary wasn't looking any perkier.

"Ms. Royale was a client of Thomas Saturne's, by the way. A pal of mine, Basil, was tailing him a while back. I checked with him – because something about her was gnawing at me – and he said he recalled a young woman by that name. Basil's got a remarkable memory and can remember names, streets, cars, diners, you name it, without referring to notes. She met with Saturne a couple of times."

I perked up suddenly. This was interesting. But where would it lead? "Why was he tailing Thomas? And why was she seeing him?"

"About three years ago, Thomas Saturne was suspected of stealing funds from a non-profit organization he represented. Nothing was ever proven – not in terms of him – though it appeared, Roblee Schnee, a guy at that org was the actual culprit. A few thousand dollars were found in a locked drawer in his desk and at his condo in a cereal box at the back of a closet. He committed suicide the day the desk discovery was made, so the case was closed and Basil's services terminated."

"He committed suicide ... how?"

"The guy jumped from his thirteenth-floor balcony."

"How neat."

"And convenient?" he asked dryly, taking a gulp of something.

"Very." Thomas would have been with Prunella then. Had they framed Roblee Schnee and opted for fresh starts?

"What about Linda? She wasn't implicated or involved in this in some way?"

"No, nothing like that. She met Saturne about family stuff related to the Smiths – who she's related to."

I all but goggled. "She's related to the Smiths who once owned my aunt's house?"

"Yes ma'am – one and the same family. In fact, Loretta Linn is the LL Smith who maintains a family blog." More paper crackled. "It's entirely possible this Chiffre guy got her started on the Smiths. She'd visited a lawyer by the name of Katt Salmon not long after they were married, seeing if she had legal claims to family cash." I could hear the frown. "The guy probably wanted drug money and thought this would be an easy way of getting it. There was a lot of correspondence between the Royales and the Smiths, but nothing happened. Salmon had no luck, either. Then the druggie-hubby died and she put it on the back burner – until she turned thirty-one last year. That's how she got to be a client of Saturne."

"I'm guessing nothing came of it."

"As Saturne's bitten the dust, you'd have to ask the lady herself for details. But no, it doesn't look like anything came of it."

"So she tried to get money again," I mused aloud, perturbed. I could see Linda as many things, but not the greedy sort.

"I believe she wanted a set amount – nothing extravagant – for some family members, including her brother, because of his slump." Gorcey moved on to May-Lee Sonit and again offered known facts. What I hadn't been familiar with was the antique dealer's two sisters and daughter. Forty-eight-year-old Marigold was a dentist in El Paso and forty-four-year-old Blanche a high-end salesperson in Miami. Daughter Karina owned a small event-planning business and lived with her eight-year-old son Guy-Marc in Seattle.

May-Lee had been married very young to Percival, but divorced within a few weeks. No new news there. Her daughter was the product of a short-term relationship with a pilot when she was twenty-four. Sammy, her last boyfriend, also an antique dealer, passed two years ago of pancreatic cancer.

"Do you want me to find out more regarding Ms. Royale and Ms. Sonit?"

"Hold off for now," I answered slowly, considering it. If he couldn't find any red flags, there

308

likely weren't any. But never say never, right? "How about the Sayers?"

Gorcey recited old news: the marriage, the writing, the employment history.

"So there are no closet skeletons, and I'm not talking about Aunt Mat's little surprises." I was discouraged and sounded it.

"Granted, there are no big closet skeletons, but I wasn't finished," he responded soothingly. "In 2010 Percival Sayers spent six months in a European spa, which is another word for rehab."

"For what? Drinking? Drugging?"

"He had a breakdown."

"What type? Mental? Emotional?"

"Both. Apparently Sayers lost it at a book signing for a friend. He ran amok, broke balloons while singing happy birthday to himself, and then munched a few flower arrangements."

"What triggered it?"

"I don't know". He drew a deep ragged breath. "They're both a bit strange, those two. Prunella Sayers spent her teen years in six different boarding schools."

"Why so many?"

"Boredom? Teenage troubles? I didn't think to find out, but I could dig around." He cleared his throat. "Moving on ... Hubert Flagstone, age sixty-seven, has been working for your aunt for decades. His folks and grand-folks were from Brighton England. His family moved here when he was six. These people lived pretty much every-day lives. His sister Miriam passed in 2010, killed by a herd of yaks when she was trekking across Nepal."

"You're serious?"

"Would I lie about a yak stampede?"

"Would you?"

He chuckled. "Beatrice Hellmutter Dorfen-feld's mother was from Switzerland and the father from Austria. She moved here in the early sixties and hasn't done anything but maid work. She worked for a couple of impressive and rich people until she took up with your aunt. In fact, she came into nice money when a theater couple she first worked for was killed in a car crash off a canyon road. She'd been with them three years. She got – let's see – right, sixty thousand dollars."

"Not bad."

"Especially in the late 50s. That wasn't chump change."

"Why'd she not retire?"

"You'd have to –"

"Ask her," we finished together.

He chuckled again. "She also got fifty thousand in 1969, when a spinster she was working for died in a fall. The mansion was built high on a hill and one day the old lady tripped and rolled down a few hundred yards. Her head smashed into a boulder at the bottom."

Ouch. "Beatrice is quite lucky. I wish I could say the same for those she worked for," I said. "Do you think they died of natural causes?"

"Do you think this woman's capable of rigging a car or throwing an old lady to her death?"

"In the last little while, I've come to believe *anything* is possible. But if Beatrice *was* responsible, why keep working as a maid? She could have taken the money and bought a house, or gone back to school."

"When you're a maid, you don't have to pay rent, food is usually taken care of, and you get perks if you're with the right folks. Maybe she likes sitting on money. Maybe she's plain greedy. Or maybe she just likes working."

"… Anything else?"

"There's one more thing you may find interesting."

I chuckled when he paused. "Okay, what *else* would I find interesting about Beatrice Hellmutter Dorfen-whatever?"

"She had a cousin who moved to the U.S. a couple of years after she did. Cousin Erich worked as a butler, mechanic, and groundskeeper. In 1985, he was arrested for triple murders in San Antonio. Self-defense the guy claimed … fours years *after* the police found the bodies."

"You mean, a guilty conscience finally caught up with Cousin Erich?" I asked sarcastically.

"It was more like a fraidy-cat witness finally came forward. Abernathy Orville Manting was the late witness' name."

"Late as in deceased? Or late as in taking his time to see the police?" I asked dryly.

"Both. A runaway golf cart smashed into the guy four days after he visited the boys in blue. He flew into a river cruise taking a river tour. He was already kind of dented after being hit, never mind what he was like when he came to rest on the helm."

"Good luck continueth – not."

Johnny laughed. "It's only a temporary road-block."

Hopefully. "Could I impose upon you to do more detecting?"

"You got the moolah, I got the time."

I chuckled. "Will you find out about two people who probably have some sort of business affiliation with the Moones and the Sayers? The names are Gruber Pathos and Santana Anna Dinero, and that's all I know about them."

"I'm not called 'Sherlock' for nothing."

* * *

Mid afternoon saw three disenchanted faces in the drawing room: mine, Rey's, and Linda's. Aunt Mat had spent most of the morning chatting with Lewis. Gwynne, surlier than usual, probably because he wasn't pleased about being stuck at the Moone mansion, re-checked the house "to be certain all was okay" and ordered everyone to "stay clear of marked and cordoned-off areas, or find yourselves in blistering hot water".

Adwin had decided to bake quiches and breads for dinner. After assembling notes chronologically, I'd returned to the Internet and scanned some of Percival's on-line landscaping and gardening articles (can you spell y-a-w-n?). I'd also discovered that the Sayers' father was a pharmaceuticals exec, Mother #1 (Percival's) a professor of medieval English literature who'd later moved to England to open a pub, and Mother #2 (Prunella's) a runway model.

Wayne, the former bookie, called just before Prunella and Percival had a blow up. It had been a short but raucous affair that resulted in a broken Cinnabar Chinese vase and swearing that turned Adwin's pale face an interesting shade of rose. Wayne said Thomas' gambling problem had run into the hundreds of thousands of dollars. He'd annoyed a few prime turf accountants and the odd mobster, including someone named Triple J, who'd died mysteriously in the eighties. Triple J had to be none other than the infamous Jimmy Jojo James. Somehow our blubbery barrister had always managed to steer clear of brass knuckles and concrete boots, but only just – hold on though. Triple J had died when Porter was still co-owner of that nightclub. And Thomas had a link to the mobster. Could the two men have known each other back then?

Come to that, where had the cook been those years he'd not been on the radar? Culinary school? Slinging hash in diners? He'd left *Le Cochon Volant* in the mid nineties and not shown up at the Moone estate until 2003.

Stepping to a drawing room window, I gazed out onto a glassy wonderland. The only life forms that might enjoy the outdoors today were Gentoo penguins. "What do you know about Thomas Saturne's personal life?"

Wayne chuckled. "Ya mean his love life? His family and all that?"

"Uh-huh."

"He loved the fillies – the four-legged kind."

I laughed.

"He had the odd gal pal when I was still in the business. One was named Alice Sinatra – no relation to Old Blue Eyes. They lasted two years. That was at the end of the 90s. Guess she didn't like playing second fiddle to a horse, because she wanted him looking at her tail, not the mare's. Then he dated here and there, but didn't seem interested in getting serious for a long time." He paused. Vintage Randy Travis started to play in the background. "About a year ago, there was a younger odd one. She didn't seem his type."

Younger odd one? Prunella? Not likely, but I asked anyway. "You mean Prunella Sayers?"

"No, not that one."

"You're sure?"

"I knew about *her* – like who'd forget a name like that? This one was, hmm, mid-twenties maybe. It was hard to tell. She was dressed in clothes someone more in her fifties might wear: classy and not cheap, but 'old world'. I bumped into the two of them at a bar in the Fens. He seemed kind of anxious seeing me there, but he was polite enough. She had this strange smile on her face, like she had a secret and wasn't going to share."

"What did she look like?"

"Creamy skin. Cool eyes. Clean, fresh; you know? She was wearing a short skirt made of nice fabric and a tight top, not sleazy though. The clothes were classy and expensive, like I said. She had nice toned arms and athletic legs that were real easy on the eyes. It looked like she was into taking care of herself."

"Was she pretty? Cute? Stunning? Did she have a tiny nose or a Jimmy Durante schnoz? Was her hair red, blonde, or brown?"

"She had shoulder-length hair. It was dark brown – like the melted chocolate you dip marshmallows and fruit into. There was a little blond in it, too. The light in the bar made her hair and fancy pins sparkle and shimmer. I remember thinking the hairpins and clothes didn't much match the face or body – not just because of the age – but because she was kinda wholesome yet kinda sporty."

He'd painted a pretty generic picture. Maybe a re-check of photos with Thomas in them would reveal a woman bearing Wayne's description. "You didn't catch a name, did you?"

He chuckled again. "Does 'Dewdrop' count?"

I cringed. "Oof, you're joking?"

"I am." He chuckled again.

Whew. I wished him well, disconnected, and sauntered to the sofa.

"Anything interesting?" Rey asked, not looking like she cared one way or the other.

"Not yet." I lay my cell phone on an armchair. "But at least phones are still functional."

She sighed loudly. "Gawd, I want to go back to my Brentwood apartment – to a palm-treed courtyard with a decent pool, a bad script, and a fitness-loving smart-assed neighbor and his fat farty St. Bernard."

Adwin and May-Lee sauntered in and took seats beside Rey. "I wouldn't mind being at the restaurant, working on a tray of treacle tarts or cherry-cashew mousse."

Linda stretched her legs. "I wish I could be sitting on my lumpy couch, watching HBO, and eating an all-dressed veggie burger with crisp sweet potato fries and a big chunk of gooey carob cake."

"And I wouldn't mind lounging in a pine-scented bubble bath in my teeny condo, with a good mystery book and a view of Mr. Black's deck … and two-hundred-and-fifty-pound Mr. Black doing his early morning tai-chi ritual in 80s Spandex wear," I said.

Rey gave a thumb's up. "Maybe we should get him together with Trevor, the fitness-loving smart-assed neighbor. Sounds like a match made in heaven."

"I'd like to be back at the shop," May-Lee offered with a smile, "talking about the joys of owning a Shaker Ladder-Back chair or a Hepplewhite cabinet."

Prunella entered. She looked like a supermarket customer who'd had a run-in with the produce manager over wrinkled peppers. "Perc should be down soon. He was trying to nap. The poor dear didn't get much sleep last night."

The "poor dear" probably got more than most of us. He'd surely not been researching on the Internet or investigating corridors, alcoves and recesses during the early hours. Speaking of, "poor dear" entered as Beatrice wheeled in an antique oak dining trolley with cookies, dates and clementines, a fat jug of water, and two carafes, one of tea and one of coffee. Maybe the siblings' fight had taken its toll: he seemed jittery, tense, and unhappy. With a quick nod, he grabbed three mocha wafer cookies and slipped into a chair near Adwin, and we settled into silent snacking.

After several quick if not anxious jaunts here, there and everywhere by the various folks who'd congregated in the drawing room, Aunt Mat still hadn't shown her face.

"What do you suppose that woman is up to?" Prunella asked upon returning from upstairs, a plaid silk scarf in one hand.

Percival's smile was feeble and swift. "That woman is probably planning another trick. Or maybe she's detesting our presence and wants to stay away."

"What's to detest? We're all lovable, endearing people," she responded flippantly.

Adwin suggested she could be talking with the police.

Rey shook her head. "Lewis is in that rear guestroom making calls and issuing orders, and going through a third pot of coffee. He said he would head out later, if the weather shows any mercy. Gwynne is in a second-floor bedroom, working on cop stuff and wiping his brow a lot. He's looking ratty and washed-out."

"Maybe your aunt's embarrassed as to what her get-together has resulted in and is staying the distance," Linda suggested.

Rey took several gulps of water and wiped a hand across her lips like a football player who'd chugged a bottle of H2O after a scrimmage. "Maybe we'd better find out if she's okay."

Linda straightened. "Where do we find her?"

"Her room would be a good place to start," Prunella responded tersely, draping the scarf around her shoulders.

We looked at one another and filed upstairs.

Then filed down again when we discovered she wasn't there. Before anyone could suggest an alternative part of the huge house to check, Beatrice's anguished shout – a cross between a bull elephant cry and a foghorn alert – summoned the gang to Reginald Moone's library-study.

A Bop on the Head is Worth Two …

A glossy bright stream of carmine red, reminiscent of the strawberry jam I'd had the other morning, trickled down Aunt Mat's right temple. She was seated on the floor, looking pained and perplexed. A crumpled, nondescript white handkerchief lay alongside.

"Keeee-rist," Percival whispered, his face growing paler than Adwin's.

Linda, Rey and I raced to her side.

"Prunella, call an ambulance and get Lewis." I dropped to my knees and peered at the wound.

Percival ran an anxious hand through his hair. "Is she –"

"Of course I'm not, you ding-dong! You have eyes, don't you? I'm far from dead. Nor am I comatose or even badly injured. I do, however, have a headache that could fell an elk." Aunt Mat scowled. "Don't call anyone, Prunella, I'll be fine." She placed a hand on my shoulder and with Rey's assistance, pushed herself into a standing position.

As if fearing loud sounds or extreme movements might distress or harm the woman, Adwin and Prunella tiptoed over.

Linda peered at the half-inch wound. "You may need a couple stitches."

She winced. "Do you think so?"

I picked up the handkerchief and dabbed at the blood. "What happened?"

"I got clunked on the head as I was reading up on – uh." She went to point and frowned. "It's gone. I was looking at a book and it's not there anymore."

"What's going on?"

We turned to the sheriff, but no one responded.

He muttered something about praising saints and hurried over. "Are you all right, Mathildah?"

She waved off his concern, but patted his ruddy, chapped hand as it gently grasped her shoulder.

Linda moved to the pedestal desk and scanned the top and underneath. "There aren't any books here."

Rey walked past the desk and scrutinized the floor. "And there's nothing hard and heavy for head-whacking."

If looks could kill, Rey'd have been dead three times over.

"I'm not imagining things, and I'm far from senseless," our aunt huffed. She turned to Percival. "Would you get brandy, bandages, and gauze?"

"Of course, Matty." He bowed his head like a loyal butler and hastened from the room.

I motioned Reginald's armchair. "Maybe you should sit."

"Come on." Lewis led her across the room and we waited until she was settled.

"You were saying you were looking at a book. What happened next?" Linda urged.

"And which book was it?" Rey. "Are you sure it's gone?"

Aunt Mat gave another withering look. "I was starting to read up on old-world poisons when I heard a soft footstep. Before I could turn, something heavy caught me upside the head and down I went. When I opened my eyes, there was a handkerchief on my face."

I sniffed it and noticed a slight, sweetish scent. "It's been soaked with something ... maybe a highly concentrated form of chloroform ... or some sort of inhalant."

Rey grabbed it and smelled it. "It certainly has an icky smell about it – like something that would keep you down and out."

Lewis glowered and held out his hand.

She shrugged and slapped it onto his palm, then studied a row of books on the shelf. "I seem to remember one really old book being here. It was thick and had a black cover, and was all about apothecaries and treatments and poisons."

"That's the one I was looking at," Aunt Mat stated. "*An Apothecary's Handbook ... The Manual of ...* oh dear, I can't seem to recall. Anyway, it's not exactly a lightweight book you could tuck under an arm and run with."

"But one you could slip into a hidden corridor with." I studied the room. Surely this somber space held a secret or two. "You didn't see anything? You didn't get a glimpse of a foot as it stepped towards you? Or maybe a sleeve as an arm or hand struck out? Did you see *anything* that could identify your assailant?"

Aunt Mat shook her head and winced.

"I'm going to call this in, Mathildah –"

"Leave it, Augustus. For now, please?"

He scanned my aunt's set yet pleading expression and nodded. "We'll leave it for now, but we'll talk again latah. I'll bag this handkerchief for what it's worth, which is probably nothing. Then I'm going to find out about Mrs. Wheelah, who's gone into labah."

He left as Percival hastened in with a fancy silver tray that supported two white linen napkins, a box of assorted bandages, a package of dressing and cloth tape, a bottle of Hennessy, and a lovely large crystal snifter that would make five goldfish happy to call home. I grabbed a napkin, poured Hennessy on it, and dabbed it against a wound that promised to turn into an ugly scab surrounded by interesting shades of blue and green over the coming days. Adwin poured two ounces into the snifter and passed it to my aunt.

"Thankfully the killer didn't do a very good job," Rey said lightly, perching herself on the edge of the desk. "You'll be sporting a badge of courage like Linda and Prunella,"

"Our killer wasn't attempting to kill her," I said. "This was merely a warning. If he – or she – wanted Aunt Mat dead, she'd be dead."

"A warning?" Adwin asked, bemused. "Like get out of town? You're next? Give me all your money or else?"

"Maybe someone didn't appreciate Matty's joke," Percival offered.

"Some 'joke'," Prunella murmured, picking at her sweater. "Matty, you are so in doggy doo with me right now."

Linda struggled to contain laughter while Adwin and I attempted to remain straight-faced. Rey gazed at the Bird Lady as if she had brains the same size as her feathered friends.

"I'm not overly pleased, either," Percival admitted quietly.

"You always enjoyed a good prank," my aunt responded, pushing aside my hand as I started to swab the wound again.

"Pretending you're dead and having the lot of us spend too many hours together goes beyond 'good prank'."

Aunt Mat laughed and stepped alongside Percival, giving him a solid slap to the back.

"So," Linda asked, opening the door, "which one of us beaned Mathilda Moone?"

"Every last one of us all slipped out of the drawing room at one time or another during the last hour or so," I advised.

"At least once," Adwin emphasized. "Particularly in the last twenty or thirty minutes, with everyone having claimed a task that needed doing."

We turned to my aunt, who extended her hands in answer to the unspoken question. "I could have been out five minutes, fifteen, or forty. I'm not wearing a watch and I hadn't been looking at the time. When I was actually hit is anyone's guess."

"Then timing-wise, it could have been any one of us," I avowed.

"Or someone still unknown." Rey.

* * *

Before joining Rey and Prunella in the kitchen for a pot of organic green tea, a favorite of the

Audubon lover, I peeked into Reginald's library-study. Thirty minutes ago we'd finished a hurried search of the immediate grounds. We'd not actually expected to have found something in terrain that had seen lots of ice and several feet, but we'd been hopeful. Besides, a bit of fresh (bracing) air didn't hurt, so we'd jokingly told ourselves. When we'd come across a men's thick black shawl one-hundred feet from the kitchen (Rey had gotten curious about the ice-layered composting units), we'd actually danced a jig – which had resulted in Rey's slim bum slamming the ground. Thankfully the howling and swearing had trailed into the windy, wintry afternoon.

No one claimed ownership of the shawl and Aunt Mat couldn't recollect one like it belonging to Reginald, so Lewis tucked it into a bag as we excitedly discussed the possibility that it belonged to the killer. The sheriff merely listened with an expression of strained patience.

"He probably lost it when he was hurrying off," Prunella suggested.

"To where though?" Rey asked, perplexed. "A waiting car – covered with ice?"

"Maybe someone was keeping it running until he arrived," Aunt Mat offered, fingering the bandage on her right temple.

"On a nearby road – covered with ice?" Rey asked skeptically.

"The shawl may have been placed there to have us assume the killer left," Linda pointed out.

With a furrowed brow, Percival looked from her to his sister to my cousin. "Speaking of 'left', as in departing, here *I* go." Off he sauntered.

One by one we followed, leaving the "Mystery of the Manly Shawl" for another time.

Lewis was chatting with Aunt Mat as they sipped coffee from oversize mugs the color of bat's blood (okay, I didn't know the actual color, but it sounded good and spooky considering the circumstances and weather). May-Lee had retreated to her room to start on yet another book: *Turn of the Screw.* The others were missing in action. Something rumbled in the distance. A plow? Train? Thunder? What wacky weather. But then, what a wacky get-together.

My aunt was leaning into a bookshelf, staring into her mug as if it might offer explanations to everything that had recently transpired. Lewis was sitting behind the desk, dunking a short-bread cookie into the mug, his expression an odd twist between sad and amused, as if he wasn't sure whether he should weep profusely or laugh hysterically at the absurdity of it all. He'd showered, shaved, and changed into a casual navy-blue wool suit belonging to Reginald Moone. The clothes were a nearly perfect fit in length, but a little snug in width; Lewis had a good twenty pounds on my uncle. Still sporting his sheriff's hat, a fashion plate he was not. Three corpses, hovering and/or nattering media folk, a group of weird guests collected for a weird week in a fairly weird house, a bump to a head: what could possibly happen next his vigilant sea-green eyes appeared to be asking. I could mention that Fred the Ghost might breeze past in fine baritone form, but that might push the frustrated man over the edge.

Another officer was expected to arrive later, whenever he or she could commandeer the right vehicle to navigate the harsh elements. I wasn't sure which was more dangerous: driving on an ice-sheathed road with limited visibility or remaining in an old ghost-inhabited mansion with an unknown killer.

"Your tea's cold," Prunella groused, motioning an elegant floral cup as I ambled to a daintily decorated table. A Spode tea set, a silver and gold platter with delicate sandwiches, a beige linen tablecloth with an aster motif and sunflower-yellow linen napkins, seemed out of place in the kitchen, but you had to give Prunella Sayers points for trying to add color and hominess to a dank, gray and tense afternoon.

I sank into a chair, feeling refreshed from a fragrant shower and change of clothes, but not overly anxious to be in the company of any one person at this particular moment. Folding hands across my fleecy jacket, I looked from one face to the next. "Emotions appear to be running ragged around here."

Rey, who'd remained in a long wool turtleneck but swapped jeans for thick wool leggings, continued gnawing on a midnight-black Twizzler. One arched, heavily penciled eyebrow seemed to say, "Can't imagine why."

"Do you think anyone else is in line to die or be walloped?" Prunella asked, topping off her tea. "Or have we truly seen the last of the killer?"

I took a sip of mine. Ugh. It was cold and way too green on the green tea side. "Is there any reason someone else *should* die or be walloped?"

"That's hard to say. It depends on what dark secrets we hold and what nefarious schemes we have planned."

I pictured her as a bad-ass businesswoman, saw her sharing an intimate dinner with Thomas, and then envisioned her going after someone with a potentially lethal fish. "What secrets or schemes might we hold?"

"They would hardly be secret then, would they?" Her smirk bordered on haughty. "Let's get back to the dead gentlemen. Thomas may well have been murdered because of his gambling problems. It wasn't mere pennies he owed. Another possibility is he planned to kill us all and collect the grand booby prize to pay off his anxious collectors and/or play the ponies in hopes of winning big-time ... but someone caught wind of his intention and bye-bye Tommy Boy."

Rey and I glanced at each other. Considering Prunella's break up with "Tommy Boy" and her penchant for unusual weapons, she'd be our first choice for lawyer whacker. I smiled benignly and looked as innocent as Dora the Explorer. "So you know about the gambling?"

"Rumors and gossip have been flowing around here like lava from Hawaii's Kilauea volcano."

I looked at Rey. The eyebrow arched again. And the Twizzler got smaller.

Prunella continued. "Jensen was about to divorce his less than lovely wife. He'd screwed up a couple of business deals, perhaps because he was thinking too much of his lover of the past five years – who, I understand, was going to make their relationship public if Jensen didn't admit to it."

Rey and I tensed. How could we have missed that?

"He had a mistress, did he?"

Prunella nodded as she nibbled what had to be a watercress sandwich, gauging from the little green leaves fluttering to her lap. "In this case it's a *mister.*"

It was my turn to arch an eyebrow. "He's … ?"

"Very," Prunella grinned. "At least for the time being. He's been said to step from one side to the other, depending on who has captured his fancy."

"That hardly seems like a motive for murder," I said.

"It would be if the wife was royally annoyed. Winda Moone always had it good. She never had to work. She shopped, enjoyed cocktail parties, and fine-dined regularly. If he had planned on coming out, that would have been the official demise of a sham marriage. She'd have been p.o.'d with the major, unplanned lifestyle change. On the flipside, it would also be a motive if Chaters Roland the Fourth – lover and fellow barrister – had determined that everything should be, and *would* be, in the open."

I gazed at her blankly, then shook my head. "It doesn't fit. Jensen's death was somehow connected to Thomas'. I can't see pissed off wifey or mister-mistress traveling all the way from England to off a spouse or partner."

"It's perfect, though, in both cases," Prunella said gleefully. "Who would ever guess that Winda or Chaters had traveled all those miles to 'off' a partner?"

"You're right that no one would think of either one as the murderer, but no matter how furtive she or he was, there would be a trail. If someone investigated diligently enough, they'd find it. But I'm not even remotely inclined to believe it's either one of them." I drew a long, slow breath. "Thomas' overdosing on quinapril could have been an accident, or been accepted as one, but the use of Poison Hemlock and a blowgun were deliberate." I leaned forward, my expression somber. "Jensen *must* have discovered something and, as a result, was silenced. The same with Porter. One schemed killing was followed by two cover-ups. It's a crazy chain of events."

"With one crazy killer now potentially off the premises." Prunella eyed me closely. "Why do *you* think your aunt was hit?"

I scanned her strained expression for several seconds. "As your brother Percival suggested earlier, someone may have been making a statement about her joke not being appreciated. Or they desperately wanted that book.... But why would they want it that badly? It's all way too vague." I accepted a cucumber sandwich from the plate she held out. "Which one in the group do you think did it?"

Her dimpled chin rose. "It certainly wasn't me. Nor was it Perc. I know my brother very well."

"Isn't he your half-brother? Or is it step-brother?" I asked with Dora's innocence.

She smiled frostily. "My my. The gossip doesn't just flow like a tranquil lava flow from Kilauea, it spews like clouds of stones and ashes from Mount Vesuvius." Her cool gaze moved from me to Rey and back again. "How about one or both of you?"

I laughed and looked at Rey. "What do you think, cousin? Should we confess?"

Rey smiled. How uncharacteristically quiet she'd been. I liked it.

I hopped to my feet. "I'm going upstairs to keep my laptop company."

Rey sipped tea, popped the last of the licorice in her mouth, and rose. "Let's pool our thoughts and observations after dinner. I could use a bit of a lie-down."

"That's not a bad idea," Prunella said. She called for Beatrice, who was in the kitchen in less than five seconds. Did the maid lurk in the shadows, waiting to be summoned? After instructing her we were finished, Prunella led the three of us up the stairs.

"Dang!"

"Keeee-rist!"

"Hey guys! We found something!"

Linda and Percival's excited voices prompted us to hasten to Jensen's room. What now? Another body?

* * *

I lurched into Rey, who stumbled into Prunella as the three of us attempted to enter Jensen's room at once. A honey-combed crystal vase toppled and its "combs" textured the floor.

"We're here, not there," Percival yelled from the next room.

Off we lurched and lumbered to the hobby-art room. Linda was by the brass-bound trunk, holding a decorative shoe box and looking smug.

Adwin shambled into the room, nearly bumping into Percival. His hair was messy and his face had bed-sheet lines. He also looked peevish, like a tot who'd been awakened from an afternoon snooze much too soon. "You're as graceful as a herd of caribou – no, make that a convoy of cement trucks rolling over a boardwalk. What's going on?"

"Murder most foul," Percival announced dramatically, pointing at the box as if it were something distasteful, like fresh roadkill or regurgitated lunch.

Rey and I peered inside. A .40-caliber blowgun and a small amber bottle with a stopper, half-filled with liquid, lay on a folded satin scarf. The bottle looked old, like a museum piece.

"Where'd you find this?" I asked.

Linda nodded to a partially draped Victorian mahogany library bookcase. "We were passing by Jensen's room and thought we'd give it a quick once-over. We found nothing so we thought it might be worth investigating some adjoining rooms. If someone's going to hide something, they may not want it in immediate grasp or sight, just in case, but maybe they'd place it within arm's reach, so to speak. We were right."

Rey frowned and stepped around the wooden divider, surveying the area. "How come the cops never found it?" What she really meant: how come *I* wasn't the one to discover it?

"They may not have known what they were looking for. It's nothing but a shoe box in a cabinet." Prunella patted Percival's back. "If they'd looked inside, they may have thought it was medicine – something a diabetic would need."

"In a shoe box?" I asked flatly. "In a room that hasn't been used in a dog's age?"

"It's a freaking blowgun," Adwin all but hissed. "People don't *blow* insulin into their necks."

We turned to Adwin and he gazed balefully back. Someone was in need of additional nappy time.

"They overlooked it," Linda said simply. "Which is easy enough to do."

Prunella murmured in agreement. "We'd better show Sheriff Lewis. He's around here somewhere."

"He's in that guestroom Matty assigned him," Percival said with a sour smile. "He should have the entire force here, not that it would do much good."

"One second." I held up a hand. "If this belonged to Jensen – and we're assuming it did simply because of its location – we have to surmise he killed Thomas."

"Makes sense."

"Sounds logical."

"Yup."

"And then someone killed him," I pointed out.

"His partner," May-Lee declared. "There has to be a partner – possibly the person who lost the shawl."

"Or purposely placed it there and who also killed Porter, for potentially seeing him – or her – with the body and/or evidence," I continued.

"Makes sense."

"Sounds logical."

Something wasn't logical though, and I couldn't put my finger on it.

"There's no need for one or both to kill anyone else, because none of us have seen anything," Adwin grumbled, leaning into a wall. "More importantly: one or both appear to have departed the premises."

Percival exhaled loudly. "Personally, I'm past caring. Let's get this box to the sheriff and let him and his colleagues figure it out. Hopefully they'll find fingerprints on the bottle and blowgun, and all will become readily apparent. To-morrow, if not sooner, I want to be back home, reading Hemingway or Chaucer by the fireplace, and forgetting the last few days happened."

"I'm with you about being home." Linda walked to the door. "I'm going to see Lewis." She left, box in hand, Percival hot on her heels.

The four of us eyed one another.

I had to say it. "It's too pat –"

"Too perfect," Rey agreed.

"Because you *want* it to be, "Adwin suggested with a sneer. "Leave it to those who do it best and know how to deal with danger."

Prunella nodded. "Rey, dear, you'll have many chances to play a detective in your movie career, I'm sure. And you, Jill, you'll make a fine reporter or journalist one day, of that I'm also sure. As Adwin said, leave it – leave it to the people who are trained to find answers."

"You tell 'em Pruney," Adwin said and the two high-fived each other.

Rey and I exchanged glances and followed the two. As my beau and his comrade strolled down the hallway, chatting about dinner, my cousin and I turned to each other.

"Leave it?" she hissed under her breath.

"In a pig's eye," we avowed quietly in unison.

22

Little Brown Jugs

Figuring the library-study wasn't likely to be occupied at 9:30 at night, Rey and I agreed to meet there. My cousin sat where Lewis had been hours before, her torso pressed into a handsome antique desk as she leaned over and scanned papers. The lawman was upstairs with Jeana, who, between coughing and sneezing fits, looked as stressed and tense as an inexperienced cross-country skier about to be thrust down a flying hill. The promise of a full-scale cold was etched on her ruby-red nose and in her glassy eyes. Gwynne was out for the count; the victim of a wicked bug, his pale face had become more ashen as he grew increasingly sweaty and sick.

I sat opposite my cousin, legs crossed, a tall glass of cranberry juice and soda in hand. We were wearing similar two-piece fleece outfits;

hers was poppy red, mine mustard yellow (we'd have been seen coming from two hundred yards).

Except for sleet persistently thumping the roof and windows, the early dinner had been a fairly silent affair. Every few minutes, gales at an aggressive seventy MPH would accelerate past like an Olympic luge team, making for deadly forces that could topple trees as if they were matchsticks and thrust aside power lines like bits of string. Crossing several states, the storm was quickly evolving from nuisance status to disruptive. It would be full-scale within a matter of hours somber-faced announcers stated before reminding viewers about the dangers of being on the roads and shoveling heavy wet snow.

Adwin's early-day baked goods had complemented a simple dinner. Herb-infused bread accompanied beef-barley soup that had been frozen for emergencies while challah buns accompanied two types of quiches: a pleasantly spiced spinach-salmon fusion and a chunky bacon-ham blend. Hubert had put together an antipasto platter and Beatrice had made up two huge jugs of iced mint tea, an odd beverage for a cold night and late fall dinner. In the drawing room afterwards Adwin, Prunella and Percival, and Linda had hunkered down over Monopoly while Aunt Mat sat in a corner with an old Jude Devereaux novel and a glass of dry sherry. May-Lee had claimed the opposite corner and opted for a mug of Earl Gray and needlepoint, with the Stars and Stripes gracing one-third of her canvas.

"You think Lewis'll let us go home tomorrow?" Rey asked.

"You mean: will *Mother Nature* let us?" My smile was as flat as my tone. "In terms of Lewis, I don't believe he can technically detain us, but law isn't my forte."

"Except for what you catch on *NCIS* and *Bones* reruns, right?" Rey grinned.

"That's forensics: a different kettle of fish."

She made a "whatever" gesture and held up pages of handwritten notes in fuchsia ink.

"Has Linda been researching again?" I asked.

"I have. She wanted down time and I wanted to learn the truth, so I decided to go it alone."

"I'm impressed."

She leaned across the desk, a patient confiding in a doctor. "The history of this place had me curious, what with all these weird cubbyholes. I tried to find out more about its history."

"It's quite a tragedy about the Smiths."

"Yeah. Sad." She feigned a shiver. "And scary."

"Some people seem to absorb bad luck. Continually."

"Like a sponge." She pushed forth a page. "I followed the family up to present day and then switched gears. Fascinating stuff." She motioned a page. "See this woman, Theresa Smith? That's Linda's mother."

I glanced down the long list of Smiths and noted the various modes of death and mischance Rey had jotted alongside each name. The stuff sagas were made of. I noted Theresa had three children and that she died fairly young, after having been mowed down by a squash truck during squally weather. "So you know about her relation to the Smiths?"

She scanned my face. "Apparently so do you."

"I only found out earlier today."

"Thanks for sharing," she sniffed.

I shrugged. "The opportunity didn't present itself."

She sniffed again. "Anyway, she was married for a short spell in her late teens to an aspiring blues musician. Chiffre Royale. Great name, doncha think? He was attractive and talented, and heavy into heroine." Her expression grew somber. "They found him in a Chicago motel with a needle in his arm." She sighed softly and shuffled papers. "Moving on. Besides our Uncle Reginald, six Moones have died in the last five years: two in fires, two in one car accident, one in a spelunking adventure, and one swimming off Myrtle Beach."

"Maybe the Smiths' bad luck rubbed off on the Moones when they bought the house."

"Maybe the bad luck was arranged?"

I scrutinized her grim expression. "Are you suggesting the deaths weren't accidents?"

"What if they weren't?" she asked with a cynical smile.

I ran down the list of names: Jackson Moone, David Leigh Moone, Harrison Moone, Franklin Moone, Helena Moone and Florence Moone-Bertolli. "The only Moone I'm familiar with on this list is Helena. I recall meeting her at a family gathering at Cousin Fitz's Mashpee home ten summers ago. She was a tall, reedy thing, very somber, and extremely snobby. She didn't mix with us much. Remember?"

"Yeah. She hovered around Cousin Petey, Uncle Carlton's youngest son. She really had a thing for him."

I chuckled. "Tall and reedy, somber and snobby meets short and flabby, silly and frisky."

"He was funny."

"Wasn't Carlton expected *not* to show? I mean, he and Reginald never spoke after Carlton ran off to join the army, so it was a huge surprise for most to see him and the kids attend. I remember Mom's face paling three shades when they strolled across the patio with wine and beer in tow in that little chuckwagon."

"Uncle Reginald wasn't fifty miles within range and Uncle Carlton knew that, courtesy of Aunt Mat. That's why he came."

"Reginald was never much in range: the man was fairly anti-social when it came to us."

"Betcha didn't know that Petey became a sought-after stand-up comedian?"

I shook my head. "There are a lot of family members I haven't kept in touch with."

"He's got a big movie deal in the works." She smiled drolly. "Now he's short and flabby, silly and frisky, *and* rich."

"And a gold-digger's dream."

We laughed and I strolled to a Palladian-style window and peered past heavy beaded curtains. Bone-numbing cold permeated thick glass and I instinctively zipped up the jacket to my chin. "It's nasty out. And it's promising to get even nastier, which is hard to imagine."

"At least we're as snug as two jailed bugs."

I perched myself on the windowsill. "Do you like living in California, hobnobbing with celebrities and doing the party circuit?"

She gazed past my shoulder. "I love being an actress."

"You always were a ham."

She grinned. "*That* was my first memorable commercial: Reynalda the hula-ing ham. I went from fruit to meat, to vegetables, and back again. My first few acting jobs included the tap-shoe-dancing turnip, tangoing tangerine, and then waltzing watermelon."

"Widget."

"Widget?" She looked thoughtful.

"It's a small gadget or doodad. You were a waltzing widget," I confirmed and laughed. "And you thought those dance classes wouldn't pay off."

"Right. I remember I had to wear a fifty-pound padded outfit... . And I met Cecil after the shoot."

"The editing guy you left at the altar?"

"He got over me," she smiled. "I wasn't getting very challenging roles back then, but the bills got paid. As for California, L.A. smog aside, the beaches are great, the food is wholesome and awesome, and shopping's fab. There's always something to do and someone to see."

"Then you're happy?"

Rey's expression turned unusually serious. "One person's happiness is another's misery. It's all relative, isn't it?"

I studied her face and she turned away. "What else do you have besides a bunch of dead Moones?"

"Not much." She shook her head and spoke to the desk lamp. "But I think dear Pruney killed Thomas."

"Where's your evidence?"

"Here's my three-part evidence: motive, timing, ability."

"In your case that equals women's intuition, and that's not enough. What we need is *incontrovertible* evidence – like a shawl with DNA and/or sewn-on name tag."

"Yeah. In our dreams." Rey's Clara Bow lips pulled into a harsh line as she scanned a couple of pages and pushed one forward. "What about this?"

I perused it. "So Percival wrote articles on herbs and apothecary treatments, and natural ways to keep a garden prime? He's a history and landscaping-gardening buff. Prunella would have read them, or any of his books and research papers. She'd have learned a few things, like what's written here." I pointed. "How Poison Hemlock leaves or fruits are inferior to the preserved juice of the herb. How the fruits yield more coniine than the leaves. How Poison Hemlock juice, if overdosed, produces paralysis." I pointed to another paragraph. "Symptoms of poisoning include nausea, weakness, paralysis, and death."

"We've always known Poison Hemlock to be dangerous, courtesy of mystery movies." Making fists, she placed one on top of the other on the desk, and rested her chin on them. She looked exhausted, maybe a little dejected.

I moved to the next page. "Curare is the common name for various arrow poisons originating from South America. There are three types: tube, calabash, pot. The main toxin of curare is dubocurarine, Attempts to use curare during anesthesia date back to 1912 –"

"I read it. I don't need to hear it again."

"Fine, but hear this: there's *nothing* that puts the blowgun or Poison Hemlock in Prunella Sayers' hands … here or anywhere else." I smacked her head playfully with the papers and placed them on the desk.

She sat upright. "Speaking of Prunella Sayers' hands, I never told you – that woman has a vise-like grip. She could break bones without trying!" She recounted the moment when she started to open the door to Jensen's room and Prunella clasped her hand.

"That still doesn't prove anything, other than she lifts weights or uses grasp springs."

"Do you always have to play devil's advocate?" She put on a pouty face and slumped back in Reginald's nineteenth-century library chair.

"I'm playing Sheriff Lewis and demonstrating what he'd say, given there's no proof to back up your allegations." Bruno Mars announced I had a call. Thankfully no cell phone towers had gone down and there were back-up power systems, so there were no major inconveniences at the Moone manse. Too bad the same didn't hold true for all the homes in nearby counties reported to be draped in frosty darkness and roads shrouded with slick ice. "Yes?"

"Hey. It's me."

"Hi 'me'." I looked at Rey and shrugged. The voice was familiar, but I couldn't place it.

"I remembered something about that young wannabe classy gal Saturne was with."

It was the former bookie. "How are you? What do you remember?"

"I'm fine. Thanks. I remember she was drinking lager. Saturne ordered her another round while we was chatting. That seemed an odd mix: lager and class. You know what I mean?" He didn't wait for me to respond. "While I was thinking on it, I do remember her voice. It was kinda sweet-sounding and young – immature young, not physically young. And she used the word 'dang' twice. That's another reason I thought her weird – dressed fancy like that, but using a hick word and drinking beer."

"What a great memory. I appreciate you calling to let me know. I owe you." And I did. "I'll catch up with you next week." I hung up and told Rey what Wayne Antici had relayed.

Rey and I eyed each other for several seconds. We opened our mouths simultaneously, but it was gale-force winds hurling ice matter against the mansion that resounded throughout the room. Then the lights went out.

* * *

Holding hands, Rey and I fingered walls to find our way to the drawing room. A fire blazed and Prunella was in the midst of lighting six tall candles standing in silver holders in a perfect row on the sideboard. Everyone, save for Percival, was there, including Fred the Cat and an old gnarly police officer Lewis had requested be sent over to take over for ailing Gerald Gwynne. Wet, cold and miserable, he'd arrived two hours late via a Chevy Tahoe currently parked one-hundred yards from the driveway entrance – in an icy snow drift.

Gnarly hoisted a thick leather belt over a pumpkin-sized paunch. Save for the perfect globular shape of the man's chrome dome, he resembled Jackie Gleason in *Smokey and the Bandit*. "Lights going out happens a lot in these old big houses." Tell us something we didn't know or hadn't heard in a dozen films.

"Where's Perc?" Rey asked casually, glancing around.

"He's getting flashlights and boxes of candles, hopefully useable, from the rear storage room," Aunt Mat said, moving before the fireplace. "With this storm, electricity will likely be out until morning. And if it ices up for as long and heavily as they're saying, it may be out for two or three days, or more."

Linda stood by a window, peering into a crystal-white night as winds howled like ravenous wolves. Rey and I glanced at each other, shrugged, and moved closer to the fire.

What was in a "dang" anyway? A lot of people used the word, right? And *if* Linda had been Thomas' drinking date, who was to say there had been anything ominous or lewd about it? But why had she never mentioned it, *if* she was the one Wayne had described?

"Have you two solved the murders?" Adwin grinned.

Rey stopped and turned. "We've come up with viable solutions."

Prunella smirked. "Dear Rey, 'viable solutions' are far from concrete facts or tangible evidence. They won't put anyone behind bars."

"Folks, I'm gonna look around and make sure everything's locked up, then check on the sheriff." Gnarly hoisted the belt again and sauntered to the door like a sated armadillo.

"I'm heading up," Adwin announced. "It's been a long day."

"I'd better see what's keeping Perc." Prunella followed Adwin, who had a candle holder in one hand and a very tranquil-looking cat tucked under the other arm.

Rey sighed and started toward Linda, and stopped. The screenwriting assistant was no longer in the room. "Where'd Linda go?" Her hands flew to her hips. "Shouldn't we stay in sight of each other?"

"That would be my advice, but who am I?" Aunt Mat responded with a tart smile.

"Who are any of us?" May-Lee asked philosophically, her smile melancholy. "I'll see you all in the morning."

Rey's arms flew up. "I give up!"

"Should we bother with Linda?" I asked, not sure I really cared one way or another at that moment. "She's probably gone to bed. She looked beat."

"Or guilty maybe?"

"Wishful thinking?"

She shrugged. "What if she did it, Jilly? What if she's a secret psychopath? What if she wants to kill some more? I'm sharing a room with her."

"Come on. Would she kill her best friend?"

Our aunt chuckled. "Methinks that imagination of yours, Reynalda, runneth rampant."

I chuckled as well.

"You can always move into one of the rooms near our friends in blue, if you want." Aunt Mat grabbed a candleholder as Rey appeared to mull it over. "I'm going to see what's keeping the Say-ers."

"Hey – what did I say about staying in sight of each other?"

She regarded her niece patiently.

Rey's curse, although silent, was audible in the expression. "Fine. We may as well all go."

I grabbed two candleholders. "I could do with a tall glass of icy-cold chocolate milk. How about you, Cousin? It seems as if you could use some-thing to mellow those tense nerves."

Her gaze narrowed and her lips tightened.

I elbowed an arm. "Let's keep things in per-spective. Crazy conclusions without justification are just that: crazy. Remember what happened in the Catskills during summer vacation in middle school?"

My cousin's frown changed into a grin. "Af-ter that, Dinde the lifeguard, and the local police wouldn't let us within thirty miles of the place. And the deputy's family never did move back. I *still* get letters."

Aunt Mat regarded us as if we'd lost it when we started tittering.

"How were we to know it was summer stock theater?" I gave her arm a playful slap. "Anyway, we made some crazy conclusions – which resulted in some majorly foolish conduct and serious repercussions – and we couldn't have been more wrong. Let's embrace logic, as well as common sense."

The three of us walked down the corridor that, except for the sounds of a seething storm, was strangely quiet. We stepped up to a small storage room door by the laundry room and found everyone there, save for Adwin and the officers. Prunella and Linda stood silent and shocked – over Percival Sayers' inert body.

* * *

The cry we all expected to burst from Prunella's lips didn't; she was too busy gaping. She stood near his head, her face drawn, while Linda was situated by his feet, her expression grim. Amber candlelight lent an eerie feel to the surreal scene.

"He's dead?" Rey.

"As the proverbial doornail," Linda replied.

"How can you tell?"

"He has a Furi Rachel Ray seven-inch offset bread knife in his heart."

"Uh. Right."

"One of us better get Gnarly," I suggested softly.

"Who?" Aunt Mat appeared bemused.

"That old geezer Lewis had sent over."

"That would be Ulysses Abbott," she said, her gaze remaining on Percival, as if anticipating that any second he might yank the blade from his chest and shout, "Ha ha, gotcha!"

"Maybe we all better go," Linda advised. "This is way too *Ten Little Indians.*"

"Little Brown Jug" resounded down the hallway.

"Fred's here," I announced.

Rey shot an elbow into my ribs. "Will you stop with Fred the Ghost? He's a figment of your imagination."

"In a pig's eye!"

"No one else has seen him –"

"He's real Reynalda! Can't you hear him?" I motioned the hallway.

"Ladies!" our aunt called, playing referee. "That's Ulysses. He loves nineteenth-century folk songs. Ulysses? We're in the back, by the laundry room."

Heavy footfalls came our way. A flashlight beam preceded his entry.

"Yes Mrs. Moone? I just – oh." He looked at Percival and frowned. "Is he … ?"

"As the proverbial doornail."

He exhaled loudly and pulled a cell phone from the breast pocket of his wrinkled shirt. "Sheriff Lewis is not going to like this one iota. I'm up shit's creek – in a cracked canoe."

23

Ring around the Rosie

During the night, sleet had morphed into snow grains and then transformed into heavy, wet snow. Winds continued to wail, but now they sounded more like tormented banshees. The group, what was left of it, was seated in various corners of the drawing room. It was just after eight o'clock in the morning.

Adwin was absently patting Fred, who was curled on his lap and snoring up a storm comparable to the one outside. Aunt Mat was idly leafing through a decorating magazine, looking weary. Linda was staring at Prunella, who was regarding the portrait of my aunt and uncle over the fireplace, yet both women appeared to be on other realms. My cousin was re-reading notes and entering citations here and there. Our spindly stern-faced maid was refilling coffee cups as Hubert stood by the door like a listing ship, waiting to see if anyone required his services. It was like being caught in a bad reality show rerun or playing Bill Murray's Phil Connors in *Groundhog Day* and living the same events over and over again.

Sometime after midnight, Gnarly – better known as Ulysses Abbott – had collected statements and was waiting for an M.E. and back-up to arrive. Lewis' cell phone had died last night thanks to a tumble over the second floor balcony when he'd slipped on the waxy wood floor. A first-floor ceramic urn in the direct path of the tumbling cell incurred a long jagged crack. With LAN service currently down, the sheriff was running around, communicating with law enforcement personnel via alternate means: tablet, mouth to mouth, and smoke signals. Okay, it was too wet for the last method, but if he could have started an exterior bonfire to get his orders out and obeyed, he'd have done so.

Gwynne was sicker than he'd been the night before. Fortunately, Aunt Mat had found Bonine to help with nausea and had brought it to the deputy with a pot of chamomile tea. She'd suggested he take one of the raspberry-flavored chewable tablets, but when her back was turned to pour, he'd sucked back five. The man would be out for a while.

Jeana was resting upstairs with a pot of peppermint tea, a bottle of ibuprofen, and a large box of tissues. She'd told Aunt Mat, who seemed to be enjoying playing nurse, that she'd come downstairs later, when the throbbing in her head subsided. The rest of us were fine with her staying upstairs; no one wanted Jeana's germs dancing around with joyous zeal. Apparently Lewis was of the same mind: he'd told the officer not to show her face until she was feeling at least ninety per cent better.

Gnarly had patrolled the household perimeter twice after Percival's body had been discovered. No doubt he'd done an A-1 job of it after Lewis' lambasting. You had to feel for the heavyset man who looked like he'd had a knife thrust in *his* chest. There was no way he could have prevented what had happened. If Percival had not received the knife at the moment he had, he'd have received it at a later time. Why Percival Sayers though? Or had he been mistaken for someone else in the dark?

I felt eyes on me. Linda smiled thinly, turned, and re-focused her gaze on Prunella, who shifted and studied a brass vase that boasted a uniquely etched geometric design.

"How are you holding up?" Aunt Mat asked Prunella quietly.

She shrugged. "It will take a while before it a sinks in. It seems … kind of … dreamlike."

"Why your brother?" Rey asked, standing.

"How would I know?" Prunella replied coolly.

"He must have ticked someone off."

"He was a nice man: he didn't *tick* people off."

Rey crossed her arms and studied the birder's pinched face. "Did it seem as if he was worried, or scared maybe?"

Her gaze narrowed and her tone grew frostier by the syllable. "Perc had no reasons to be worried or scared … no more than any of us, given what's been happening. He has always … he *had* always been a conscientious, kind-hearted person who'd accepted most people at face value."

Rey didn't seem fazed. "Did he mention anything earlier in the day?"

"Like what?"

"Like having seen something or heard something. Maybe *learned* something … or *knew* something."

Prunella frowned, rose stiffly, and began pacing. Tension was thickening like quickly-whisked roux.

It was time to return to my laptop upstairs. "Is there any reason we need to stay here?"

"Yeah." Linda's smile and tone were parch-dry. "So we don't get offed."

"The way things are going, *any* one of us could be 'offed' next," Adwin murmured, scratching his fuzzy friend's head. "Apparently the scarf in the compost area was merely a ruse."

"Apparently?" Prunella's smile was sour. "If you're next on the killer's list, you're next. That's it. There's no escape."

"We're like those duck targets at the carny," my beau declared. "I'm all for leaving."

Linda looked from one face to the next. "I know the sheriff said we could head to the station if we don't feel like staying here, but I'm not about to risk navigating through cement-like snow and treacherous road conditions. Even the medical examiner has to take extreme measures to get here I heard – by coming in on the tail of a plow in a sturdy Jeep Rubicon."

"It could take hours to get there, *if* we get there. We could spin into a ditch or wrap ourselves around a tree. And who wants to be stuck in a small police station? At least here, we can keep an eye on one another, or run and hide, if we're so inclined," May Lee stated with a frown. "I'm with Linda. I'd prefer to stay put."

Rey turned to Aunt Mat. "You keep any guns?"

"There are half-a-dozen hunting rifles. Why?"

"We should arm ourselves."

"I'm sure Lewis and company would love having us meander around, ready to shoot at any movement or sound that startles us." Adwin placed Fred on the rug and hopped to his sneakered feet. "Since we're all staying, I'm going upstairs to get some sleep seeing as I only got about two hours of it last night. Then, I'm packing so I can leave as soon as this brutal weather lets up." He grabbed two ham-and-brie sandwiches, wrapped them in a napkin, and turned. "So are you."

I looked at Rey and smiled. "Don't you love a man who exudes authority?"

She smiled impishly in return and together we responded, "No-ot."

Adwin glanced from her to me and left, Fred padding immediately behind.

"I think I'll do the same," Linda said. "I like you guys, but I'm getting kind of sick of looking at you. Nothing personal."

"Ditto," Prunella said.

Both strolled from the room. May-Lee shrugged and followed.

"That leaves the three of us," my aunt announced. "I'm tired, but far from sleepy."

"Ditto," Rey laughed, motioning Beatrice for more coffee and grabbing a pecan cookie. "I could do with more caffeine and sugar."

"Ditto." With a weary smile, I stepped closer for a refill.

Aunt Mat instructed Hubert to see if Lewis required anything and requested Beatrice brew another pot of coffee. Then she turned to us. "Ladies, let's recap."

* * *

"We agree Prunella's involved?" Posed on the sofa like Theda Bara in *Cleopatra*, Rey sounded as histrionic as she looked.

Aunt Mat sat in the armchair that Thomas had expired on. I was seated by a fire I'd enlarged by three thick logs a few minutes ago, enjoying the warmth that veiled like a soft, flannel sheet. The two of us turned to each other and nodded.

"And we're not sure how Linda plays a part," she continued, "*if* any."

I said, "We need to confirm that the 'dang gal' with Thomas in that Fens bar is *our* 'dang gal'. Do you have a photo of Linda that we can forward to Aunt Mat's private detective? Let's see if Johnny can tie the two together."

Rey's eyes darted like whizzing pinballs. Finally she smiled. "There aren't many, but there is a pretty good one from early last year. She was sitting on a gaffer's lap at an industry function. It was out of character, but then so were the five bourbon shooters she and Roadhouse – he's the gaffer guy – threw back." She motioned the laptop I'd grabbed from the bedroom.

Two minutes later we were looking at a very happy Linda Royale perched on a hulking bulk of a male. The name Roadhouse suited him to a T. Her highlighted hair was longer and had seen a straight iron. Dressed in a tight-fitting lilac sweater and long flowing black skirt with gold filigree, gold hoops, chain and bracelet, she looked very different. And pretty drunk.

"What's Johnny's email address?"

Aunt Mat gave it and off it went.

"While we're at it, let me see about sending one." I got a phone number from my contacts, made a call, and promised Wayne a "reward" (courtesy of my aunt) to make up for disturbing him. He'd eaten a bad batch of clams late last night and was lying in bed, and through the moans and groans, promised to check out the photo. Off it went.

Rey looked contemplative, then enthusiastically announced, "I've got an idea." After locating two email addresses for television companies, she keyed in two short paragraphs.

I read the request regarding vacation timeframes and slapped her back. "Smart thinking."

She pitched forward, looked like she might curse, then shrugged and grinned. "I'm not all beauty, you know."

Who wanted to go there at this time of the morning? Feeling optimistic, I leaned into the sideboard. "Now we wait for replies to arrive."

Aunt Mat paced before the fire. "What if Johnny confirms he's seen Linda? Or this former bookie does? Does that then confirm that she and Prunella are in cahoots?"

Rey nodded. "In terms of Percival's murder, Prunella *had* to have been there – she and Linda left together. If Linda was the one with the knife, Prunella certainly didn't stop it and if Prunella was the one with the knife, Linda did nothing to stop it, either. The question, though, is *why* was Percival murdered?"

"For that matter, why any of them?" our aunt asked quietly.

"Unfortunately, we still have a lot of suppositions and gut instincts, but no bona fide answers or proof," I sighed.

We eyed one another, glumness shrouding our faces like Niagara Falls mist.

* * *

"Sure is quiet," Rey whispered as we headed down a second-floor corridor later that afternoon.

"Everyone's resting or napping. Lewis is on the other side of the house, conducting 'official' police matters, which translates into stay-out-of-my-hair-ladies business," I pointed out, "and you haven't uttered a word in the last few minutes, which is very unlike you."

"Ha, ha." Rey offered one of her raspberries.

"Ha, ha, ha, you and me, Little brown jug, don't I love thee!"

Grinning, Fred the Ghost moseyed past.

Rey's eyes were as wide and round as ping-pong balls and she made some sort of sibilant sound, as if she wanted to say something or shriek, but her tongue was pasted in place.

"Fred, you devil, you're frightening my niece," Aunt Matt scolded softly, wagging a playful finger.

"Ha, ha, ha, you and me, Little brown jug, don't I love thee!" Into the wall he disappeared.

"You have to believe me now," I told my cousin.

Rey merely glanced from one face to the next, took a faltering breath, and careened into Aunt Mat's bedroom.

"She's in denial," I said.

"I'd rather keep Fred our secret, anyway. Who needs paranormal types hanging around the gate?" My aunt slipped her arm into mine. "I'm sure Fred would prefer it that way, too."

We stepped before the door.

"Does he ever talk to you?"

She gazed back at the wall he'd entered. "Not usually."

"Do you have any idea how he ended up here in this house?"

"Yes." She smiled mysteriously and tugged me into the bedroom.

Rey was on the far side of the queen-size bed, under a satin quilt, a down feather pillow pulled over her head. There was no way she'd speak of Fred again in this lifetime.

* * *

An early, casual dinner was served in the small dining room around 5:45 p.m.

My cousin and I had taken showers and slipped into clean jeans and sweaters, while our aunt opted for designer slacks and turtleneck. Adwin was wearing his favorite sweatshirt and jeans, while May-Lee's attire, a gray pin-striped pants suit, was classy and costly. Linda and Prunella, seated at opposite ends of the table, were both sporting long wool skirts with heavy sweaters. I'd always thought people, when caught in dire situations, didn't much care for how they looked or smelled. Obviously I'd been wrong.

Lewis, Jeana and a young ruddy-faced officer named Budd were also having dinner, but had opted to eat in the kitchen. Budd, whose full name was Buddy Barnabus Budd (and here I'd been thinking the Fonnes held the record for kooky names), had hitched a ride on a plow the M.E. had been following in a Jeep. Meanwhile, Gnarly had snagged a ride back to the station.

Lewis stuck his head in. "The autopsy's going to get underway later this evening," he said, eyeing each one of us warily. "Fenton's pretty certain Percival Sayahs died from the knife in the hawht … after a hit on the back of the head with what was likely a hammah or similah implement. Just thought I'd let you know, seeing as you all but made me promise to keep you up-to-date." He retreated.

"Ouch, that's gotta hurt," Linda murmured, chomping into a piece of steamed parsnip.

Adwin drew a deep breath. "Someone smashed in the back of his head, then fatally stabbed him – without a thought or a blink. How cold-blooded is that?"

Aunt Mat sighed softly. "Evidently there was no remorse."

"Killing comes easily for this person," Rey murmured, taking a sip of cranberry juice.

"Or persons," I threw in.

"So who at this table did it?" Linda regarded faces like a drill sergeant attempting to detect insubordination.

"Cuckoo."

Everyone's gazes swept across the room to the Swiss-made clock and watched a cheery little bird announce the time. Funny, it had never cuckoo'd before.

"*You* did, Linda my dear," Aunt Mat announced.

"Mathilda Moone, that's absolutely absurd." Prunella waved a hand in dismissal.

"And so did *you.*"

Prunella's mouth dropped to the table.

24

That's the Way the Cookie Crumbles

Linda stared at my aunt for several seconds, looked at Rey and then Prunella, and then bah-hah-hahed. "Dang. That's hysterical."

Prunella's expression was a cross between surprise and disbelief. "Surely you jest? My dear, this isn't at all amusing."

"We know it *has* to be someone in this group," Aunt Mat responded tartly. "You've said so yourself, and even pointed a finger at different individuals – away from yourself."

"We were *all* thinking aloud." She took a sip of hibiscus tea and leaned back, looking very calm, even amused. "We also thought it could be an uninvited person, or persons." She held out her cup as Beatrice stepped alongside with a fine white porcelain Noritake teapot. "Why pick on the two of us?"

Aunt Mat was sitting at the head of the table, looking like a CEO conducting an annual shareholder meeting. She leaned forward and grasped the edge of the table, her expression stern. "Johnny Gorcey has a witness or two who will swear Linda was at Thomas' office on at least two occasions."

Rey started to speak, then appeared befuddled. "What's that bookie-runner guy's name again?"

"Wayne Antonici," I replied. "He knew Thomas very well in his bookie days. He confirmed he saw Linda *with* Thomas at a Boston bar."

Linda's gaze turned ten degrees cooler, but she remained mute.

"And thanks to helpful people in the personnel departments at two companies you worked for in the last ten years, we have vacation dates." I pulled a folded list from my jeans pocket and held it up, "as well as dates you called in sick."

"It appears privacy clauses have been broken. I'll have to check with legal sources." Leaning back, Linda smiled coldly and arched an eye-brow. "So?"

"So they coincide with the times six Moones died."

"What about it Ms. Royale? Were you present when those Moones died?" Lewis stood in the doorway, his air and tone neutral.

Budd, standing behind him, picked up his eye-balls from the floor.

"Go ahead. Try proving I had anything to do with those deaths," she sniffed. "How ridiculous."

Budd leaned forward, completely absorbed in the moment, while Lewis ambled to the side-board and poured a glass of warm tomato juice. He turned slowly, tumbler in hand. "What would happen if we ran checks on planes, rental cars, buses and the like? Would we find you'd headed to the same destinations where – and when – the Moones died?"

"Go for it," the screenwriting assistant dared.

This one was as cool as a cucumber. Maybe she thought no one would actually verify. Or maybe she had covered her tracks very well. Two cucumbers could play this game of cool. I sat back and crossed my arms. "We have two sources ready to substantiate that you were with Thomas Saturne."

She mirrored my pose. "I'd met Thomas Saturne back when. I used his services twice: after Mother met with an unfortunate accident and a time after that. Yes, we met at a Boston bar one afternoon. We both happened to be shopping in Copley Place, bumped into each other, and thought we'd have a drink to catch up on each other's lives. Thomas mentioned a little bar he liked and off we went. There's nothing illegal or suspicious about that."

Rey held up her cup as Beatrice went around pouring more tea. "Then why not tell us you knew him?"

"No one asked."

"But you both pretended like you only met here at the house."

Linda offered a salty smile. "This group loves to natter over nothing. We had no desire to give wagging tongues more to wag about. Besides, we *weren't* friends – just a professional service provider and his client."

"I'm no tongue-wagger," Prunella snapped.

"I'm no natterer." Aunt Mat appeared affronted.

"Don't look at *me*," Rey puffed.

"How did you get involved with a New York lawyer in the first place," I asked "considering you're California-based?"

"He came recommended. I happened to be living in New York – Queens to be precise – when we'd first met."

"There seem to be a lot of coincidences going on," Rey declared bluntly. "Too many, if you ask me."

"We didn't ask you," Linda all but snarled.

"Ladies, please." Lewis held up a hand and turned to Budd. "It appears we have allegations and facts to check. Maybe you can use the computah in Reginald Moone's office to set wheels in motion." He glanced at Aunt Mat for affirmation and she nodded. "See what you come up with and do what you have to to get information, if possible without heading out in this God-awful weathah. And look in on Gwynne. Maybe bring him some leftovah soup. Then tell Jeana to give you a hand, if she seems bettah. With four bodies," his eyes rolled upward, "we have our work cut ount for us."

"I don't care how bad it is out there, I'm going home – with Reginald's vintage trapper snow-shoes if necessary. I've put up with and been in-sulted enough," Prunella huffed. "I've got to see to my brother's services, too."

"You won't be burying him tomorrow, Ms. Sayers," Budd told her quietly.

Prunella's stare held the heat of a flamethrower; the officer should have resembled a charcoal-broiled burger, heavy on the charcoal.

"We may be wise to scour every room and hid-den hallway again."

"Why Sheriff, that would suggest you didn't do a good job the first few times." Linda's tone was as sweet as chrysanthemum soda.

His tone was equally honeyed. "Then why not confess, ma'am, and save us time and trouble?"

"Dream on."

A thought flew into my head much like that Harris Sparrow had into Prunella's the other day: fast and furious. I jumped up and mo-tioned Lewis into a corner of the kitchen. Jeana was spooning up a couple of mandarin sections, heavy on the syrup, from a big bowl.

"Feeling better?"

A sneeze sounding like a detonated squib answered my question.

"Budd will be needing help," Lewis informed her.

With a quick blow of the nose, she rose and left the room with her half-finished dessert.

He eyed me curiously and waited.

"Has anyone checked out these dead people's insurance policies and wills?"

He hesitated, then nodded. "Being a mystery buff and aspiring detective, young Budd researched histories and families, wills and insurance. Not that we wouldn't have, but we've been overloaded and short-staffed, and he was just a lot quickah." He pulled a small thick pad from his back pocket. "This is Jeana's. She got the rundown from him and jotted notes." Narrowed eyes ran down the first page. "Saturne had no will and no current insurance policy, but he did have one a while back." His eyes scanned mine. "Your friend Prunella Sayahs was beneficiary."

"When did he cancel it?"

"Nearly two years ago."

Before the break-up. Interesting. "No one thought that strange?"

"When Budd brought this to our attention, we didn't think much of it. There wasn't a valid policy, so she wasn't going to collect."

"Maybe she *thought* she was going to collect."

Lewis' jaw shifted and he looked back at the next page. "Jensen's wife had been cut out of the picture some time ago. He had a fellow named Chatahs Roland listed as chief beneficiary. The will leaves money to Roland as well as three educational institutions."

"Did anyone check May-Lee Sonit?"

"Mathilda's long-time friend has a will, leaving all to a daughtah and grandson. She also has coverage for the shop, and a modest policy for herself. I heard something about her having been an old girlfriend of Percival Sayahs."

"Wife – of short duration."

The man's expression meandered from rapt to perturbed to bemused. "We bettah re-check policies and wills for Percival Sayahs. Maybe Budd missed something."

"And check the cook," I advised. "Porter was a chef at Prunella's San Francisco restaurant several years back. She hasn't, however, ever claimed to know him."

He scanned my face for several seconds. "Do you think she'll show up in the cook's will or policy?"

"That's not likely, but it would be worthwhile knowing who was important enough in the ex-con's life to warrant beneficiary status ... if he even had a will or policy."

"Ex ... con?" Lewis looked far from amused.

Quickly, I brought him up to speed about Porter's notorious past. "But getting back to Prunella, I'm not sure she'd have killed Percival for money – if she was the one who performed the deadly deed."

"Money's great incentive for murdah," Lewis declared.

"If that were the incentive, she'd have done so years sooner."

"She may have been waiting for the right time and finally found it when bodies started piling up. This could work in her favah."

"Are you suggesting the murders aren't related? That there are different killers?"

Lewis' smile was apathetic. "Right now, I'm simply tossing around ideas, and not very good ones. Until we have us some real evidence – a confession or two would be welcome – we can only speculate." He tucked the notepad back into his pocket. "While we're speculating, let's consider Linda Royale. You were talking about her having something to do with six dead Moones. Are you thinking she might also be involved with what's been happening here?"

I leaned into a wall and gathered the tidbits of facts we'd uncovered so far. There was a link somewhere. What was it? "What if my cousin is right and she and Prunella are both involved? One of them would have to be the instigator – most likely Prunella, because she's a powerhouse in her own right. Let's say Prunella collects the payoff and Linda, in return for assistance, receives a percentage."

"Is she the sort who'd take money so easily and become an accessory to murdah?" He frowned. "My gut feeling says she isn't."

"She may be harboring a major grudge." I told him about the relation to the Smiths and estate.

"Damnation." He rubbed his temple and suddenly appeared ten years older. "Let's go back to the payoff you were mentioning. Where would the Sayahs woman get the money to 'pay off' your friend?"

I considered it. "There are two possibilities. One, she thought she would inherit money – lots of it – from Thomas Saturne. Two, she thought she would receive payment from an angry bookie or loan shark – earned for the termination of a debt-heavy gamester whose losing was becoming a horrible habit."

"And the others were what – collateral damage?" he smiled dryly. "One more vital question: when did your friend and the Sayahs woman get togethah? It would have to have been *before* this bizarre affair started."

I drew a deep breath. Suddenly the reasoning seemed lame and pedestrian.

Noticing my dejection, the sheriff chuckled and gave my shoulder a gentle pat. "We'll get there."

* * *

An hour and a half later three super sleuths (in our dreams) were conferring in the library-study.

Rey whistled and pulled a photo gently from Aunt Mat's fingers. "Johnny 'Sherlock' Gorcey sure has a great memory, and even better sources."

"That looks like proof to me," our aunt said triumphantly.

The photo showed a well-dressed very different looking Linda Royale sitting by a tall French-style window in an upscale Manhattan restaurant with Thomas Saturne. It had been taken maybe sixteen months ago. Her hair was neatly arranged in a chignon and she wore a metallic brocade jacket with mandarin collar and red seamless tank. He was dressed in typical Thomas Saturne frump-wear: an ill-fitting ash-gray striped suit with an off-the-rack white shirt and drab gray tie. They were drinking red wine and nibbling tapas. From the smiles, it looked more personal than business, but the photographer may have caught them during a casual moment.

"I wouldn't call that proof. Curious yes, condemning no," I warned. "She admitted having met him re legal business. Nothing here suggests otherwise."

Rey sighed. "Too bad we don't have an *after* dinner photo."

"I can't see Linda and Thomas romping in the sack. That's too repugnant an image," I said.

Another sigh. "You're right. She's not his type."

"She's stylish in a mature and conservative way, but young emotionally," Aunt Mat advised. "She wouldn't be romantically interested in a stuffed shirt like Thomas."

Rey strolled to the door to answer an insistent knock.

"Phones are still down in places. Powah, too. It should be getting bettah out there, nawt worse." Lewis ambled to the windows and peered out with a frown. "Jeana's a real troopah and getting bettah by the moment. Gwynne's nawt faring well, and I'm worried." He exhaled at length and turned.

"The flu can be quite debilitating," Aunt Mat said lightly.

"I had one last spring that kept me in bed for four days," Rey acknowledged with an emphatic nod.

His smile was as brittle as a stack of long-discarded pine needles. "Did you ladies find anything?"

Aunt Mat motioned Rey, who held up the photo still clutched in her hand.

He took it, studied it, and passed it back. "Where's the smoking gun? Or in this case maybe I should say the *blowgun*?"

"Do you think we could play one gal against the other to get one or both to slip up?" Rey asked.

"It would never work. Prunella's too shrewd. Linda's potentially screwed up for all we know," I responded.

On the next floor, immediately above, a thud like a body contacting a hardwood floor was followed by a crash of ceramic or heavy glass.

Several seconds later, Budd's bass voice boomed from upstairs. "Sheriff!" Another thud followed.

Lewis' lips drew into a dour line and he whirled, hastening into the hallway.

"That doesn't sound promising," Aunt Mat murmured.

"So not promising," Rey agreed.

We glanced at each other and scurried after him like children chasing an ice-cream truck.

* * *

"What's the ruckus about?" Sheriff Lewis demanded as we stormed into Jensen's bedroom.

Adwin, prone on the floor not far from the door, had split lips and a bruise on his forehead. The cherry-framed mirror and silvery fragments were lying beside him, as were his glasses. Budd was ten feet away, his face to the floor.

"Cupcake!" I dropped beside the injured man. He stirred.

Aunt Mat hastened to the washroom and returned with two wet facecloths, one which she passed to Rey. Quickly she dabbed Adwin's pale cheeks and forehead; Rey did the same to Budd.

Lewis bent over him. "What happened? Did you and my deputy get into a fight?"

"No." Adwin pushed aside the facecloth and struggled into an upright position as Lewis moved over to Budd.

He leaned close and inspected the young man's face. "Did you trip ovah Mathilda's niece's boyfriend's body?" he asked dryly.

Budd grimaced and felt his chin. It, like Adwin's forehead, would soon be sporting several colors. "I heard voices from the next hallway. They seemed pissed, uh-angry, so I thought I'd check it out. When I got to the corner, the voices stopped, but I kept walking. Then I heard a noise from this room and looked in. I found him like that, but didn't see no one else." He got up slowly. "But ..."

"But?"

"There *must* have been someone, 'cause I got a whack to the back just after I shouted for you, which sent me sailing."

Lewis gazed around. "I can't imagine some phantom did this."

I glanced at Aunt Mat. She looked like she was going to say something, then thought better of it.

"Like Officer Budd, I heard voices. They sounded heated and seemed to come from here.

I thought maybe your Cousin Reynalda was irritating someone again, so I decided to step in." He smiled dryly, grabbed his glasses, and shakily put them on. "When I did step in, there was no one in sight, but a light was on." He motioned a tortoise-shell urn lamp. "I was about to turn and leave, when someone shoved me hard." He pressed a hand to the top of his head and winced. "Then, for good measure I got hit as I was going down."

"You heard voices?" Lewis asked absently as he surveyed the room again.

"Yes sir." He eyed blood on his fingertips and grimaced. "Whoever was in here obviously heard me approaching." He motioned his heavy leather shoes. "They're not the quietest things."

I checked his scalp and forehead. A minor cut and major bruise respectively, Tylenol #3 would be in order, but stitches would not.

"Do you think it was the cousin here?" Lewis asked, eyeing Rey.

Adwin gazed from him to Budd and then to Rey. "Not likely. She'd have stuck around to take credit or offer another challenge or two."

Rey glowered.

"She was with us," Aunt Mat reminded him.

He kept his eyes on Adwin. "But it *was* a woman?"

"I'm inclined to claim at least one woman." Dejection darkened his face. "There may have been a third voice. Maybe even a fourth. I can't swear to anything, sir." With a soft groan, he got up slowly, ignoring my extended hand.

Lewis turned to Budd, his tone shy of exasperated. "What was it? One woman? Two women? Three? *Four*?"

"I'm not sure," he said quietly, appearing apologetic. "I was focused on my Blackberry, getting an update on things at the station and on weather conditions. Things are going nuts there, Sheriff."

He rolled his eyes. "I can imagine. Are roads getting cleared yet?"

"The area's still filled with outages." He smiled reassuringly. "But there haven't been any major crimes."

"I expect not – they're all happening *here*! Including this here little free-for-all!" Lewis inhaled deeply and turned back to Adwin. "You're certain you didn't see a thing?"

"Yeah, I saw stars. Lots of them." His smile was feeble. "As I said, I was hit almost as soon as I stepped inside the door." He looked at Budd.

Who shrugged.

"What about *you* three?" Lewis asked.

"I'd hardly bean my boyfriend," I snapped.

"Jill, Reynalda and I were together in the library before and *when* you arrived," Aunt Mat stated tersely.

He scowled. "Have your maid get a large pot of coffee going. We're going to need it." He turned to his deputy. "Budd, round up those othah ladies and herd them into the dining room. I'll be down in a few minutes." Lewis stepped alongside Adwin and inspected the wound. "You'll live. You may want to take some Aspirin, though." He glanced around. "Does anyone have any idea how she, he, or they could have snuck past without being seen?"

Aunt Mat shook her head. "There's no hidden passageway in here."

"That we know of," I emphasized.

She eyed me for several seconds and nodded somberly. "That we know of."

Rey spoke up for the first time since leaving the library-study. "Let's see if we can find one." She started fingering a nearby closest wall like the consummate pro she'd become.

* * *

Several minutes later, Rey stood akimbo, looking triumphant if not smug. "Am I good or what?"

A cherry panel above the four-poster bed revealed shadowy darkness. Aunt Mat went into the bathroom and returned with a Mag-Lite flashlight, which she handed to me.

I aimed it forward and a bright beam showed five steps leading to a corridor no more than three feet wide. Indistinct footprints were visible in the dust, suggesting it had been used previously, and more than once, but by whom? Whoever had hit Adwin and Budd?

Lewis peered over Rey's shoulder. "I suppose we should head down."

"*We?*" Aunt Mat asked.

He glanced rearward. "Right. Budd's gone to get the women. I guess it'll be me."

"We'll come with you." I gestured Rey and my-self.

"I don't need back-up, but thanks."

"We'll only follow," I warned.

He scanned our set expressions. "Fine, but it could get real dark down there, so you'd bettah get lights."

Aunt Mat hastened from the room and was back before anyone could say Harry Houdini twenty-two times. She handed me a nifty Pelican flashlight and hung a floral canvas beach bag from Rey's shoulder. I peered inside to find it held two similar flashlights, extra batteries, a package of long-burning emergency candles, matches, and two lighters.

I took a deep breath and followed Lewis while Rey took up the rear.

"Ouch. What a place to put a pipe," Rey groused.

I swung my light around and found her rubbing a shoulder. "You may want to keep a closer watch on where you're walking."

"Yeah, like I've got nocturnal vision," she puffed, then exhaled slowly. "This reminds me of the corridor leading to the secret room. Maybe this one'll take us there, too."

"They all pretty much look the same: narrow, long, dark, and gloomy."

We continued behind Lewis. There wasn't much to see along the descending path but concrete, pipes, and more concrete – and a nearly invisible opening. It only garnered our attention because Lewis had slipped and stumbled into it, and the resulting sound held a metallic ring.

Rey rubbed a palm against the divider. "This doesn't have a wooden or stone-like feel."

"Let's see if it can be opened," Lewis proposed.

We struggled with the thin and tapered barrier, and finally managed to open it. Our lights, pointing into the distance, revealed a familiar entrance. Rey had been correct about the tunnel: it was a narrow extension of the other one and led to the secret room.

"We're kind of at a dead end," my cousin muttered.

"We discovered this barely visible door; why can't there be another? Look, we already know what's down here, so let's move upward a few feet, over there," I instructed and walked over.

"Start feeling around, Ms. Magic Fingers. You're bound to discover something else."

"Long as I don't 'discover' any creepy-crawlies."

Several minutes and grumblings later, another wall slid silently sideward.

"It's well oiled," she commented. "If Aunt Mat isn't aware of this secret passage, someone else sure is."

Lewis stepped forward and we followed, entering the laundry room via a tiny narrow panel. "Interesting," he murmured, awed.

"Not *that* interesting." Rey appeared annoyed.

I glanced back at the wall we'd stepped through. It was well concealed by a small slim shelving unit that had moved with the wall. It supported a sundry of cleaning products. Who'd have guessed? Evidently, not us.

"We've found yet anothah corridah leading to anothah room, and anothah route of escape." A preoccupied Lewis moved ahead while Rey pulled me back.

She waited until he disappeared from view and then grabbed my elbow and led us into the pantry. "Any thoughts?"

"Prunella and/or Linda could be attempting to creep us out."

"You think they staged that heated conversation upstairs? For what purpose?"

I considered it, then threw up my arms in defeat. "I haven't got a clue.... Maybe they're playing mind games."

"With whose minds?" She smiled wryly, inserted the flashlight into the canvas bag, and passed the bag to me.

I tucked mine inside as well and slung the bag over my shoulder. "Who was the third and/or fourth voice, do you suppose?"

"There may not have been a third or fourth. That was only a guess by two beaned boys. And who's to say it wasn't one woman pretending to be more? Maybe a loony-tunes one?" My cousin grabbed a can of Coke from a shelf and gulped back half of it.

With a tiny burp, she moved to a huge heavy unit holding cereals and fiber bars on the topmost shelf, bags of rice and noodles on the second topmost shelf, and countless packages of cookies on two middle shelves. She fingered several, then peered closely. "What? No peanut-butter ones? How can you have fig cookies, coconut cookies … marshy-mallow cookies, pecan and shortbread cookies, but no friggin' peanut-butter ones? Am I the only one who loves peanut-butter cookies?"

With her head and shoulders jammed inside the middle-most shelf, my determined cousin pulled and pushed. "Holy crap!" Bags and boxes of sandwiched and disc-shaped sweets started flying every which way.

"Rey! Get a grip! Adwin will bake you a batch of peanut-butter cookies if you're craving them that badly."

"There's someone tucked back here!"

I leaped forward and peered past the mess she'd created. "That's not someone. That's some-*thing*."

"This keeps getting weirder." She eyed the skeleton that had previously graced the hobby/art room.

"That, Reynalda Fonne-Werde, is an understatement."

We turned to each other. I shrugged, she gestured, and at the top of our lungs, we released simultaneous bloodcurdling shrieks.

25

Murder They Wrote

With the prowess of a froghopper bug and the steeliness of a vulture, Lewis soared into the pantry. Hot on his heels were Aunt Mat and Beatrice with opossum-wide eyes and marmot-curious expressions. Hubert limped in ten seconds later, May-Lee and Linda tramped in ten seconds after him, and Prunella strolled in five seconds after them.

Looking both worried and wary, Budd shoved through the small crowd. "Sir?"

Lewis looked from him to my cousin and me. "Those screams surely traveled down the driveway and then some. What's the mattah now? Are you ladies wanting to get on the evening news?"

Rey gave a nudge. "You gonna tell him, or am I?"

I nudged back. "You found it, you should –"

"Ladies!"

Rey slid rearward and flourished her arms like a game-show host displaying a grand prize. "Another body."

"It's not possible," Aunt Mat murmured in disbelief, bringing a hand to a drawn mouth.

Beatrice anxiously stroked liver-colored lips while Hubert, bewildered, squinted at the molested cookie packages.

As Lewis stepped forward, a soft curse drifted backward. "Who put this here? Maybe more importantly, whose bones are these?"

Aunt Mat's smile and tone were almost contrite. "That's Wolfgang, a welcome-to-the-estate helper."

"We met him in one of the rooms upstairs." I draped an arm around her shoulders. "He's a very vocal fellow – for no vocal chords."

Rey grabbed a dented package of mocha wafers, eyed the box briefly, and then ripped into it. "You didn't move Wolfie here ... did you?"

"To what end?" the grande dame sniffed.

Rey bit a wafer in half.

"Praise be to God it wasn't a real body this time." Lewis peered closer. "Hold on. What's this?" Removing a pen from a breast pocket, he fumbled to retrieve a small notepad tucked between the skeleton's clavicle and scapula, and finally held it gingerly by poking the pen through the spiral coil. "This is Jeana's. But I had it with me." He felt side and back pockets and frowned. "I must have left it somewhere."

Budd eyed it anxiously. "It sure looks like hers."

"It is," I confirmed. "You showed it to me in the kitchen, Sheriff."

He frowned again, carefully pocketed the notepad, and turned to Budd. "When'd you last see Jeana?"

"… I guess … fifteen-twenty minutes before I entered the upstairs bedroom and found Mr. Timmins on the floor." His brow puckered. "She told me she had to check something. When I asked what, she said maybe it was something, maybe nothing, but until she was sure she'd rather not give details. She slapped my shoulder, smiled, and headed to the back, and I moved on."

Lewis' sparkling eyes dimmed as he stared at Wolfgang. "This doesn't bode well."

"Maybe it's a message," Rey stated dramatically.

"Maybe," he agreed stiffly. "Budd, see if you can find her. Hopefully she's simply gone investigating and is in one of the tunnels, lost or wrapped up in something interesting. She can't be that hard to locate and she hasn't been missing that long … but if she can't be found within a reasonable amount of time, you best call the station and see if one or two of the boys can get ovah here." He exhaled softly and scanned the ceiling. "I sure hope it doesn't come to that."

"What's going on?" Adwin asked, his cheeks ruddy and moist, a fleece jacket slung over his right shoulder and a wool hat scrunched in his left hand.

"Where have you been?" Lewis demanded.

"I took something to calm the ache in my head and felt a little spacey, so I went outside to clear the fog."

The sheriff eyed him suspiciously, then focused on Beatrice. "You bettah put on anothah pot of coffee, ma'am. I suggest we move to the drawing room and stay togethah until we hear back from young Budd." The tense-faced man

regarded each face distrustfully and then motioned forward.

As the others followed, Rey and I took a hurried detour upstairs. We grabbed the canvas bag
with lights, tucked in tissues, plastic baggies and
both cell phones, perfect for photos and emergency calls, and headed to the hidden corridors.
It would be a while before Budd got to them; he'd
be searching rooms first.

"Don't forget about the slope and the –"

"Frig!"

"Steps," I finished.

"Ouch." Rey winced and straightened. "When
we get to the tunnel that leads to the cottage,
let's aim to locate more entrances. They have to
be there."

"How many passageways could there be
on one estate, for heaven's sake? This isn't
the Tower of London or a sixteenth-century
monastery."

"Remember, there used to be stables and a
coach-house. They probably had underground
connections. I'm betting there are more," she asserted as we started walking at a snail's pace.

I repeated what I'd told my aunt not long ago. "It seems like overkill."

"I read somewhere that old Mr. Smith had a black streak. He may have been a scientist, but I bet he didn't use these corridors for scientific purposes. Weird and crazy experiments would be more likely. Like maybe he operated on people and they ended up maimed and/or nutzoid, walking these dark passages like –"

"Old sci-fi movie mutants," I concluded, laughing.

"Okay, mutants aside, there could have been escaped slaves, robbers and other villainous sorts traveling these dingy walkways." She poked my shoulder. "I'm betting he was as twisted as that writer suggested."

"Writer?"

"Albert Humpelmeyer … or whatever the frigging guy's name was. He's some sort of historian."

I stared blankly. "I have no idea what you're talking about."

"This Albert guy wrote a few essays on old New England families and estates. I came across some when I was researching the house and family. He'd said that Caine Granton Smith was a known eccentric, among other things. Caine's father had been placed in an asylum when Caine was ten years old and the mother had been rumored to be into black magic or sorcery, or something like that."

"Eccentric is a long away from twisted," I advised.

"Scientist plus eccentric, plus loony-tunes dad and witch-mother, equals twisted," she contended. "All these below-ground corridors couldn't have been for good Samaritan causes."

I tried to imagine the place one-hundred-plus years ago and what Rey's "twisted" scientist could have been up to. "It's possible he had these corridors built for personal privacy – like monks or smugglers did back when – or for visitors so they could be discreet."

"'Discreet' like when visitors or servants have trysts with the master – or mistress – of the house?" She smiled wryly. "Maybe so, Cousin Jilly, but I'm prime for more sinister reasons."

"Unfortunately, no one's alive from those days to confirm or deny your theories." I motioned.

"We'd better find something soon. Lewis is probably having a fit that we've gone off again."

My cousin waved off my worry. "He knows us well enough. He's got more important stuff to concern himself with than two wayward cousins." She stopped and aimed her flashlight. "Feel that?"

I aimed mine, too. "Yes. A draft."

Cousin Reynalda peered closely. "Whoa Nelly! Another door."

"A very well concealed one." I ran a beam over a heavy studded iron door with pintles mortised into the frame. To the far left was a thumb latch featuring heart-shaped cusps and a four-inch grip. "And an old one. Do you think you can manage to open this, Ms. Magic Fingers?"

"Step aside, Useless One." Rey blew her fingertips like a retro TV safecracker. She pressed, prodded, poked, broke two fingernails, and pressed some more. A loud, blasphemous curse flew from her lips; had she been Catholic, she'd have to say two-hundred Hail Marys. Facial expressions moved from frustrated to angry to livid to determined. Finally, the inch-thick door crashed inward, triggering dust particles and rust flecks to sprinkle legs and feet like jimmies on ice-cream. "Ugh. Smells moldy."

"It smells like something," I agreed, shining light ahead and noticing a narrow, low-ceiling walkway. Old cords and tools, and two iron wagon wheels leaned against one wall while something resembling a heretic's fork and other items I didn't want to guess at leaned against another. They looked ominous and deadly. Of course, they could simply have been antique farm implements for all I knew, but somehow I doubted it. "This looks like a psychopath's dream."

"The dirt and cobwebs add a nice touch," Rey concurred, peering over my shoulder. "This pretty much proves Smith was a crazed wingnut."

"We don't know what the space or tools were used for." I swung away from the walls and focused on the short, dank walkway ahead. "Are we ready to move on?"

"Ready." She didn't sound overly eager.

I glanced over. "Come on. Let's find that proof we've been talking about since the first body fell."

"This place looks like no one's been here in decades. But as you're always saying: never say never." She released a long exhalation. "With our luck, we'll only find red sardines."

"The phrase is 'red herrings'. And haven't you suddenly become the pessimistic one?"

She stuck out her tongue and eyed the wall, then pulled down a short-handled hoe. "May as well play it safe and protect ourselves if necessary."

"That thing won't do much good against an otherworldly ghost or deceased body."

"It will if it's a *live* body ... because if we run into a live one down here, then we've run into the *killer*."

"Point taken." I grabbed a wooden mallet.

* * *

"Pretty gruesome."

"That's an understatement," I murmured, staring into Jeana's still face. We'd found the officer sixty feet farther down the corridor, opposite the direction we'd come from. I positioned the flashlight on the ground so that it illuminated the body, which was propped against a dark and fusty wall, and examined it more closely. Crushed cranium aside, her face seemed almost serene; she'd not been surprised or startled. Like Jensen, how could she not have seen or heard her attacker? Or had she faced someone familiar, a person she'd never have expected to turn on her? "She looks like she's napping."

"Yeah, except for the side of her head," Rey said sardonically, "where one-third of it is caved in."

A thick winter police-issue jacket, unbuttoned, was worn over a heavy army-green sweater and jeans. A loosely draped scarf of drab olive hung from her thin neck. It appeared the deputy had intended to venture outside. Why? And what had brought her down here? "I wonder who she ran into."

"Someone who didn't like having her down here and wanted her to stay quiet – permanently." Rey frowned and studied the body. "She's got some serious cuts on the top of her hands."

I scanned torn, bloodied skin. "She appears to have been scratched or clawed, and yet there doesn't appear to be any signs of a fight. Her knuckles aren't bruised, as if she'd punched someone. Her face has no marks. This may have happened elsewhere, and earlier. The blood is dry."

My cousin shone the flashlight around. "There seem to be scuff marks there. See? She must have been dragged."

"She's not exactly ballerina petite. It would have had to have been someone with strength."

"It could have been two people. Or someone insane. I've heard that crazy people have amazing strength."

"It's possible," I murmured. "The suspect list is pretty small. If you had to choose, who on the list of two do you suppose is powerful enough, or insane enough, to do this?"

Rey took a deep breath. "Linda's in good shape and Prunella is strong. And either one could be certifiable. We're not sure yet. But we do know that Linda killed those Moones –"

"We *assume* she did, Rey. We only have coincidences and no proof." I rubbed the back of my neck where tension was creeping in with the dampness. "Jeana can't have been dead long. We saw her at the end of dinner –"

"Around 6:30 or thereabouts," Rey nodded.

"And Budd saw her fifteen or twenty minutes before he and Adwin were clocked in Thomas's room. That would make it ... two-and-a-half hours, give or take."

"It may be hard to tell the actual time of death. Casper's Law, or Ratio, says when there's a free access of air, a body decomposes twice as fast than if immersed in water and eight times faster than if buried in earth."

I could feel my eyebrows leave my forehead. "Thank you Dr. Max *H5-O* Bergman."

"I was trying out for a forensics role – a pathology student actually – and did some research. Hard as it may be to believe, Jilly, I *can* remember details and stats." She smiled drolly. "And sometimes I even *understand* them."

I offered her shoulder a gentle punch and looked back to Jeana Malle. "In this case, we can state unequivocally that she hasn't been dead for more than three hours, and that everyone has been in and out of sight at least a couple of times during that period."

"Death is starting to fascinate you, isn't it?"

"It's the search for facts and evidence that is fascinating me." I scrunched down, balancing the mallet on my lap. "In this instance, where better to find both than on or around the body? Pass me one of those little plastic bags, will you?"

Tucking the handy-dandy hoe under one arm, she rummaged in the canvas bag, pulled one out, and thrust it in my face.

I gave her a look, slapped it aside, and reached for Jeana's clutched hand. Before this crazy Connecticut week had begun, I'd never been within twenty feet of a corpse, much less touched one. The thought of doing so would have repulsed me; now it seemed part of an abnormal norm. There was a story some somewhere in all this I absently thought as I unfurled the officer's long fingers.

Tucked between were three connected, twisted links. Tiny, dark flecks on them could have been blood. "Do you recall seeing a chain like this on anyone or anything?"

She stared for several seconds. "No. That looks like something from a fancy belt. Or a tool maybe."

"This is gold."

"A *fancy* tool then," she said with a grim smile.

"Cute." I took another look, certain I'd seen it somewhere before, stood and stretched my neck and shoulders. A tube of Bengay would be welcome right now.

Rey tucked the links in the bag. "Now that we've handled it, we can discount fingerprints."

"I don't know how much of a print you could get, considering the size and grooves, but there could be some of the killer's DNA."

"We know the killer is pretty meticulous, so I'm betting there won't be anything convicting to be found," Rey contended. "And I'm also betting that whatever this came from won't be found, either." She held up the bag and eyed it critically.

"You're probably right. It would be kind of like searching for a tiny needle in a huge haystack." I rubbed my tense neck. "But I can't help ..."

"What?"

"Feel like I've seen that piece of chain somewhere before." I sighed. "We'd better get Sheriff Lewis."

"Hey, what about a weapon?"

"Huh?"

Rey offered a tired smile. "Why don't we look for one? That hole in her skull had to be made with something: a hammer, a gun handle, or maybe a brick. What do you say we check rooms as soon as we can? Prunella or Linda may have been rushed and tucked whatever was used under a bed or in a closet or wardrobe."

"I can't see Jeana's killer racing around the house with a weapon or brick, or anything else incriminating in the frantic search for a hiding place, but why not? We have nothing to lose. Let's make sure to ask Lewis if one or both left the drawing room at any time."

"What if they both left?"

"Then we're still down to two suspects."

"Unless there's someone we don't know about," she reminded me.

"Possibly, but not very likely. Didn't we agree on that – even if the shawl may have suggested otherwise?"

She pressed a finger to my chest. "You're the one who always says 'never say never'."

"I'll take the bag, Reynalda."

We spun slowly. Prunella stood fifteen feet away with a twisted smile as chilling as the tone and gaze. She'd been as quiet as a church mouse (or we'd been too absorbed in useless chatter). A hand-crank flashlight shone in one hand and a Beretta Tomcat 32ACP in the other; it resembled a toy, but wasn't for play.

"You'll have to kill me first."

The birder raised the weapon.

"No need to take me literally," Rey scowled.

She smirked, raised the weapon a little more, and nodded to the bag.

"So you're our killer, Pruney?" I turned to my cousin. "I was leaning toward Linda, what with the Smith connection and particularly the Moone deaths, but maybe they truly were accidents."

Rey offered a you-could-be-right look.

"Lewis has to be wondering where we are –"

"He may be wondering, but he won't be *looking.* He knows you're both always off on a sleuthing adventure. Besides, he's given up on keeping the group together, thanks to you two, so he's gone to check on Gwynne, who according to Deputy Budd, 'is groaning and moaning and looking like absolute crap'."

"You may have thought to scurry off with the weapon, but you got careless with the links."

She scanned my face. "Do you even know where they're from?"

I scanned hers in return – and remembered. "They came from that pendant you wore when you arrived. Percival said you wore it almost always – you had for years – yet you weren't wearing it for very long here in the house."

"That's right!" Rey exclaimed.

"You're good," Prunella smirked.

"Did you lose it when you were killing someone? Jensen perhaps?"

She appeared to consider what she wanted to reveal, then shrugged. "Jeana found what was left of my lovely antique necklace in a corner of the cellar. She looked preoccupied, as if she were set on a critical mission. I asked what was up and she told me she'd found something potentially peculiar and was going to head over to the station."

"Naturally she had no reason to suspect there was anything to your casual, curious question," Rey said sarcastically.

Prunella's smile was smug. "I convinced her to show me what she'd found, emphasizing how long I'd know the Moones and how often I'd been in the house. In all likelihood, I could identify what she'd found, and possibly even put it into perspective." Her expression was reminiscent of a mouser that had cornered its prey: focused, gauging. "When I saw what she had, I said I had a good idea where it came from and told her to meet me in the pantry so I could show her. I requested she not mention it to anyone because I had a suspicion who the killer might be, but didn't want to reveal anything until I verified something before we met. I suggested she dress up for a quick departure to the station in case I was right. She bought it." She glanced at the body and snickered. "Literally."

"So Jeana wouldn't have suspected anything, like you swinging at her," Rey commented dryly. "But then I guess you don't look like a typical murderer or fucked-up fruitcake."

"I'm quite affable," Bird Lady simpered.

"As a person? Or a partner?"

"Come on Prunella, tell all," I coaxed.

"In your dreams, my darlings." Another simper. She gestured the bag. "Enough chit-chat, Ms. Weather-Girl."

"I prefer Ms. Meteorologist."

Rey stepped back and I tried to buy more time in the hopes that a plan of attack and/or escape would fly to mind like one of her swift-swooping feathered friends.

She looked from me to Rey and back again. "Give me the bag. I'm not asking again."

"Prunella, even if you've left DNA or some identifying substance on the chain, why risk –"

"Coming back down here?" she snapped, then inhaled sharply. "I needed to take another look to ensure nothing else had been left behind, including two nosy aspiring detectives. Although I must admit, I'd not have expected you to find her ... at least, not so soon. Back to the bag: please hand it over."

"You could just shoot us dead and take the stupid thing," Rey suggested hotly.

"Hey!"

"Sorry, Jilly, but she *won't* shoot us. It would bring people down here."

Prunella burst into laughter – that haunting hyena sound again. "They would never hear the shots, Reynalda."

She lifted her chin. "Sure they would."

"You aren't the brightest bulb on the marquee, are you honey?"

My cousin offered a dazzling smile before spinning and screaming, "Do like Cousin Chucky!"

A crazy summer episode during our teens had banished us from the Catskills. It flashed before me (why and how I recalled it after all those years I'd consider for days to come). Rey threw herself into the wall while I gripped and swung the mallet like a pro hitter presenting one awesome swing arc. Prunella Sayers' head did a backspin.

Skin split and teeth cracked, and red oozed onto a caramel-colored cashmere jacket. Her gaze registered shock as she peered down at the carmine that resembled Rorschach inkblots. She pointed the gun, but before she could pull the trigger or I could throw up, I jumped forward and propelled her into a concrete wall like a Caterpillar D9 running amok. Hitting cement with a bone-splitting clack, she fell like a bag of wet grain.

"Is she dead?"

"If she's not," I answered, "she's a foe worthy of *The Terminator*."

"It never happens that fast in the books or in the movies."

We gazed downward.

"Pretty gruesome."

"That's an understatement," I murmured, staring into Prunella's still, hideous face.

26

Who REALLY Did It?

Lewis' office was a 10' X 14' room painted edamame green and parsnip white, and was filled with furniture that could have come from the Sally Ann. Crammed inside, it felt as if we were in a *Murder She Wrote* episode, waiting for the murderer to be unveiled – after we went around the group a few times, of course, and challenged each other with pointed, accusing fingers.

It was 4:00 a.m. Tuesday, and hours since Jeana and Prunella had been transported from the passageway to the morgue and hospital respectively. Gwynne had been taken to the same hospital. The flu he'd been experiencing could actually have been food poisoning – emphasis on "poison". It was a good thing Lewis hadn't met the same fate; obviously he'd avoided ingesting what the deputy had. Had Bird Lady engineered the entire Connecticut caper? Or had she had a partner, sharing equal – and evil – responsibility? Had that been Porter perhaps? Or had he merely been an errand boy?

It was an investigation Augustus Jacob Lewis was not looking forward to conducting. Jeana had been family and Cousin Hermeena, Jeana's mother, was not going to let anything or anyone slip through any legal cracks. She was prepared to take on the town, county, and state if necessary. In terms of Prunella, however, he was ready to write her off as mastermind and executioner, and no one felt much like presenting an argument.

A young pug-faced man carried in a long cardboard box filled with large cups marked coffee and hot cocoa, small cartons of milk, thick egg-salad sandwiches, containers of maple oatmeal, pastries and cookies. Everyone, including a dispatcher and mechanic, dove in. The remaining Moone mansion guests and their hostess buried tired faces into the tasks at hand: appeasing grumbling tummies and avoiding one another.

"I hear main roads in the area have been plowed and salted, and are travelable, if ya'll drive with care. Some trains and buses outta be moving by early-morning rush hour," he announced with a pronounced Waco accent. Tiny lips sporting remnants of an ugly cold sore smiled wearily and with a nod, the sapling-thin rookie left.

Lewis sauntered in, grabbed a hot cocoa, flipped the lid and took a noisy gulp. "We must have set a record for the numbah of killings in one location in five days."

Aunt Mat put down her oatmeal, got up, squeezed his shoulder, and ambled to a small narrow window. "What? Only one media van?" she asked flatly, peering through faux wood blinds.

"It's still early. A couple of TV crews are ten blocks ovah at a bakery fire. The place has been known to bake the best breads and buns for miles, and has been in Beth Seth's family for three generations. It's big news. So's the roof cave-in at Mort's Mad Mattress Mezzanine. It crumpled under a mass of ice like it were a house of cards. There's nawt one bed left. Othah media folks are likely stuck behind plows or storm chasing."

Lewis started to sit when Budd, carrying an industrial-size coffee and sporting a colorful scabbed chin, peered in and gestured. All eyes followed the sheriff as he closed the door behind him and joined the broad-shouldered man in the hallway. They chatted in low tones and ignored us as we, brimming with curiosity, ambled up to a tiny interior window with partially drawn plastic blinds and watched.

Rey, the only one standing smack-dab in the middle of the window, sucked on an almond croissant, her gaze affixed on the two gents like a cheating student keeping a leery eye on the pre-siding professor. "What do you suppose they're discussing?"

"Maybe they've discovered something," Aunt Mat replied astringently, retrieving the unfin-ished oatmeal and dropping into Lewis' mesh-back chair. "Like *solid* evidence for a welcome change."

Rey continued to watch. "I'd like to know how Pruney Sayers found out about the passage-ways."

"We had rather 'liquid' affairs over the years, which sometimes resulted in overnight stays. There were numerous opportunities for her to snoop around and get into old blueprints and plans. Or she may have learned of them through Porter, who may have discovered them while in my employ. Or maybe Reggie mentioned them at one time or another," our aunt offered casually, adding sugar to a cold cup of coffee. "As I told Jill initially, I'd suspected her – along with Percival and/or Thomas – of replacing authentic pieces from my husband's collections with fakes. The passageways were ideal for transferring items secretly from one place or home to another."

"That seems like an awful lot of work and risk, never mind the laborious task of actually transferring the items," I announced. "I'd be more inclined to believe the fakes were shipped after Percival made the purchases."

"Whenever the trades were made is irrelevant." Aunt Mat's expression grew solemn. "I wished I'd been wrong about all this, because I'd considered her such a ... a precious friend."

"I'm sorry," Adwin said with a placating smile.

"As the saying goes, shit happens." Her expression bordered on dejected.

"When they investigate Prunella further," I mused aloud, "they'll probably find funds in various accounts and/or business ventures. She had to have stashed that ill-gotten money somewhere and I'm wagering it wasn't in a mattress."

"Percival must have discovered something while we were at Aunt Mat's house, but what?" Rey looked thoughtful. "Had he seen his sister move through a wall? Had he found bank statements or receipts in a purse or drawer? Had he overheard her talking to a crony?"

"Whatever it was, he lost his life for it," I responded.

"Which goes to prove that love or family *isn't* thicker than blood," Rey said wryly. "She killed her half-brother, and long-time lover."

"She killed *two* long-time lovers," I clarified. "Thomas Saturne was one as well, as you so eagerly and frequently stated. But what her actual relationship with Porter was may never be known."

"He had a small stake in *Le Cochon Volant*, so there was a definite business relationship, even if only minor," Linda reminded us. "You know, given her knack for cheating and stealing, and his past, the two of them could have been working together back then to defraud Wiffleton, the co-owner. Maybe they were running a scam like substituting high quality foodstuffs with low-grade items, and pocketing the difference."

"I wouldn't put anything past her. Maybe those San-Fran days were when her interest in thieving began," Rey said. "I'm still curious about the whys, though – like, why Jensen and why Porter?"

"Why Percival? Or for that matter, Thomas?" Linda added.

Adwin dipped a madeleine in cream-laced coffee. "If you don't mind me playing Joe Mannix for a minute, how about this? Who better to help Prunella gain regular access to the house than the household cook? It's a slam dunk. They most likely had blackmail material on each other from those San Francisco days. Maybe Prunella had more on Porter than he did on her, what with the bomb or whatever caused the explosion, but either way, they had stuff on each other that bonded them for life … until one bond, and life, had to be terminated for the other to continue."

Linda eyed him curiously, as if considering his assumptions, then nodded. "Once you dance with the Devil, you're his partner for life."

"But who's the Devil? Porter or Prunella?" Adwin bit into his little sponge cake carefully, trying to avoid contact with scabbed lips. He gazed around the room before stopping at me. "You mentioned that nothing could be proven in terms of the explosion, so it's anyone's guess as to whether it was an actual accident or not, but considering what you've told me about Porter's past, I'm inclined to think he had a self-centered, dark streak. Let's go back to that scathing restaurant review. As a proud chef, he would have been angry and humiliated, so he'd have wanted payback. I'd want the same if some-one claimed my Cherry-Berry Chiffon Cloud Cake was bland or boring."

"But you'd never act on it," I said.

"Wouldn't I? It's amazing what you can do with butter cream or a roux," he responded with a strange smile. After another bite, he contin-ued. "Regardless whether Porter knew the critic

432

would be at *Le Couchon Volant* with Prunella, or alone, he wasn't going to stop with his plan to exact revenge. If Prunella was a casualty, it was no skin off his nose."

"But it *was* skin off her chest and sites unknown," I said matter-of-factly. "Believing he was responsible, which wouldn't have been hard to assume, she kept silent –"

"Until she needed something," Rey jumped in, "and that was Porter's services here at the mansion."

"What about the frozen fish episode?" Linda asked, bemused. "Had she done it in retaliation for the explosion, or had she simply become super stressed or manic as she was recuperating?"

"It may have been a spontaneous act – strain and anxiety taking its toll – or it may have been strictly for show. Prunella had made her point." I smiled wryly. "Or rather the swordfish had."

Aunt Mat leaned her head one way and then the other, as if absorbing the validity of what had been put forward. "In retrospect, it does seem odd that over the years Prunella never went into the kitchen or had any interaction with Porter … not that my guests normally did, what with the man's self-proclaimed shyness. But Percival managed to exchange a few words with Porter whenever he went to get water or soda, which he was always pleased to announce upon return. I believe he felt privileged or something."

"How did Prunella react when he did that?" Linda asked.

A groove deepened below Aunt Mat's hairline. "She ignored him and moved on to other topics."

Rey said, "Obviously she wanted it to seem as if they didn't know each other."

"That was probably fine with Porter," Adwin acknowledged. "I'd certainly want to stay out of someone's way if they held something threatening over me. The guy undoubtedly came here to turn over a new leaf and had no idea who lived nearby. He settled in nicely and was happy in his new private cook role. And then what happened? Queen Dragon Lady re-entered. Suddenly, everything was turned upside-down. He must have felt a stiff noose tighten around that thick neck."

"And the only way to loosen it was to do Queen Dragon Lady's bidding," Linda frowned. "Did that make him a poor misfortunate chump or a cold-blooded conniver?"

May-Lee put down a partially eaten trail-mix cookie and gazed sadly at her friend. "How awful for you to have conspiracy and collusion under your very roof – from people you cared for and trusted."

"Conspiracy, allusion, *and* murder." Linda rose and stepped alongside Rey. "Dang, that was one *kooky* lady."

Rey's unspoken comment was registered on her face: takes one to know one.

Lewis reentered, Budd on his heels. "We're going to put you up at a cornah hotel for today and tomorrow. We'll have a couple of officahs keep watch, just in case, uh … just in case."

"That Augustus Jacob Lewis, sounds suspiciously like 'you're under house arrest'," Aunt Mat sniffed.

"Mathildah Moone, I'm simply being vigilant and ensuring your warmth and safety. With no powah at the house, you're much bettah to remain in town for a couple of days. As you're aware, buses are on holiday schedule today. A train has derailed four miles east of here and it looks like signal lighting at the station is faulty, so there's no service at the moment. Who knows when they'll have everything cleared and fixed. It'd be best to remain in town, and I'd prefer that you do, but if you all *really* want to return to the house –"

"No!" rang the unanimous responses.

* * *

By the time we'd gotten settled in the hotel rooms it was after 6:00 a.m. Mini shopping excursions, quick naps, and light snacks during the windy, gray day quickly brought us to six p.m. The weather had finally cleared and warmed up a couple of degrees, but it promised to be cloudy and blustery for at least two more days. No matter. Even if it hadn't obliterated unpleasant memories, being away from the Moone mansion had quelled stress and tension.

"Man, this thing's as comfortable as a cheese cutter." Rey, grousing, was lying on a single cot in a corner fourth-floor hotel room she, Aunt Mat, and I were sharing. A heavy wool blanket was draped over bare legs.

"You can always share my bed," I offered.

"Why don't *you* take this thing and I'll take the bed?"

"Because *you* lost the coin toss."

She stuck out her tongue.

"Will you stop? It's a nice room: warm and antique-y." I was lying on my stomach on a comfortable double bed that would have made Mama Bear happy. "We've got dinner coming, a cute guard in the hallway, and a selection of good shows and movies."

Rey peeled off a huge thick camel-hair sweater that had belonged to our uncle. She'd found it folded among several others on an upper shelf in the first-floor rear closet when she'd decided to do a little more snooping. "The blond one is hunky, isn't he, but I'm not getting why we need a guard."

I shrugged and continued to brush my hair. "Maybe the sheriff thinks crazy Prunella will find a way of exacting revenge."

Rey snorted. "Yeah. I can see the woman – dressed like Madam Mummy – escaping the hospital confines."

"The water's still hot," Aunt Mat announced as she stepped from the bathroom, a large plush towel draped around her head and a thick fleecy bathrobe enwrapped around her lilac-scented body. She'd purchased the cranberry robe with matching spa slippers in a designer bed-and-bathroom shop across the street, and had bought me an ivy-green ensemble and Rey a watermelon-pink one. My cousin hopped to her feet and grabbed hers from the back of a wingchair in the corner.

Our aunt moved before a maple mini bar resembling a bisected globe, opened it, and surveyed the contents. "The wine selection is dubious, but the gin, vodka and blended Scotch are drinkable. Would anyone else care for an aperitif before dinner?"

"Make mine a double gin with lots of ice and a touch of tonic." Rey stepped into the bathroom.

"Mine, too." What the heck? A good stiff drink could be just what the doc ordered. I tossed the brush onto a nightstand, rolled onto my back, and eyed the French patterned ceiling relief made of traditional hand-cast plaster. "I'm surprised Linda opted to share a room with May-Lee."

"Why wouldn't she? May-Lee's very likeable." After Aunt Mat prepared the drinks and placed them on an end table, she sat down on a caned French bergere-style bow-fronted bed, propping two huge pillows against a curved walnut head-board. She leaned back with a contented sigh. "Linda must be tired of the whole nasty business and if she's going to get any peace, she knows May-Lee's a better choice for a roommate. The three of us won't cease talking about it."

I sat upright and took a long sip. The icy-cold floral-toned alcohol warmed a path from my freshly scrubbed face all the way down to my newly painted gladiola-red toes. I wiggled them and absently noted how nicely the red worked with the green robe.

"I'm surprised Adwin didn't suggest you two share a room."

I grinned. "*He* must be tired of the whole nasty business, and knows we won't cease talking about it."

We laughed and toasted each other across the room.

"He was pretty adamant about having quiet and lots of sleep. He knew he'd not get either if we stayed together, so he selected Fred the Cat as a roommate." I took another sip and sighed softly. It felt good to sit back, relax, and be free of the madness of the preceding days. "Do you think Lewis is keeping close watch on the Bird Lady from Hell?"

"He'd be a fool not to," Aunt Mat responded. "I wonder how she'll do once – if – she recovers."

"The early morning surgery was successful. Lewis called while you were in the shower to say the doctors were more optimistic than not."

"I was referring to her mental state. That mallet may have caused facial disfigurement, but the knock to the head had to have resulted in some cerebral damage. And you have to wonder: just how sound or stable was she to begin with?"

"You've known her a long time –"

"Apparently not long enough," she sniffed, "to realize she wasn't who I thought she was."

I smiled dryly. "She was either a great actress or a truly demented individual. Or likely a little of both. Whatever the case, no one would have – *could have* – been the wiser."

My cell phone announced a call. I grabbed it from the corner of the bed where it had been tossed earlier. Caller ID informed me that Johnny Gorcey was calling. "Hey Sherlock."

He chuckled, then sobered. "I heard about the murder."

"I'd make a joke about 'dropping like flies', but I might actually laugh."

"Laughter's a good cure-all." He drew on something, maybe one of those cigarillos I imagined he might smoke. "I got something on those two people: Gruber Pathos and Santana Anna Dinero. It took a bit of prying and delving."

"I'm all ears, my friend."

"Pathos appears to have been 'born' ten years ago. He showed up as a major client for a Spanish company ... owned by Percival Sayers."

I sat pillar straight. This was getting interesting. "Major as in purchaser of countless antiquities and the like?"

"That's right. I managed to get a list of items this guy bought. My investigator instincts told me to see what exactly had been purchased by friends and relatives of Sayers. Don't ask how I got the lists," he advised. "Are you sitting down?"

"I am."

"Almost all the articles purchased by Pathos were the same as those purchased by your aunt's hubby ... at discounted prices."

Stunned, I couldn't speak for several seconds. "This has to mean that Gruber Pathos was the scammer, the replacer of authentic pieces with fakes."

"I'd have to agree. He was purchasing replicas."

"What other details have you got? Is there a photo?"

"There's no photo to be found, but he resides in Zurich and heads an offshore investment company headquartered in the Commonwealth of Dominica. He also oversees a non-profit agency with a focus on eco-friendly manufacturing in Latin and South America."

"Curious. Thomas Saturne did pro-bono work for non-profits."

"There may be a connection if we dig deeper."

"What about Dinero?"

He grunted. "There's no information on her before she became a board member of a Swiss investment firm."

"Does she reside in Zurich, too?" I asked blandly.

"Geneva."

I smiled dryly. "Was she recently 'born', too?"

"Almost to the day Pathos was. Do you want me to keep searching?"

"At this stage, I'm not sure it would prove of much value save for appeasing curiosity," I responded. "Still, we should tie up loose ends. With intensive investigation, I'm fairly sure Pathos and Dinero will somehow link to Prunella. Will you try to find that link?"

"You bet – even if it takes me in-person to the land of army knives and high-end watches."

* * *

A light but persistent knock on the heavy oak door sounded like a determined woodpecker. Aunt Mat arched a shaped eyebrow and got up to see who it was. Linda, dressed in freshly washed jeans and a thick taupe wool cardigan, sauntered in. Her hair was pulled back with several pretty crystal deco hairpins.

"I thought I'd drop by before dinner arrived and see how you're all doing." She glanced around. "This is larger and warmer than my room. And ..."

"Antique-y?" I asked drolly.

She smiled and noticed our drinks.

"Help yourself." Aunt Mat gestured the mini bar.

"Thanks." She pulled out a Bud, unscrewed the top, and took several swigs like a pool player who'd been engrossed in a marathon match or a person who'd had a rough time at the office. "What a day, huh?"

"What a week. But it's certainly been eye-opening," Aunt Mat responded casually, getting another Scotch.

"We're all so calm, considering." Linda leaned into a wall near the mini bar and regarded us intently. "I'm curious. Do you guys still believe I killed those Moones?"

"Did you?" Aunt Mat sat on a high-back, shrimp-colored mohair couch between two oriel windows. It was a lovely Louis XV styled piece, with cabriole legs that curved into the arms and frame, and would have nicely complemented the grande dame's drawing room. With slim legs crossed and dainty hands folded, she certainly looked regal sitting on it.

"Don't be silly," she scoffed. "And I didn't help Prunella, either. She did what she did on her own accord, with assistance from Porter and probably Percival."

Aunt Mat all but snorted. "If that were true, why would she kill Perc?"

"Because he no longer wanted to help, or she thought he was a liability." Linda took another swig and leaned forward, her expression intense. "The woman has no conscience, no sense of right and wrong. For her, everyone is a means to an end. Literally."

"True, she has no conscience," I conceded, draining my icy drink. "We'll never know the entire truth unless the police find written documentation, bank records or something concrete, or she confesses all, which I have serious reservations about."

Wet hair slicked back, Rey stopped just outside the bathroom door and regarded Linda with evident surprise. "Oh."

"Linda was offering her take on Pruney," I explained.

"Oh." She hugged the robe tighter, as if it were a protective layer or device to ward off evil spirits, noticed the beaded glass by her cot, and grabbed it.

"We've all agreed that Porter helped Prunella. He had access to the house at all times and could have let her in whenever I and/or Reggie weren't there," Aunt Mat said. "If Reggie were alive – good heavens. I couldn't even begin to imagine how he'd react once the shock dissipated." Her expression grew dark. "Even if Prunella were blackmailing or threatening Porter so he'd assist, I'm fairly confident she'd have ensured he'd received a decent cut. Financial incentives make for less disgruntlement and more loyalty."

"Better a rich blackmailee than a poor one," I concurred.

"Receiving financial incentive is definitely motivating." Linda showed signs of relaxing as she moved into a smooth faux-leather rocker recliner. "But why murder in the first place – why now, this past week, at the Moone estate?"

"Prunella had a thing with Thomas and he betrayed her by opting out of the relationship. She'd probably planned revenge for a long while, but had been waiting for the most fitting moment. The inheritance get-together – for reasons only Prunella can confirm – proved the perfect opportunity," Rey said simply, settling back on the pillows Aunt Mat had claimed minutes before. "She had easy access to Thomas at the house, and a helper to make sure all went smoothly."

The scriptwriting assistant's brow creased as she considered it. "You know, you're right. She'd have to have been waiting for an opportune moment, like this get-together. It would have taken a great deal of planning and accuracy to do it elsewhere, like at the New York office or his Long Island home. Too many people would have been around and too many things could have gone wrong."

"Makes sense," Rey agreed quietly, studying her gin and tonic.

Linda frowned. "What doesn't make sense is Percival being an accomplice to sticking a stake in someone's chest – or possibly even doing it himself – not to help a half-sister, lover, or any-one else. He was many different things, but a killer? I don't see it."

"Like Porter, he could have been coerced," I re-sponded. "If he'd been involved in the larceny, the theft, call it what you will, he may have wanted to protect Prunella."

"From who? Her own unhinged self?" Rey scoffed.

"Maybe he did it to guarantee her silence. I could see her threatening to spill all and impli-cate him, whether he was involved or not," Linda asserted.

"Good theories, ladies, but we're just flapping lips," Rey exclaimed.

I shrugged and turned back to Linda. "Why don't we get back to those Moones?"

"I *didn't* kill them." Linda paced around. "Yes, I took time off work. I called in sick, had an ill relative, needed dental work, or whatever. I lied a half dozen times in five, maybe six years so I could go on trips to relax and unwind, to have "me" time. If I was nearby at the time of the Moone accidents, then it was coincidental. Strangely but *truly* coincidental."

Pursing her lips, Aunt Mat studied the young woman.

I smiled dryly. "With everything that's happened, I'm sure the police will be investigating those 'accidents'."

Linda plunked the bottle loudly on a night table, her gaze as frosty as Rey's glass. She was about to say something when there was a rap-rap-rap at the door.

Rey elected to see who it was.

A scrawny, mouse-faced man murmured a greeting and rolled a laden cart to a large round maple table in the corner.

Rey turned to Linda. "You know the truth always comes out eventually, so –"

"You're impossible." She scowled and stomped from the room like a spoiled birthday girl who'd not received the slice of cake with the sweet, creamy rose.

"Something I said?" Rey asked innocently, closing the door with a sledgehammer-striking-concrete bang.

27

Three on a Dare

Four Scotches and four hours later, Mathilda Reine Moone was fast asleep. She reclined to the far left, her face serene, almost joyful, as if she were dreaming of tiptoeing through a vast sunny field of daisies. A couple of sedatives on top of the Scotches had undoubtedly contributed to the feeling-no-pain slumber.

There was some serious sleep to catch up on, so Rey and I had seen no reason not to get to bed early. But sleep wasn't coming easily, maybe because of the over-fatigued factor. Certainly the trucks chunka-chunking past and the guard pacing past the door and chatting sotto voce on a Smartphone weren't helping. My cousin, I was pretty sure, was mentally rehashing the events of the last few days, because she was normally a restless sleeper, and at the moment she wasn't moving a muscle. Her brain, like mine, was probably on overdrive.

The day I'd arrived at the grotesque Moone manor, the film *Two on a Guillotine* had invaded my thoughts. If I'd been born male pre-1960, I might have had a thing for Connie Stevens, who played Cassie Duquesne in the film directed by *Jake and the Fatman*'s William Conrad. I'd have wanted to be reporter Val Henderson, played by the ever-cute Dean Jones, who befriended the ever-cute blonde. For those not in the know, the premise of the film bore a familiar storyline to the one we'd been experiencing of late. Ceasar Romero, wonderfully eccentric as the magician-father, had an unusual clause in his will. As a result, a week-long stay in the creepy Duquesne manse resulted in several scary moments, where skeletons and strange little bunnies popped up at the darnedest moments.

The film had been a favorite of my mother's and the first time I'd seen it I'd been four. I'm sure Mom had always dreamed of being Connie Stevens (she'd worn her hair in a similar fashion for the first six years of my life). The film had creeped me out, but in a fun way: a kid seeing a horror film for the first time. It hadn't been gory or grisly, but entertainingly frightening. It played upon your senses and made you squirm. Nothing was what it appeared. Everything had been a pretext, much like Aunt Mat's crazy scheme. Only she'd not wanted to lop anyone's head off; she'd wanted to ensnare whoever had been cheating her. So she'd claimed.

I rolled on my side and eyed the attractive woman. She was a walking encyclopedia, her head filled with "trillions of tidbits of junk" (as Aunt Ruth June had once claimed). Wacky, lovable Aunt Mat had remained hidden while we'd dealt with the initial mayhem and murder. If anyone had had a perfect opportunity to help Prunella Sayers, she had. After all, *she* knew the passages, had access to medical, botany, and gardening books and manuals, and knew what made people tick.

When thoughts and musings refused to cease tumbling and colliding, I slipped from the bed, grabbed my robe and Rey's, and tiptoed to her cot. She shifted and was about to say something when I tossed the robe onto her chest and motioned her to follow.

Pocketing change and a hotel key card, I closed the door softly behind us, and nodded to Rey's "Cute Blond", who stood twenty feet down the overly warm hallway, before an arched window shrouded with condensation, phone in hand. Despite acne scars and a huge Terry-Thomas gap between the front teeth, he was oddly attractive when he smiled.

"We thought we'd stretch our legs … and maybe grab a late drink."

He scanned our garb.

"Too casual?" Rey asked with a sultry smile.

"If no one else is down in the lounge, you may get away with it." The remnants of a southern accent hung in his words, as if he'd been born and raised in Mississippi but had made an attempt to lose any trace of dialect or drawl. Close but no cigar.

"Maybe we'll just walk around a wee while."

"Ladies, I don't think that's a good idea –"

"We can't exactly leave the hotel dressed like this," I interjected. "Even if we dared, it's way too cold outside. We'd be Popsicles before we reached the end of the block."

He chuckled and motioned us onward.

"What's up?" my cousin asked when we reached a vending-machine niche three floors below. Her gaze focused on a section featuring chocolate bars. "You got any –"

Change found its way into her hand before she could ask.

Two PayDays dropped from their comfy little compartments. She passed one over.

It was fairly fresh and delicious. There was nothing better than a mix of salty peanuts and sweet caramel. "I'm going to run ideas by, based on what Johnny conveyed today. Don't interrupt, okay?"

An eyebrow arched. Mouth full, she held up a finger and I waited until she could speak. "How many bits of information have you received recently and not shared?"

"Only what I received today. Do you want to hear or not?"

"I'm all ears," she sneered, taking a big bite.

"What if Thomas was killed *not* because he'd dumped Prunella – and we've tossed this around previously – but because he was the chief, or counterpart, behind the misappropriation? He had access to Aunt Mat's and Reginald's accounts and contracts, and all things legal. He helped Reginald set up businesses, wrote up agreements and organized deals, oversaw financial dealings and arranged for antiquity shipments. He handled imports and exports. It wouldn't have been difficult to siphon funds, to switch authentic artifacts, antiques and antiquities with fakes *before* they arrived, especially if he had a couple of phony cohorts whose identities he used to do all the dirty work. Over the years, performed at a practical pace, the substitutions would never have been obvious. And they still wouldn't have been if our uncle's old friend and advisor hadn't visited and detected the fakes."

"So Prunella figured it out at some point and wanted in?"

"Or *he* wanted her in at some point to help smooth and conceal transactions ... a partner to make it work on both sides of the big pond. He invented Gruber Pathos and Santana Anna Dinero, and when necessary, he played Gruber and she Santana." I gave a quick rundown of the Swiss twosome.

Rey chewed thoughtfully and noisily, obviously relishing the sugary rush the candy was providing. "I wonder how and when they became lovers. Was it fraud first and romance second?" She eyed the half-eaten bar. "So-o, when he dumped her, that lucrative business venture they shared was a done deal, and a large source of no-tax income dried up. He'd cut her out of the picture and she was pissed."

"Very much so, I'm sure," I agreed. "The sweetest revenge would have been to use something against him to let him stress and stew. Killing him would have been too easy and not very gratifying."

Rey waved what was left of the PayDay. "Do tell, Cousin Jilly, *how* or *what* would she have used against him?"

I waved my bar in return. "This brings us back to the first hypothesis. She'd tell our aunt, knowing it would incense her. Prunella was totally banking on that."

"Which resulted in incensed Aunt Mat deciding to carry through with revenge." As if she were a deflating beach ball, Rey exhaled slowly. "Aunt Mat could have told Prunella to be patient, that she or they would strike when the moment was right."

"Maybe they set that perfect 'moment' in motion when our dear aunt and her equally dear friend planned a fabulous balcony death scene and inheritance get-together. Thomas topped the bequest list."

"What I'm not getting is why she would tell you about her suspicions regarding the thefts in the first place if she knew – courtesy of Prunella – that Thomas was involved. If they'd planned revenge, she'd have been smart to remain silent."

"She may have wanted to divert suspicion by pointing a finger elsewhere. She may have believed the thefts or substitutions would be discovered at some point, especially with the crazy goings-on. If she had me – us – believing there are several potential thieves, the truth may have simply become obscured because the focus would have been on the murders."

"I don't know, Jilly." Multiple lines wrinkled Rey's brow. "Aunt Mat's possible knowledge of, and/or involvement aside, we've thrown these ideas around in one form or another. There are way too many maybes. Do you have any fresh questions or hypotheses?"

"Just a continuation. What if *Aunt Mat* killed Thomas? She could easily have done so from a concealed room or niche. What if Prunella, in on the plan, grabbed the deadly dart from Thomas' neck and hid it, or had Porter dispose of it? What if Percival had seen his half-sister near Thomas' body, only at that time, he wasn't aware he was witnessing anything criminal? It dawned on him later. Maybe something said or done triggered the memory and he confronted her."

"I don't know, Jilly." The lines deepened. "What about Jensen? And Porter?"

"Again, I have to go with Jensen having learned something. He had documents in a brief-case in his room. Some of them listed company names and dollar figures, which is how I stumbled on those two names: Pathos and Dinero. If he'd found evidence and someone discovered this, his fate had been sealed." Eyeing the last of my treat, I reflected on arrival day. "I wouldn't have thought anything if I'd seen Prunella casually saunter past Thomas in the drawing room. And if I'd seen Porter and Prunella chatting in the kitchen, why would I have thought some-thing underhanded was going on? If Prunella were tucking something into a shoe box, would that have seemed suspicious? No. Simple every-day actions don't equal nefarious doings."

My cousin eyed her fingertips and then licked them slowly. "Next."

I leaned into a pineapple-yellow wall. "I'm in-clined to believe Porter was involved with rob-bing the Moones, pressured by Prunella or oth-erwise. We were saying Prunella was the one to coerce him, but it could have been Thomas who'd done the intimidating. I found an old photo of Porter in Thomas' room."

Rey's eyes grew so round she resembled a Philippine tarsier. "How come you didn't men-tion that?"

I offered a lame shrug. "It slipped my mind."

"Care to search those malfunctioning mem-ory banks and locate other things that have 'slipped'?" She slapped my shoulder. "Tell all and don't leave out a thing."

I provided a rundown of the two room searches. When she remained silent, either an-noyed because I'd not invited her on the quest or she was digesting the meager findings, I moved on. "I'm also inclined to believe the theory that at some point Porter developed cold feet – undoubtedly when bodies started piling up. As a result, *he* became one."

Rey held up a finger. "What if Percival was helping his crazy beloved Bird Lady *and* our aunt?"

"Then we have four of them –"

"A team?" She exhaled slowly and scanned the wall. "One mastermind, one accessory, and *two* co-conspirators."

I started to laugh at the absurdity, then stopped. Maybe it wasn't far from the truth.

"It still boils down to this, Jilly: we have no proof. You've been saying that often enough over the last few insane days."

"It's merely more conjecture, you're right." A tiny grain of doubt had been parked in the back of my mind for the last hour and it started to sprout.

"You've got that infamous Fonne I've-got-an-idea look. What's up?"

"Linda."

She groaned. "What? She's part of the murdering quartet? We have a *quintet* now?"

I smiled. "She's the scapegoat, Rey."

My cousin looked blank. "You've lost me."

"There's no arguing that she went on those trips, but what if someone arranged for them? What if someone paid for them?"

"What are you talking about? She called in sick and made excuses to have time off."

"What if they were just that – excuses? Her traveling to the places where Moone members died could have been arranged. There are coincidences and there are coincidences: *calculated* ones."

"Then you're saying she *wasn't* involved?" She looked as confused as a contestant on a game show having to choose between three prizes hidden behind three big boxes.

"What if she was *meant* to be in all those places when the Moones died so that at some future date, if events were questioned or accounts crumbled, it would appear as if *she* was responsible for those deaths?"

"It all seems so mindbogglingly fantastic," Rey said with a deep sigh, eyeing the vending machine. I bought two more PayDays and we regarded the space above each other's heads as we munched and ruminated. "Do you really think it was Aunt Mat behind the deaths?" she asked once she reached the next-to-last bite.

"There was no love lost between the lot of them. She so much as said so. People kill for lesser reasons."

Rey wiped nut fragments from her lips. "Maybe she's a true kook, like most of the family has claimed over the years." She frowned. "The Fonnes didn't think much of her marrying Reginald. I wonder why none of *them* died, other than from old age or ailments."

"The Fonnes weren't overly vocal about their feelings, at least not when our aunt was around, which wasn't often. Nor did they visibly shun her. The Moones, on the other hand, were arrogant and cruel. They ill-treated her, snubbed, and betrayed her."

"Okay, I'll buy killing judgmental, in-your-face-rude relatives. But now – brother-in-law Jensen aside – she starts killing *non*-Moones? Is she that crazy or blood-thirsty?"

"If you were zany to begin with and then you became super pissed off –"

"And had someone *fuelling* that pissed-off state – sure," she declared, straightening. "Yeah, you might just snap."

In contemplative silence we got into the elevator and found a grim, weary-faced Budd leaning into a mirrored wall, a cardboard tray of coffees in one gloved hand and a large take-out bag in the other. He looked us up and down.

"We needed to get out of the room for a bit," I said with an casual smile. "It looks like it's been a very long day for you."

He managed a weak smile in return. "It's been a very long *week*."

* * *

Linda peered into the winding corridor, blinking against the bright hall light.

Rey pushed her way into the L-shaped room and I followed. It was smaller than ours, its eighteenth-century replica furniture bathed in topaz thanks to raised stripe-print Roman shades that enabled a huge neon cocktail lounge sign across a quiet snow-lined boulevard to shine through. On the farthest four-poster oak bed, May-Lee reclined on top of a gold-and-peridot striped quilt. She was wearing Natori animal-print pajamas and engrossed in an old Jonathan Kellerman novel.

"No early night for you two?" Rey asked with a sassy smile.

Dressed in a baggy mustard-yellow T and flannel pants with huge sunflowers on them, Linda jerked a thumb at the wall. "Who can sleep? Frick and Frack keep alternating between high-school lovemaking and gang war-zone hate. I'm not sure which is more disturbing: the groaning and moaning or the swearing and slapping."

"A good book helps distract," May-Lee held hers up. "To a point."

Rey switched on a fake Tiffany bedside lamp and sat on the edge of a second four-poster oak bed. "It's quiet now."

Linda smirked. "Give it five or ten seconds."

Sure enough, "Frick and Frack" started swearing and yelling like agitated guests on a Maury Povich episode. Rey regarded the lamp beside her, shook her head, and reached into a nightstand drawer. Extracting a Bible, she thumped it twice against the wall.

"That's sacrilegious, isn't it?" Linda asked, moving alongside a wheat-shield wall medallion, her expression grim.

"What's sacrilegious is the way those two numb-nuts are behaving at this time of night."

Someone banged back.

Rey's brow shot up. She rose and stamped from the room.

Linda smirked. "Trouble's on its way."

I had to chuckle. Two minutes later, Rey returned, her expression smugly triumphant. "They'll be behaving more like Bert and Ernie on Valium now. Where were we?" She dropped into a boxy, padded armchair in a far corner of the room.

I turned to May-Lee. "Do you think we could talk to Linda in private?"

"You could," she smiled dryly, "but at this point are there any reasons to keep secrets from one another?"

"There's no reason May-Lee shouldn't stay," Linda stated firmly.

I dropped into a plush recamier sofa across from Rey. "I'm going to bet the trips you took at the time of the Moone deaths were arranged by someone other than yourself. Who?"

Linda's eyes widened. Then, she sighed. "That 'someone' is a good guy and I don't see that it matters *who* arranged the trips."

Rey looked surprised. "A guy? Who?"

"A distant cousin … John Jonah Smith." Linda moved to the window and stared onto the street. "I haven't seen John since I was a kid, but he's been nice enough to send me on a few spa retreats over the years. He and Mom had always been close. A few months after the accident, he sent a letter explaining he'd once promised Mom that should she not be around, he'd check regularly on my brother Lido, my sister Loretta, and me."

"I hope you're not ending the story there," Rey said after several seconds of silence, then held up a hand. "Hold on. John Jonah Smith? … I've heard that name before. Where?"

"Maybe when we were hanging out in the evenings – you memorizing lines and me emailing or writing." She scanned her friend's face. "I think I recall mentioning him a couple of times way back when. Anyway, there's not much of story. Cousin John had always been shy and awkward with people, so his idea of checking in was two or three times a year. End of short, dull story."

"He's a writer or something like that, right? Where's he live?"

Linda crossed her arms. "He was a freelance writer, right – primarily of articles and manuals related to engineering, aviation, and science. I used to read his stuff now and again. It was very dry, but kind of fascinating. He had residences in New York and Atlanta, but since he retired from writing and the world a few years ago, he's been living outside Portland, Maine." She looked at me. "In the beginning, he'd send a postcard every six months. Then a few years later, when I was in my twenties, he'd started to send how-are-you-doing emails.

"He'd also started sending sweets: primarily chocolate-covered almonds and salt-water taffy. His favorites maybe. And starting about six years ago, every ten months or so, he sent an airline or train ticket to a nice little spa, as well as a hundred dollars. He said he had contacts and got good deals, so I shouldn't worry about it or question it, just accept and enjoy.

"In terms of Lido, he sent theater and film tickets and books, because Lido loves both. Loretta would get Hummel figurines, because those were her thing. He claimed it was the least he could do for the family, especially because he had so much, thanks to his successful real estate broker dad, and we had … well, lots less."

I asked, "When did you last receive a gift from him?"

Linda frowned. "A couple summers ago, I guess."

"He sent you to Myrtle Beach, the same week that Helena Moone died?"

"Yes, I suppose," she replied quietly.

"Has he emailed you since?"

"Yes, three times."

"In recent years, he usually gets in touch through emails. No calls?"

"There were no calls, ever, but I do have a telephone number somewhere. And it's a Yahoo address before you ask."

"You didn't think it strange that he never picked up the phone?"

"Cousin John suffered from laryngeal cancer eight years ago. He once wrote that he shied away from speaking because he sounded like a toad with a bullfrog in its throat." Linda regarded me for several seconds. "I come from an unusual family. We never did – or do – things in a 'normal' way. We've all been known to be quirky and some may even say eccentric, like the Moones."

Rey snorted. "You obviously haven't heard enough about the Fonnes. Now there's eccentric if not crazy."

Linda chuckled, as did Rey and I, while May-Lee regarded us with something akin to sadness.

I turned to the lounge sign, which started flickering, then died. So did most of the lights on the other side of the boulevard. "Throat cancer's a great excuse for not picking up the phone and talking."

"I was ten or so when I last saw him at Aunt Nora's and nineteen when he got in touch again. I don't think I'd have recognized his voice one way or the other, if you're trying to suggest it may have been someone pretending to be Cousin John."

Rey leaned back and scanned the scriptwriting assistant's face. "You might have recognized Aunt Mat's, even if it had been disguised."

Linda looked dubious. "I don't think I'd have recognized hers, either. I'd only met her once before coming here – when she visited you for a week – and talked to her twice on the phone." Her eyes widened. "Are you suggesting your Aunt Mat is involved?"

"My good heavens," May-Lee murmured, sitting upright. "*Are* you?"

Rey gazed from one to the other, her expression solemn. "It's a strong possibility."

Linda looked as perplexed as a recently-elected politician being questioned about broken campaign promises. "I'm officially confused."

Rey nodded to me. "Jilly thinks Aunt Mat killed those Moones."

May Lee's "why?" came out as a shriek.

"Vengeance. She hated the Moones."

"But Reginald loved her," May-Lee said. "… Didn't he?"

"I wonder," I murmured.

"You think he married her for what – money?" Linda appeared perplexed. "She had none. Isn't that what you told me, Rey? He, on the other hand, had tons."

"He did," she affirmed.

"She was young and pretty, and quite a character," I pointed out. "Very tempting and desirable for an older, unsociable gent."

"She was full of jokes and pranks, and silly-fun ideas," Rey added. "An old, cold fart meets a pretty, young thing full of whim –"

"Vim," I corrected automatically.

"Whatever. She was the type of woman he thought he'd never attract in a hundred years."

"Not 'attract'. Own," I emphasized. "He collected things, remember?"

"He collected *oddities*," May-Lee affirmed quietly.

"And she is pretty odd." Rey smiled wryly. She gazed from one face to the next and slammed a fist into a palm. "First thing tomorrow Linda, I want you to track down your cousin. Let's see if he's one and the same who's been sending you on retreats."

"I can do that." Linda glanced from Rey to me. "But who's going to prove any of it if John denies it all? Who's going to prove I didn't go after those Moones, now that you've served that crazy idea to the police on a silver platter?"

Rey rose, stretched, and paced the thick French beige carpet. I did the same.

"I suppose pawing through rooms at the Moone house isn't going to do much good," Linda sighed. "As if there'd be proof to be found."

I halted. "You're right, there'd be no proof. The rooms have already been searched – for different reasons, at different times, by different people. There'd be nothing incriminating lying around."

"How about Porter?" May-Lee asked.

I shook my head again. "He may have kept something incriminating to protect himself, but it would have been related to Prunella – his 'just in case' if she trod on his toes too heavily. And it would certainly have been removed when he died. There'd be no loose ends."

Rey ceased pacing. "What about under floor-boards –"

"Or in hidden drawers?" I finished with a smile.

She arched a shoulder. "If there are secret passageways, why not secret drawers and compartments?"

"If they exist, all evidence would now be gone as Jill said. Your aunt is smart, and from what you're suggesting, pretty damn crazy," Linda responded grimly. "Like Prunella."

"Who's to say she knows *every* nook and cranny?" Rey persisted.

"She'd have known; she's lived in the place forever – a"

"But she didn't know about all the passageways –"

"She *claimed* she didn't. Drop it, Rey," I insisted.

Determination crossed Linda's face. "What about the Sayers' place?"

"What would we be looking for there?" May-Lee asked, curious.

"Something implicating." I moved back to the sofa but didn't sit. "Finding proof will be next to impossible. Getting a confession from our aunt: same."

"I hear a 'but'?" Linda coaxed.

"If Mathilda Moone believed we knew *what* to find and *where* to find it, because Prunella revealed something in the corridor while she was waving the gun."

"Something like a diary maybe?" Linda suggested eagerly with a gleeful smile.

"That's perfect Linda!" May-Lee smiled brightly. "A diary could detail transactions and doings, and *names*."

Rey clapped. "I love where this is going."

"Saying the two women *are* partners, I can't believe your aunt would have allowed Prunella to kill you. Besides the fact you're blood relatives, she's truly very fond of you." May-Lee's brow puckered. "I'm also finding it difficult to believe that we're talking about two potentially insane women having gone on two different killing sprees. What are the odds?"

Rey eyed me. "When May-Lee words it that way, it does seem unbelievable."

"In terms of Prunella, I'm fairly sure she was only planning on frightening us. She was probably going to lock us in an underground room and then inform someone where to find us once she was well gone. As for Aunt Mat, we're only theorizing. Again, those deaths could have been true accidents."

Rey appeared uncertain. "Maybe."

"If Prunella *had* killed us, she'd have had Aunt Mat to answer to. As May-Lee suggested, and we're inclined to agree, she *is* fond of us. I can't see Aunt Mat letting Prunella get away with murdering Rey and myself." I turned to May-Lee. "As for the Moone murders, *if* they were that, Aunt Mat can be the only other candidate if Linda didn't –"

"I didn't!"

I smiled at Linda. "Prunella would have had no reason to kill those Moones –"

"Other than the fact she's f'g nuts," Rey sneered.

"It doesn't fit," I said with a firm shake of my head. "The Moones lived in various cities in different states. How could the birder have known them? She kills for a reason, with purpose."

Rey's expression was grim. "We should check with Lewis about Prunella in the morning. Maybe she's revealed something since surgery."

"I doubt she'll awaken any time soon. Or be coherent anyway. She'd have to have been pretty doped up since they brought her in," Linda said.

"Even if she did speak, why would the sheriff be inclined to share the information with us?" May-Lee asked.

"Why would he *not*?" Rey challenged.

May-Lee smiled and rose. "I want a soda." She moved across the room and returned with four Cokes and straws. "I thought you might all like something cold, sweet and fizzy."

We did.

"Jill, perhaps this is the scenario you have in mind?" She took a quick sip. "You and your cousin are cornered in a cold, damp subterranean passageway. Prunella discloses something – such as her having kept detailed diaries over the years – because you asked or she wanted to boast. She decided to share this information, as either you'd be dead soon and the secret would die with you, or you'd be languishing in a hidden room until she was faraway gone. Then it wouldn't matter." Her gaze locked on mine. "Here's the ten-thousand-dollar question: why didn't you say anything about diaries to the police? Your Aunt Mat is going to wonder, if not ask. I certainly would."

"Easy peasy." I chuckled. "I always wanted to say that –"

"So Ms. Easy Peasy, why *didn't* we say anything earlier?" Rey demanded.

My smile bordered on the saucy. "Because we wanted to sneak over to the Sayers' house and get those diaries before the police did. Everyone – Lewis most of all, right? – knows we enjoy playing amateur detectives. We're inquisitive and persistent enough to want to solve the crimes."

May-Lee slipped onto the edge of the sofa, her expression eager and alert. "Why would it be in our best interests to be the ones to retrieve those darling little telltale books and not allow the police to find them, if they existed?"

I grinned. "Because we're inquisitive and persistent enough to want to solve the crimes."

May-Lee laughed while Linda looked pensive. "Maybe we better put our heads together and get our ducks in a row."

"I believe that's *Anas platyrhynchos* in a row."

Rey smirked. "Prunella would be *so* proud."

28

If the Diary Fits . . .

Seated at a large corner table by the only two windows in the hotel dining lounge, the group gulped back tar-strong coffee and devoured fluffy blueberry pancakes with homemade cherry preserves and local maple syrup like there was no tomorrow. Reminiscent of a coastal B&B, the place was cozy-quaint, warm from a log fire in a corner glass fireplace, and fragrant with sweet and savory morning cooking smells. Sheer pale-blue chiffon-like panels hung in one corner by a huge maple hutch filled with empty jam and Mason jars from various decades. Watercolors of valleys, gardens, and farms lined two walls; colorful ceramic vases and plates made by local artists on floral-carved pine shelving lined another. Predominant colors were soothing shades of copper rose and moonstone blue.

The four-lane main street was quiet. Testing freshly shoveled sidewalks were a happy looking middle-aged couple and their playful Collie and Schnauzer. All four sported similar plaid coats, which I found heartwarmingly cute and May-Lee thought inanely comical. The only vehicles to have passed in the last ten minutes were a slow-moving police cruiser, an electrician's van, and an old multi-dented Volvo that looked as if it had been parked in the middle of a golf driving range for a month.

Adwin and Aunt Mat seemed energetic if not animated compared to May-Lee, Linda, Rey and myself. Clearly they'd received restful nights of slumber while the four of us had had maybe two hours.

Linda had made two calls to her cousin: one to the number he'd provided years ago and one to a Portland address she'd located courtesy of the Internet. Both netted nothing; he wasn't there or wasn't answering. At the old number, a tinny emotionless female voice had provided a generic "please leave your name and number" message. The Portland number had no answering service, so Linda determined to try again later. In terms of the first one, it would be interesting to see if someone called back. And if they did, would it be Aunt Mat pretending to be Cousin John? Instinctively I gazed across the table.

She and Adwin were laughing over his favorite story: a piggies-in-a-blanket brunch turned food-fight fiasco at the restaurant last year, in which a chairperson had ended up wearing a "piggie" in both ears. I forked up the last piece of pancake and waited for the pastry chef to finish a story he never tired of telling.

Rey caught my eye and was far from discreet with the scrunched nose, questioning brow, and anxious tic. I glared at her and requested Linda pass a fruit basket. Rey rolled her eyes and popped a piece of syrup-heavy waffle past stiff lips as I bit into a tart pineapple spear.

Linda took two more pancakes from a huge platter and casually asked, "Do you think we'll be able to go home today – as in *home* home?"

"I hope so. Has anyone heard from Lewis?" Adwin looked across the dining area. A burly bear-faced officer of fifty-plus years, who we'd not been introduced to, sat in the opposite corner by the fireplace, sipping coffee and perusing a newspaper.

Aunt Mat glanced at her Tag Heuer. "It's nine-thirty. He should be here soon."

"Good. Then we can grab our gear and go." I winked at Rey and she gave an exaggerated wink in return.

Aunt Mat regarded us, but refrained from asking about the exchange.

"I bet you'll be glad to get back to the TV station, my little rhubarb cobbler," Adwin smiled, squeezing my hand.

"Actually, my darling apple crisp –"

"Oh, for the love of Pete," Rey snorted. "Will you two *fruitcakes* knock that off? All this cutesy love talk is sickeningly sweet."

Linda tried to swallow her laughter, but ended up sounding like a hippo expelling water. Aunt Mat chuckled and Adwin grinned. The reactions were contagious and the corners of Rey's mouth started twitching. "Okay, okay. Whatever turns the cupcake couple's cranks."

I turned back to Adwin. "I was thinking of staying a while longer, if Aunt Mat doesn't mind."

"I'd love to have you," she responded casually, "but why would you want to stay in a house that's seen so much … unpleasantness?"

"I don't mind if you don't," I replied nonchalantly.

"I'd like to stay, too," Rey announced.

"And me." Linda.

"As enjoyable as that sounds," May-Lee twittered, pouring the last of the orange juice from a thick glass pitcher, "I have a shop and clients to tend to."

Adwin's eyes grew wider while Aunt Mat's drifted from one face to another, stopping at Linda's. "The more the merrier, but why? If it's down time you're looking for, we'll do West Palm Beach for four days – my treat. I'll call my travel agent when we're back upstairs."

"That's very sweet," Rey said, leaning toward her. "Maybe we could do that after."

"After *what*?" Adwin demanded, bemused.

"After we check out Pruney's and Percy's place," she gleamed.

Aunt Mat didn't bat an eye. "Why would you do that? The police went through it yesterday."

Linda nodded and voiced confirmation. "While I was waiting for the elevator this morning, I overheard the one Jill calls 'Gnarly' talking to Charlie, the officer Roy's hot for. He said something about the roof-to-cellar search of the Sayers' place not yielding anything of note, and joked that it was obvious the owners were sufferers of serious OCD afflictions."

"There you go. Nothing was found. And there's nothing else to discover," Aunt Mat declared with a smug smile.

Adwin's fingers started drumming the edge of the table and his forehead developed a few deep creases. "What are you up to?" he demanded.

I gazed at Rey.

She arched a shoulder, feigning indifference.

"Rey, just spill the beans," Adwin ordered, switching from edgy to irked. "You know you want to."

She stuck out her tongue and pulled her chair near. "Okay, Jilly's boyfriend, here's the scoop: we're going to locate Prunella Sayers' diaries."

"She told you she had *diaries*?" Linda's puzzlement seemed genuine.

May-Lee's, on the other hand, seemed off. "Really?"

Rey slipped into B-movie-actress gear. "We did manage to ask a few questions before she started waving the gun like a demented bad-ass. It was like … like one of those old weekly mystery series endings."

"That's very true, but once we offered compliments about her talent at deceit and manipulation, she felt a need to brag," I added.

While we waited for a fatigue-faced waitperson, sporting a bronze name tag that read "Rolphie", to replace coffee pots and juice pitchers Rey leaned close. "Is this going to work? Last night we were saying that Aunt Mat may have been helping Prunella. What if we're wrong?"

"Let's bank on the fact Prunella is crazy and that she would not have shared everything with Aunt Mat," I whispered in return. "Let's go with it and see where this all takes us." I nodded to the waitperson after she refilled my cup and turned to my aunt. "Prunella proudly, if not arrogantly, stated she'd killed Thomas because a) he'd deserved to die for dumping her and leaving her flat, and b) he'd cheated you."

May-Lee looked dumbfounded and this time the emotion seemed real. "Are you suggesting she was claiming innocence and that it was purely Thomas Saturne switching authentic art pieces and collectibles with forgeries?"

"She diddn't actually discuss involvement in the switches, or swindling Aunt Mat." My expression changed from grave to earnest. "Maybe we'll learn more about her part, if any, when she's fit enough to speak."

"*If* she's ever fit enough," Adwin murmured.

"What about the other deaths?" Linda asked, leaning forward, her expression intense.

Rey popped a fat ruby-red grape into her mouth and looked from one face to the next. "She didn't discuss that, either."

"What *did* she discuss? Other than giving some quick details about needing to kill Jeana and Jensen, she must have mentioned *something*." May-Lee was pouring it on a tad thick with the imploring tone and rounded eyes, but at least she was steering the conversation in the direction Rey, Linda and I had hoped it would go.

"Lewis had advised us not to relay any more than we already had about what had transpired in the passageway while he waited for Prunella to provide comment. Based on what the doctor had communicated, he figured she'd likely be available for questioning a day or two after they investigated the Sayers' place."

"If he wanted you to keep it to yourselves, why share *now*?" Aunt Mat's tone was cool and her gaze frosty.

"We didn't feel it fair to keep the information from you indefinitely. Besides, Reynalda couldn't keep her lips sealed much longer," I replied casually.

Rey glowered.

I smiled cheerily, and mentally crossing my fingers, continued. "We thought we should locate the diaries."

Aunt Mat took a mini bran muffin from a dwindling pile and flatly asked, "Really?"

"Really." Rey smirked and gazed at me. "Jilly, tell the gang what Pruney said about them."

Nothing like being put on the spot. Discreetly but not gently, I jammed my foot on hers. "I'll paraphrase. Let's see... . Right. I've been recording dealings and transactions, names and dates, in my diaries. One never knows when one needs insurance or ammunition. Those you trust most are usually the ones to deceive you most."

Everyone gazed suspiciously around the table. Linda was the first to speak. "To think, if Jeana had been a little less trusting, she might have solved the mystery without having had to die in the process and Prunella might not have ended up in the hospital."

"Prunella's an odd duck – pardon the fowl reference – but who'd have imagined in their wildest dreams she was capable of multiple murders?" Adwin asked with a pensive brow.

Rey looked grave. "Obviously none of us."

"Think of all the lives that could have been saved." Adwin sighed woefully and sipped coffee while Aunt Mat started poking the muffin.

"Poor Porter," was all she said, and so softly, it was barely audible.

"Poor Percival," Rey said with a lengthy sigh.

I eyed my aunt. "Did Prunella know you were around and that this get-together was a sham?"

Her smile was lean, her gaze wary.

Rey leaned forward. "Do you *think* she knew?"

The grande dame frowned. "How could she? I kept myself well hidden. No, *no one* knew, not even the servants. If she'd had a hunch or suspicion, she'd have come looking. Remember how she appeared when I first walked in? She was *genuinely* surprised." The frown deepened and she stared into the street, where a courier and shopkeeper were conversing. "Of course, she could be one outstanding actress." Placing a hand to her chest, she appeared distressed.

I restated, "We can't be sure of anything at this point ... other than she kept transaction-based diaries."

"What about another angle? Maybe this was nothing more than Prunella wanting the entire inheritance for herself and that's the reason for the killings," Adwin proposed. "She killed Jeana because she had to – what with the piece of chain having been found – but maybe she'd planned to take out each and every one of us."

"Porter wasn't part of the inheritance-collecting crowd," Rey pointed out.

"But he was proving to be a problem," Linda stated with a tense frown. "Porter and Jeana aside, it's not as if she'd collect ten million dol-lars. The full amount – if she were the last one remaining to collect – wouldn't be enough to live in luxury for more than a year, at best... . No, I don't see the inheritance serving as motivation for Prunella Sayers committing murder."

May-Lee exhaled slowly. "This is becoming all so complicated."

"And vague." Adwin.

"And odd," Aunt Mat scowled.

"She was an odd woman," I reminded her.

"A real nut job," Rey said emphatically.

"Certifiable, certainly," May-Lee agreed.

"No question. That woman was a few feathers shy," Linda said, struggling to contain a smile.

Rey and I chuckled.

"What about Percival? Any new theories there?" Adwin asked, reaching for a slice of peameal bacon.

I took a stab, but it wasn't a terribly original theory. "He confronted his half-sister about what he suspected. He presented her with an ultimatum: confess or pay the consequences. Remember: he knew her extremely well. They'd been living together for years, and had had an intimate relationship. He believed she'd do the right thing and tell all."

"Or wanted – hopelessly – to believe that she would, the stupid fool," May-Lee said quietly.

"How wrong could one lovesick brother-lover be?" Rey.

Aunt Mat grimaced while Adwin's expression grew sour and he took a long sip of water, as if the action might wash away an acrid taste in his mouth.

"But Prunella didn't admit any of this, did she?" May-Lee asked.

Rey shook her head.

"Unfortunately, there are a lot of uncertainties when it comes to who did what and when," I added.

"And to who. Or is that whom?" Rey looked confused.

"Hopefully these many unexplained details will be clarified soon," May-Lee murmured over her coffee cup.

"Her diaries should clarify some of them," I said. "She'll be able to wrap up the rest when she's compos mentis."

"Huh?" Rey looked dumbfounded.

"Lucid."

"If she's ever lucid," Adwin said. "And only if she wants to."

"True. She doesn't seem to have much of a conscience. I could see her taking great pleasure in having everyone coax and beg for answers and her never providing any," Linda declared.

Adwin jabbed the crisp slice of meat with a fork. I could tell he was extremely upset and angry, even if it didn't register on his face or in his tone.

"I'm still puzzled by the diaries. Why would Prunella need to keep records?" Aunt Mat's tone suggested she didn't believe her former best friend would be so imprudent.

"Maybe she wanted to make sure she wouldn't take the fall alone should she ever be caught."

"Why detail your own involvement?" Aunt Mat demanded. "Why risk having someone find damaging evidence?"

"Who's to say she detailed her own? Maybe the purpose behind the diaries was to detail others, to hold something over them. Until we see what she's written, we can only surmise," I replied. "Maybe she simply listed names and transactions. November 1st: Thomas Saturne replaced bone saint applique with fake. March 23rd: Thomas pocketed £4500 from sale of Tang Dynasty camel."

"And you're sure she didn't bring these journals to the house?" May-Lee asked.

Rey and I exchanged glances, and my cousin offered, "We didn't ask, but can you see her risk having a diary fall into the wrong hands?"

"That couldn't happen at her own place?" Aunt Mat mocked.

"It's not as likely," I replied. "She'd know where to conceal things in her own home so they couldn't be found." It was hard to tell if she was buying any of it. Now that I heard it being vocalized, drama included, it did lean toward the fanciful – not impossible, but definitely fanciful.

"Pruney did seem to enjoy talking about how brilliant she'd been," Rey added.

Aunt Mat's head tilted one way and then the other, and then she smiled. "Yes, that's Prunella Sayers. If you get her started talking about herself or her charities and hobbies, she'll natter your ear off." She studied Rey. "You intend to locate the diaries, you said?"

My cousin leaned back and a trace of arrogance crossed her face. "Her plan was to zip home, pack a quick bag, and leave the country. Movie-time agenda. This means they have to be easily accessible, so how hard can they be to find?"

"If they are *that* accessible, my dear, why didn't the police find them?"

Rey smiled prettily. "They wouldn't know what they're looking at. Neither would you, if we hadn't told you. You'd see diaries and assume they're just that: dull daily journals."

"Interesting," our aunt murmured, eyeing her closely. "Just why do *you* want to find them? I believe it's illegal to tamper with or steal evidence."

"Who's stealing?" I asked simply. "We're merely helping prove that you were the victim of long-term theft and that Linda *didn't* kill those Moones."

Rey patted her longstanding friend's hand. "We realized that there was simply no way Linda could be a conniving murderess. Sure, she's held a long-time grudge against the Moones for what happened decades ago, because the property did once belong to some great, great relatives of hers. She was bitter when it came to the Smiths. With the curses and all that bad luck – *and* her mother's unexpected death – a person would want payback, wouldn't they? Not that they'd necessarily act on it. But they'd sure think it. No, we couldn't imagine she'd be so riled or that brainy to plot the murders."

"And successfully make them look like accidents," I put in.

"Thank you ladies," Linda said with a touch of brininess.

Rey extended both hands apologetically.

"Never mind." The scriptwriting assistant's tone and gaze were as icy as the recent storm. She was definitely not a bad actress by half. "What else did you talk about down in that dark, clammy corridor?"

I appeared suitably distressed. "Rey was distraught and on the verge of tears, and asked Prunella what she planned to do with everyone – us, and then the three of you."

Rey didn't care to be painted as emotional or sensitive and shot a you-bitch look.

"What did she say?" May-Lee pressed.

Rey's expression turned overly dramatic. "Not much except that people and circumstances were not necessarily always what they seemed."

"How curious," Adwin murmured, appearing perplexed. "Well, anyway, thank the Good Lord you two stopped her before anyone else died or suffered."

Aunt Mat drank coffee, her thoughtful gaze on the table. Suddenly, her face brightened. "When do we go find that bizarre woman's incriminating diaries?"

Rey and I grinned. "As soon as possible."

29

It Always Works Different in the Movies

The preceding hour had been spent touring an immaculate six-bedroom house that confirmed a taste for quality furnishings but not quality taste. Almost everything was dark and oppressive and heavy, perfect for an old English manor owned by a lineage of dreary lords. The only room that offered color and light was the solarium, Percival's domain and, according to Aunt Mat, his unequivocal pride and joy. It was filled with beautiful orchids, lush ferns, numerous herbs, and an abundant array of geraniums; it seemed out of place in the somber house. When I commented about the plants being left unattended for the week my aunt explained that Percival had hired a local professional and writing associate named Parr S. Lee to tend them. From the look of things, he'd done an ace job.

An officer had dropped us off at the Moone manse, courtesy of a crabby sheriff's terse request. After a tense conversation about meddling and foolhardiness, my beau had packed the rest of his stuff, gathered Fred and the feline's food, litter items and bell-filled toys. Taking the Sebring, he drove May-Lee home and himself back to the hotel, where he'd spend another night. I'd collect him and his new pet the following day and we'd return to Wilmington. Boyfriend and cat had bonded for life, which meant a visit to an allergist topped Jill Fonne's to-do list back home. Aunt Mat would miss the "fuzzy gent", but he did seem to prefer Adwin's bony lap to hers.

Taking the least amount of time as possible, Rey, Linda, Aunt Mat and I slipped into comfortable "detecting" clothing, collected flashlights, a digital camera, candles and matches (in case the electricity wasn't working or went out), a kitchen bread knife, and old Colt Thunderer with actual bullets from Reginald's modest nineteenth-century gun collection (in the improbable case an unknown crazy was in the house). Thirty minutes after the drop-off we were scooting out of the abode.

"Kind of creepy," Linda murmured, slipping off a heavy black cardigan and hugging it tightly to her chest as if it were a protective shield.

Spinning like a Lazy Susan rotating tray boosted by a bored kid at a Sunday family dinner, Rey pulled off a modboy hat and scrutinized a huge forest-green room with fifteen-feet high ceilings that accommodated dozens of rosewood shelves stacked to well-ordered capacity. Her expression was just shy of aversion.

The room, like the rest of the Sayers' house, was warm and stuffy. It was reminiscent of an early nineteenth-century college library where everything was carefully aligned and the air was thick with bygone knowledge and practices. Several birch logs lay in a large Greek-styled Victorian cast-iron fireplace that sported intricate detail and unusual bosses, a perfect fixture in a Boris Karloff movie. Dark paneling and oil paintings of English and French countrysides lined walls where shelving didn't exist. On the west wall were two multi-paned arched-head windows and a large rectangular stained-glass window depicting among other things a family crest: a pheasant and a magpie. Apparently the bearers of feathers and wings played a part in the Sayers' family history. That explained the bird fascination.

Bright mid-day sunlight did little to cheer up a room best described as stodgy. Three knights guarding three corners didn't make for a friendly feel, either. Had Reginald's taste for the medieval influenced the Sayers? Or vice versa? Or could it be, more people than imaginable were fascinated by the dark and dour Middle Ages?

The four of us stood in the middle of the library on a medallion in the center of an immense rectangular Persian rug. Suspended above was a Two-Tier Paris Flea Chandelier, a heavy antique fixture that could better have served a ski chalet dining room. Had we been in a movie, I'd have expected it to start swaying uncontrollably and crash to the floor in ominous warning.

"Where does one start?" Aunt Mat asked in awe, scanning a wall that surely held no less than five-hundred books. "Did Prunella give any indication where she tucked the diaries?"

Rey shook her head. "None. But they have to look different from all these leather-bound books, which pretty much look like legal or library collection type books. Right Jilly?"

"They're probably smaller or slimmer than most of the books here."

"The word 'diary' *won't* be embossed on the spine," Linda offered.

Aunt Matt looked around dubiously. "This will be like searching for a flea on a camel."

"Rey and I will each take a wall. You and Linda share one. There are two rolling library ladders, so we can alternate. Two of us will start at the top, two at the bottom," I instructed.

Aunt Mat eyed me critically, as if she thought I might be bereft of sense, but finally nodded. She turned, then stopped, her gaze on a rosewood partners desk beneath the stained-glass window. "Would she have hidden them in there?"

Linda frowned and turned on an Aladdin lamp on a Victorian library table. "That's too obvious, don't you think? It would be too easy to stumble across them."

"What if there's a hidden compartment? Those old desks usually have one or two."

"Good thinking, Aunt Mat," Rey said cheerily. "Let me check the desk."

I smiled drolly. "You do have those magic fingers."

She stuck out her tongue and stepped behind a tall back office chair.

Aunt Mat strolled toward the east wall. "Let's take this one, Linda. It's as daunting as any other. What a shame May-Lee opted out of helping."

"She's not much into playing detective," Linda said. "Besides, she does have a business to tend to."

Aunt Mat's smile was dry. "Yes. The customers are out in droves with this lovely summery weather."

Rey and I dove into the task. Would we actually find a diary? Yes, in approximately five minutes, give or take. It had to look good and real – or as real as calculating amateur detectives could make it look. Scheming and conspiring had extended into the early hours of the morning. We had no experience with criminal masterminds or psychopaths, or the mentally challenged, and Rey had never appeared in a legal or private eye series, so she'd never researched that realm.

What did we know about snaring a villain? Nothing. But we were eager to make a valiant attempt and condemning, detailed diaries seemed a worthwhile ploy.

The plan of attack involved Linda and I, both quick typists, keying Prunella's "observations" and "findings" into two laptops. Time being of the essence, we caught minimal shut-eye – a few minutes here and there – and then hastened to the print shop around the block, which fortunately opened at eight a.m. Everything was printed on different types of paper, cut and pasted and stapled into two heavy, fat blue leather diaries Linda had purchased at a card and gift store in the hotel lobby. We'd also inserted clippings from on-line newspaper articles – anything we could find in those hours that could add weight and believability to the crazy scheme. It hadn't been that difficult to put ourselves in Prunella's Birkenstocks, and Rey's overactive melodramatic imagination helped bring Bird Lady's madness to life.

Aunt Mat would doubtless question why Prunella had typed most of the entries, but Linda's reason was as (un)sound as any: Prunella liked things clean and neat and readable. Who could argue with that? What effect or result the diaries actually created remained to be seen.

"Eureka!" Rey's right-on-cue scream grabbed our attention. "Look!"

We scrambled to her side and gathered around. "Is it Prunella Sayers' diary?" Linda asked breathlessly.

Rey grabbed the journal that we'd stepped on, bent, and sprinkled with tea. A hair dryer had assisted in giving it a used, timeworn look. "It seems to be. Look, here's a clipping of Reginald Moone's obit. And Helena's and David Leigh's. And the others."

I took it and leafed through several pages. "She's listed meetings with Thomas, documented calls and get-togethers with Porter, who she refers to as Crackers, and there's reference to – hey, look Aunt Mat." I showed a page. "It says here Prunella was certain you would get even with Thomas after she'd discovered you'd found out about his stealing from Reginald's collections." We'd remained vague to avoid any blatant inaccuracies.

"Of course I was going to get even – during my inheritance extravaganza," she snapped. "I was going to *scare* him, though not the same way I was going to scare the rest of you." She grabbed the diary. "Odd, I don't recall sharing suspicions or intentions – of any sort." She started to leaf through it, stopping here and there. Finally she flipped to the back, where Linda had entered a few hastily scrawled notes, marred by watered-down whiskey. Could it fool Aunt Mat at first and second glances? We'd find out soon enough. Instinctively I moved into grade-school mode, crossed my fingers, and silently promised to be good for a week.

"It's proof of Prunella's involvement," Linda said with a weary smile. "I bet there is enough in here to shift suspicion from me. She held an interest in the Moone deaths that went beyond casual."

"Yeah." Rey gazed at our aunt curiously. "Any idea why Pruney would keep the obits?"

Aunt Mat smirked. "A sense of perversity?"

I reached for the diary, but Aunt Mat pulled away and strolled to a thickly padded burgundy leather sofa, and sat on the armrest. Then she regarded us closely, as if waiting for us to make the next move.

Rey looked around. "Odd. There's no phone in here."

"There's one is in the kitchen," Aunt Mat explained. "They cherished their privacy. Neither was big on talking to the outside world when they were at home, so it's the only one – for emergencies."

"I'll go call Lewis," Linda volunteered.

"What's the rush?" Aunt Mat asked casually. "You can call from my house." She glanced around and offered an exaggerated shiver. "This place makes me feel peculiar."

"It's kind of spooky, isn't it?" Linda agreed.

She offered a droll smile. "I wouldn't mind having an opportunity to read what Prunella claims people have done before it gets buried in police red tape." She turned to me. "I thought there were a few diaries?"

Rey and I exchanged glances.

"Let's keep looking," my cousin suggested.

"I could do with coffee, so while you're snooping around, I'm going home and read. I'll have a pot ready for your return. It will be burned and tarry, as it tends to be when I prepare it. I don't have Beatrice's or Hubert's touch, and I'd arranged to have someone collect the poor dears early this morning. They desperately need a week of R&R."

Linda and I looked at each other.

"Sure, go ahead."

"Sure," Linda repeated with a shrug.

I ignored Rey's are-you-nuts look. "As soon as we find the others, we'll join you – pronto."

Diary in hand, our tense-looking aunt ambled from the room.

"We didn't have a choice, Reynalda," I stated before she could comment or condemn. "She'd have become suspicious if we didn't let her go."

"Jill's right," Linda affirmed.

Rey frowned, then sighed. "Let's 'find' the other diaries."

"You mean *diary*?" Linda pulled it from her knapsack and we departed the library.

* * *

In the Sayers' foyer we started to slip on coats for the return jaunt through the cold when Rey made a dramatic proposal. "Why don't we sit in the Sayers' kitchen for a few? It has to be fully stocked."

"A change of venue wouldn't hurt," Linda agreed. "But what about your aunt?"

"I doubt she'll be doing much more than what she said she'd do. And we can't head back too soon. We're supposed to be on a hunt."

"You don't think she'll make a run for it as soon as she's read everything?" Linda asked worriedly.

"I don't believe she will, as long as she thinks she's the only one to have read the contents," I replied. "Besides, nothing in there out and out states she's responsible for anything. There are only ... suggestions."

"But she knows we're looking for more diaries and she's bound to think we're going to read them and assume –"

"What she'll assume is that we're going to bring them back as soon as we locate them. We promised to return pronto," I reminded her.

Rey re-hung her wool coat on an antique six-peg walnut coat tree. "Linda, you're doing sandwiches and appetizers. Jilly, you're in charge of beverages. I'll find treats and set the table."

"Follow me, kids." Linda pointed and took the lead like a self-assured hall monitor leading pupils toward the auditorium.

The rustic kitchen was as large as an outdoor public pool, darkly decorated, and glazed with heavy detail. Hardware merged with exposed stone and metals and carvings of milk and honey. It was well laid out and, like the entire house, immaculate. A cook's dream. Who wouldn't want the lovely Tierra Negra cookware that neatly lined high-gloss shelving between two arched windows?

"Hey-ho, crackers and cookies third cupboard, left of the stove," Rey announced, shaking a box of poppy-seed biscuits.

Linda opened the fridge. "We've hit pay-dirt! Milk and cream. Juice. Italian soda. Different cheeses and cold cuts. And bread – and it looks fairly fresh."

"Placemats and napkins and cutlery have been located. Put your table-setting skills to use, Rey." I pulled them from the middle drawers of a wood cabinet and strolled to a chrome coffee machine on a granite counter. "I could do with a caffeine jolt right now. Any coffee in there?"

"Three types. Let's go with the Kona." She started removing items.

A mango glow warmed the room when I turned on track lighting above a kidney-shaped island in the middle of the kitchen.

Rey began rummaging through boxes and packages in a cupboard. "What? No one likes *un*-healthy cookies?"

As Linda and I chuckled, I glanced out a window behind a large rectangular table in the corner. A large pond, wandering pathways, evergreens and two rock gardens were in immediate view. At the far end of the expansive yard were two dozen beautiful handcrafted bird-houses. With the blankets and drapes of white, it held a certain austere beauty, but in summer had to be absolutely stunning.

Linda started preparing sandwiches while Rey set the table.

"Do you think she's buying it?" I asked, watching fragrant coffee fill the pot.

"We'll know soon enough," Rey replied, regarding a pheasant motif on the placemats. "I'm surprised she doesn't have any stuffed feathered friends around the house."

"She's into the real thing," Linda responded. "I'm sure she'd find taxidermy sinister if not cruel, even if the plumed creatures had died of natural causes and not a hunter's gun."

I brought jars of mustard and mayonnaise to the table. "I'm getting a little nervous, to be honest. The diary details are pretty vague."

"You need fuel," Rey declared, directing me to a chair. "You'll be fine and fully positive in a few. Linda, where's our feast?"

"Here, my lady." She bowed and brought over a tray supporting a platter of thick crusty sandwiches and a plate of cheese and crackers.

Rey poured coffee and we toasted.

"Here's to de-throning a bone-chilling, killing queen."

"Here's to three women having some explaining to do."

We turned slowly, guiltily, knowing that Massachusetts accent anywhere.

"Why, Sheriff Lewis," Rey smiled gaily and extended her arms in welcome, looking like a presenter greeting a crowd at the Golden Globe awards. "You're just in time for an impromptu and very nummy lunch."

30

Almost Always

After an angry Sheriff Lewis had chewed out the three of us for trespassing and tampering, yadda yadda yadda, we'd dived into a tasty late lunch. Forty minutes later, he'd left with a respect-the-law message and us wondering how he'd known to find us at the Sayers (he'd pleaded the Fifth). Then three suitably chastised souls trundled back to the Moone manse and a warm, sunny kitchen where we found Aunt Mat looking relatively relaxed.

Rey's nattering and ill-tempered attempts at baiting, however, had soon worn thin on the sexagenarian, and hadn't set that well with Linda and myself.

"I'd like to look at it." Rey reached across the breakfast nook table for the diary our aunt had returned home with. The one we'd brought back rested alongside it.

Aunt Mat slammed the first volume on top of the second, then pressed a tiny hand on them, her hold secure and her gaze as frosty as the ice-clasped exterior. "Reynalda, we've had enough for the moment, thank you."

My cousin was taken aback. "Excuse me?"

"I've had enough of your petulance and impatience," she retorted. "These diaries belong to someone once considered a dear friend. I'd like to reassess what I've read so far, and peruse this new one. Leave them with me. They won't go far."

Taking a sip of tepid grit-your-teeth coffee, gaze fixed and tone measured, I leaned toward my tetchy aunt. Maybe Rey's exasperation was infectious. "We've gone through a few days of hell. It's been grim and gloomy, and it's been mysterious – hell, it's been a *nightmare* – but we should learn Prunella Sayers' secrets, and we should do it here, with all of us present."

Aunt Mat's delicate jaw shifted, but she remained mute.

Rey finished chewing a Medjool date and leaned across the table. "Suck it up, Matty

Moone. Like Jilly said, we've gone through hell. We want – and deserve – to know what's in there."

Aunt Mat's jaw shifted again.

Rey slapped the table. "Hand them over, Mathilda Moone!"

"Come on, Mrs. Moone, pass them over," Linda coaxed, giving her friend a peeved glance.

She gazed at me, as if seeking support, then cursed softly. "Fine." She propelled both across the table, causing two full cups to topple and cookies to crumble. French Roast splashed dried fruit and stained a taupe linen tablecloth and cornmeal-colored placemats.

Jumping up, Linda grabbed a roll of paper towels and started dabbing and wiping. Rey and I only managed to gape; this was a side of the older woman never seen.

"Something tells me you don't want us to know what's in there," I challenged.

Her smile resembled Jack Nicholson's The Joker: sinister. "I believe you already know what's in there."

Linda passed me the diaries, tore off more paper towels, and continued wiping up the mess.

"You've been playing me since we got back ... and even before."

"Playing you?" Rey's mien was innocent, but her tone held an edge.

The evil smile deepened. "You're a good actress, Reynalda. Almost as good as Prunella."

My cousin regarded her for several seconds, then tossed her head and smiled angrily in return. "What about you?"

"I am the queen of thespianism. No one holds a candle to me, my dear." She rose and straightened, holding her carriage regally. "I'm going upstairs – with the diaries."

"Mrs. Moone, aren't you feeling well?" Linda asked with exaggerated concern, looking at her best friend. "Maybe you should accompany her."

"Maybe *you* should *all* stay here," Aunt Mat replied dismissively. "I'm extremely tired and am going to lie down. I trust you can amuse yourselves for a couple of hours?"

"You seemed to have had a good night of sleep," Rey commented dully. "How can you be tired?"

"There's being physically tired ... and there's being mentally and emotionally tired."

"You know, sharing mental and emotional burdens can lessen the weariness," Linda advised nonchalantly, piling coffee-soaked paper towels on a plate. "It's like when you confess to a priest. You feel uplifted."

"And burden-free? I'm not Catholic, although I believe a few of the Fonnes converted over the years. But I'll consider it." She chuckled, then brightened, and glanced at the sardine clock. "Later on, we'll order Caesar salads and two or three types of pizzas. Benton's parlor has probably reopened now. He makes the best in the state."

* * *

Quarter of six found us in the drawing room. Linda and I were seated on opposite sides of the long sofa, my legs hooked over an armrest, hers on an ottoman. Rey reclined in one of the plush armchairs. The room was dim, the only light courtesy of a roaring fire. My cousin was indulging in rye-and-ginger with slices of lime, Linda a large snifter of Grand Marnier, and I a smooth, easy-drinking Australian merlot. Anyone viewing the scene would have thought: what a simple and pleasant way to spend an early Wednesday evening.

Despite the warmth from the fire and alcohol, our faces looked as glum now as they had when we'd entered the room fifteen minutes ago.

"Do you think she's having a fitful lie-down?" Linda asked, sucking on a maraschino cherry, the fourth of eight she'd plopped into the orangey brandy.

"You mean a *guilt*-free lie-down?" Rey's asked tartly.

"She saw through the lame attempts at depicting Prunella Sayers' diaries," I said flatly.

"Ya think?" Linda asked drolly as she got up and refilled the snifter.

"Mind, hon?" Rey held out her empty rocks glass and Linda saw to her bidding.

"I wonder what she'll do with them," I mused aloud.

"Hopefully she won't go to Lewis," Linda murmured.

"It was bad enough to be lectured about intruding and tampering-with-evidence charges," Rey declared with a sulky face. "Can you see us explaining our efforts as diaryists to the sheriff, without sounding as crazy as Prunella?"

I could see the man's grave face when he'd tramped into the Sayers kitchen earlier. I didn't believe for one second he'd actually have thrown the book at us, but I was sure he'd have had no qualms about locking us up behind bars for several hours to teach a lesson.

"It was kind of humiliating," Linda acknowledged, passing Rey a filled-to-the-rim glass that looked more like rye than ginger. Her snifter was a few fingers deep, too.

Rey snorted and sank lower into the armchair, relaxing like someone finally relieved of a big burden. "But it's over now ... even if Aunt Mat won't confess to anything."

"It won't ever truly be over, but let's just sit back and enjoy this quiet time," Linda recommended.

I got the bottle of merlot and filled my crystal goblet nearly to the brim. If ever there was an occasion to be mentally and physically numbed – okay, *blottoed* – this seemed to be it.

"You'd think she'd be nervous or something, knowing we believe she's involved." Rey looked bemused.

I watched the crackling fire in the grand Citizen Kane fireplace, wishing I were back home in Wilmington. The last twenty-four hours had left a taste as bitter as dandelion greens in my mouth. "She's a calm and wise lady, and calculating without question. Not a lot would affect or throw her."

"All the more reason to leave the game a winning loser than a *lost* winner," May-Lee avowed.

We turned to find the antiques shopkeeper standing in front of closed doors. Odd that we'd not heard them shut. Too engrossed in our own silly selves, no doubt. As always May-Lee was dressed smartly, this time in gray flannel pants, pink wool turtleneck, patent leather studded ankle boots, and a cashmere trenchcoat, buttons and belt undone. A textured cloche was perched on her head, and to complete the ensemble, a Webley MkIV gripped in one hand.

Rey's "whoa Nelly" and Linda's "dang" collided with my "damn".

519

"Are you heading off somewhere or dropping by for a casual chat?" I asked blandly once the shock passed.

"I'll leave it for you blundering detectives to discover." She grinned. "You'd do the Three Stooges proud, my dears."

"The Three Stooges? Us?" Rey huffed.

"You're quite the comedic trio. Linda's Curly: childlike with a hint of charm. Rey, you'd be Moe: always smart-alecky, slapping and poking your friends with retorts and sarcasm when they don't see your way. Jill, you're Joe Besser, the only one who dared hit Moe in reprisal and put him in his place."

If Rey had had enough hair to flip, it would have covered her entire face. Instead her short spikes shifted from left to right and then stood up straight again, like daisies being caught in an erratic gust. I could only gape, while Linda's lips remained adhered to the snifter, her eyes plum-round.

The attractive woman smiled self-consciously. "My father loved those three. He grew up with them and, consequently, so did I."

Amazement evolved into concern and Linda gestured the weapon. "You're holding that gun because … you're going to kill us?"

"No, I'm not. Well, not if I don't have to." She appeared contemplative. "They'll figure out it was me if I do, but if I don't, you'll inform the sheriff. Either way I'm screwed…. But no, unless I'm provoked, I won't kill you. The 'death list' is growing a bit long."

"Seeing as we'd prefer to remain breathing, how do we *not* provoke you?" I asked crisply.

"Simply remain calm and everything will be fine," she responded sweetly.

Rey resembled a badger ready to lunge. "Why return to the scene of the crime, uh, crimes? I'm guessing you're involved in some way?"

May-Lee chuckled. "Foolishly enough, I left my wallet here. I'd forgotten I'd tucked it in the bottom of the chest of drawers in my room. I won't get far without it. My life's in there."

"You didn't come just to get your wallet, did you?" I asked. "You wanted to know how Aunt Mat had reacted to the diaries."

"And maybe tell us you're Prunella's partner," Linda added, regarding the woman closely.

"The wallet *was* my priority. I'd simply intended to sneak upstairs to get it, which I did, but then, yes, curiosity began nagging me. It started when Sheriff Lewis dropped by the shop to ask how my fingerprints happened to be on Deputy Malle's notebook." She leaned into the sideboard and smiled prettily. "I offered a viable reason, which he accepted."

Rey exhaled softly. "He can be a trusting soul, but then, why would he doubt a successful, community-minded businesswoman?"

"Why *were* they on there?" Linda asked curiously. "Why would he have yours on file?"

"I was the one who tucked it in Wolfgang," May-Lee explained with a lame shrug. "My fingerprints were on file because of a B&E that happened three years ago at the shop ... and a little tussle with one of the robbers, who managed to get his foolish self stuck in a pillory. Curiosity can be *such* a bitch." She chuckled. "They took my fingerprints at the time to weed out the non-guilty from the guilty."

"So, you are ... *were* Prunella's partner. Why place Wolfgag in the pantry?" Linda persisted.

"I don't like the word 'partner', because that would mean I also assisted with the murders and other schemes – well, I suppose I did. Still, I don't like thinking of myself as her *partner*," she replied nonchalantly and shrugged. "Putting Wolfgang in the pantry was part of the game. Prunella's. I thought it silly, but she felt it was a worthwhile taunt, a fun little 'head' game."

"Game?" Rey, Linda and I asked in chorus, surprised.

"Her mind works a bit differently from the norm, as we know," she said with a tired smile. "She found it quite hysterical."

"You know, if you'd not come here today, no one would have been the wiser about your involvement," I pointed out.

The shop owner tilted her head one way and then the other. "Maybe for a day or two. But Prunella wouldn't have allowed me to get away with anything if she was, among other things, going to be arrested on multiple murder charges. She may not reveal her involvement in everything, but she'd certainly reveal mine. I'm screwed, no matter what, so confessing my role is neither here nor there." She offered another tired smile. "But I'd rather you learn the truth – the *real* one – from me. Her truth will consist of out-and-out fabrications."

Linda drew a long bracing breath. "It must have been you who informed Sheriff Lewis we'd be at the Sayers."

She seemed to stifle a yawn.

Rey tossed back half her drink. Great. Retraction: now was *not* the time to be blottoed.

"So, Mrs. Moone had nothing to do with any of ths?" Linda's Grand Marnier disappeared. Wunderbar. Now we had two-and-a-half drunks and one clear-headed killer.

"Mathilda Moone is guilty of only one thing, besides being eccentric. Like Augustus Lewis, she's too trusting."

"And you pay back that trust – and kindness and generosity – by setting her up," I said coolly.

She waved the top-break revolver. "The police, slow as they can be, would have figured it out eventually should it have come to an arrest. She'd not have been on the hook for long."

"Do you mind if I get up?" I rose slowly and stretched, my thoughts racing. How would we extricate ourselves from this nasty dilemma? Unfortunately, the only thing that came to mind – charging the shop owner like bulls during the annual Pamplona run – didn't seem the best or most rational course of action. I stepped alongside the hearth and scanned the expansive room. It had no solutions to offer.

"Why obscure those pretty faces? Turn on the tall lamp, will you Jill?" May-Lee requested cordially.

Linda held up a hand like a keen town-hall attendee. "I have a question!"

May-Lee looked happy to play the Q&A game. "Yes, Ms. Royale?"

"This is undoubtedly an inane question at this point, but for the record: who killed Thomas Saturne?"

"Prunella, of course. She truly was enraged at having been dumped by the man. She loathes not having the upper hand. Vengeance is always hers. I don't believe she has ever lost – at anything. And yes, she was in on the pilfering with Thomas. They'd set up some shell companies overseas several years ago with different purposes. Porter assisted later on – and yes, she had coerced that assistance, but he was handsomely compensated for his services. The illicit dealings were extremely lucrative, but as happens with most thieves, the devious duo grew greedier with time. They didn't know when to stop. Poor Porter had no choice but to schlep along." She appeared fleetingly woeful.

Rey finished her drink and spoke to the empty glass. "How did you two bond? Prunella and you didn't care for each other, that was obvious. Or was that the master plan: to give the impression you were repelled by each other?"

"We've hated each other since Percival and I'd first started seeing each other. She had a thing for him long before he did her. At the time, I simply thought she was an over-protective sister – excuse me, *half* sister. It took only a few weeks after the divorce to realize how besotted with him she was." Slowly, she moved to the chaise longue, removed the cloche, tucked it into a pocket, and sat primly, like a lady at an English manor engaging in high tea. Her hands were remarkably steady, as was her gaze. "That zany woman had tried to drive a wedge into our relationship the moment she'd heard about our first date." She smiled with rue. "Too bad she'd not tried more diligently."

"But you and Prunella did have a bond," I prompted.

"Yes. A purely financial one."

"What? You're going to have us beg for details?" Linda asked when the woman ceased speaking, her expression waffling between disbelief and amusement. I suspected the latter was brought on by the Grand Marnier, but maybe she found the entire scene darkly humorous.

May-Lee chuckled. "One weekend during a Mathilda Moone extravaganza, I couldn't sleep, so I decided to stroll around the house. I came across an open door – the den, as I recall – and Prunella and Thomas were arguing over who should handle a Byzantine bronze phalera. Naturally, my ears perked. I know, listening into private conversations is boorish, but I was captivated and heard enough to comprehend what was going on. As I was about to return to my room, I saw them embrace and kiss. It was disturbing, to say the least." She shuddered. Was she referring to the crime or the kiss?

"So you confronted her?"

"I kept an eye on her and started poking around. After several weeks I'd uncovered enough to present her with details. I wanted a cut. The money would enable me to buy more pieces for the shop and travel overseas and all that. I wasn't being overly greedy. Really."

"I suppose the fact you had exploitable connections in the ways of antique dealers, warehousing, and shipping helped influence Prunella's decision to cut you in," I proposed.

May-Lee smiled like someone who'd won a one-thousand-dollar wager. "She did see the logic and merit of accepting the proposition."

"Was Percival in on it?" Rey asked, leaning forward. Her eyes were glazed, but her bearing and disposition appeared solid.

"Not to his *knowledge*. Prunella did use a couple of his companies for certain undertakings and cover-ups, but he wasn't any wiser for it."

Sporting similar measuring expressions, the three of us crossed arms simultaneously and surveyed May-Lee's cheerful countenance. While we resembled three travelers awaiting a long-delayed flight, May-Lee Sonit could have been sitting in a lounge or bistro, awaiting the arrival of a frothy, chilled cocktail.

31

Going for It

"No more questions?" May-Lee's Joan Crawford lips drew into a Cruella De Vil smile. "I'd have thought you'd be bursting at the seams to learn everything."

Rey's tone was brackish. "We don't want to seem over-eager."

The shop owner's laughter held a theatrical resonance; she could have been a glee-filled villainess thrusting a dagger into a victim's heart during the climax of a play. Was she doing it for show? Or was she as unhinged as her hospitalized partner?

"Oh, what the hell. *I'll* go for it," Linda announced, executing her best friend's dramatic flair. "Prunella made sure Thomas died three ways. Did you help?"

"The monetary incentive to *help* was too great to refuse."

"She administered the quinapril, am I right?" Linda continued.

"Yes Curly." May-Lee grinned. "It was easy enough to accomplish, but she wasn't sure the dosage was enough to cause *fatal* damage, so when the moment presented itself, she slipped Poison Hemlock into a beverage."

"Then to be on the safe side, she shot him with a blowgun," Linda added with a Cousin Rey snort.

May-Lee shrugged. "That's Prunella Sayers – always wanting to ensure a one-hundred-and-twenty-five per cent success rate."

"Of all weapons, why a blowgun? Where'd she learn to use one?"

"She'd gone on a few South American bird-watching expeditions. She learned the art in Brazil, I believe. Being the woman she is –"

"The *nutso* she is," Rey interjected.

"Being the woman she is, she opted for a blow-gun. It was a more challenging and entertaining murder weapon than a conventional gun or knife, and less detectable."

"If there'd been no Poison Hemlock or quinapril overdose, and that miniscule mark on the neck had gone unnoticed – and subsequently the curare not detected – Thomas' death may well have been tagged a natural one."

Linda grinned. "Would you care to run that by one more time, Jill?"

"I couldn't if I tried," I confessed with a slim smile and turned back to our keeper. "Who removed the dart? You?"

She nodded once.

"Did she put the blowgun in the shoebox and hide it in the room upstairs?"

"It was a spur of the moment decision and that room seemed as good as any place to leave the box until it could be properly retrieved and disposed of."

"Did Percival see either of you doing your thing?" Rey asked.

She nodded again. "He did notice Prunella and I exchange a few quick words, which surprised him, but he didn't mention it until much later."

"When he *realized* what he might have seen?" Linda prompted.

A third nod.

Linda and Rey glanced at each other before the scriptwriting assistant asked, "The know-how regarding the biennial herb came from one of Percival's articles – maybe the one I read recently?"

"A book, actually." May-Lee crossed her legs and settled back.

I started to say, "The one on poisons and herbs that was removed from the library –"

"And resulted in a clunk to Aunt Mat's head," was finished by Rey. "Plus a handkerchief soaked with a dangerous chemical placed to the face."

"Prunella had run upstairs for something or other and saw the door ajar, and Matty in the room, perusing the book. It was crucial to get it right then and there, not because of the pages devoted to that herbaceous plant, but because Prunella had left sticky notes in there ... or thought she had. As it turned out, she'd hastily, if not clumsily, tucked them into the latest copy of *Bird Watcher's Digest.*" The sigh and tone expressed irritation. "All that panic for naught. I mean *really.*"

"Who poisoned Gwynne?"

May-Lee offered the slightest of smirks. "Besides being overly nosey, the man rubbed Prunella the wrong way."

"He rubbed most of us the wrong way," I responded wryly. "Say, do you know anything about the cigarette butt in the corridor? Did Percival remove it to cover his tracks?"

"No, as I said, Percival had nothing to do with any of the goings on here. It was Porter's. He'd dropped it the last time he was down there. That Davidoff stub could have easily been traced back to him, so Prunella retrieved it as soon as possible. She wanted to keep him out of any potential spotlights."

"Huh?" Rey squeaked. "None of us even knew he smoked."

"Your aunt did," May-Lee said solemnly. "He'd been an off-and-on smoker for years, but more on than off. When you saw it, Prunella nearly had a stroke. She was sure you'd pick it up and keep it as evidence."

Rey held up her empty glass. "Could I get a refill?"

"Go for it, as the saying goes," she twittered like an American Goldfinch, "but don't make any sudden or stupid moves."

Rey sauntered to the sideboard and poured ginger ale, no rye. "What about Jensen? Did he tell Prunella about his findings or that Aunt Mat was alive?"

"He had no idea that your aunt was alive. He did, however, stumble across the curare and Poison Hemlock in the cellar. Prunella had brought enough to kill ten people – a 'just in case' reserve – and tucked them between boxes of sound-effect CDs and silly, rubbery creepy-crawlies. At the time she'd had no idea they were items Jensen would be using to help Matty scare the dickens out of us." She gestured with the Webley. "Please pour some soda and leave it on that side table over here."

Rey did as requested, her gaze and actions cautious. May-Lee Sonit was being civil, even pleasant, but you never knew what a killer could or would do if incited. Linda gestured the bottle of Grand Marnier. Rey shrugged and poured a small amount in a new snifter. Linda gestured again. More streamed in. "So, Prunella more or less confronted Jensen?"

"She slammed the stake into him and he grabbed her necklace as he was going down. Would you care to fill in the blanks?" I urged gently with a benign smile.

It was Linda who responded. "Prunella suspected he was in the cellar, readying for a prank, and she quickly headed down there while we were refreshing ourselves. She should have left it be. He'd have had no idea who'd put the poisons there."

"But he might have brought them to the police and *they* might have dusted for fingerprints," Rey offered.

"That's spot on." May-Lee nodded. "Not knowing of her involvement – or how dangerous she could be – he told her what he'd found and that he was considering informing the sheriff because there was no doubt in his mind that the items had been stashed by the killer." Another finch-like twitter.

"Huge mistake," Rey said flatly.

"Huge *and* foolish," I concurred. "The stake in the heart certainly proved just how dangerous –

and unhinged – the woman was. I'm surprised he didn't see it coming."

"He probably thought she was simply going to swat him," was May-Lee's casual response. "She's exceptionally strong and vicious, and quick. By the time he realized it was a stake flying at him with the velocity of the Shanghai Maglev, it was in his chest, and way too late."

"But he grabbed the necklace, in a final flash of hope and purpose."

"I'd never have believed her to be the vicious type. Peculiar yes, maybe even creepy, but vicious no." Linda nodded thanks as Rey passed the drink. "Let's get back to Porter, a.k.a. Crackers. When did she start enlisting his services?"

"It was a little over four years ago that she discovered the man was an old, not-so-dear associate. As you well know, he was an introverted sort who always disappeared when guests were around. Try as Matty did, he simply refused to greet guests and accept compliments or permit people into his kitchen. He was exceptionally accomplished at avoiding people."

"Except for Percival," I reminded her. "Who did speak with Porter on a few occasions."

Recall shrouded her face like a widow's veil. "That's right."

Entrenched in the moment, Linda leaned forward. "Porter's most recent services included helping with moving bodies and concealing evidence, right?"

"Yes." She took a sip of soda and waited for another question.

Rey's smile was dry. "I guess once a criminal, always a criminal."

May-Lee looked skeptical. "What choice did he have? Once Prunella recognized him, his fate was sealed."

"Notorious pasts and nasty deeds have a way of catching up, even when lives have traveled new paths." I envisioned a strident, unpleasant confrontation between the cook and birder. "The quiet, normal existence he'd embraced by moving to Connecticut eventually proved to be anything but."

"Shit happens," Rey said dully.

Linda took the helm again. "Like we'd discussed, he obviously developed cold feet at one point and she had no option but to ensure his silence. Out came the blowgun again ... right?"

"The curare, not the blowgun. She mentioned he was becoming increasingly nervous. He's a thief, an embezzler – or at least he was – but cold-blooded murderer? No. He had a great stomach for food, not killing."

"But he did bomb the restaurant he worked at in San Francisco," Rey stated.

"He never admitted that, even when Prunella pressured him, so it's anyone's guess whether he actually did or not."

"The curare didn't fell him as she'd schemed, did it?" Linda inquired.

May-Lee scanned the room, as if collecting thoughts. "Let's back up. Prior to the garage episode, maybe a half hour before, she'd asked him to move Jensen's body from the cellar to the garage. The barrister was in one of the large trunks, in case you were wondering; she'd put him there herself, believe it or not."

"I believe it," Rey affirmed. "She grabbed my hand once and man, she had a vice-like grip. She seemed to have Superwoman strength."

"Why the change of shirt?" I asked, curious.

"She bandaged the hole so it wouldn't ooze and leave telltale trails; a fresh shirt would keep the binding in place. That was her thinking."

Linda paled.

"Anyway, the cook placed the body in the trunk of the car, little knowing that she'd strategically placed a curare-dipped pin where he'd not see it, but feel it. Unfortunately it either didn't prick him as deeply as planned, or she'd not administered the right dose, so it didn't have the full, intended effect. Knowing how she'd killed Thomas, Porter immediately realized what had happened. He'd shrieked and we came."

Linda nodded. "She was the first one at his side."

"Percival was there pretty quickly, too," I reminded her.

"Under her breath, Prunella told Porter it was merely a warning, but if he attempted to leave the estate for good, she would find him no matter where in the world he went and ensure that he received enough curare to cut short his life … after she lopped off certain parts of his body."

"Percival knew this?" Rey asked.

"He'd suspected she'd been up to evil doings because she'd been missing on a couple of occasions just prior to the discovery of bodies. That, and a couple of other trifling actions put him on – what shall I call it? – *vigilant alert.* She'd hastily mentioned the pin after we'd heard Porter, and he felt compelled to remove the evidence."

Linda looked perturbed.

"That formally sealed that sibling bond, didn't it?" Rey asked flatly.

"To a point. She told me a little later he'd demanded an explanation of everything she'd gotten herself involved in. After she obliged, he instructed her to go to the police and plead insanity. He'd pledged to stand by her side every step of the way."

"That must have gone over like a swarm of locusts," Rey snorted.

Linda leaned back with a furrowed brow. "We know the answer, but let's ask anyway: did she chop Porter's head off?"

"She'd failed with the curare. It was possible he'd been scared enough to keep his lips forever zipped, but she couldn't risk it. So while he was in bed, she – well, it only took three whacks she claimed." May-Lee sighed, appearing both resigned and dejected. "The woman was embarking on a serious murder spree and showing no signs of letting up.... If anything, she was becoming more self-assured with each killing. I could envision her lopping off the heads of everyone here, including me."

"So you had no choice but to comply." Rey's expression and tone were as acidic as apple cider vinegar.

The shopkeeper sipped more soda, her expression genuinely remorseful.

"Then she moved on to her own brother," Linda prompted.

"Actually, I did. It was payback time." May-Lee offered a regretful smile. "And to be honest, it was rather hard not to get caught up in the killing frenzy – it almost seemed like, well, sport."

Stunned, I glanced at my comrades. Rey looked surprised while Linda appeared stoic. "Was this payback for being spurned all those years ago?" I asked.

"It was payback for Prunella having interfered those many years ago ... for Prunella going killer-crazy... . For Percival being a colossal idiot."

Rey eyed her skeptically. "She didn't want to do you in to retaliate?"

"I have no doubt she'd loved to have blown a dart my way, but we had a bond, remember?" May-Lee smirked. "She needed me, loathe as she was to admit it."

"Who hit Jilly's boyfriend and Officer Budd upstairs?"

"Prunella, of course."

Rey gave a go-ahead sign.

She looked at Linda. "It's been on my mind to ask, but with the ongoing excitement, I've never had the opportunity: you're part of the Smith family, the ones who originally owned this place?"

Linda studied May-Lee's expression, a cross between curiosity and challenge. "It's not a major secret."

The business owner gestured Rey. "It seems a bit strange that you end up being friends with Reynalda Fonne-Werde, whose aunt happens to own the very estate your great, great relatives did."

Rey and I regarded the scriptwriting assistant with astonishment. Why had we not considered how the two had ended up steadfast friends, given the familial connection?

Linda crossed both arms, drew a deep breath, and stared into a corner. Finally, she spoke. "My brother, sister and I had heard the family history when we were young. Mom had only revealed some of it and the rest was relayed by cousins she'd kept in contact with over the years – ones that, like us, weren't rich or successful."

"Your mother must have been very resentful. Surely the cousins were as well?" May-Lee asked with a sympathetic smile.

"I suspect she may have been – a little. The cousins? That's hard to say… . It wasn't easy raising three kids as a single mom. Dad died when I was four. That no one from the Smith family reached out financially may have soured Mom a bit, but I don't know that for a fact. Sometimes I caught her looking at old photos and she seemed either sad or angry, sometimes both." She sighed softly. "Lido, Loretta and I once took a four-day Greenwich vacation. We came to check out the estate. Always curious and courageous,

Lido actually got inside the grounds. He checked out the house, took photos. Nothing happened while he was doing so, fortunately. Anyway, we returned to town, talked about what happened and what might have been, and that was that."

"You knew Rey was related to Aunt Mat and you made friends with her on purpose?" I asked, unable to fathom Linda as the calculating sort.

"Yes and no.... Not really."

The three of us waited for her to expound.

"Several years ago, I'd read Rey's bio in a magazine featuring the cast of that show that bombed big-time: *Frolic and Flings in Fresno.* I was curious to meet someone related to the Moones so I went to the studio. Oddly enough, I managed to walk into a job when an insensitive director fired his production assistant as I was standing nearby. He grabbed me, asked me if I could fetch coffee and handle mega egos. I managed to squeak 'yes' and was hired on the spot. I officially met Rey at a company barbecue a month later."

"Yeah, you were eating ribs on the far side of the pool. You were staring at me as you were sucking on the bones like you'd been stuck on Gilligan's Island for a month," Rey snickered.

"At least I didn't look like I'd been licking clean bowls and platters. Those globs of sauce –"

"Hey, I did not –"

"You sure –"

"Ladies, there'll be time to reminisce later." May-Lee raised the Webley, looked beyond us, and grinned. "I see you're not sleeping the evening away. You didn't touch the tea I left on the nightstand. Tsk."

A strained-looking Aunt Mat stood at the drawing room entrance. A glazed gaze traveled from one face to the next before fixing on May-Lee. "I did take a few sips. Poisoned?"

"Tranquilized."

She nodded and drew a hand-knitted Fair Isle cardigan tightly around her.

May-Lee waved the gun. "Do join us."

Aunt Mat bowed her head and strolled across the room, and sat on the armchair alongside Rey. "What have I missed?"

"Prunella killed everyone except Percival," Linda explained. "May-Lee was in a payback frame of mind and took care of her ex."

She smiled dryly. "This promises to be much more entertaining than any of my murder mystery weekends... . Although with mine, people do walk away and return for more."

"Spontaneity has its merit."

Aunt Mat rubbed her face slowly and leaned back. "Is it possible that Prunella arranged for Reggie's death?"

We turned to our hostess with the mostest (not).

"Anything is possible, of course, but she's never confided that. I do recall her mentioning something about him having contacted a private investigator, and she'd seemed concerned. But it was only in passing and she never brought it up again," May-Lee answered.

"That Rajastoni stone figure falling on him truly was a mishap. Happenstance," she answered. "The carpeting on the staircase was loose and when one of the renovation fellows tripped, the stone figure tumbled onto Matty's beau. It was an ugly accident."

"You and Prunella didn't have anything to do with the 'loose' carpeting?" Rey asked distrustfully.

"We did not," she affirmed, pulling her shoulders back. "I liked Reginald, strange and distant as he could be. He'd always been a gentleman. He was incredibly knowledgeable and always had items of interest to share. I believe Prunella was of a similar mind."

"The woman may have been killing for decades," Linda murmured, perturbed.

"Having known her all these years – and after all that's transpired – I wouldn't put anything past her," May-Lee said softly. "She's complicated ... complex ... and crazy."

"She's a serial killer," Rey said bluntly. "A *female* one. That's a rare breed."

"Fascinating," Aunt Mat whispered.

"Eerie," Linda murmured.

"Very," May-Lee agreed, and we all stared. "Well, it is eerie. I killed out of necessity, not desire or fun like Prunella."

Aunt Mat asked, "And what was Percival?"

"A need for vengeance."

Rey, Linda and I looked at one another and agreed simultaneously, "Necessity."

"That makes it all peachy-keen," Aunt Mat snapped.

"This'll sound like a corny B-movie line," Rey stated, "but they *will* catch you."

"I doubt it."

"Wow, now *that's* confidence."

"That's *luck*, Reynalda. For the last few years of my life, nothing's gone wrong. It's as if I've had an angel sitting on my shoulder –"

"I wouldn't call it an angel," Aunt Mat sniffed.

"Fine, call it a little red, trident-tailed gremlin, but I've had incredible good fortune. Okay, I've never won the Powerball pot, but absolutely everything has always worked out in my favor."

My aunt waved a hand dismissively.

A forgotten question popped into my head. "Who put Snakey in Thomas' bed?"

May-Lee appeared surprised. "Who else?"

"Prunella, of course," I answered. Why had I bothered asking? "But why?"

"You tell us why," she urged with a smug smile. "I know you have it in you to figure it out."

I considered it and chuckled. "Because she thought he was a snake."

"So it was a message." Linda appeared confused. "But he was already dead, wasn't he? So what was the point?"

She shook her head. "Prunella had placed it there early the first afternoon. Regrettably, he never had an opportunity to find it. The message was so clear. And rather clever."

"Both of them were, yes," I said.

"Both?" Linda appeared even more bewildered. "Both *what*?"

"Messages. Not only was Prunella calling Thomas a snake, she was informing him he was dead."

Linda pursed her lips and appeared meditative. "I get the first message, not the second. A dead snake doesn't necessarily signify *death*. Evilness maybe, but death, no."

"Whatever the case, maybe he'd have left the place at a rapid run if he'd actually seen it," May-Lee shrugged.

"Or, at the very least, scampered as fast as his tubby self would allow," I said with a dry smile.

"Hey gang, I have to use the little girl's room," Rey announced.

Linda and I looked at her as if she were as demented as Prunella Sayers.

32

The Best is Yet to Come

May-Lee's feather-soft sigh floated across the expansive room. "Linda, you've been elected group leader: please guide the way down the hall. We're all going to go, but do remember who's holding the gun. As I said, I don't want to shoot anyone, but will if necessary."

"You can't shoot all four of us at once."

"No, but I could get a least one of you. Who'd like to be the 'special one' to receive a .455 cartridge in the face? I believe that may hurt, never mind what it will do in the looks department."

The four of us exchanged glances. Apparently none of us wanted to be that "special one".

Like someone embarking on a two-week Caribbean vacation, May-Lee's face lighted up and she smiled gaily. She motioned the double doors and we fell into single file with the shop-keeper taking up the flank.

"Do you enjoy killing?" Rey asked over her shoulder, curious. "Do you hear voices in your head?"

"No, Reynalda, I do *not* hear voices. Prunella, on the other hand, most certainly does."

"I'd bet dollars to donuts on that," Linda exlaimed.

May-Lee signaled Rey to open the thick, oak-veneer bathroom door. She complied and froze when we started to follow.

"You don't think I'm about to leave you alone in there, do you? I'm not having you sneak out the window, or finding some obscure weapon like a toilet brush to use on me. I watch cheesy movies too, you know."

My cousin exhaled loudly and marched into a marble-heavy bathroom. "Privacy, if you don't mind."

We all turned, save May-Lee. "I've seen it all before."

Rey grumbled and we took quick turns fresh-ening up, biding time as notions of flight ran through every head. Four anxious women contemplated ways of escaping an oddly lucid woman wielding a Webley revolver and one considered how to gain freedom from said four anxious captives, three of whom smelled like a bar and one a perfumery.

"Before I forget: put your cell phones on the counter, please."

Linda was the only one who had brought one. On the counter it went. With a clunk.

As we filed back into the hallway, with a trace of sarcasm, I instructed May-Lee Sonit to send a postcard.

"Of course, darling," she winked. "I'll send a few."

"You know, you remind me of someone," Linda murmured, clearly perplexed as she considered who it was.

"Hannibal Lector," Rey responded coolly.

"Come now, Reynalda," May-Lee cajoled. "That's hardly nice or fair."

"It is a bit much," I concurred. "May-Lee is more like Mallory Knox of *Natural Born Killers* or maybe Catherine Tramwell of *Basic Instinct.*"

"I'm stunned, Jilly. That's amazing." Rey's tone expressed approval. "I thought your butter tart was the movie buff?"

"I've picked up a lot watching Friday late-night flicks."

With a fleeting smile, she turned back to our captor. "What now? Are you going to lock us in a closet or something?"

"I'm going to have you tie each other up. See the rope on the duet stool over there? Linda, be so kind as to get it. I'll fasten the last person – you, Reynalda. Now, where would you like to be locked up: the cellar or the tower?"

The simultaneous response: "Tower!"

"The cellar's too dark and damp," Rey added blandly.

"And spooky." Linda.

"Toxic and claustrophobic." Me.

"Cluttered." Aunt Mat.

"Wonderful. You're all in agreement and I'm happy to comply. Linda." She gestured and the scriptwriting assistant hurried down the hallway to retrieve the rope. When she returned with the sizeable cord, May-Lee signaled us to proceed. "Start strolling upstairs single file, ladies."

Up to the tower we tramped. Overthrowing one slim woman with one impressive revolver wouldn't have been that difficult, but who wanted to risk it? The worst case scenario: we'd be locked in the antiquity-filled tower for a couple days, but we'd be alive. Sheriff Lewis and his deputies would start wondering when they'd not heard from us and come looking. She said she'd not kill us, and I tended to believe her. May-Lee Sonit took lives out of necessity – and vengeance – not desire or fun. Whatever floated Prunella Sayers' boat was another story.

Per May-Lee's instructions, Rey began to secure Linda's hands behind her back, after which she'd fasten her to one of two large limestone obelisks and then Aunt Mat.

"Who is – or was – Fred?" I asked Aunt Mat as we watched.

"He was a hired hand, someone Edward, the house steward, liked and gave a job to. Fred proved to be quite a decent stableman and carpenter, so I understood from one of Reggie's Madeira-induced stories. Unfortunately for Fred, he developed a crush on the housekeeper, and she on him. Well, Fred wasn't the only one in love with Valentina – yes, that was her name. The 'master' of the house had it bad for the woman, too." Aunt Mat smiled sorrowfully. "It was a love affair destined for tragedy."

Her eyes on Rey, May-Lee agreed.

I peered around casually. Most mystery movies had a dramatic ending. The one to a madcap collect-your-inheritance get-together shouldn't be any different. As Reynalda moved to Linda's ankles, which would eventually be tethered to Aunt Mat's, I surveyed the room filled with my uncle's oddities. What luck. The candelabrum Adwin had handled the other evening was ten feet away and still in the gauntlet of "Lancie", the 16th-century knight. Casually yet watchfully, I maneuvered over, clutched the large branched candleholder behind me (it might as well have been a stuffed wombat for all its heftiness), and casually moved back again. Thankfully, May-Lee's gaze was still fixed on my cousin and her best friend, implying my aunt and I posed little threat.

"May-Lee?"

"Yes Jill?"

With the velocity of a 90 MPH baseball, the candelabrum struck her upside the head. Before I could think twice, or she could react, it whizzed around to clout the other side. (It was truly amazing what one was capable of when caught in a perilous situation.)

Ignoring blood and ragged flesh – just as I valiantly (desperately) had when I'd struck Prunella Sayers in a corridor several floors below – I grabbed the revolver as Aunt Mat instinctively caught the antique seller's descending body.

"Dang," Linda whispered, eyes billiard-ball round.

"Double dang." Rey regarded the inert body. "Man, you have a thing about beaning people, don't you?"

"Is she dead?" Linda studied the woman hanging heavily in Aunt Mat's slender arms.

"No." I peered closely. "But she'll need tending."

"She'll need a few stitches for sure. She can take a bed beside Prunella in the hospital." As Rey hastily untied her friend, Aunt Mat flew down the stairs to call Lewis. Soon the three of us were carrying May-Lee downstairs to her former bedroom.

"Get some towels and a large container of warm water," Linda instructed Rey as we laid her on the bed.

Rey sprang into action.

"She's looking awfully pale."

"She's not looking well," I agreed quietly.

Rey raced back in with Aunt Mat seconds behind. Linda dampened a towel and began dabbing open skin as Aunt Mat dropped into a carved walnut Regence armchair in a corner.

"You know," the older woman said wryly, "if I weren't so happy at having this be truly and *finally* over, I'd give you three a piece of my mind for having believed *I* was the guilty party."

"Jill, see if you can find gauze, alcohol or disinfectant, and adhesive tape or something similar. I'm going to practice non-existent nursing skills."

"I'll go – I know where to find those items." Aunt Mat leaped up and hastened into the hallway.

Rey leaned into the wall beside the bed and looked equally elated and exhausted. "Who'd have expected her to be Prunella's little helper?"

"Apparently, none of us," I replied. "Let's not get any crazy notions about quitting our day jobs and becoming private investigators."

"Considering we've never solved a mystery, we did pretty good," my cousin declared.

"We did *okay*," Linda corrected.

Face flushed, Aunt Mat re-entered the room with a large zebra-print plastic cosmetic bag. Dropping it alongside May-Lee, she returned to the armchair. "Those diaries, by the way, weren't bad. Not great. But not horribly bad. Next time, be consistent, and use handwriting. That would make them look more like bona-fide diaries."

Rey extended her hands. "We had a lot of suppositions, not enough time to investigate, and only a few hours to pull them together."

"Prunella's insanity must have fuelled May-Lee's," Linda said, dabbing disinfectant on and around the wounds.

"Was she really insane ... or simply audacious?" I wondered aloud.

"Both, even if I don't know what aww-dacious means," Rey said. "With a whole whack of gutsiness thrown in."

I had to laugh. "Did Lewis say how long he'd be?"

Aunt Mat shook her head. "No, but I told him to get here as soon as possible and to dispatch an ambulance because May-Lee Sonit has been injured. Then I hung up. There'll be time to talk later... . He'll be disappointed to hear about May-Lee. He really liked her. She's done quite a lot with local charities. But he'll also be thrilled to have a multiple murder case solved." She released a long exhalation. "It's over, my dears."

She and Rey exchanged tense smiles as Linda concentrated on administering "non-existent nursing skills".

"When'd you become the doctoring sort?" Rey asked, curious, stepping closer for a better look.

Linda eyed May-Lee, who hadn't stirred but was still breathing, albeit shallowly. "I felt a need. Strange, huh? Maybe I've found a new calling?" With a slim smile she stopped wrapping her patient's head with thin gauze. "With the way things have been going, I wouldn't be surprised if a supernatural being crashed through a window or sucked us all through a wall."

I chuckled. "Or maybe Fred the Ghost could appear and congratulate us on a job not so well done."

A raucous crash from the front of the house caused us to jump and all but kiss the ceiling.

"Dang!" Linda's face was whiter that Adwin's celebrated five-layer coconut cake.

Rey's face made Linda's look like it sported a Brazilian tan. "Shit. It's *not* possible."

I was too astonished for words while Aunt Mat's eyeballs seemed to bounce from their sockets as if attached to helical springs.

* * *

"Was that absolutely necessary, Augustus?" Aunt Mat demanded, motioning the damaged ebony doors when we reached the base of the stairs. There was no battering ram in sight, but the entrance seemed to have been smashed by one. Beyond splintered wood was a patchy, starless sky that looked drab and bleak, fitting for the moment.

"You said – screamed – to come quickly, that May-Lee Sonit was injured and down, so we hurried on ovah. We didn't know what to expect," he responded curtly, scanning the foyer. "Where's her body?"

"She's not a 'body'. She's upstairs and she's injured as I said and you heard."

He jerked a thumb over his shoulder. "An ambulance is a minute away."

"Is it true, Mrs. Moone," Deputy Budd asked, removing his hat. "Is she Ms. Sayers' partner?"

"It's true, sadly." She cocked her head. "I didn't mention that. How did you know?"

The young man leaned closer. "Ms. Sayers was talking an hour ago. It was hard to speak with all the stitches and tubes, and medication, but she did manage to spit out that Ms. Sonit was 'a partner', that she was a, uh, 'bitch', and that there was going to be 'all hell to pay' when she was up and walking again."

Aunt Mat's eyes widened and she looked from him to Lewis. "That is one spirited woman."

"An audacious one," I said with a slim smile.

"A major whack job," Rey snorted.

Aunt Mat peered past the sheriff's shoulder. "The paramedics are pulling up. Rey, show them to May-Lee's room. I'll make a couple of big pots of coffee. I suspect everyone will be needing major amounts of caffeine."

33

All's Well that Ends Well ... Sort Of

The last twenty-four hours in Connecticut had proven to be informative ... and startling.

Lounging in the kitchen nook later that night, after Lewis et al had departed, Aunt Mat casually delivered a confession that held the impact of a glide bomb. *She'd* done the deadly deeds: killed Moone family members.

Rey, Linda and I could have used spatulas to scrape our jaws off the table while Aunt Mat hadn't seemed the least bit upset or traumatized or repentant. The statement was as smooth as the liqueur-laced cocoa we were indulging in. "By the way girls, I'm the one who dethroned those Moones." Then the grande dame explained how she'd set up Linda.

John had died nearly seven years ago. He fell off (jumped off or was pushed off) Portland's Casco Bay Bridge and into the Fore River. Linda's recent search for John Smith had been based on a contact number search, nothing more; hence, the death had not come up in the search and she'd never been the wiser.

Aunt Mat's idea about covering tracks had merely been a kernel when she'd overheard Linda telling Rey about "nice Cousin John" a few years back, but it germinated quickly. If he was thoughtful enough to send boxes of sweet treats, why not other gifts – like books, figurines, a little trips?

The need to establish a scapegoat had become a necessity when Mildred Trapusking-Moone had an electrifying experience one Saturday afternoon while drinking orange-pekoe tea. Faulty wiring caused a short and subsequent (fatal) shock. Apparently her hair was spikier than Ethan Hawke's 2013 bleached-out blond do. This had occurred a year before Jackson Moore was found charcoal-broiled, so we'd missed (at least) one person on the "Moone Murder List".

According to Aunt Mat, Mildred had been a self-absorbed bitch who perpetually peered down a long W.C. Fields proboscis at everyone not born with five million in a trust fund. Very long story short, Aunt Mat had never expected Linda to actually be convicted of anything. It had been just as we'd bantered about – that setting up Linda was a means of diverting attention elsewhere should something have gone wrong and the Moone deaths discovered not to be accidents.

Aunt Mat was a thorough woman, smart and, well, kind of crazy, yet rationally so. If Linda have actually been handcuffed and mug-shot, Aunt Mat would have plotted another course of action. Legal forces would have been continually confounded.

She'd rather enjoyed the covert game of playing Cousin John while terminating Moones. It proved an amusing pursuit and entertaining challenge. Lucky for her, Linda took it all in stride, but maybe she didn't want to tick the old gal off and end up becoming an "amusing pursuit" herself. Smart thinking.

After the confession, we'd opted for doubles in mugs the size of well buckets, heavy on the whipped cream. If Aunt Mat wasn't feeling anything, either would we (our friend Tia Maria would ensure that).

Who'd have thought creamy hot cocoas could cause such intense hangovers? Around eight the next morning, Rey, Linda and I dragged ourselves into the kitchen wearing jeans and heavy wool sweaters, and lots of concealer (bags with designer labels were much desired, those under the eyes were not). We shared a bottle of Advil, pot of coffee, and minimal conversation. A half hour later Aunt Mat, wearing casual pants and a lovely cashmere sweater of ivory white, entered. Her make-up was flawless, but red-rimmed eyes suggested some suffering. Linda made more coffee and I boiled eggs while Rey toasted and buttered slices of rye. Conversation again was minimal.

Sheriff Lewis had arrived at eleven and stayed for a light lunch, filling us in with nonessential details about what the future held for two "wigged-out killahs". Suffice it to say, psychiatric assessments and lock-ups were part of the equation. The subject of the murdered Moones wasn't brought up. Why? No one wanted to put the quirky woman behind bars. After all, she was the Fonnes's grande dame, a gentlewoman, and a likeable one at that (killer streak aside). But could we, should we, would we (continue to) look the other way? Time would tell.

What about Sheriff Lewis? He'd heard our suspicions regarding Linda being the Moone killer. Would he pursue them? Or would he chalk them up to the ramblings and unfounded (unsound) reasoning of detective wannabes? Again, time would tell.

Johnny had dug deep enough to discover that the two Swiss folks, Gruber Pathos and Santana Ana Dinero, had indeed been fabricated by Thomas and Prunella. He'd even found a photo taken at a charity event in Geneva that showed the lawyer and bird lover mingling with a bank president and a telecom CEO; underneath the smiling foursome decked in designer evening-wear were the names Gerhardt Spatz, Kurt Heinrich Vogel, Gruber Pathos, and Santana Ana Dinero.

Various entities, including the IRS, were currently investigating. As for closed-mouth

Prunella, she had recuperated and was awaiting trial. Mental evaluations had deemed her fit. May-Lee, on the other hand, had suffered a breakdown and was weaving Shaker baskets when she was giggling or doing bird imitations. Yet again, time would tell if the show owner would return to "normal".

And speaking of time, it was hard to believe that the Connecticut Caper – as Rey laughingly called it – had happened nearly a month ago. Yet in some ways, it felt like a year. The entire episode seemed dreamlike and distant.

I dropped onto the only piece of furniture I'd purchased for the Brentwood apartment so far: a beautiful two-piece leather sleeper sectional sofa that set me back a lot more than budgeted for. But it would serve as a perfect focus piece and last for years, and I wasn't planning on being that extravagant with anything else. It rested to the side of a large deep-set fixed window with solid panel shutters. Sitting here, I could gaze four stories below onto a lush courtyard with two burbling fountains.

Christmas was around the corner and it felt strange to not have my nephew Quincy racing around, trying new seasonal recipes, or sticking Quincy-would-like gift suggestions in obvious places. The first week of December, Mom usually had the B&B decorated with lights, holly and ivy, and a couple of tinsel-trimmed Christmas trees. A stunning silver menorah rested on the dining room sidebar for Jewish friends and guests.

I'd made a move to California. Sold all belongings, put the Wilmington condo up for sale, packed clothes, and wondered what I'd gotten myself into besides a three-day weather-forecasting job at a local community television station. I'd have to find other work, of course, if we didn't make money serving as professional sleuths (which I had doubts about), but it was a start. Rey was planning on getting the detective agency going in the next month or so.

Yes, that was correct: detective agency. Back at the Moone manse, as the three of us were packing and making promises to stay in touch, Rey had revealed a plan that she'd been considering since May-Lee had been wheeled away: opening a private investigation agency in California. To make her happy and keep me sane for the remainder of the brief stay, I'd said I'd consider the wild notion that seemed as probable as a Minnesota drought in January. But somewhere and somehow over the weeks, I'd decided maybe it wasn't that wild after all.

Even Linda had gotten caught up in Rey's enthusiasm. I wasn't quite sure how to inform them about California's strict licensure. They'd be devastated to learn they weren't going to be private investigators any time soon. Among other things, we'd need a combination of education in police science, criminal law or justice, experience equaling three years or 6,000 hours, and to pass a criminal history background check. Oh yes, we'd also have to receive a qualifying score on a two-hour written exam. It was surprising that Rey hadn't yet discovered that; or maybe she had and had simply refused to accept facts. In any event, at present, in addition to scouting offices, my cousin had signed up for a business course. Kudos to eager and determined Cousin Reynalda.

The drive back from Connecticut had afforded Adwin and I time to talk about life, goals and objectives, feelings and family. By the time we'd reached Wilmington, we'd decided that moving in together was probably not a great thing. We truly weren't that compatible or in sync, and that was fine we both acknowledged. I loved Adwin, and he loved me, but in the grand scheme of things we weren't really a romantic couple or marriage material; we were more of a buddy-bud duo. We'd remain in touch and he'd visit California, and I'd see him – and Fred – whenever I returned to North Carolina. We'd take the odd vacation together. Pledges were made and, with a bit of luck, they'd be kept.

I stretched bare legs onto the sofa, and sipped mango nectar from a bottle via a straw. It was thick and sweet and perfect for the sunny weather outside, and seemed to work well with little, decadent mouthfuls of a Red Velvet cupcake I was enjoying. I'd been off sweets since Connecticut – hadn't wanted to see another cookie to save my life, but this morning, after a three-mile power walk, I'd dropped by Suzee-Sooz's Cupcake Houz and bought the sinfully delicious treat that was nearly the size of a soccer ball. (Okay, a bit of an exaggeration, but not by much.)

"Hey you." The door opened with a bang.

"Hey yourself and watch it. I don't want to buy a new door, thank you," I groused, watching Rey all but dance into the small L-shaped living room, Linda in tow.

Both were dressed in the same Chip & Pepper jeans and similar Aloha shirts. While Linda sported colorful Converse runners, Rey wore strappy sandals. I half expected them to have the same polish on their toes and fingers. Maybe they'd both been deprived of high school friendships and were making up for missed girly-girl BFF moments.

I looked back at the shirts. Hawaiian wasn't Rey or Linda's usual taste. Oh-oh.

"What's up ladies?" I asked suspiciously, putting my drink aside but keeping the cupcake on my lap. I suspected I'd be needing sugar-enhanced comfort momentarily.

Linda closed the door and followed Rey. They leaned into the kitchen counter comprised of pretty pale blue and dusty rose ceramic tiles. I liked the cozy, bright kitchen, but why did I suddenly suspect I'd not be enjoying it for long?

Rey moved into melodramatic mode. "The licensing requirements to become private eyes in California are tough."

"We'd don't have the qualifications or background," Linda affirmed.

Oddly, neither looked deflated or upset. I smiled dryly and said nothing.

"I know, you're thinking that our detecting days are over before they've even begun."

Not really, but I eyed Rey expectantly.

"They're not!" she announced gleefully, hanging an arm around her friend's shoulders. "Guess what?"

"I couldn't even begin to," I responded wryly, gazing from one to the other.

Rey grinned. "We're going to become ..."

"Hawaiian P.I.s!" Linda finished with a jubilant grin.

"Pack your bags, Jilly!"

The Red Velvet cupcake caught Rey in the middle of the forehead.

An index finger sporting neon blue polish removed some of the frosting clinging to her brow. She licked it and smiled. "Delicious. *Mahalo.*"

* * *

Yes, I'd made a move to Hawaii … packed up
and wondered what I'd gotten myself into, besides a weather-forecasting job at an Oahu television station.

Dear reader,

We hope you enjoyed reading *The Connecticut Corpse Caper*. Please take a moment to leave a review, even if it's a short one. Your opinion is important to us.

Discover more books by Tyler Colins at https://www.nextchapter.pub/authors/tyler-colins

Want to know when one of our books is free or discounted? Join the newsletter at http://eepurl.com/bqqB3H

Best regards,

Tyler Colins and the Next Chapter Team

The story continues in:

Can You Hula Like Hilo Hattie? by Tyler Colins

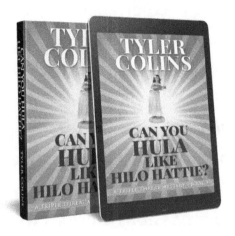

To read the first chapter for free, please head to:
https://www.nextchapter.pub/books/can-you-
hula-like-hilo-hattie

About the Author

On the professional side, Tyler Colins possesses over 15 years of experience in freelance writing, copywriting, editing and proofreading, as well as training in business communications and technical writing. Her current focus is fiction, film and television. On the personal side, she plans to reside in Hawaii permanently and embrace America, a country she's been enamored with since before she could read. Her passions, besides writing of course, include the aforementioned land of Aloha, animals in all shapes and sizes, fitness and athletics, the Good Lord and spirituality.

Connect with Me:
Twitter: https://twitter.com/UsBound3
Friend me on Facebook:
https://www.facebook.com/tyler.colins.9
Visit / Subscribe to my blog:
www.creativespider3me.com/creative-spider-3

Discover other titles by Tyler Colins:
Can You Hula Like Hilo Hattie? (coming summer 2015)
Coco's Nuts (coming fall 2015)

The Connecticut Corpse Caper
ISBN: 978-4-86747-522-5 (Large Print)

Published by
Next Chapter
1-60-20 Minami-Otsuka
170-0005 Toshima-Ku, Tokyo
+818035793528
28th May 2021

Lightning Source UK Ltd.
Milton Keynes UK
UKHW041239060622
403916UK00013BA/94